Praise for
New York Times and USA Today Bestselling Author

Diane Capri

"Full of thrills and tension, but smart and human, too."
Lee Child, #1 New York Times Bestselling Author of Jack Reacher Thrillers

"[A] welcome surprise....[W]orks from the first page to 'The End'."
Larry King

"Swift pacing and ongoing suspense are always present...[L]ikable protagonist who uses her political connections for a good cause...Readers should eagerly anticipate the next [book]."
Top Pick, Romantic Times

"...offers tense legal drama with courtroom overtones, twisty plot, and loads of Florida atmosphere. Recommended."
Library Journal

"[A] fast-paced legal thriller...energetic prose...an appealing heroine...clever and capable supporting cast...[that will] keep readers waiting for the next [book]."
Publishers Weekly

"Expertise shines on every page."
Margaret Maron, Edgar, Anthony, Agatha and Macavity Award Winning MWA Past President

RAW JUSTICE

by DIANE CAPRI

Published by: AugustBooks
http://www.AugustBooks.com

ISBN-13: 978-1-940768-50-2
ISBN-10: 1940768500

Original cover design by Michelle Preast
Interior layout by Author E.M.S.

Published in the United States of America.

Visit the author website:
http://www.DianeCapri.com

ALSO BY DIANE CAPRI

The Hunt for Justice Series

False Truth (Serial)

Fatal Error

Fatal Demand

Fatal Distraction

Fatal Enemy

Due Justice

Twisted Justice

Secret Justice

Wasted Justice

Raw Justice

Mistaken Justice

Cold Justice

The Hunt for Jack Reacher Series:

Don't Know Jack

Jack in a Box

Jack and Kill

Get Back Jack

Jack in the Green

For Robert

RAW JUSTICE

CHAPTER ONE

GILBERT IRWIN DROVE AWAY from Tampa through the vicious thunderstorm. Away from Denton Bio-Medical. Away from everything. Tears coursed down his ruddy cheeks while rain hammered his car. He couldn't see through the steamy windshield. He turned defrosters on high and swiped foggy glasses with a grimy napkin. The napkin smelled like Annabelle. He began to cry again.

"How could she? How could she?" he wailed inside the cabin where no one could hear him. He'd been blubbering like this for days, and he couldn't seem to stop, no matter what he tried. This is how a broken heart felt. He knew he'd never get over her and he didn't want to. He wanted Annabelle back. She'd loved him, too. He knew she had.

His Miata swerved on the interstate's slick pavement and slid quickly across two lanes. Then a blasting horn jerked Gilbert out of his self-pitying fugue.

"Ohmygodohmygodohmygod," he shouted. Shaking, he slowed to fifty-five. Planted thick paws firmly on the steering wheel at ten o'clock and two o'clock. Felt sweat dot his forehead, dampen the fringe of brown curls around his bald crown, trickle from his armpits, chafe his crotch.

The driver of the boxy green Kia alongside shook his fist as he sped past.

"Sorry," Gilbert mouthed, although he knew the driver couldn't see his apology.

He glanced into his rearview mirror. A midnight blue Jaguar stalking.

"Bemorecarefulbemorecarefulbemorecareful," Gilbert cautioned, noticing mucus dribbling toward his upper lip. His hands slipped on the steering wheel after he took a swipe at his nose. Another quick jab under his glasses smeared all remaining vision.

His spiffy red Miata kept moving, speeding up again, sliding on the wet roads, and the Jaguar stayed close behind.

Gilbert saw the flashing sign at the entrance to the Sunshine Skyway Bridge as he passed. "Warning: High Winds," it said. Good. Not "Closed." The bridge was closed when wind was too dangerous. He would make it across and keep running to the highway's end. To the Southernmost point. The end of the earth.

And then what? Keep going?

He entered the tollbooth line, opened his ashtray. Found four quarters; moved into the exact change lane. The last thing he wanted was to talk to anyone.

On the other side of the booth the bridge suspension struts swayed. They looked like yellow sails on a huge yacht, catching gusts. Cars sped past Gilbert in the other lanes, but he'd slowed, trying to be careful. Not so much for himself. He didn't want to hurt anybody.

He rolled into the toll plaza but landed too far away from the toll basket, so he opened the car door and edged his body closer, prepared to toss his quarters into the hopper. The Jaguar skulked behind him, waiting; its menacing engine seemed to growl at him, barely tempered by the storm. Impatiently, the driver gunned the engine. Gilbert dropped one coin onto the ground and felt the Jaguar disapprove.

Gilbert fumbled slimy fingertips to retrieve the quarter from the concrete. He managed to pick up the coin and dropped all four into the basket. Closed his door. Waited. Green light; okay to pass through. He moved ahead to escape the Jaguar's menace.

Rain pounded his roof in a mesmerizing cadence. Gilbert's attention faded out again as he approached the highest point of the bridge. Annabelle wasn't coming back. Someone took her. Maybe she was dead, Gilbert worried. She'd have contacted him if she could. He knew it.

His white-knuckled grip suggested control, but Gilbert was unaware; the Miata drifted toward the center line. A horn, louder than before, blasted briefly into his fog, but he dipped into preoccupation once more while another angry driver passed, honking.

Gilbert looked down, noticed his speed was too slow, so he accelerated.

"It's not better. It's not. It's not," he repeated, arguing aloud with his absent friend, Blake Denton, who quoted 'twas better to have loved and lost than never to have loved at all. Without Annabelle, Gilbert knew, life was not worth living.

Where was Annabelle? Maybe she wasn't dead, but why hadn't she called him? What had she done with the formula? Gilbert began to cry again as he wallowed. Damp-hot breath re-fogged the Miata's windows.

The Jaguar's front bumper, coming around now, too close, on Gilbert's left. An explosive thunderclap slapped Gilbert awake too late.

He swerved away from the vicious Jaguar, but the Jaguar seemed to leap forward to butt him out of the way.

Quick, hard impact jarred Gilbert's rigid grip. His horrified glance noticed indelible bright red paint slashed across the Jaguar's front grille as if snarling with Gilbert's blood.

The Jaguar rushed past. Never slowed. Never noticed the Miata, propelled like a hockey puck across the slick pavement.

Gilbert was sobbing now; his nose dripped mucus onto his shirt. Blinding tears masked the bridge's center rushing toward him, barely visible from the steamy interior.

Panicked. Confused. He jerked the steering wheel sharply to the right, sending the lightweight car too quickly in the opposite direction, toward the looming guardrail at the bridge's edge.

Horns blared and tires squealed as traffic scrambled to avoid collision.

Before he could right the small red vehicle the deafening storm exploded rapid cannon thunder.

Startled again, Gilbert pushed the gas pedal hard to the floor instead of mashing his brakes. The Miata jumped forward as if it were giant-spring propelled.

Fully aware now, Gilbert struggled but failed to regain control. The Miata hurtled, hydroplaning through sheeting rain and caromed the concrete abutment guardrail. Quickly, but feeling like the slow-motion Matchbox toys he'd owned in childhood, the little car bounced. Tumbled forward. Lifted. And sailed beyond the bridge's edge as if the Jaguar had tossed it across the veldt.

Gilbert and the Miata plummeted two hundred feet into churning whitecaps and slipped into the channel.

Wind-whipped Gulf of Mexico brine erased the splash point immediately.

The Miata sank to the bottom and settled gently where Gilbert, stunned and confused, yet feeling his first peace since Annabelle disappeared, resigned and closed his eyes in the muffled quiet to rest.

After long, slow minutes of breathing the last bit of air in the cabin, Gilbert's eyes popped open. Gasped. Blunt fingers flailed desperately to release the seatbelt latch as he thrashed against its restraint.

Too late.

CHAPTER TWO

JENNIFER LANE SQUINTED AT the computer screen as she reviewed the latest draft of the executive summary she'd been working on nonstop. She was scheduled to attend the biggest meeting of her career tomorrow—a new case Jennifer knew nothing about, except that she'd be working for the firm's most important new client. The opportunity astounded her. This case would change her life forever. She knew it.

Given the chance, every lawyer at Tampa's Worthington, Smith & Marquette or any other firm for that matter would kill to represent Russell Denton and Denton Bio-Medical. But Jennifer had been selected for the interview. Sometimes, a girl just gets lucky. She felt the excitement humming in her veins. She was running on pure adrenalin now, and she simply wouldn't allow herself to blow this chance.

After hours of labor, the five-page summary and longer full report were shaping up. She'd promised the senior partner that she'd have the information on his desk by six o'clock tomorrow morning. He wanted to review everything before their seven o'clock breakfast, when they would discuss her work in preparation for the big meeting. Her report had to be perfect. Nothing less would suffice.

She glanced at her watch, a gift from her parents for her law school graduation five years before, and saw it was just nine-thirty. A grin stole across her face as she realized she might finish up in time to grab a couple of hours of sleep.

Jennifer ran a quick hand through her short, curly hair and gnawed on a hangnail as she read through her straightforward prose. She'd created her boss's favorite kind of report: quick and to the point, all essential information present. It flowed nicely with succinct, economical sentences. A warm glow passed through her, beginning at her toes and working its way up. This was some of her best work ever. She could feel it.

Her eyes traveled backward up the words now from the end, making sure each was perfect, commas in place, no semicolons where periods should be, nothing misspelled, extra spaces eliminated.

Wait. There.

About the middle of the first page, she saw an empty spot she'd left a few hours ago. She'd forgotten to fill in an essential fact because she needed to look it up. Where had she seen that reference book?

Right. She'd left the heavy volume of *Who's Who in American Business* in the small conference room up on the next floor. No problem. She grinned again. Just one last date, a few more passes over the lines, and ready to print.

"Sleep, here I come," she said aloud to the empty room. Stood. Sore feet yelped. Still wearing pumps.

Stretched the kinks out of her back caused by too many hours in the lumpy chair. Winced. Not that she cared. She loved her job, her work. Her back was young enough to take it.

The once-pressed white blouse long ago had pulled loose from her gray skirt. Earrings on the desk where she'd tossed them hours ago.

Jennifer glanced up and caught her reflection in the small mirror hanging behind the door. She'd chewed off her lipstick. Mascara under her eyes created an unflattering raccoon look. Grimaced.

She kicked her pumps off and headed around the battered wood desk down the corridor in her stocking feet. Didn't worry about her bedraggled appearance. No one important was likely to see her at this time of night anyway.

Stopped at the closest coffee pot counter near the stairs hoping for stale coffee. No dice. The pot was empty, except for long-burned scum on the bottom. Spied a Styrofoam cup about one-third full of black liquid perched on the counter.

"Better than nothing, I guess," she said aloud.

Flipped the burner off under the pot, rinsed the scum, and set it aside for tomorrow. From experience, she figured she'd be the first one to make coffee in the morning when she was much more likely to need it.

Carrying the cold coffee, she rounded the corner and bounded up the stairs.

Hallways were dimly lit by emergency lighting. No matter. She could find her way around the familiar spaces in total blackness. She'd spent so much time at work over the past five years. Sometimes she wondered why she bothered to have a home, she was so rarely there.

Exit lights cast an eerie red glow in the darkest corners. Where office doors had been left open, the last vestiges of twilight and weak street lighting offered enough illumination to navigate. Jennifer had never felt safer.

Petite fingers kneaded her forehead to stave off the stress migraine's sharp edges behind her right eye.

She patted around in her pocket for an eight-hundred-milligram ibuprofen caplet as she walked. Put the bitter painkiller on her tongue, washed it down with unexpectedly sweet, cold, black sludge left by an earlier paying client. Grimaced at the appalling taste.

"There," she said aloud into the empty corridor. "That should do it."

When she came around the last corner, Jennifer noticed that the door to the small conference room, like several other doors along this corridor, was closed. Not slowing her pace at all, she reached the door, put her hand on the knob, turned to open it and, glancing down at the carpet, pushed in.

Three steps into the room, Jennifer stopped, startled. Seated around the table were senior attorney Melanie Stein and two people Jennifer had never seen before.

CHAPTER THREE

MELANIE LOOKED UP, ALMOST as startled. Jennifer began to apologize and back out, but Melanie waved her forward. "No, come in. I'd like to introduce you to our new clients."

Mortified, Jennifer wagged her head back and forth, attempted to decline and back the hell out.

"This is Ronald and Lila Walden," Melanie said, as everyone stood to exchange greetings. "And this is one of our top associates, Jennifer Lane."

Both clients stared at Jennifer as if she was an apparition.

When Ronald spoke, Jennifer could smell his breath across the table. The faintly acrid odor of metabolized alcohol when he exhaled churned her already queasy stomach and aggravated the budding migraine.

"Pleased to meet you," he said, while his wife merely nodded.

Stubby fingers he drew through dark wavy hair sported yellow smoker's stains; nails bitten below the quick. Raw flesh unhealed.

Once, Ronald Walden might have been handsome in a boy-next-door kind of way. The years and the mileage combined to produce a used and weary man.

Partly because these were pro bono clients, Jennifer guessed at first he was a workingman who had never been inside a blue-chip, silk-stocking Tampa law firm like hers before and was probably nervous.

No.

He shook not because of nerves. Alcohol withdrawal. Jennifer recognized the signs. Her father, too, had been a drinker once.

Lila Walden remained still, primly restrained, ankles crossed as she'd no doubt been taught in the church where she'd been baptized and married. The way she styled her hair and dressed reminded Jennifer of aged photographs in her mother's albums.

An old-fashioned, imitation leather purse rested on Lila's lap under hands holding a delicate lace handkerchief. Narrow gold wedding band her only jewelry. Quiet. Controlled.

"We'll be helping Mr. and Mrs. Walden with a guardianship proceeding," Melanie said, as if Jennifer were a part of the team. But she wasn't. She couldn't be. Jennifer's time was already promised to other clients.

"Our baby just up and disappeared, ma'am," Ronald Walden told Jennifer. "We been lookin' for her for weeks." Ronald waited, figuratively hat-in-hand, pleading for Melanie or Jennifer to work a miracle. If only she could.

"They're concerned about their daughter being evicted from her apartment while she's gone because the rent hasn't been paid," Melanie explained. "And they want to use her funds to hire a private investigator to find her."

Melanie headed up the Community Services team and Jennifer was grateful not to be assigned to the often desperate clients who lived too near society's edges. She envied Melanie's objectivity; something Jennifer could never master. She quickly recalled what

Melanie had said about this heartbreaking, hopeless new case yesterday at lunch.

Almost as if she'd been abducted by aliens, Roxanne Walden had vanished three weeks ago. She'd left her tony apartment full of expensive furnishings and everything else she owned behind. She'd even left her purse, complete with wallet, credit cards, and cash.

Tampa PD had done what it should have, Melanie said. Missing women had become a high priority to American law enforcement agencies. For too long, too many victims had been presumed missing but later discovered dead, usually at the hands of husbands or boyfriends. The police had tried to find Roxanne by using all their normal means.

When the Waldens first reported Roxanne missing, local police had checked her credit card charges, ATM withdrawals, and bank account activity. There had been none. Roxanne's car was still in the parking lot of her apartment complex. All airline, train, bus, and cruise ship lists of passengers departing Tampa had been examined. Friends and colleagues were interviewed. Even unidentified bodies that had found their way to the morgue in the intervening weeks were, one by one, considered. But none were Roxanne.

Now, standing in the small conference room in the presence of Roxanne Walden's parents, Jennifer felt herself being pulled into the vortex of a family tragedy, one she had no power to change. Except that it would have been incredibly rude to do so, Jennifer would have tried again to excuse herself from this nightmare.

She knew she was the antithesis of the warrior goddess, Cyrene, for whom she'd been named: Cyrene Jennifer Lane. Maybe the ancient Cyrene had fought a tiger with her bare hands, but the modern Jennifer Lane had no illusions about her own bravery. She was a hardworking lawyer, honest, sincere. Maybe even intelligent. But she was certainly not brave. Jennifer had never been brave.

When Melanie insisted that Jennifer take a seat at the conference table, she didn't have the strength of will, or the right, really, to refuse. She tucked her blouse back into the waistband of her skirt and ran her fingers through her hair. Rubbed under her eyes, to minimize the black mascara rings. Jennifer knew she still looked foolish, but it was the best she could do.

Jennifer listened through half an hour of Ronald Walden's lament, feeling more disheartened with each passing second. There was no way Roxanne's story would ever have a happy ending. She felt that as strongly as she'd ever felt anything.

Ronald tossed a small cell phone from one hand to the other, then pushed a stack of pictures toward her.

Jennifer flipped through the color photographs. The scene suggested Roxanne had only run outside briefly. To the mailbox, maybe.

Nothing about the pictures of Roxanne's two-bedroom apartment, only a few miles from where Jennifer now sat, screamed murder. Designer clothes still hung in the walk-in closets, while boutique toiletries implying pleasant floral scents rested on the dressing table in the master bathroom. A high-end computer perched on an ebony ergonomic desk in the home office.

Big screen television gleamed like a black hole from the wall where it was mounted opposite a glistening oil on canvas. Speakers remained poised to serenade from the corners of the main room.

Ronald handed a grubby Manila file folder to Melanie, who opened it to review the contents.

"Here's the notice of eviction," Melanie said, handing the

document that had been tacked to the door of Roxanne's apartment over to Jennifer.

Skimmed the notice. Management would be removing Roxanne's things from the building after five more days.

"I knowed the gal felt real sorry for us," Ronald continued in his heavy Southern drawl. "That's why she called. She said if we just paid the rent, everything would be okay."

"Was Roxanne married?" Jennifer asked. Chagrinned to realize she'd used the past tense.

Lila made a small snorting sound that might have been mirth, but Ronald said simply, "No."

"Children?"

Ronald shook his head back and forth. No children, either.

Jennifer struggled to maintain a safe emotional distance. She couldn't get swallowed now. Not tonight. Melanie would be handling the Waldens' case and she'd be great for them. Jennifer still had mountains of other work to do.

She left as soon as she could reasonably excuse herself. It was the migraine that scared her, Jennifer told herself, not intuition that Roxanne Walden would never be reunited with her parents above ground. Jennifer couldn't change the outcome. Just like the last time.

CHAPTER FOUR

RUSSELL DENTON SETTLED HIMSELF deeper into his leather wing chair and ignored his fatigue. Outside, Tampa's daily summer thunderstorm raged. Oblivious to the relentless pounding of the monsoon-like rain, the savvy, self-made billionaire focused yet again on Jennifer Lane's short dossier, and noted little with which he was able to find fault. At least, nothing that he was capable of changing. He checked the information he'd already memorized, comforting himself with its familiarity.

She was young but smart. University of Florida law graduate five years ago. Summa cum laude—if not from an Ivy League school. And she craved approval. Excellent. He liked insecure overachievers. He understood them well.

The next notation concerned him the most. Jennifer Lane suffered from debilitating migraines for which she took prescription medication. Her condition was well controlled, he'd been assured. Not that he believed.

Russell examined the candid photos. Jennifer wasn't beautiful, although the resemblance to the other woman was clear if you knew what to look for. A certain tilt to the nose; crinkles around her eyes; brown, curly hair. Those physical traits were the same. The dimple in her chin seemed identical. Jennifer was well groomed, but plain. Nothing particularly out of the ordinary. The other one had been something special. Flashy. Irresistible. Maybe Jennifer's ordinariness would mask the similarities. He hoped.

A small frown formed between his eyes as Russell reread the next line on the page. *Single.* Too bad. He'd made that mistake once before. Married would be better.

Make the best of it. Single. No husband or children to distract her. And this one was nothing like the other. Not a party girl.

He stared again at the pictures. Definitely not glamorous. Not his nephew's type at all. Single could be all right this time.

It had to be.

Russell forced his brow to relax and the frown faded slightly. He nodded to himself. Yes, Jennifer Lane looked good to him on paper. Besides, he'd already rejected all of the other options and he didn't have the luxury of starting over, even if Jennifer wasn't perfect.

Russell closed the slim yellow folder and placed it carefully on the coffee table in front of his chair. Then he picked up the blue folder and sat back to review once more the memorized dossier on Stuart Barnett.

Russell's memory was his great ally. He memorized everything. Lately, though, he'd noticed his own increased mental confusion. He memorized material but couldn't recall it quickly when he needed to.

Forced himself to concentrate. Rain pelted the windows of the high-rise as strong wind gusts rattled the panes, but Russell didn't notice the weather outside.

Stuart Barnett was older than Jennifer, of course. Fifty. Experienced. The black sheep at a good enough law firm. Despite strong talent, Barnett was underappreciated by his partners and had been passed over for promotion several times. He was bitter and had something to prove. Excellent.

The frown returned to Russell's face as he reread the facts. He picked up the four-color driver's license photo and another picture the investigator had collected.

Barnett was too good-looking a man, his wife was too wealthy. The combination meant the lawyer wouldn't be easy to control. A definite problem. One that couldn't be helped.

Russell tapped the blue folder against his knee. He reexamined his plan.

The package *could* work perfectly. Jennifer the face; Barnett the experience. Would it, though?

Russell could find better legal talent, but as a team the two of them might do the job.

Still, Russell's intuition was almost as essential to him as his memory. And something about this decision nagged him, just didn't feel quite right.

If his other efforts were unsuccessful, everything would depend on Lane and Barnett's success. Denton Bio-Medical was the only thing Russell truly cared about—besides his nephew. He'd worked too hard, for too long, to lose everything now.

Lane and Barnett. Could they do it? If he was wrong—no, he wouldn't even consider that. He pushed the thought away. He needed to be certain.

Russell tested his own decisions in the way a highly successful man surrounded by sycophants must: proceed objectively. He'd made his own way in the world since he was sixteen. He'd learned the hard way to rely only on himself.

Now was not the time for a crisis of confidence.

Russell felt hot in the heavily air-conditioned room. Ignored his rising fever. Replaced the blue folder on the table next to the yellow one. Looked straight ahead, facing the hidden camera behind the large mirror, as if he could see through to the camera's lens and its operator in the other room. At least he would have an accurate tape. He could examine it later. He would be able to reassure himself objectively. Or develop alternatives.

An exceptionally loud crack of thunder snapped Russell back to full attention. Raised his glass of iced tea in a toast to Tyler, the unseen camera man, and then sipped. Checked the time.

"Exactly four o'clock. We're ready," he said, testing the microphone again.

"Are you tired?" Tyler asked via the small, invisible microphone inside Russell's ear.

"A luxury I can't afford," Russell insisted.

"Have you eaten today?"

"No appetite." Russell heard the disapproving silence. Lane and Barnett would be prompt, regardless of the weather. Everything about them in the recorded dossiers told him so. He glanced again at his watch. No one had dared to keep Russell Denton waiting in decades.

Russell sensed his life coming down around him with the same violence the storm outside. But fifty years in business had taught him never, ever, to show his emotions. Poker face. Essential.

"You could still change your mind," Tyler's disembodied voice suggested.

Russell gave a quick negative head shake. Tyler was wrong. Russell Denton couldn't change his mind. Because if he did, he would die.

CHAPTER FIVE

EXACTLY FOUR O'CLOCK.

Jennifer stood slightly to the side and behind Stuart Barnett on the Executive Club's plush gold carpet. Damp clothes pressed to her skin. Wet wool smells teased her recently departed migraine's return. Anticipation and anxiety in equal measure coursed through her body.

Thunder exploded. Reverberated. Drowned Stuart's fisting raps on the heavy wood.

Average looking man opened the door. Wearing an oversized Chinese-red silk golf shirt and baggy but sharply creased trousers. Feet clad in whisper-thin socks and well-shined cordovan loafers. Glasses emphasized shrewd hazel eyes; bruised circles and pouchy bags accented. Thinning brown hair, grey at the temples, parted on the left in sharp contrast to his politics.

He could have been an ordinary businessman.

But Jennifer knew he wasn't.

Invited entry.

"Stuart Barnett?" Russell Denton asked, extending his hand.

"Yes," Stuart answered, accepting the greeting.

"And Ms. Lane?" Presented his hand to her.

"Call me Jennifer," she said. Genuine smile accentuated the dimple in her chin. Shook warmly. Southern gentlemen of a certain age rarely offered to shake hands with women. His gesture was another indication that this man was different.

"Thank you for coming over in this storm. I hope you didn't get too wet." He indicated two gold-leaf arm chairs upholstered in rich blue brocade; waved Jennifer toward the head and Stuart to the side of the low coffee table. Three glasses of iced tea waited.

"Let me take that," Russell said, collecting three thin folders—one blue, one yellow, and one green—from the section of table in front of her seat.

"I can move over there." Jennifer offered.

"You're in the perfect spot," Russell said, as he placed himself opposite Stuart.

Jennifer and Stuart lunched at the Executive Club almost daily. She didn't need to assess or admire the comfortable surroundings.

She also knew exactly how she looked sitting on the edge of the oversized wing chair, her feet firmly planted on the floor. The decorative mirror directly opposite attracted like a horror movie but failed to improve her appearance.

Jennifer watched herself study Stuart Barnett. He was nice to look at, but not the reason she cared. The best lawyer in her firm, maybe even in all of Florida. Brilliant. Never predictable. Always fascinating.

After five years, she still loved working as Stuart's protégée. Absorbed his tutelage like a white cloth soaks up red wine: never to become as deep as the wine itself, but infinitely more colorful than she could ever hope to be otherwise.

Stuart confided this morning, "I want Russell Denton and his company as my clients, Ms. Lane. We will do whatever he asks to make that happen. Understand?"

Indeed, she did. Russell Denton was the biggest fish in Tampa's business community. His name on Stuart's new business list would vault Stuart to the prominence he deserved. Jennifer planned to be in the co-pilot's seat.

Stuart had said, "Stick with me, kid. The next twenty years will be my best. Won't hurt your career, either."

"You have a gift for understatement, don't you?" She replied. Felt like an insider. Unusual. Intoxicating. She loved it; craved more.

For the past five years, she'd been embattled and often defeated. Competitive peers, jousting opponents, relentless bosses, demanding judges, ravenous clients. Many times, she'd have quit and run back home if not for Stuart. He had been her shield and her sword. Coach and friend. Working for Stuart, advancing them both, suited her plans perfectly.

None of which she admitted to him. His ego was big enough already.

She noticed her nervous smile reflected by the mirror; replaced it with rehearsed confidence. *Fake it 'til you make it, Baby.*

"You're familiar with my company, Denton Bio-Medical," Russell said. It wasn't a question.

Jennifer nodded. She'd prepared an extensive file; knew everything about the man and his business. Ran through the highlights in her head.

Offspring of uneducated, middle-class parents. Prodigy. Developed his first patented medical device at age twenty-three. Owner and sole shareholder of Denton Bio-Medical, Incorporated. Wife deceased. One nephew lived and worked with him, the heir apparent.

Russell Denton wasn't as sensationally successful as an oil tycoon, but in the Tampa business arena, he was a Goliath. If you had a cold or a headache, or something serious like diabetes or cancer, Denton Bio-Medical products provided treatments of choice. The community and the world were lucky to have him.

Which made him a perfect client in every respect. Jennifer repeated her internal resolve not to blow it.

"We need the best legal talent in Florida for a critically difficult case," Russell said now, unnecessarily stroking Stuart's ego, tempting him.

"What kind of case?" Stuart asked, playing it cool, as if anything Russell Denton answered would matter in the slightest.

CHAPTER SIX

"SHE'S CONCERNED, CONFUSED. MAYBE scared," Tim Tyler's voice said into Russell Denton's earpiece.

Russell nodded slightly. Good, but curious. Nothing scary disclosed yet.

"What I'm about to tell you must not leave this room," Russell said, looking directly at Jennifer. She stiffened.

"You've pissed her off." Tyler's voice came through the earpiece again. Information didn't make sense, but Russell signaled that he'd heard clearly. Trusted his technology to read Jennifer's bio-reactions accurately. The software was infallible.

She sat poised, waiting, anger concealed.

Good. Just the reaction he'd counted on. Confirmed Tyler's investigation data. Her desire for Barnett's approval and advancement triumphed over visceral reactions.

"Goes without saying," Barnett replied.

Russell turned to Jennifer, expecting agreement.

"You think we might violate our ethics and your trust?" she asked, sharply.

Tone raised his antennae; simultaneous understanding

dawned. He'd offended her honor. Perhaps she had more backbone than he'd believed. *Even better.*

"My terms are not negotiable," he said. "This is a bet-my-company case. A fight I can't lose. I will be in complete control. Every move will be handled my way." Russell held out his hand, two fingers extended, and waved between the two of them, but he looked directly at Jennifer to dangle the carrot.

"If you accept my terms, you are the right team for the case."

Barnett interjected. "We're pleased you've selected us for a matter that's so important to you. We'll put the full power of Worthington, Smith & Marquette behind the case."

Russell said, "That's exactly what I don't want. Not obviously, anyway."

He and Tyler had crafted and rehearsed the lines; tested for persuasiveness; revised and honed. The point was critical. No margin for error.

Russell spoke to Barnett but Jennifer was the crucial one. "Our opponent is an individual. A young woman. We're a large corporation. American juries notoriously grant undeserved sympathy to underdogs and ignore the truth as well as the law in our favor. We are the aggrieved party here, but to win, she *must* appear at least evenly matched." He nodded in Jennifer's direction. "I want Jennifer first chair. To demonstrate equality. Insure a level playing field. We're entitled to fairness, aren't we?"

Russell's testing had proved the excuse plausible. It was partly true.

Tyler's voice said, "She bought it."

Barnett answered Russell's question. "We'll need to know what's involved first. Right, Ms. Lane?" Barnett turned to her as a matter of feigned courtesy, Russell suspected.

Her agreement didn't come immediately. A beat passed. Two.

Russell pressed her. "I can live with those terms if you can, Ms. Lane."

His lips curved a reassuring smile.

Jennifer lifted her iced tea glass and brought it to her lips. Russell noticed the slight tremor she couldn't suppress. Sipped to wet her parched throat, leaving a small lip print curve on the rim.

Excellent. For a while, he'd thought her too nervous to drink anything. Now, he'd have fingerprints, and saliva for DNA testing. He'd demand a blood sample later when she was more comfortable.

Awaited her response. Based on her merits alone, the opportunity was too good to be true. By every objective measure, she was too young, too green. She lacked experience, which Barnett's guidance would supply. Her expertise was irrelevant to Russell. He didn't plan to rely on her legal skills.

"Okay," she finally said, her voice cracking.

"You've got her. She's in," Tyler's voice in the earpiece whispered.

Russell signaled Tyler, continued, "A former employee has stolen something that belongs to me. I want you to get it back."

"Sounds like a matter for the police," Barnett responded, smoothing his tie and folding blunt hands over the starched shirt that covered his flat, athlete's stomach. Gold wedding band twinkled in the lamplight.

Jennifer asked. "What did she take?"

Russell's face flushed to the bright red of his shirt. He stared into Jennifer's eyes. Cold anger no longer suppressed. "She took everything I've worked for: my reputation and the future of my company."

Jennifer flinched. The storm raged outside. Lightning flashed. Thunder followed. Rain drenched.

When decibels fell Barnett smoothed again. Even tone and relaxed pose proved his reputation for unflappable calm well deserved. "Surely she signed an employment contract?"

"If this were as simple as suing a former employee for breach of contract, I wouldn't need pricey lawyers, would I? There is no contract. And right now, there's no employee to sue, either."

"Easy," Tyler's voice cautioned in Russell's ear, coaxing down his impatience. "You're scaring her."

Abruptly, Russell switched gears. Barnett wanted Russell's name and his money. Easy to proffer. Simple business deal. Lane wanted to please Barnett. But Russell needed more from her. A personal promise, too.

From the dossier, he knew how to hook Jennifer Lane deeper. She still had stars in her eyes about doing good in the world. Appeals to altruism motivated her, but groundwork was required.

"What do you know about hepatitis Z?" He asked.

Barnett raised his right hand, his thumb and forefinger touched together: zero.

Jennifer said, "It's a virus that attacks the liver, right?"

"Hep Z wasn't actually identified until 1989, although it's been around longer." Russell breathed deeply. Tired. "They call it the silent killer because it can lie dormant in the body for years. Similar to HIV, the AIDS virus. You can have it right now and not know you're sick."

Jennifer lifted the glass to her mouth again, taking a longer gulp this time.

Russell watched. "Hep Z symptoms can make you wish you were already dead. About four million Americans have it now and the infected population is growing every day." Jennifer looked a little green. Gentled his tone. "Do you know how many people that is? It's three times more than those afflicted with HIV. Five times more than Parkinson's. Ten times more than MS."

He made it personal. Saw her earrings peeking from beneath brown curls. "If you've donated or received any blood product, or been tattooed, or pierced? You're at risk."

She blanched. Dropped her gaze to the floor.

Barnett listened without comment, detached.

Russell directed his fire to Barnett. "You or your wife and children could have been infected when they received routine vaccinations. *Anyone* can have Hep Z. The virus is everywhere. Doesn't respect your occupation. Or your wealth."

He allowed his message to soak in a few moments. Drank iced tea. Left his bait on the line.

"What are the symptoms?" Jennifer asked, her voice a little hoarse.

Russell answered matter-of-factly, "None for a long time. If you're lucky. But it usually starts with fatigue, maybe a little right-side pain and loss of appetite. Gets worse. Then liver function declines. Cirrhosis, followed by jaundice, other skin changes. Next comes vomiting blood, mental confusion." He stopped a moment. "It goes downhill from there."

"You've scared her sufficiently now," Tyler's voice cautioned in Russell's ear.

Barnett cleared his throat. "Is Hep Z always fatal?"

The grandfather clock ticked in the corner of the room.

"Russian roulette." Russell paused. "When you have Hep Z, every day is another click of the gun's trigger, pointed directly at your gut. Today could be the day."

Pelting rain invaded the room's silence.

Barnett and Lane exchanged wary glances. Russell knew their work usually didn't concern matters of life and death. As civil lawyers, all they normally did on a daily basis was push paper around and collect hourly fees. This case would raise the stakes. Were they capable enough?

Russell drove his point home. "Hep Z is a virus. There is no cure. You get it, you own it and it owns you. The man who cures a virus, any virus, will be a hero to the entire world."

Jennifer seemed to understand at last. She cleared her throat. "Have you done that? Figured out how to cure a virus?"

A smile barely lifted his lips. He'd convinced her of Hep Z's importance and the need for a cure. Hooked her into the case. First piece accomplished.

Russell stated his appeal. "We haven't figured out how to cure a virus yet. But that's why I need your help. We've developed a new product we call HepZMax. Close as anyone has ever come." Russell wouldn't exaggerate, but if HepZMax was as good as they thought, he might win the Nobel Prize.

"What does HepZMax do?" Barnett asked.

"About ninety percent effective. Puts patients into Hep Z remission. Minimal side effects. Compared to existing treatments, it's as good as a cure." Russell stood, walked to the window, stared at the sheeting rain flooding Tampa's streets and rooftops. Hands clasped behind his back.

"Hep Z diagnosis is devastating," Russell said, quietly. "Liver transplant is the only partially effective treatment. Between eight and ten thousand Americans die each year from liver failure caused by Hep Z. Rate expected to triple by 2015."

He turned around to face them, allowing all of the anguish he felt to color his words. "Unless you find Annabelle James and retrieve my HepZMax formula, each of us, or someone we love, may suffer needlessly and die. Certainly, our fellow Americans will die. And the worldwide death rates are staggering."

Silence lasted a full three minutes this time. Russell waited while she searched her heart and her conscience. He wouldn't force her, and he wouldn't hire her if she failed to care.

Barnett was first to recover. "It's far too much work for one attorney. Jennifer's going to need a lot of help."

True. But irrelevant. An army of Worthington, Smith & Marquette lawyers working for Denton Bio-Medical would inflate the firm's revenues by several million dollars and probably lift Barnett all the way to CEO.

Russell remained still. Biding time.

"She's beginning to thaw," Tyler's voice predicted in Russell's earpiece. "She'll do it. She wants to be Barnett's hero."

Russell signaled again that he'd understood. "As much as I appreciate your reputation, Stuart, we must be clear on this point. Jennifer is the one I want. Up front. Head of the team. In first chair. No one else. Behind the scenes, do what you want. But whenever there's a person attached to this case from your firm, it's her. Alone."

Barnett turned to Jennifer. Whispered.

Russell couldn't hear Barnett's pleading over the storm's rage, but he didn't need to. All he needed was her answer. Only one answer would he accept. But she had to get there on her own. His plan would fail otherwise.

"I'm flattered, Mr. Denton—" she said.

"Russell."

She began again. "I'm flattered…Russell…to be chosen. I'll do my best for you."

Solid commitment. Russell's belly uncoiled. She would put 100 percent into his project. He could count on her now. *Excellent.*

"I know you will," he said. "I'm betting everything on you."

Russell picked up the green folder and tapped it against his palm. “There’s only one reason to steal a formula like HepZMax. Annabelle will sell it to a competitor. When she does, the buyer will announce it. The formula will only make its owner wealthy once it hits the market.”

Jennifer said, “I understand.”

“I’ll need you to do two things,” Russell continued, listing investigative work first. “Keeping everything confidential, figure out how to flush Annabelle James out of hiding. And get my formula back from her before she sells it.”

“I’ll do my best,” she promised.

He paused a moment before he offered a legal solution. “If that doesn’t work, stop the buyer before he submits my formula to the FDA.”

“We’ll get a temporary restraining order preventing anyone from marketing HepZMax. And then an injunction until the court awards you full title to the formula,” Barnett suggested.

Jennifer shifted uncomfortably in her seat.

“What’s wrong?” Russell asked.

Tentatively, she said, “A TRO—temporary restraining order—of any kind is very hard to get. An injunction is even more difficult. Courts usually reject applications for both. The judicial system is poorly suited to prevent people from breaking the law before final rights are determined in a trial. You’ll need to prove that HepZMax belongs to you. And you’ll have to show that you have a substantial likelihood of success in the case against your former employee. Can you do that?”

Russell’s dossier showed Jennifer’s results on TRO requests were dismal. She’d won a couple of times, albeit in smaller matters. He knew the odds were against him. Didn’t expect her to win.

Russell handed her the green file folder. “You’ll need this to get started. After you've looked at the records, you tell me what I have to do to get HepZMax back."

Jennifer reached for the folder, hesitantly, a perplexed look on her face.

"Something wrong?" Barnett asked.

Jennifer shook her head, as if to break some kind of spell. "No."

"And one more thing," Russell's tone as intense as one whose very life might be at stake. "You report only to me. You are not to discuss my business with anyone else, inside or outside the company."

"Of course," Barnett replied automatically.

"Not anyone," Russell reiterated. "Including my nephew, Blake."

He waited until Jennifer agreed. Hoped she'd be strong enough. His nephew could be a very persuasive man.

CHAPTER SEVEN

TIM TYLER HELD THE racquet in his left hand and slammed the squash ball against the court with the full force of his frustration.

Slam!

Right hand. How in the hell did Annabelle James run off with a formula that would make her a Nobel Prize winner and a multibillionaire?

Slam!

Left hand. Why in the hell would Russell trust her in the first place if the damn formula was so important?

Slam!

Right hand. How in the hell was Jennifer Lane ever going to get the damned thing back? *Slam!*

Waiting for his opponent to show up at the Athletic Club, Tyler used his considerable intellect to ponder the problem that had been bugging him since he left Russell Denton's office the day before. He punctuated each sentence by slamming the ball with the racquet and posing the next question as he waited for the ball's return. Alternating the racquet from one hand to the other with every stroke, he tried to place each shot, moving his lanky frame very little. He called this exercise the Squash Meditation. He'd been using it for years. Sometimes it worked.

Slam!

The formula for a potentially lifesaving new treatment for Hep Z was being chased by several bio-medical companies.

Slam!

They were all racing to be the first to submit an FDA premarket approval application.

Slam!

Denton Bio-Medical was the front-runner.

Slam!

Denton had the secret weapon, a genius researcher named Gilbert Irwin. He'd been so close.

Slam!

But, then this flashy young woman had come in and finessed both Gilbert and Russell by finishing her research first. But Tyler didn't believe these young people, especially the young women, were any smarter or better than the previous generation. He knew something had gone wrong, he just hadn't figured out what that something was—yet.

Slam!

She did beat the hell out of old Gilbert, Tyler reminded himself, and shook his head, whiffing the racquet through the soft air and missing the ball for the first time.

Tyler thought she had probably just been lucky. Although he'd looked for another explanation, he hadn't found one.

It could have been luck. Tyler never discounted the luck factor. He'd had too much luck himself to be a doubter.

Barely breathing hard, he picked up the ball, changed his

location on the court, switched the racquet into the other hand, and started again.

Slam!

He'd known very little about Hep Z before he'd watched and listened from behind the one-way mirror today at Russell's meeting with the lawyers.

Slam!

Who would have thought that his own foolish behavior, so long ago, could potentially be deadly to him now? The thought jarred him and Tyler whiffed again.

He repeated his set-up routine as if it were a religious ritual, picking up the ball, moving to a different location on the court. He'd started to sweat. He rubbed his face with the special towel his kids had given him for Father's Day and began again.

Slam!

Now that he knew this much about Hep Z, he'd be getting tested in the morning.

Slam!

He'd already made an appointment for his kids.

Slam!

Somehow, he'd convince his ex-wife to get tested, too.

Whiff!

He missed the ball again. His ex-wife always interrupted his concentration. Tyler tried never to think of her during squash. Or sex.

He retrieved the ball and set up one more time.

Slam!

He'd be damned if he was going to have anybody dying of an undiagnosed fatal disease on his watch.

Slam!

This time, Tyler slammed the ball with such force it returned immediately and hit him hard in the stomach. He didn't even feel it.

His opponent, Roger Riley, walked onto the court in time to witness the last ball slam into Tyler.

"Hey, buddy," Roger called as he approached. "You're not planning to kill me here today, are you?"

Roger laughed as he delivered the line with the diction of the well-trained actor he happened to be. Roger, in fact, looked like a movie version of a squash player. *Always in costume. Always playing a role*, Tyler thought.

Tyler shook hands with the club's only squash player who could give him a decent game.

"Killing you would be a service to the community, Riley," Tyler told his opponent, not altogether in jest. "Think of all the corporate fat cats who would influence the governor on my behalf."

"Hell, you wouldn't even be prosecuted," Roger said, agreeably. The two men laughed.

Rabid Roger Riley was proud of his reputation. He'd worked hard to earn it. Riley was Tampa's most famous or infamous, depending on your point of view, plaintiff's attorney. He viewed himself, Tyler knew, as some sort of Robin Hood.

As in the original tale, most of the people Tyler knew viewed Rabid Roger as a thief in designer clothing. But the two men had never battled each other except on the squash court, where their skills seemed to be quite evenly matched, if you didn't know to watch Roger carefully for cheating.

"Man, it's raining like a monsoon out there," Riley said as he started to warm up. "I could barely see the road on the way over." The two men began with a slow volley. "I sure hope no poor SOB is driving over the Skyway."

Riley referred to the eleven-mile suspension bridge—the Sunshine Skyway—which joined St. Petersburg with the other side of Tampa Bay.

"On second thought," Roger said, laughing as he gave the ball another soft volley, "if some slob goes over, I could sue the engineer and construction company for sure. Could raise my net worth by a few million."

"Like you need the money," Tyler said, lobbing the ball again.

"Money isn't everything," Roger told him, hitting the ball hard, bouncing it off the wall and slamming it into Tyler's stomach for a second shot of the day. But this time, the stinging ball left a message Tyler knew he'd feel for days.

CHAPTER EIGHT

JENNIFER HATED TO BE late, so she'd left the office thirty minutes before the time scheduled for her to arrive. Denton Bio-Medical's corporate facility was located out near the University of South Florida campus, about a twenty-five minute drive from downtown Tampa in light traffic. But Jennifer had trouble finding the plant because she wasn't that familiar with Bruce B. Downs Boulevard or the surrounding campus area. She turned right instead of left from Fletcher and ended up on the boulevard too far from the medical buildings.

The digital clock on the dashboard mocked her as it marched relentlessly past her appointment time, unconcerned. She could feel her internal anxiety mounting and tried to stuff her discomfort back down. She hated being late. Tardiness meant a failure to start on time, and disrespect for others. She'd already waited hours for judges and other lawyers in her short career, but no one ever had to wait for her.

After a few U-turns, she headed in the right direction, and followed the signs to the facility's visitor parking lot. Now forty minutes late, she felt her anxiety ratchet up to near screeching pitch.

Jennifer slid her deep purple PT Cruiser into one of the empty spaces in the lot, locked the car, and hurried about one hundred yards up the sidewalk to the front door. She quickly checked her appearance reflected in the glass as she tried to calm herself before she entered.

Her curly hair had begun to spring out of its well-sprayed order in the summer humidity. She didn't try to pat the curls back into place; she knew from long experience that resistance was futile. Her plain blue business suit and neat white blouse had already started to wilt on her slight frame. Jennifer took three deep breaths and said sotto voce, "I am calm," but the technique didn't work. She gave up the effort and entered the building like a Christian about to encounter her assigned lion.

The lobby was sparsely furnished and utilitarian-looking in comparison to the lobby of Worthington, Smith & Marquette. Denton Bio-Medical was, so far, a disappointment. After her meeting with Russell Denton at the University Club, she had anticipated opulence. Instead, all she saw was a few low vinyl and chrome couches and a couple of chrome and glass tables lining the walls. On the tables were magazines like *The New England Journal of Medicine* and *Time*. Nothing about the place looked as if a multimillionaire owned it.

A receptionist sat behind a small desk in the corner farthest from the door. The woman was on the telephone and asked Jennifer to wait by holding up a hand with her index finger extended.

Two doors led off the lobby on opposite sides of the reception desk. While she waited, Jennifer watched a couple of people come in and go out these doors. Each used a pass card connected to some kind of security system to release the door. The employees wore these cards on chains around their necks, so they had to stoop to hold the cards in front of small black boxes mounted waist high.

"May I help you?" the receptionist asked at last, drawing Jennifer back from her focus on the security doors to give her name and her contact—Blake Denton. The receptionist handed her a visitor's badge and told her to wear it at all times. The woman watched like a hawk as Jennifer peeled off the backing and stuck the badge onto her suit jacket, over her left lapel. Only then did she ask Jennifer to have a seat, adding, "I'll let Mr. Denton know you're here."

Jennifer sat down and picked up an old copy of *Newsweek*. Not a full magazine—inside the cover was just a single article, one that had originally appeared in April 2002. "Hepatitis Z," the headline on the cover said. "Over 3 Million Americans Are Infected with the Stealth Virus. Most Don't Know It."

An involuntary shudder went down Jennifer's spine as she vowed, again, to have herself tested—just as soon as she got up the nerve. After her meeting with Russell Denton, she'd done enough research to realize that absolutely anybody could be infected and not know it. Was it better to know that one had an incurable, probably fatal disease? Or was ignorance bliss, as Russell Denton had claimed? She began to read the frightening information.

If she hadn't been hired to find Annabelle James and to help Russell Denton get HepZMax back on track and distributed to the patients who needed it, Jennifer would have volunteered for the job after completing the research she'd done since her meeting with Denton yesterday. She felt as if she should be venturing out into the world only when fully encased in body armor. This article was no less scary.

HepZMax simply had to be manufactured and gotten into the

hands of the people who needed it. It wasn't an exaggeration to say that people would die if Jennifer should fail. Every day that the formula remained lost was a day that victims continued to suffer. And those victims might be people Jennifer knew and loved.

Jennifer barely noticed her toe tapping in nervous impatience to get started with the work she'd come here to do.

"Amazing, isn't it?" a deep, raspy voice startled Jennifer from her reading.

She squinted up at six feet of the tallest, blondest, and maybe most handsome man she'd ever seen. She struggled to get out of the deep vinyl couch that had swallowed her.

"I'm Blake Denton. You are Jennifer Lane, right?" She took his offered hand, while he pulled her up the rest of the way, and then held on just a little longer.

"Jennifer, right," she answered haltingly. Her hand felt cool and lonely when he let it go. She dropped her arm back to her side and closed her fist to hold his warm greeting a little longer.

"You can keep that article, if you'd like. We have hundreds of them." His friendly smile charged her nerve endings like an electric jolt.

Jennifer stuffed the old article into her briefcase and stood up straight. With her gaze level, she looked squarely at the middle of his chest. She doubted his view of the top of her head was as fascinating to him as his broad chest was to her.

"My uncle asked me to show you around today, introduce you to the folks you'll be working with. I've been told to answer any questions you might have, too." Blake stretched out his arm, indicating that Jennifer should precede him toward one of the two entry doors.

He reached into his pocket, pulled out an access card, and held it in front of the small, rectangular box on the doorjamb near the door's handle. Jennifer heard a soft click and then Blake pulled the handle to open the door. He gestured her to walk inside what appeared to be the main office area and followed behind.

"Did you get a chance to read all of that article?" Blake asked, as they continued to walk down the corridor. She glanced quickly at him again, this time taking in his casual attire and relaxed style.

He wore the summer uniform of a Florida businessman, but with more than the usual flair. Instead of a golf shirt, he wore a Hawaiian silk shirt with a sage green background and a bright coral tropical pattern on it. His deeper green trousers were a soft fabric that held a knife-sharp crease. His loafers were worn without socks, but they looked as if he'd put them on new just this morning.

Altogether, Blake Denton was one of the best-dressed men she'd ever seen, and Jennifer worked with lawyers who selected their outfits from fashion magazines. Blake's style made her feel dowdy by comparison, totally out of her element.

Jennifer's mouth was so dry, no words emerged. She cleared her throat and tried again. "Not all of the article, but most of it," she croaked.

Blake smiled. Jennifer figured he knew women found him attractive and he expected that she did, too. He wasn't wrong. Jennifer knew Blake was way out of her league, though, so she just stuck with the business she came to conduct.

"Can you show me the lab where Annabelle James worked? And maybe explain to me a little bit about where she kept her research and the other things she took with her when she left?" Russell had given her permission to ask Blake these questions, but she was not to tell him anything about the results of her own investigation or her recommended course of action. This was a concession Russell Denton had demanded without an explanation.

Blake looked at her quizzically. "Sure. Let's go back this way and out onto the research floor." *He must find it unusual for a woman not to flirt with him*, Jennifer thought. Not that she would mind flirting with Blake, if she knew how to flirt effectively. All of her prior attempts at the mating dance had wound up in disaster. Jennifer decided not to think about the past right now.

Blake led Jennifer down a corridor lined with offices on the outside and secretarial stations on the inside. Like many corporate offices she had been in, Denton Bio-Medical tended to the sparse-efficiency mode, populated by the ubiquitous cubes that decorators called "office landscaping." Not at all like the opulence of her firm's law offices, she thought again, pleased that she'd chosen a more comfortable atmosphere to work in.

They passed through several intervening doors, having to stop each time for Blake to put his security card in front of the infrared card reader to release the electronic locks. Jennifer noticed video cameras placed in every room through which they traveled. *How did Annabelle James get anything out of this mini-Fort Knox, anyway?*

Blake smiled and answered the question Jennifer hadn't realized she'd asked aloud. "We don't know. This is Uncle Russell's first facility and our oldest. But it's been fully updated with the most current technology available. Annabelle's security clearance would not have given her access to the computer files or the original formula documents. Those are all stored in a vault in the executive offices we just passed through. Only a limited number of employees are allowed in here. Which is why there are two doors into the inner portions of the building off the lobby. One entrance goes directly to the remainder of the building, and the one we took allows passage through the offices first."

"I wondered about that," Jennifer said.

"We've been investigating the weak links that allowed Annabelle to take everything with her, but we haven't quite got it nailed down yet. Our security people told us that theft from this facility would be impossible, but we know that's not true—now."

Jennifer and Blake had come to a stop outside a room labeled "R&D Lab." A sign above the now familiar black security card reader said, "Proper Attire Required," just like a fancy restaurant. They stared through the glass at the workers, but didn't intrude.

This room looked like a television show laboratory with two lab benches, equipment resembling the stuff from Jennifer's high school chemistry class, and several computers placed around the room. A few people dressed in blue surgical scrubs, from the tops of their heads to the bottoms of their feet, stood around the room working at various stations.

Since the workers wore blue paper caps on their heads, masks over their noses and mouths, gloves on their hands, and even paper booties over their shoes, telling the men from the women wasn't easy. Jennifer didn't know any of these people, but she wouldn't have recognized even her best friend in those getups. They were effectively neutered and made anonymous by their protective coverings.

"Annabelle worked in here. Only six people had access to the lab besides me and my Uncle Russell. Annabelle was one of those six."

"Does that mean Annabelle had a security clearance that would allow her unlimited access to other areas of the company?" Jennifer asked. This security setup was all foreign to her. At her law firm everybody could walk around anywhere. The most confidential client files were available to anyone who worked in the firm. They had some pretty lax security that kept outsiders from the common areas of the office, but insiders were trusted. Only the money was put in a locked safe.

But then, research and development was the heart of a pharmaceutical company's future. Maybe this department was Denton Bio-Medical's equivalent to money, the equivalent of Worthington's steel safe.

"No. Annabelle's access was strictly limited to this room. The computer files are password protected and the sensitive ones are also protected by retina scans," Blake explained.

Jennifer said, "What?" She felt as if she'd entered the twilight zone, where the world was off-kilter and not exactly like the one she lived in.

"Industrial espionage. Surely you've heard of it?"

Jennifer nodded. Of course, she had. Jennifer went to the movies once in a while, just like everyone else. Her clients tended to be businesses that operated in less sensitive areas. This was her first case involving a pharmaceutical company. She had a lot to learn.

"Medical research is big business, Jennifer. Hundreds, maybe thousands, of researchers are working around the clock on the big medical issues. Like hepatitis Z. Several researchers have grown hepatitis Z or 'HZV' in a laboratory and are studying how the virus reproduces. We've isolated special enzymes of HZV called helicase and proteases. Our competitors are also working on specific drugs that inhibit these enzymes and will be highly effective in treating HZV." Jennifer listened closely to his explanation, wishing she had her notepad on hand.

"We'll develop our own products and then we rush to beat each other to market with them," Blake clarified. "With HepZMax, we got there first on the research end, and then lost our edge when Annabelle James took everything." He made medical advances sound like child's play.

"The stakes are awfully high for gamesmanship, aren't they?" She was mesmerized by the sound of his voice and by the sight of those anonymous human robots behind the glass performing mysterious experiments. They looked more like toys than soldiers in a deadly war against viral contagion.

Blake smiled. "Not much of a capitalist, are you? Yes, the system is fairly inefficient. Yes, we could do more if we all worked together, more cooperatively. No, that will never happen in our lifetime." Blake said these things in the kind of voice that let Jennifer know he'd been asked the same questions many times, and that the suggestion of cooperative development, or "partnering" as the management types called it these days, bored him.

"Look at it this way. Why don't Olympic athletes just get together and draw straws to decide who gets the gold medal? Why not simply toss the coin at the beginning of a football game and declare the winner?" Blake said, catching her eye. "It's a game, a competition. Accumulating more money than the competition is only the way we keep score."

Competition. Did Jennifer understand competition? She wasn't much of a competitor. That approach did seem so inefficient—and frightening—to her. Surely, in the end, biotechnology was not about games. Lives were at stake.

Since she'd been hired to figure out how to get the HepZMax formula back, Jennifer had spent hours, day and night, examining every word of the file Russell Denton had sent her and she had come to a standstill. She was frustrated and could feel the clock ticking.

Much of the file materials were completely unintelligible to her. The documents were filled with formulas, numbers, and symbols she couldn't even read. She'd have to hire six experts just to understand what the documents said. Jennifer was mired in minutiae and she felt as if she were trying to move through molasses on her knees. Coming here today was supposed to help her clarify things for herself.

"Look, Jennifer. Denton Bio-Medical is a local research firm. We're successful, but we're not on top of our industry. We're a big fish in a relatively little pond here in Tampa, but there are much bigger, better-financed companies than ours. We do the best we can and that's pretty damn good. We discover and develop some of the most effective drugs available on the market today. If we win the Hep Z race, we're propelled to the very top of the heap—we're the winners. We go public. We begin to acquire our old competitors, one by one. We eat them up. We become as big as Microsoft in our industry, and I get to be as rich as Bill Gates. Get it?"

No. She really didn't. Oh, she wasn't an idiot. She realized that a patented cure for hepatitis Z would catapult Russell and Blake Denton into international prominence and generate more money than both men could ever spend in this lifetime. But was that more important than bringing the product to market for the benefit of mankind, regardless of who got the credit for it? Was Russell really asking her to find Annabelle James and the missing formula just so he could make more money?

The one thing Jennifer definitely did understand, though, was that HepZMax was too valuable to remain lost somewhere. Annabelle James, if she took HepZMax, would definitely surface sooner or later. Jennifer was determined to make that happen as quickly as possible, and she'd been strategizing the most effective way to accomplish her goal as she'd worked through the night.

Blake began walking away from her now. "Let's go to my office and I'll give you a crash course in virology and try to explain HepZMax a little better to you," he said. Jennifer gratefully followed him back through the locked doors and down the corridors to the executive offices, where they had started.

CHAPTER NINE

TYLER WOKE UP THREE hours later than he'd planned to. His head was groggy. He felt as if he'd been swimming through Jell-O all that time.

Tyler was experienced as a detective. He knew his subconscious would solve all problems, if he could just get out of his own way. He thought of his process as a door that opened inward. While conscious, he felt his efforts to solve his cases remained as ineffective as if he were pushing on that unyielding door. The information he needed, just on the other side, couldn't get through until he stepped back and let the door open by itself. This he accomplished in a sleep state.

Tyler had begun this practice while still with the FBI. A knotty problem meant that he'd need at least an hour of deep sleep. He kept a recorder near his bed, always, so that the second he woke up, he could dictate what had been revealed to him. He also slept with the voice-activated recorder turned on so that if he talked in his sleep, his words would be recorded automatically.

The extra hours' sleep made him feel more tired than before. He wasn't refreshed, and if he'd received any insights while sleeping, they eluded him now. He looked at the recorder's tape. Nothing had been recorded. Damn! He'd wasted three hours, and he didn't even feel better.

Worse, he was losing this game of beat the clock. Finding Annabelle James and HepZMax had at first seemed like an easy task. After several weeks of trying everything he could think of, he'd finally recommended that Russell hire Jennifer Lane. Tyler realized how desperate he'd become that he'd recommend such a long shot of an idea. Only he and Russell were aware of the full gravity of the situation, but they wouldn't be able to keep the matter out of the public eye indefinitely.

Tyler dragged himself to the coffee pot and forced himself to pour the six-hour-old mud from the bottom into his cup. As soon as he put the thick, black stuff in his mouth, he spat it out again. No one could drink that crap, no matter how macho he might think he was.

As the new pot brewed, Tyler went into the small bathroom in the corner of the room he had dubbed "the Cellar" and splashed cold water on his face. He looked at the shower stall and decided a ten-minute shower under some stinging needles of hot water might make him feel human again.

Turning the water on, he stood beneath the pounding stream. As the shower washed the grime out of his brain, he began to work again on the problem.

How had Annabelle gotten all the data out of the computers, out of the plant, completely off the radar?

Tyler suspected that Gilbert had given her the formula, put her name on it, but he had no proof. But would Gilbert have stolen it? Unfortunately, Tyler hadn't asked Gilbert the question before he'd driven his car off the Skyway two days ago. But Tyler thought not. Gilbert had been as loyal to Russell Denton as an old hound dog.

In fact, that's what Gilbert had always reminded Tyler of—an ancient bloodhound. Loyal as the day was long, as good a hunter as existed on the earth, but completely stupid when it came to everything else about living.

And how did Annabelle erase the data? These were the missing pieces that he hadn't been able to find. So far.

Tyler finished his shower, poured a fresh cup of coffee and returned to his desk and the pile of video and audiotapes. He thought about it: The security department operated 236 cameras in the plant. He'd looked at the video from the lab and the computer rooms. He'd looked at the tapes from the locker room where Annabelle stored her personal stuff while she worked.

But he'd never found any evidence. *Where else could the information be accessed? How'd she do it?* If Tyler could figure out how Annabelle stole the backup data on HepZMax, then maybe he could fix this mess before it got any worse. And if he couldn't, then at least they had Jennifer Lane, their ace in the hole.

Seated in a corner of Blake's office at a small, square conference table, Jennifer looked over the room while he collected materials to demonstrate his explanations. Blake's office was larger than Jennifer's but not palatial. Some of the partners on the forty-second floor at Worthington had much bigger working offices. Stuart's office would be more than twice this size when a victory for Russell Denton moved him into the CEO's chair. Blake's office was not impressive. Jennifer had expected something more.

The room was furnished with Danish modern, natural-wood pieces, which were more legs than drawers. One small bookcase, half empty, sat in the corner. He wasn't a reader. The only extravagance here seemed to be the three computers Blake had up and running: two fancy laptops and one sleek desktop computer with a high resolution, flat-screen monitor on his credenza. All three computers had screen savers displaying the floating blue and white Denton Bio-Medical logo Jennifer recognized from the few over-the-counter painkillers she bought regularly to supplement her migraine prescriptions.

Blake pushed a button on one of the PCs. A large screen on the wall immediately opposite slowly revealed a slide from the computer—again depicting the Denton Bio-Medical logo. Jennifer watched Blake click an infrared mini-mouse to display a slide show program while he talked.

"Interferon is the current treatment of choice for HCV." Blake flashed a graph and several pie charts up on the screen while he explained the various treatments. "Unfortunately, only ten to fifteen percent of patients treated with standard interferon monotherapy cleared the virus."

Jennifer interrupted. "I'm sorry, what does that mean?"

"It means the virus didn't show up in their blood after further testing." He switched the slide. "Combination therapy with ribavirin clears thirty-eight to forty-seven percent. Adding pegylated interferons increases that clearance to fifty-five percent."

"Does that mean the patients are cured?" Jennifer asked.

"Depends on what you mean by a cure. If a patient makes it for six months, then ninety-five percent of them will remain symptom free, based on what we know now." Changing to another slide, he added, "But at what cost?"

Blake went through the next set. "Patients must inject themselves subcutaneously with interferon. This requires learning about storing and preparing the drug, sterile technique, injection sites, and needle disposal. Many aren't able to handle this emotionally. Just as for diabetics who take insulin. Sure we have oral drugs now, but they're not for everyone."

Jennifer shuddered to think about the prospect of having to inject herself every day. She wouldn't be able to handle it. She was even squeamish about paper cuts. "Are there any side effects to the therapy?"

"Unfortunately, yes." Blake switched to another slide. "Side effects vary, but they can include chills, muscle aches, nausea, diarrhea, fatigue, weight loss, skin reactions. Some patients experience depression, mental changes, and hair loss. Then there's the frequent blood tests to monitor the effects of the therapy."

"What are the blood tests for?" Jennifer was beginning to feel like a pincushion just hearing the list of horrors that came with the "cure." If she'd ever considered getting a tattoo, she struck the thought from her mind in that instant.

Blake pulled up another slide and kept pouring on the misery. "The treatment affects white blood cell and platelet counts, so the patient is more susceptible to infection."

Jennifer gave a shaky laugh. "Gee, is that all?"

"No," Blake told her, no humor in his voice. "I haven't gotten to the side effects of the ribavirin and the pegylated interferons yet."

For the next fifty minutes, Jennifer found herself riveted to the chair as Blake gave her the quick rundown on the various scientific methods used to research a cure for hepatitis Z and the future of improved treatment as well as ribavirin and pegylated interferons—words she couldn't even pronounce. Finally, Blake seemed to wind down his presentation. When he turned off the projector from his remote mouse and brought the lights back up, Jennifer tried not to sigh with relief. How was she going to survive this case, let alone win it?

"Thanks for that explanation, Blake," she said.

Jennifer had come here today hoping to find something—anything—that would help her understand Annabelle James and why she stole the HepZMax formula. If there was information in what Blake had just told her to help her achieve her goal, Jennifer had completely missed it. What kind of woman would knowingly put so many people in such peril by denying them a potential cure? And why? The depravity of such a theft was almost more than Jennifer could fathom.

Blake nodded. "I know it's dry. But I hope you'll remember some of it, anyway. I'll print out the slides for you, if you like, so you can flip through them again when you come to these concepts."

"Would you?" Jennifer wanted to hug him, but her reaction was probably not related to his offer. She hadn't stopped wanting to hug him since they'd met. "That would be so helpful." She glanced down at her watch and was not surprised to see that it was already past six. "I need to get going. Can I take the copies with me, or would you rather send them?"

"I'll get them to you later," he told her. Jennifer agreed and gathered up her purse and briefcase. Then Blake accompanied her back toward the lobby. Jennifer found herself easily falling into the rhythm of his walk and the cadence of his stopping to pass the security card over the reader before opening the doors.

The offices they passed were empty now and the receptionist gone. Jennifer left her visitor's badge on the desk and signed out. Blake unlocked the front exit for Jennifer to pass through.

As Jennifer went through the door, she turned to face him. "Blake…"

"Yes?" He was too close behind her and his warm breath brushed her face with the intimacy of a lover.

"Just out of curiosity, why didn't you simply go after Annabelle James and get HepZMax back?" This was the question that had been bothering Jennifer. Going after Annabelle directly seemed as if it would have been a simple solution.

Blake's face hardened and his voice became angry. "We tried. She's disappeared. No one knows where she is. We even hired a private detective to find her. No luck. It's like she took the formula and vanished off the face of the earth."

Jennifer felt the small hairs rise on the back of her neck, but she put that down to her physical attraction to Blake and ignored her intuition. "How long has Annabelle been missing?" she asked.

"Several weeks," Blake said. "That's why we finally hired you and decided to take the legal route. We thought we could find her and handle this privately. But it turned out we couldn't."

CHAPTER TEN

RUSSELL WENT INTO THE master bedroom and checked his bag again. They weren't staying overnight, but he'd need a change of clothes anyway. He and Blake never missed the Yankees and the Braves. Baseball played a long season, but the two men rarely had the chance to see the two great teams compete because they played in different leagues. Most years the Yankees and Braves wouldn't play each other at all.

Traveling to every contest had become a ritual between Russell and his nephew back when such an experience was a real stretch of their resources. Now, of course, they could afford much grander pastimes, but it was the nostalgia for his old relationship with Blake that Russell was after. Russell wanted to believe that relationship could be rekindled.

He had considered skipping today's game. "No," Tyler had said. "You need to go—and take Blake along." Russell didn't ask why. He didn't really want to know. While they were gone, Tyler would have his opportunity to do whatever he needed at the plant.

This afternoon, the game would be played at Yankee Stadium. They'd decided to take a quick trip up to watch the game in the mayor's box seats, then have dinner at the Gotham Bar and Grill. They'd return late tonight.

Things might have been different if Blake had made the team. He played well in high school and then in college. For a while, it looked like he would make it to the majors. Blake was easily as good as most of the talent Tampa's Devil Rays had managed to collect.

But Blake himself had lost interest in the game as a career. Changed his mind. "I've decided to go directly into business," he'd said at the time. And Blake, being Blake, now wanted to buy a baseball team. Any team. But, so far, none were for sale, even for the wildly unreasonable prices sports franchises commanded. "I can wait," Blake said, "for the right team, at the right time. Maybe Steinbrenner or Turner will sell one of these days. Stranger things have happened."

Russell wondered about Blake's conversion to unencumbered capitalism and his desire for excessively lavish lifestyle. Blake had been such a happy young boy. Russell recalled Little League games when the sunlight seemed to bathe Blake in its ethereal glow on the small pitcher's mound. Blake had been a good athlete then. He'd won more games than he'd lost. And he'd been gracious in both victory and defeat.

Russell's thoughts brought a dark frown to his features. All of that had changed. Abruptly. And recently. At work, it seemed that every choice, every decision, hinged on how much money Blake could generate. His competitive drive was on steroids, out of control. Yesterday, when Russell tried to reason with him, Blake had lashed out. "You have your fortune already, old man. Why don't you get out of my way? You want me to die broke, in the gutter, like my dad, is that it?"

Russell drew back as if he'd been punched in the gut. How could Blake think such a thing? "Come on, Blake. You know that's not true. I've always had your best interests at the top of my agenda."

"Oh, really? That's why you reacted to Annabelle James the way you did? Don't bullshit me. Just get out of the way, while you still can." Those had been Blake's parting words and Russell hadn't spoken to him since. Whether Blake would show up today remained to be seen.

If Russell could find the HepZMax formula and get that project going again, he would have more time to work on his relationship with his nephew. Russell still worried about him, but Blake was a man now. Russell could only hope he'd been a good enough substitute father and that Blake would eventually come around.

A few minutes later, Blake popped his head into Russell's study. "Ready?" he asked, in the brusque tone he'd been using in all conversations with Russell lately.

Russell breathed a sigh of relief. After yesterday's scene, he'd thought Blake might skip today's ballgame. Perhaps Blake was willing to give him another chance. "I'll be right there."

Russell shut down his computer and patted his jacket pocket to make sure the small cell phone was there. He didn't want to be out of touch with Tyler—even for a day.

Russell looked out the tall windows of his home on Hillsborough Bay and across to Davis Islands as he descended the stairs. How beautiful the Tampa area was. He loved living here. He would never move, even though Tyler thought he should. Tyler had said that HepZMax would catapult Russell into the realm of the superrich and make living a relatively normal life impossible. Russell hoped not.

He put his arm around his nephew and Blake didn't pull away. "Let's go."

They walked through the foyer to the front door and headed to where the limousine driver and two bodyguards waited. Since Gilbert had died, Tyler insisted that Russell travel everywhere with protection if Tyler himself was unavailable. Russell thought the concept preposterous, but he'd hired Tyler for his expertise, so he allowed the intrusion into his privacy.

In the car, Russell and Blake talked about the game, the evening. Their conversation was an undeclared truce of sorts. They'd been arguing so much lately, Russell was glad for the momentary respite. He hated arguing with Blake. And he rarely won.

In the Denton Bio-Medical private plane, they watched a video of the last matchup between the Yankees and the Braves. On request, the plane's steward served them beer and Chicago-style hotdogs for lunch. The experience once again filled Russell with a longing for the past.

Russell wished Blake were still ten, still fifteen. But he wasn't. Blake was an adult now, and Russell was responsible for molding him into the man he had become. Once again Russell went over the territory: Where had Russell gone wrong? Was it possible to overcome genetics? Was Blake destined to follow the same miserable path his father had trod? Russell didn't think he could go through it all again. He didn't have the strength. Or the will.

Watching the game, rooting for their favorite players, and making small talk with the others kept Russell and Blake apart most of the day. The flight home, afterward, was spent sleeping.

Once they'd arrived back at the Denton mansion, and Russell was laying his head on his Egyptian-cotton sheets, he said his silent prayers for health, safety, and good luck. He thought about how much he'd loved being Blake's uncle. He would have loved nothing more than to do this one job for the rest of his life. But Blake wasn't going to let that happen, and Russell's last thoughts before sleep were of the giant emptiness in his heart where his nephew's love used to be.

CHAPTER ELEVEN

JENNIFER CRAVED MELANIE'S SELF-CONFIDENT presence like a chocolate addict craves a candy bar. Melanie was almost six feet tall and had the prettiest coffee-colored skin and large, expressive brown eyes. Everything about Melanie was smooth and well put together. Her clothes and composure reflected the kind of style that Jennifer could only dream about.

Melanie could have been a model; she was that stunning, Jennifer thought. But she had chosen law and she was good at it.

Melanie's combination of beauty, brains and talent might have made some of her other female colleagues jealous, but not Jennifer. The glow of Melanie's friendship bathed Jennifer in a more glamorous life than she would otherwise ever have. With Melanie, the best-looking lawyer at Worthington, and Stuart, the best lawyer and on his way to being CEO, as her friends, Jennifer felt something close to acceptance from her colleagues. People spoke to her in the hallways, invited her to lunch sometimes. Acceptance was a feeling Jennifer wasn't used to, and she liked it.

Melanie had told Jennifer she had more power than she realized because of her relationship with Stuart. But Jennifer didn't feel that power on a daily basis. She thought she would feel it once Stuart was actually CEO. For now, she heard the veiled criticism of Stuart by his colleagues in the hallways, even if Stuart didn't hear it. Stuart wasn't a powerful man—yet. The Denton case would change all of that.

Now, while Melanie sat across the table from Jennifer at the Wine Exchange in Old Hyde Park Village, they sipped Chardonnay and Jennifer listened as Melanie discussed her complex love life. Jennifer had no love life to discuss—a fact that, at the moment, was a very good thing. If there had been a man in Jennifer's life, she would have had no time for him right now.

Relationships, especially romantic ones, required nurturing. Jennifer spent all of her time working. Her efforts to find Annabelle James and, simultaneously, to anticipate every legal argument she might use to get a TRO against any potential buyer of HepZMax took up every waking minute of her time.

She still smiled at the old joke about the lawyer who died young because God looked at his time charges and thought he was ninety. When she'd first heard that joke while still in law school, Jennifer didn't understand the humor. Now that she was living the irony, she had the insight to acknowledge it.

For romance, Jennifer lived vicariously through Melanie.

By the time their salads were brought to the table, Melanie finally wound down on the subject of her latest lover's deficiencies and transgressions and turned her attention to Jennifer.

"You're pretty quiet tonight. Still thinking about Russell Denton and his case?" When Jennifer's face flushed embarrassment, Melanie admonished, "Do you ever think about anything except work? Get a life, girl!"

Jennifer tried to hide her discomfort in a mouthful of spinach leaves. She didn't have the grace to pull off a lie, so she said nothing. Melanie knew her too well.

"All right, then. You aren't going to have anything to say unless we talk about what's on your mind, so just tell me what the problem is. I already know it has something to do with Stuart."

Jennifer knew Melanie wasn't nearly as exasperated with Jennifer as she sounded.

Her friend—her best friend for the past five years—had always been willing to listen to Jennifer's breathless fixation on work, and, more specifically, her fixation on Stuart Barnett. Every facet of Stuart's life was fascinating to Jennifer. Melanie tolerated Jennifer's unrequited crush on the man with patience because Melanie believed Jennifer would eventually get over it. So far, though, after five years of daily contact, what Melanie thought of as Jennifer's lovesick mooning over Stuart Barnett hadn't abated. Jennifer followed Stuart Barnett the way an Orthodox Rabbi follows God. But Melanie was wrong about Jennifer's feelings for Stuart. She loved him, yes, but she would never have a romantic relationship with him. She wanted something more permanent than that.

Jennifer swallowed her spinach and pushed away her plate. She wasn't really hungry tonight. She'd only been waiting for an opening to discuss the Denton case with Melanie and to get Melanie's thoughts so that she could test her own. Jennifer's confidence in her own lawyering skills was still building. Some day, she believed, she'd be an excellent lawyer. She already knew she wrote the best briefs in the firm. The rest would come. When she took her anxiety medication regularly, she was sure of it.

Now, she relied on more experienced colleagues as she found her way. Like Stuart, Melanie Stein was a brilliant attorney. She could see, incisively, what other lawyers struggled to discover. It was a gift. Jennifer had something of the same talent, too, although Jennifer's skills were less developed. Their love for the law was really the only common bond between the two women.

"Russell Denton is a very powerful man. He's used to getting what he wants and keeping what's his. I'm amazed that anyone would have the nerve to steal anything from him," Jennifer explained her thoughts. "I mean, you'd have to know he could squash you like a bug, wouldn't you?"

Melanie said nothing, just ate her salad and listened to Jennifer. This was their pattern. One rambled on while the other listened, a form of friendship that suited them both. Jennifer continued for another ten minutes.

"I mean, this woman was an employee. Denton supported her team's research for five years. And then, she leaves and steals the formula and all the backup data so that it can't be duplicated? How could she do that? How disloyal can you be?"

Jennifer, finally taking a breather, was genuinely outraged. She could never be so disloyal to Stuart or to Melanie. Loyalty was one of life's most important virtues. Either you were loyal, or you weren't, to her way of thinking. And if you weren't, then Jennifer had no use for you.

Jennifer had been betrayed in her life. She knew how much it hurt. But those were only small betrayals, little things like a two-timing boyfriend in high school, a cat that ran away, a doctor who tried to hit on her. A betrayal of the magnitude that Russell had suffered at the hand of Annabelle James was too devastating to think about. Not to mention the very real harm Annabelle James was causing to Hep Z patients.

Melanie looked up. "You're asking me?" When Jennifer nodded, Melanie swallowed, put down her fork and took another sip of her wine. "Well, first of all, sounds to me like the work belonged to this woman. What's her name again?"

"I shouldn't say." Jennifer knew she had already said too much, but no one could go without discussing these things with a friend. She certainly couldn't. Stuart had been in court constantly since they'd received Russell Denton's case, so she hadn't been able to talk to him. Who else was there?

"Right," Melanie continued. "Anyway, she did the work, didn't she? She could have just thought it was hers. She's not a lawyer. She might not realize that the company—" she interrupted herself. "She didn't sign any kind of employment contract, right?" Melanie leaned closer to argue the facts, since Jennifer seemed to have the better argument on the law.

Jennifer looked uncomfortable now. "I think she did, but we can't find it."

Melanie gave her the look. "In litigation, Jennifer, if you can't prove it, then it didn't happen. There's no contract."

Jennifer started to protest and Melanie hurried on. "I mean, if you left the firm…" At Jennifer's shocked expression, Melanie backpedaled. "I know you would never do that, but if you did, wouldn't you take your files with you? Your research, your memos, and the briefs you've written over the years? I mean, you've been paid the whole time you've worked at Worthington. But, still, you'd think the stuff you created was yours, and you'd take it, wouldn't you?"

"It sounds so reasonable when you say it like that. But it's not. Stuart says it's not." Stuart agreed with Russell Denton. If Stuart said so, to Jennifer the answer was as good as it gets. Stuart had never lied to her. Moreover, Jennifer's job was to advance the client's interests. That was what she intended to do. Stuart would expect no less. She expected no less of herself, either.

Melanie swallowed and set down her fork. She took the big sister tone she often used when Jennifer was being myopic about reality. "Look. Maybe she never signed the agreement at all. Maybe she signed under duress. Maybe there's another agreement that gives her an enforceable interest in this formula. There are a thousand facts you don't know here."

Jennifer shook her head. "No. Stuart asked about all of that."

Melanie lost it. She slapped her hand on the table, making the plates lift up and crash back down. "Look. Just because Stuart Barnett says so doesn't mean it's written on the tablets, brought back from God by Moses. Stuart has been wrong before." Jennifer ducked down as if Melanie had thrown the dishes at her, personally, and dropped her fork on the tile floor with a loud clatter.

Melanie had nowhere near Jennifer's level of affection for Stuart Barnett. The man was married, for one thing. Married men were completely off limits. Melanie had been down that road before, with disastrous consequences. Jennifer had realized long ago that Melanie was jealous of Jennifer's relationship with Stuart. Not because Melanie wanted the same relationship with Stuart that Jennifer had, but because Melanie wanted Jennifer's first loyalty to be to her.

"Well, the contract issue is a moot point right at the moment since Annabelle has disappeared and we can't ask her. We can't do much of anything, in fact, until we figure out how to find her and the data she stole." Jennifer's tone ended that discussion. Melanie's color was high underneath her lush cocoa shading. Her vehemence against Stuart was too upsetting. Jennifer didn't want Melanie to be angry with her.

Jennifer knew she could be a loyal friend to both Melanie and Stuart. But, somehow, Melanie didn't seem to be sure. Jennifer had tried to work this out, but she had finally just accepted it. She kept so many of Stuart's secrets to herself, she could keep Melanie's insecurity to herself, too. Anyway, Jennifer believed Melanie would never acknowledge her own jealousy.

Jennifer tuned out Melanie's warnings and changed the subject to the missing Roxanne Walden case Melanie was working on, then tuned Melanie out as she chatted. Stuart was never wrong, Jennifer believed. And he wasn't wrong now. Jennifer intended to prove exactly that. Annabelle James had stolen that formula and Jennifer was going to get it back. Melanie would be sorry she'd doubted Stuart. They all would.

CHAPTER TWELVE

STUART WAS IN HIGH good humor. He was standing in the hallway at the Sam M. Gibbons Federal Courthouse on a twenty-minute break from an important evidentiary hearing.

The hearing must be going well, Jennifer thought. She sat on a bench just outside the courtroom with papers piled in her lap and looking up at her mentor.

Today, he wore a crisp white shirt and an expertly tied yellow print bow tie. His suspenders, or "braces" as he called them, were littered with colorful hummingbirds that peeked out from time to time as he moved around in his navy suit jacket. The whole "man at court" image seemed suitable for a high fashion catalog or a movie. Stuart's wardrobe was one of the reasons his partners scorned him. They thought he was too flashy, which was somehow a character flaw.

No matter what anyone thought, though, Stuart was a genuine genius. Jennifer was bright and worked hard, but Stuart was not only older and more experienced, his IQ was above 170. Jennifer had formed the habit of jotting the great man's words of wisdom, verbatim—quickly—for later analysis. Her shorthand skills had saved her butt more than once in carrying out a partner's orders, and Jennifer knew from past experience wisdom would sooner or later be forthcoming from Stuart, although often what he said was completely bewildering to her.

Now, however, he was reading, his half-glasses perched low on his nose, and didn't look up at Jennifer who had already been speaking for more than a minute.

"Give me the short version, Archie," Stuart said with his usual preoccupied friendliness.

The two had discovered early in their relationship that they were both fans of the old Nero Wolfe books. Stuart naturally assumed the role of the rotund genius detective, Wolfe, while Jennifer preferred to act the smart and sexy go-fer, Archie. Truth be told, Jennifer thought Stuart was a greater genius than Nero Wolfe. But when Stuart called her "Archie," Jennifer felt bonded to Stuart, as if she was important to him, and she liked it.

Jennifer began to read her previously prepared summary to Stuart, feeling more than a little like the law student she'd once been. She'd spent countless hours researching the law for the Denton case and pouring over the documents Denton had provided. She'd read so much about hepatitis Z that she felt as if she could single-handedly defend all humankind against the dread virus. Unfortunately, she hadn't made a lot of headway on the case and she'd missed Stuart's deadline once already.

"Denton Bio-Medical is in the medical research and development business. Denton has a reputation for sprinting to the finish line on big new drugs, beating out its competitors. Denton has built its collection of patents into one of the few large family-owned businesses in America." Stuart hadn't looked up from his reading yet. Obviously, Jennifer hadn't snagged his attention. She skipped down a few paragraphs in her notes and continued.

"Denton's internal policy is to have all employees when they join the company sign an agreement that protects Denton's secrets and gives Denton full title to any products or research developed while the employee is working there." The courtroom deputy walked out into the hallway and told Stuart the judge would be back on the bench in ten minutes, then walked over to the other litigants standing down the hall and gave them the same message.

The facts Jennifer reeled off had seemed salient when she was formulating her report. Now, they appeared irrelevant because Stuart wasn't interested and they were short on time. But without a plan B, Jennifer had no choice but to continue on her now-failing path.

"Annabelle James developed a potentially successful formula for HepZMax, a new drug that would treat hepatitis Z without the terrible side effects most patients suffer from the current medications. Her formula would also be about ninety percent effective, compared to the current treatments that only clear about forty percent of Hep Z sufferers."

If Stuart had been pretending to listen, this was the part where he would have feigned a yawn. Jennifer could tell. She took a sip of water, then skipped a few more paragraphs of her prepared speech and got closer to the bottom of the page.

"Somehow—they don't know how exactly—Annabelle managed to enter secured computer databases and hard-copy storage rooms to which she was not entitled access. She took everything related to the research she and a coworker named Gilbert Irwin had been doing on the HepZMax formula. She removed the information from the computers and deleted all of the backups. Then, two days later, Annabelle vanished."

Stuart looked up at Jennifer for the first time. "What do you mean, she vanished?" His piercing blue eyes shot beams directly toward her, reminding her of the laser-sword weapons in science fiction movies.

Jennifer wet her lips. "Just that. They can't find her. Denton even hired a private investigator, but that guy hasn't been able to find Annabelle, either. So far."

Stuart shrugged and went back to his reading. "Maybe she's dead," he said, as if he was unconcerned. "That might make things easier."

Not for Annabelle, Jennifer thought, but didn't say so. Stuart's morbid directness had amused Jennifer on other occasions. And it fit the Nero Wolfe routine. But Jennifer was having trouble with this whole project. Melanie's words at dinner haunted her. What facts existed that Jennifer didn't know?

She'd been hired to do two things: find Annabelle James and get the formula back or wait until the buyer surfaced and be fully prepared to sue him. Jennifer's legal career had been short, but one thing she'd learned so far was the law could not force Annabelle to do anything she didn't want to do. The easiest, fastest solution to Russell's dilemma was to make Annabelle want to give HepZMax back. But Jennifer couldn't figure out how to do that exactly.

Annabelle James had worked on the formula with Gilbert Irwin. Her creativity and intelligence had helped him produce a truly revolutionary treatment, one that would save millions of lives and reduce the misery caused by traditional Hep Z therapies. Somehow, Annabelle had acquired Gilbert's interest in HepZMax. And Gilbert's car had gone off the Skyway and he'd died—probably a suicide. It was easy to see why Annabelle might think she owned HepZMax now, if she'd never formally agreed to the assignment, as Melanie had suggested.

But if Annabelle believed HepZMax belonged to her, why steal all the data and disappear?

Jennifer's job was to get HepZMax back to its rightful owner. How could she do that? It seemed to Jennifer that the best answer was a settlement.

All cases are settled, she'd heard Stuart say more than once. It's just a question of whether the parties settle their disputes themselves or whether they let a judge and jury do it for them.

Russell Denton was a multi-millionaire and Denton Bio-Medical owned enough medical products to keep it afloat in its field indefinitely. Annabelle was just a young woman, barely out of graduate school. She and Russell should work together. Maybe he could buy HepZMax from her or let her have this product to sell to the highest bidder. So long as someone had it, the cure could be produced.

And, furthermore, even though Russell thought he already owned HepZMax—and maybe he did because Annabelle was his employee—every day that he couldn't wrest the formula from Annabelle James was a day that he wasn't making money. Litigation could take years. Another researcher was bound to derive a competitive product in the meantime. A settlement was the only real solution Jennifer had come up with, the only one she thought might actually work.

Russell could buy HepZMax from Annabelle, at a fair price, if he thought he had to have it so badly. The cure would reach the people who needed it; Annabelle would get the credit, and a great deal of money. Everybody would win.

The way Russell was going about this case, no one knew where the formula was and no one would benefit. A different, more creative approach was called for. Of course, such a quick and simple solution would also severely limit the amount of attorney fees Russell Denton would pay Stuart Barnett and his firm. Jennifer said none of this to Stuart, but thinking it through emboldened her.

Jennifer picked up the ubiquitous yellow legal pad that rested on her stack of papers and grinned. "Oh great one," she intoned, "speak." She noticed the other lawyers and spectators wandering back into the courtroom. "Quickly," she added.

"Okay," Stuart said, looking up again. Jennifer sat, poised with pen over her pad, ready to take down Stuart's words. "You've got two problems," he summarized, holding up two fingers, one a time. "First, you have to find out what Annabelle James did with that formula. Then, you have to get it back. Any ideas?"

Ideas were what she didn't have. At least, none she was willing to share. That was why she was sitting there. Jennifer waited.

Stuart glanced at his watch. "Okay. Draft a complaint for conversion, interference with prospective economic advantage, breach of implied contract, whatever else you can think of. Get it on my desk tonight. Prepare it for federal court. We'll serve a notice of deposition *duces tecum* with it tomorrow." Stuart looked toward the door. "We're behind on this project, Jennifer. Russell Denton can't wait forever."

A complaint for conversion, or civil theft, would start a lawsuit and the notice of deposition *duces tecum*, or "with documents," would require Annabelle James to show up, bringing the formula with her. But it wasn't as if Jennifer hadn't thought of this solution herself. She had simply rejected it.

"We can't do that," Jennifer said, sipping water from the bottle of Zephyrhills she'd brought with her and holding Stuart back from entering the courtroom with her objection. He had five minutes yet.

"Surely Denton can give you a list of the documents he wants back?" Stuart asked with surprising patience.

"Yes," Jennifer agreed. "But that's not the problem."

"No?" Stuart reached over to pull the door to the courtroom open, giving Jennifer a glimpse of the crowd of lawyers and exhibits inside. The other lawyers were milling around at their places, but none of the court personnel had returned just yet.

Jennifer shook her head. Stuart raised his left eyebrow, mocking her, his attention clearly focused on the remainder of his hearing.

She'd thought this through and decided to stick to her original plan. She spoke quickly, urgently, lowering her voice, now that he'd opened the courtroom door. "First, what gives us federal court jurisdiction? More importantly, whom do we serve?"

You couldn't just file anything you wanted in a complaint in federal court. Strict rules existed about what kinds of cases could be brought there. Jennifer had analyzed this case seven ways to Sunday and she couldn't come up with a handle for claiming federal jurisdiction.

Stuart said nothing, so Jennifer wet her lips again and said to him, laying out her logic. "There's plenty of money at stake for federal court. Millions, if Russell Denton is to be believed. That's not the problem. But we don't have a federal statute to rely on. We don't have two citizens of different states, and we don't have a constitutional issue. So we can't get there from here." Jennifer shrugged. "We're stuck going to court in Hillsborough County."

Jennifer knew Stuart would never, ever represent a plaintiff in a case filed in the local circuit court. The state court system was not the high-powered arena in which Stuart now wished to play. To Stuart, only the less important cases were filed in state court. Stuart Barnett had graduated from that platform for his talents long ago. Knowing how he felt, Jennifer tried to use the threat of a state court action to dissuade Stuart from pursuing an ill-advised lawsuit against Annabelle James and consider a settlement. From the aggrieved look he gave her, her ploy wasn't working.

Stuart knew the federal jurisdictional requirements better than Jennifer did. He could probably recite the statutes in his sleep. Stuart loved competition. He had long since passed the stage in his career when he needed to do anything for any other reason than because he chose to do so.

"How to use the law to enforce rights and create remedies for deserving clients is what we're getting paid for here, Archie. The woman stole something that didn't belong to her, isn't that so?" Stuart sounded like a teacher explaining the alphabet to a dim first-grader.

Jennifer didn't answer him. She heard the court officer intone, "All rise." The judge was making his way back to the bench, but she saw him stop to have a quiet conversation with his law clerk.

"Jennifer, I've got to go," Stuart said. "I'm sorry."

He glanced up toward the judge. "There's a way to file a case in federal court and get her attention along with a quick hearing and a speedy decision. You know if we file in state court we'll be mired there forever. Let her know that we mean business. Use your brain, Jennifer. Hit the books. Look at the Food and Drug Act. That's a federal statute. Maybe we can use that. Consider the patent and trademark laws. Rico, maybe. Trade secrets law. You'll find something."

"Mr. Barnett, are you joining us or not?" the judge asked Stuart in a very unfriendly tone, even though he had not resumed his proper place. Like many judges, this one expected the lawyers to wait for him, not the other way around. Stuart began to move through the door into the room.

Jennifer followed him, continuing to whisper while the judge was preoccupied with a cell phone call he'd just answered. "Who will we serve? We can't even find the woman. How will we get her into court?"

Jennifer could be just as stubborn as Stuart could. She had been a lawyer for five years now. She had seen lawyers get into trouble by blindly following orders without making their own decisions.

Beyond that, Jennifer had begun to believe that Annabelle James might not have stolen anything that didn't belong to her. In fact, Jennifer didn't believe that suing Annabelle was the right thing to do. She couldn't exactly articulate why, but she thought maybe, just maybe, if she could find Annabelle James, she could work all this out. And to find Annabelle, Jennifer would need more time.

"Sometime today, Mr. Barnett." The judge was still talking on the telephone, but he was losing patience quickly.

Stuart turned and made his way to counsel table. Jennifer followed him and sat directly behind his chair in the gallery. "I'm sorry, Your Honor. Ready," Stuart said when the judge had finally finished his telephone call.

When one of the other lawyers went to the podium, Jennifer risked Stuart's wrath by pulling on his sleeve. He turned to listen with one ear on his opponent's argument.

"Was she married?" Stuart asked, flipping to the next page of the file open in front of him, making it look as if Jennifer were talking to him about the matter before the court.

"No." Jennifer said.

"Serve her parents, then." Stuart turned his back on her and refused to pay her any more attention.

CHAPTER THIRTEEN

LILA WALDEN SAT AT the psychic's table, uneasy being away from home so long, feeling the same anxious anticipation she had felt while waiting for bad news from her oncologist.

Her narrow fingers silently opened and closed the top clasp on her small, pastel pink handbag. Lila had picked out this purse because it looked like one that Jackie Kennedy had carried while First Lady and because it matched her pink suit.

She and Jackie had a lot in common. Lila looked like Jackie. Everyone said so. When she was on the homecoming court at Plant High School, she'd had her hair done in an updo just like Jackie wore at State dinners. Lila adopted Jackie's upswept style with just a little bang slanting across the side of her forehead, crossing above her left eyebrow and tucking securely behind her ear. Lila had been wearing the same style since 1963. It suited her just fine.

Before leaving home, she'd slipped on her pumps and checked for any scuffs or runs in her stockings. Lila wore pantyhose, of course. She wouldn't go out of the house in a skirt with bare legs. Common women did that. Sure, the day was hot. In Tampa, mid-summer, the weather was *supposed* to be hot like this. But that was no excuse for being common. How many times had she told her daughter Roxanne Mae that very thing?

Thinking of Roxanne Mae reminded Lila why she had come to this house today. She needed guidance from the psychic about her daughter. She'd heard Ronald talking to her on the cell phone out in the garage last month. He'd answered on the fifth ring. Ronald was so hard of hearing from years of working around noisy machinery that he had the volume on the phone turned up loud enough to be heard across the street. She hadn't meant to eavesdrop from where she stood, hiding behind a storage bin, but she'd heard the entire conversation—at least Ronald's side—and had filled in the rest.

"Hey, baby. Everything okay today?... You know I do worry, though. As long as you call me every day, I'll know you're all right... Yeah. I figured out how to do that. You should have left the cell phone charger where I could find it, too... Don't worry. What kind of trouble are you in, baby? Man trouble? Let Daddy help you. Then you can come home."

The pleading in his voice was almost more than Lila could stand. She nearly turned away. But then, she wanted to know, needed to know, what the two of them were up to.

"I don't care what you say. You need to leave that Blake Denton alone, honey. He's too high-profile for you. And he's got a mean temper, too... Married? Are you sure about that? Is he just promising you something he thinks you want to hear?... Well, I love you, too, baby." Ronald said into the empty air.

After Ronald hung up, Lila realized that she'd heard the ringing before. Ronald must have been talking with Roxanne Mae every night, late, while they thought Lila was sleeping. Ronald was right. Blake Denton did have a mean temper. But it took one to know one.

Once she'd heard the first call, Lila began to listen for the others. She knew when the police became involved that Ronald honestly hadn't heard from Roxanne Mae in the last few weeks. He kept the cell phone on, charged, and by his side at all times. Lila realized he didn't know where Roxanne Mae had been calling from. If he'd known, he'd have gone looking for her already. She thought that, with every passing day, her husband was becoming more convinced that his daughter was dead. Maybe that was why he'd agreed to see the lawyer about the guardianship.

He'd been drinking constantly in the last few weeks, sleeping only one or two hours a night. Every time he woke up, he'd gulp down another beer and then pass out again. Each day, he was more difficult to deal with, hot tempered and nasty. Lila was more afraid of him now than she'd ever been.

She needed to know what was going on. Roxanne Mae had been away for too long. She was up to something, but Lila had no idea what her daughter might have gotten herself into. Lila had used all of what she liked to consider her own psychic abilities, but she couldn't get a clear picture. She needed professional help. She needed to know what to do.

Now, she looked across the small table covered with a long floral tablecloth that touched the tops of her shoes. The young psychic, who gazed at her with dark eyes, was slightly built and had a coronet of wispy black curls; she resembled a gypsy all right. She dressed in clothes Lila wouldn't wear to clean the house. Her feet were bare in clunky suede sandals that looked like something you'd expect on a Tibetan monk, as far as Lila was concerned.

Maybe coming here had been a mistake. The psychic couldn't properly dress herself, how could she help Lila with Roxanne Mae and Ronald when so many, more competent, professionals had not?

Lila looked around the room while the psychic prepared for the reading, lighting candles, dimming the lights, and starting quiet music. She handed Lila the Tarot cards and Lila took them, removing her left hand from her purse, but continuing to work the clasp with the bony fingers of her right hand.

"I'll need you to shuffle the cards slowly. You're right handed, so hold the cards in your right hand and shuffle with your left," the psychic instructed.

Lila reluctantly released the purse clasp and did as she was told. She felt awkward shuffling with her left hand. She had trouble with it. The cards didn't want to cooperate. She ended up lifting a few cards from the front of the deck and moving them to the back. It was the best she could manage. After a little while, she was performing this task rhythmically, without thinking about it.

Smiling a tiny smile, the psychic bent down to pick up a small terrier and held the dog in her arms while she silently watched Lila shuffle the cards for a few moments. Between them on the table, the flickering candle provided mysterious illumination sufficient to allow them to see each other—though Lila didn't look at the psychic. She simply continued to shuffle the cards and wait.

After a few minutes, the psychic asked Lila a question. "You're concerned about your daughter?"

"Yes." Lila had given this information when she'd made the appointment.

"She is an adult, right?"

"Yes." Lila had told the assistant this, too.

"She is missing?"

Now, Lila looked startled. This was information she hadn't given the assistant. She stopped shuffling the cards, and the psychic motioned for her to continue. Maybe the psychic could help her; maybe the woman did know something.

Lila began shuffling the cards again. "Yes."

"Yet, you're not worried about where she is." The psychic wasn't asking a question this time, so Lila said nothing. They understood each other.

"You're more worried about what she's doing." This was not a question, either. The psychic continued to pet the little dog. She didn't ask Lila to select any cards.

"You think Annabelle is involved in criminal activity of some kind." Lila shuffled the cards and stared hard at the flame in front of her. How did the psychic know that people called her daughter Annabelle? Lila hadn't told her. In fact, Lila hadn't told the psychic her daughter's name at all. A small shiver ran through her, causing her hands to tremble slightly as she continued to dutifully shuffle the cards. Lila said nothing, though. She couldn't bring herself to speak.

A few seconds later, the psychic gasped, causing Lila to raise eyes to look the "gypsy" full in the face. Lila could see that the psychic knew. Lila was relieved that she wouldn't have to actually say the words aloud, words she had not said to anyone. Lila nodded her head in agreement, her hands stilled, holding the cards in front of her heart.

The psychic looked extremely troubled. "If you know Annabelle has committed murder, you must go to the police," the psychic told her sternly.

Lila didn't answer.

"If you don't go to the police, I shall be required to do it for you." The psychic spoke formally, as if English wasn't her native language. Lila wondered where the psychic came from. Romania, maybe? She'd read somewhere that gypsies were from Romania.

"Who did she kill?"

"I don't know." Lila spoke for the first time since the psychic had mentioned Annabelle's name. She whispered, "But she was seeing a man whose car went over the side of the Skyway and drowned."

"That sounds like an accident." The psychic paused. "Why do you think your daughter's a murderer?"

Lila sat perfectly still, not moving except for returning to the mindless, rhythmic shuffling of cards, staring into the steady flame for several minutes. The psychic, also saying nothing, petted her terrier. She waited, perhaps, for Lila to share in her own time what the psychic already knew.

"Because," Lila started, and then stopped. How could she explain Roxanne Mae's problems? Her daughter's complicated personality confounded her. Just as confounding were Lila's feelings about Ronald. She couldn't really explain her feelings, but she knew they were real. She had no information—none at all—but she knew she was right.

In a few moments, she'd made up her mind. Lila whispered the only answer she knew. "Because her father is a killer, too." Something violent and twisted lived inside of Ronald. Lila knew that much for sure.

CHAPTER FOURTEEN

MELANIE STEIN MARCHED INTO Jennifer's office unannounced and banged the door shut behind her. She threw a file folder at Jennifer's chest, and the folder bounced onto the floor. Melanie slammed both hands on the desk, and leaned six feet of anger in a sleeveless green dress toward Jennifer, supported by well-defined biceps.

"What. Do. You. Think. You're. Doing."

Jennifer backed away in her chair, seeking distance from Melanie's cold fury. Melanie wouldn't actually hit her—she hoped. "What are you talking about?" She had no clue.

"I'm talking about you. You and that cretin Stuart Barnett. And you know it." Melanie's eyes were almost literally spitting fire. Jennifer shrank further in her seat and moved her chair as far away from Melanie as she could get.

Jennifer had never been in a physical fight with anyone. Because of her diminutive size, she knew she couldn't win unless she fought with a sleeping infant. Melanie was far from sleeping and she towered over Jennifer under the best of circumstances. Maybe the Greek goddess who was Jennifer's namesake had fought a lion with her bare hands, but Jennifer had yet to attempt such a challenge.

"Look, Melanie, have a seat, okay? I don't have any idea what you're talking about. What's the problem?" Jennifer was truly at a loss. She was frightened. She had no idea why Melanie was so incensed.

Melanie paced around the tiny room—only about six steps in either direction, given her long legs—like a caged animal. "You didn't look at that file, I suppose."

Jennifer glanced down at the file folder Melanie had thrown at her. Jennifer recognized it as the one Ronald Walden had handed over when she'd met him and his wife here in the Worthington offices just a few days ago. "No, I didn't look at it. Why?"

"Well, look now," Melanie hissed with such viciousness that Jennifer was afraid to bend and pick up the folder. "Look." Melanie leaned over the desk again, glaring as if she could strike Jennifer with sheer force of thought. Jennifer kept her gaze on Melanie as she picked up the grimy folder and began to leaf through the pages.

There wasn't much information on the few sheets of paper Ronald Walden had included. Jennifer glanced at a couple of smudged newspaper articles from the *Times* and the *Tribune* without reading, and examined some pages of someone's handwritten notes that she couldn't have deciphered even with an hour's time to attempt the chore.

Jennifer looked up at Melanie, who glared and nodded abruptly back to the file. Jennifer continued to skim over the well-thumbed pages covered with grimy fingerprints to the back of the folder where she found a birth certificate and a pay stub.

A few seconds later, Jennifer blanched. She felt faint. When had she eaten last? Her empty stomach meant she wouldn't vomit, at least. It couldn't be true. Jennifer looked up into Melanie's livid features, hopelessly silent. The pay stub was the bottom half of a check with the now familiar blue and white logo embossed on it. She read the full name of the employee to herself: Roxanne Mae Walden James.

It took only a nanosecond for her to connect the dots. "Annabelle James is the Waldens' missing daughter?" The question whispered out of Jennifer's mouth, barely audible.

"Damn straight," Melanie confirmed with a quick nod. "And you will withdraw from the Denton Bio-Medical case against her right this second or I'll have you before the ethics grievance committee so fast your head will spin." Melanie's outrage had not abated since she first stormed into the room, and now Jennifer didn't blame her whatsoever. "What were you thinking? Didn't you even bother to read the file?"

"How is that possible? Her name…" Jennifer squeaked the words out around vocal chords tightened by the impending firestorm.

"Yes, *Roxanne Mae Walden James*, right there in black and white. Who cares how she has a different last name? She just does." Melanie's voice lacked any sympathy.

Jennifer dropped her head into her hands. She sat immobile behind her desk with churning thoughts, each more catastrophic than the last. Now her stomach felt as if she'd swallowed a squirming snake.

"The Waldens trusted you, Jennifer. They are our *cli-ents*. Melanie emphasized the syllables. You sat across the table from them and *prom-ised* we would help them. Now you tell me Stuart wants to sue these people? Do you want to lose your license to practice law before your thirtieth birthday?" Melanie didn't let up on Jennifer for a minute. "What is *wrong* with you?"

She continued to pace the small room and to berate Jennifer's unethical behavior. Sensing Melanie's fear, Jennifer could feel her own fear rise to her throat.

She could lose her license to practice law over this. Without Stuart's protection, she would at least be suspended. The firm's malpractice carrier would have to be notified. She'd be embarrassed in front of all of her colleagues. And someone would have to tell Russell Denton. Jennifer Lane might have the shortest legal career in history.

Jennifer hung her head and tried not to cry. She had made a rule for herself, long ago. She would not cry at the office. She simply would not do it. A tear threatened to leak out of her closed eyelids, and she wiped it away without letting Melanie see. She would not cry.

Her intercom buzzed. "Blake Denton is here to see you, Jennifer," her secretary said. Melanie darted her gaze to the intercom. Jennifer was horrified. *How could he be here now?* Why were the Furies raining down on her head today?

When Jennifer said nothing, Melanie pushed the button and told Jennifer's secretary to escort Mr. Denton to the small conference room. The one where Jennifer had sat with the Waldens and discussed their daughter's guardianship.

"I can't see him now," Jennifer objected when Melanie had lifted her finger from the speaker button.

"Oh yes you can. You're going in there and withdraw from this case before you do any more damage to my career. Or yours," Melanie told her, coming around behind the desk to pull Jennifer to her feet. "I will not be disbarred over this, Jennifer. I'm a damn good lawyer, and I'm not going down with you."

Jennifer refused to budge. "Look, Melanie. Think. Stuart Barnett is the partner on this case. If you want to throw your job right in the trash can this minute, you can do it by screwing up Stuart's chances of collecting a million dollar fee and getting to CEO. He's counting on this client and this case."

Melanie sat down for the first time since she'd entered the room. Her shoulders slumped and she lowered her chin to her chest. Now it was Melanie's turn to knead her eyes with her long, elegantly manicured fingers. Jennifer thought she actually heard Melanie groan.

"Jennifer, you cannot represent clients on the opposite side of the same case. It isn't ethical. You know this." Melanie spoke as if she were trying to convince a mentally handicapped adult of an undeniable truth that any two year old would understand.

"I know. But I'm not representing the Waldens. You are," Jennifer's excuse was feeble and they both knew it. Melanie didn't even bother to answer her. Two lawyers in the same firm couldn't represent opposite sides in a lawsuit without the consent of both their clients. Ethical issues were a big yawn to the general public, but the Florida Bar took them as seriously as a heart attack. A clear ethical breach like this always, always did damage. It could be fatal to the lawyers involved.

"Look at the conflicts sheet," Melanie said quietly.

A conflicts check was something done every time a new client approached the firm and before any new matter was undertaken. Of course, they didn't actually have a physical "sheet" anymore. Now they used a computer program to check for conflicts. But Worthington lawyers had been "checking the conflicts sheet" for over a hundred years. The words had entered the firm's lexicon and would not be eradicated by a mere modern convenience like a computer. Every day, Worthington rejected new clients and new matters because of the mere possibility of conflicts, however remote they might be. Worthington prided itself on never, ever, even approaching the sometimes very gray line between ethical and unethical behavior. Worthington lawyers were subjected to lectures on legal ethics on a regular basis.

If the Florida Bar didn't end Jennifer's career, the Worthington executive committee would do so in a hot minute if they ever got wind of this complete screwup. They'd do it just to make an example of her, if for no other reason, and Jennifer knew this wasn't just her anxiety talking.

Could she possibly say she didn't know about it? Jennifer pulled up the sheet on her computer screen. Fifty or more potential new matters came into the firm every day. Jennifer had never brought in a single piece of new business herself. She'd never used the conflicts sheet and never looked at it.

"Search," Melanie said. Jennifer used the search function to find the Waldens' new-matter inquiry data. When she found it, her heart sank to her feet.

The sheet showed clearly that the Waldens had been clients of the firm before Russell Denton had hired Stuart and Jennifer. There could be no question that firm's first loyalty was to the Waldens. Jennifer's law career was as good as over. An honorable lawyer would resign now and save everyone the consequent embarrassment, not to mention the lawsuits.

The Florida Bar was one of the most exclusive clubs in the country. Getting admitted to practice law here wasn't easy. The old guard thought Florida had too many lawyers already. Lawyers were suspended every month for conflict of interest infractions. The job, and the work Jennifer loved, was about to be tossed out of the window. She seriously considered leaping out after it.

"It doesn't matter that you didn't know Roxanne Walden and Annabelle James were the same person until now. You should have known it. You're supposed to look at the conflicts sheet every day." Melanie was lecturing now.

"But I don't look at it. I never need to." Jennifer's voice sounded whiny, even to her.

"Who cares? What matters is that we are representing the Waldens, and Annabelle James is their daughter." Melanie stated the obvious. Jennifer knew that Melanie was right. The empty head—clean heart defense wouldn't get Jennifer out of this particular mess.

Jennifer picked up the phone and dialed Stuart Barnett's number. When his secretary, Hilda, answered, she said, "Is he there, please?"

Melanie looked up, alarmed. "What are you doing? You need a plan of action before you talk to Barnett."

Jennifer shook her head. "Blake Denton is in the conference room. I can't keep him waiting forever. Denton Bio-Medical is Stuart's client. This is his decision."

But Stuart wasn't in his office and Hilda couldn't reach him. Now what?

Jennifer squared her shoulders and walked around her desk. She took a deep breath to infuse herself with mock courage. She'd been told it was impossible to feel stress and breathe deeply at the same time. *Hogwash.*

Melanie lifted her head. "What are you going to tell Blake Denton?"

Jennifer was surprised. "Nothing. I don't work for him. Russell Denton made it quite clear that he was our client and I was to report only to him. I don't know why Blake's here, but I'm not telling him anything until I talk to Stuart and then to Russell."

Melanie's anger bubbled over again. "Jennifer, we're friends. But I will not let you screw the Waldens just because Russell

Denton is rich and Stuart has delusions of grandeur. I'm warning you. If you don't resign from this case and let Denton Bio-Medical find another lawyer, I will do what I have to do. I won't go down with you."

Jennifer pulled herself up to her full five feet and walked through the door, leaving behind the woman she'd considered her one true friend at the firm. There was no reason to look back. Jennifer knew Melanie had made up her mind.

CHAPTER FIFTEEN

THE DOORKNOB TO THE small conference room felt hot in Jennifer's hands. She turned it anyway, and released it quickly, as if it would burn. Blake Denton's charisma pulled her into the room like honey attracts bees.

He was looking out the window, his hands clasped behind his back in a pose she'd seen his uncle hold on the first day they'd met at the University Club—a lifetime ago. She admired Blake's tall, straight back, the way his hair curled just above his collar, the fine cut of the expensively casual tropical shirt and slacks he wore today. Jennifer's heart skipped a beat or two as she watched him.

Blake Denton was the most gorgeous man she had ever imagined might show the slightest interest in her. During her time at the Denton Bio-Medical plant, he'd smiled at her a little too long. When he shook her hand or touched her briefly to guide her steps, his hand lingered momentarily. Jennifer hadn't realized, until just now, that she'd been remembering those minor gestures so tenderly.

With Melanie's ultimatum fresh in her mind, Jennifer

wondered how she could possibly give their budding relationship a chance? Ten minutes ago, her world had been normal. Subconsciously, she'd believed she'd have many hours of working closely with Blake Denton. And she'd craved that connection. Her biggest problems had been to find Annabelle James and get the HepZMax formula back. Those were the goals that had occupied her night and day.

Now, she felt everything she'd worked for, everything her life had been about for the past eight years, had come to an abrupt end. She would lose her job and, maybe, her license to practice law.

Although the thought of no longer working at Worthington crushed her, she realized she'd also lose her daily connection to Stuart, whom she really did depend on. He would never speak to her again. To save himself, he'd have to let her take the blame. Which was as it should be. This was her mistake. She was responsible.

Blake felt her presence and turned to lighten up her gloom with his smile. "Hello, Jennifer," he said. "It's a pleasure to see you again."

Jennifer was breathless and still. Her mouth was dry, but whether from her physical reaction to Blake or fear of Melanie's wrath, she couldn't say. Blake held out a large, white envelope embossed with the Denton Bio-Medical logo. "Here are the papers you asked me for. I was in the neighborhood and decided to drop them off myself."

When Jennifer took the envelope from him, she felt a faint electric charge, like a shock, pass from his fingers to hers. Their hands jerked back and he apologized. "No problem," Jennifer said as she took the envelope calmly and placed it on the table. She was relieved to see that the envelope was sealed, and made no effort to open it. She was afraid to gather any more information on this case.

She should tell Blake right now, let him know that the firm would not need these documents because Worthington would not be representing Denton Bio-Medical in a case against Annabelle James. She should tell him she would not be his uncle's lawyer. Only Russell's explicit instructions that she tell Blake nothing about her activities on his behalf and her loyalty to Stuart kept her silent.

In a moment of blinding clarity, Jennifer realized that the one thing she found personally distasteful about withdrawing from this case was that she wouldn't see Blake again.

Even though it had represented a breakthrough for her career, Jennifer didn't really want the case. She found herself emotionally on Annabelle's side. She'd tried to muster support for Russell Denton's point of view—even defended it to Melanie, she thought—but she hadn't been able to back his cause. Of course she might be missing quite a few important facts, but Jennifer's intuition told her that Annabelle, if she was still alive, deserved HepZMax, and, if no valid employment contract existed, Annabelle might even own the formula.

If Annabelle owned the formula, Denton would lose the case anyway. Jennifer didn't mind losing the case over something that Denton and Annabelle had done long before Jennifer and Stuart were hired. Stuart would be angry, but he'd get over it.

But if they lost the work for the firm because she'd screwed up something as simple as checking the conflicts sheet, Stuart would not forgive her. Stuart was many things, but unethical was not one of them.

No, they could get out now and save their careers. Melanie would keep quiet if Jennifer did what she asked. Jennifer would get a slap on the wrist from the bar if they ever found out about it. For a brief moment, she almost persuaded herself that she might salvage her relationship with Stuart, as long as she turned herself in and took her punishment alone.

Jennifer glanced down at the white envelope and saw a yellow post-it note on the front with Blake's monogram, "BDP," and a one word question written in strong black ink, followed by his initial, "B." Jennifer blushed to have her fantasy confirmed.

"Well," Blake said, "I need to get going." He made no move to leave.

Jennifer wasn't strong enough to resist. She knew she'd be better off spending as little time with him as possible at this point. But she wanted to see him. She nodded toward him in answer and opened the door, preceding him into the hallway and leading him toward the front door.

"I'll pick you up at your place at seven?"

Jennifer turned and nodded again. She felt his smile light up the room like the floodlights at a circus.

When they reached the lobby, she held open the door for him. Crossing the threshold, Blake said "See you tonight," and left.

Jennifer allowed a small sigh to escape her lips when the only man who had attracted her physically in years walked out the door. She thought grieving now would be good practice. She knew Blake Denton would have nothing to do with her once she withdrew from the case and once she got fired.

CHAPTER SIXTEEN

JENNIFER FORCED HER THOUGHTS away from Melanie's threats. She had to get some distance from the impossible position she now found herself in. Continuing to worry about her problems wasn't going to solve them.

She left work at five o'clock, six hours earlier than usual, to prepare for her date with Blake. It had been months since she'd had a date of any kind. A date that *mattered* hadn't been on her agenda in years. Maybe since college. She'd had no time for dating during law school. Jennifer had worked her way through school, so every minute had been spent either in classes, studying, or doing secretarial work at night.

Since she'd graduated, Stuart had filled her days with work she loved. A serious date was something exhilarating—and frightening. Jennifer wasn't prepared for the intensity of her feelings, though she'd realized, long before the electricity literally flew between them today in the office, that she was seriously attracted to Blake.

Just for tonight, Jennifer promised herself, she would have a good time. She had a date with a handsome man. She liked him—

more than liked him, actually. Jennifer was determined to enjoy the experience even if it killed her. Tomorrow would come soon enough. Tomorrow the world would force her back to solitude.

Tomorrow, she would tell Stuart that she could no longer represent Denton Bio-Medical. That would put an end to her relationship with Blake. He would find a more interesting woman fairly quickly. He probably had several lined up already.

While she parked the car in the gated lot of her apartment building, Jennifer imagined a queue of women as long as the line of fans hoping for a movie star's autograph waiting to date Blake. She lifted her briefcase out of the covered area of her PT Cruiser that she called the trunk and made her way to the elevator.

When Jennifer reached her apartment, she let herself in and pushed the code to turn off the alarm. If she were lucky, after she told Stuart about their conflict of interest and he lost Russell Denton as a client—and his best chance to be CEO—she'd still have a law license and a job. Either way, life as she'd known it would end tomorrow. But tonight, she'd try to live in the moment for a change. She tossed her briefcase in the corner.

Jennifer drew the bathwater in the deep oval garden tub of her apartment's master bathroom. The oversized garden tub at the center of a forest of houseplants was something she used for daydreaming or to escape her problems.

Jennifer lived an exciting life in these daydreams. Buoyed to near weightlessness by the deep water, she would be transported to the forbidden places her fear would otherwise never let her go. In her garden tub, Jennifer conquered the world, and enjoyed every minute of the experience.

Jennifer added to the water the expensive bath salts Melanie had given her for Christmas. Lavender—supposed to calm the nerves. She needed calming today, all right. Her hand trembled as she poured the salts.

"Oh, for Christ's sake!" she said, disgusted with herself. "It's a date. Stop being such an idiot!" She stomped off into the bedroom to hang up her suit as the water released the aroma's peaceful perfume.

Sitting in the scented bath water, enjoying quiet meditation music filtering in from the living room, and with ten of her favorite candles flickering in the semidarkness, Jennifer began to relax. She thought about Blake, the way his blonde curls just reached his collar, how his blue eyes danced with mischief and the sheer joy of living. She imagined his life as blissful in contrast to her own. How much she envied him that difference.

She allowed her thoughts to float off into an unimaginable romance. They would travel, lie on the beach, drink wine, dance. The movie she created in her thoughts had a happy ending.

An hour later, Jennifer surveyed her apartment with a critical gaze as she straightened up the few items that were out of place. She'd hired a decorator last year. When she'd finally paid off her law school loans, she'd taken a chance and replaced the early law student's squalid décor. Now, she stood back and admired her home.

For years after she was hired at Worthington, Jennifer wouldn't spend any of her salary unless she absolutely had to. She'd worried, every day, that she was about to be fired and she'd be unable to support herself. She'd end up living out of a grocery cart under the Crosstown Expressway at the corner of Ashley and Brorien. Every morning on her way to work, Jennifer drove by the spot where Tampa's homeless gathered.

"A lot of women have that nightmare," Melanie had scolded her. "It's ridiculous."

Shaking the visions from her head only kept them at bay until she passed the same location on her way home from the office.

After she'd saved almost all of her salary for five years, Jennifer finally felt she could afford to spend a little of her money. Surely, if she got fired, she could find another job of some kind within a couple of years. She lived frugally. Maybe she could avoid moving into the "Casa Crosstown," as she thought of it, if she were careful.

A psychiatrist might have noticed that Jennifer's home was figuratively as far as it was possible to get from the Casa Crosstown. No more luxurious apartment living existed in South Tampa than the Paradise Apartments in Olde Hyde Park Village.

Jennifer loved it here. For the past two years she'd felt like she had a real home. She loved the vivid red of her walls, and the vibrant jewel tones of the fabrics suited Jennifer's own dark coloring. As the decorator had said, the rooms looked good on Jennifer, although she would never have chosen anything so bold if left to herself. Her home was the one place she felt safe, secure, and entirely at ease.

The buzzer sounded at a quarter after seven, when Blake pushed the intercom button downstairs. He was fashionably late, but the perpetually timely Jennifer wasn't ready. She had tried on every outfit in her closet, changed her pantyhose three times, and still wasn't satisfied with her makeup. Whatever serenity she'd managed to gather from her bubble bath had disappeared along with the long-vanished lavender fragrance.

The buzzer again—more insistent this time. Jennifer couldn't just leave him standing there, although she was sorely tempted to do just that. She was a mess. She knew it. And soon Blake would know it, too.

"Oh, what the hell!" Jennifer said aloud. This was one night, one date, and then they'd part forever, her Cinderella daydreams notwithstanding.

She limped quickly over to the intercom, wearing her right shoe while holding her left, and pushed the buzzer. She didn't say anything to him. What would she say? *"C'mon up, Big Boy?"*

Jennifer laughed out loud at the thought as she rushed a brush through her hair, slapped on one of the red lipstick colors she had previously tried and discarded about six times, put her shoe on, and took a few deep breaths.

She looked at herself in the mirror, amazed at what she saw. "Who are you and what have you done with the real Jennifer Lane?" she said aloud in wonder to the glamorous creature she saw reflected.

In a few too short minutes, Blake's knock sounded at her apartment door. Now wearing three-inch heels, she could just barely reach up to put her eye to the peephole. She felt a smile spreading over her face, and her whole body tingled with the heat of anticipation. She'd turned down the air conditioning earlier, but now it seemed like ninety degrees in her apartment.

Blake knocked again. Jennifer whispered to herself, "Courage," and opened the door. Blake turned around and looked at her.

He simply stared for what felt like a full minute. Jennifer began to think she should have chosen the other red lipstick and the smile slipped from her mouth. Did he think she looked like a complete hag? Was he sorry he'd come? What would she do if he changed his mind? Should she just close the door right now and get back into her sweats and forget the date?

When Jennifer's anxiety had reached about a nine on her

personal Richter scale, Blake finally said, “Wow! You look great! You look like a completely different person!” and she was able to ratchet back a couple of notches. Maybe this was going to be okay, after all. Maybe she’d survive the evening.

CHAPTER SEVENTEEN

SEATED AT THE SAMBA Room in the Village, sipping her second Mojito Martini, Jennifer felt the effect of the rum on her inhibitions. Or maybe it was the effect of Blake. Whatever the cause, Jennifer couldn't remember the last time she'd been as relaxed and happy, while, at the same time, every nerve cell was humming with excitement. Jennifer imagined Melanie must experience this every day with her busy love life. But, for Jennifer, these were totally new feelings.

Jennifer and Blake had been talking for hours, as if they were soul mates separated at birth. Jennifer's nervousness was still there, but it was totally different now. Jennifer admitted to herself that what she felt for Blake might be love. Not that Jennifer knew that much about it. If Melanie ever spoke to her again, she'd say that what Jennifer felt was lust. But Jennifer thought she knew the difference. She was in love with Blake, and wasn't it just like her to choose someone she could never have. How predictable.

What would a man like Blake, a man who could have any woman on the planet, want with her? Jennifer knew the answer to this, too: nothing. Jennifer was a distraction for him, or a job given to him by his uncle to find out more about her, to see whether Russell Denton had chosen the right champion for his cause.

Jennifer freed herself to ignore both Blake's imagined motives—and his uncle's. Because she would be resigning from the case tomorrow and probably losing her job right after that, it didn't matter what Blake reported back to Uncle Russell. So she basked in the feelings she had for Blake and, as much as she was capable of doing so, she willed herself to relax and have a good time.

"Tell me something about yourself," she asked him. She'd have listened to him talk about himself all night. If she was only going to have this one date, she wanted it to give her as much food for a continuing fantasy as possible.

He took her hand across the top of the table. "What do you want to know?"

Everything, she thought. "Tell me about your parents."

His smile faded and he released her hand, taking a gulp from his drink. She sensed she'd asked the wrong question, but she didn't know how to take it back. "My parents are deceased. I've lived with Uncle Russell for years."

Desperate to change the subject because she now realized how much this one had spoiled the romantic mood she craved, she said, "Well, I'm glad of that. Otherwise, we'd never have met."

To her relief, he smiled again and returned to the lighthearted banter they'd been sharing before. "Besides that, what is there?" he said, putting a finger near his temple as if he were thinking of something profound. "Oh, I know. I'm crazy about you." The statement took her breath away.

CHAPTER EIGHTEEN

THEY STAYED UNTIL THE restaurant closed, then walked back toward Jennifer's apartment, stopping at the fountain in the center of the Village. The lighted fountain and its splashing sounds set a very romantic mood, Jennifer thought. She was reminded of those old movies where Audrey Hepburn and Gregory Peck would walk in the moonlight, stand by a fountain, and, finally, kiss. Jennifer had grown up escaping into the romance of old movies. She loved *Gigi* and *My Fair Lady* and *Sabrina*. Jennifer loved love stories, mostly because she knew they would never happen to her.

And, now, here she was, in her own love story. Just like the movies. "Make it last just a little longer," she whispered silently to the universe, praying someone or something out there would hear her. *Give me this one perfect evening and it's all I'll ever ask for, for the rest of my life.*

Blake cupped his right hand under hers and with his left pulled a quarter from his pocket, holding it out to her. "Care to make a wish?" he asked, as if he had read her mind.

Jennifer smiled and took the quarter from him. Making wishes in this fountain was a ritual she performed almost every night, although she wouldn't tell Blake that. She measured her wishes by the value of the coins she'd throw. She only used quarters for the biggest, most improbable wishes. Like when she wished her mother's breast cancer would be cured. And it had been. This was a magical fountain.

Still holding Blake's hand, Jennifer closed her eyes and repeated the wish she'd just made in her silent prayer. She threw the quarter into the fountain and heard it make a satisfactory splash. Then, before she could open her eyes, Blake kissed her.

The kiss was tentative at first. Blake kissed her as if he thought she might break in his arms. But Jennifer knew an answered wish when she felt one, and this was definitely an answered wish. She twined her fingers through Blake's fabulous blonde curls and put all of her considerable passion into returning his kiss.

After several moments, a car went by. A teenager leaned out the window and shouted, "Hey! Get a room!"

Blake and Jennifer broke up laughing, and he held onto her hand as they continued to walk toward her apartment. When they arrived, he said, "Let me walk you upstairs."

It was only one night, Jennifer reminded herself. One perfect night. If she was ever going to find some courage, maybe this was a good place to start. She punched in her security code, opened the gate, and allowed Blake to follow her. He held her hand all the way to her front door, where he took the key from her. He opened the door and stood at the threshold, a question on his face.

It was only tonight, she thought. Jennifer smiled and invited Blake inside. Inside her home. Inside her body. Inside her heart.

The most perfect night.

CHAPTER NINETEEN

THE LIGHT STREAMING IN through her bedroom window awakened Jennifer before six o'clock. As she stretched her aching muscles and felt the soreness within her, a slow contented smile spread across her face. Blake was gone now. He had to leave, he'd said, because he still had some work to finish. But he'd been here, in her bed, until three this morning. She could still see the indentation his head had made on the pillow, still smell the faint traces of his cologne, a fresh scent that suited his Greek god clean good looks. Surely he had been Apollo in another life. The ancient Jennifer had been carried off by Apollo, who named a city after her. Could it be coincidence that Blake was a blue-eyed god? She thought not.

They had spent the one perfect night she'd promised herself, like a gift to a well-behaved child. Jennifer vowed to cherish the memory always. She wasn't sorry. She didn't feel embarrassed. She only felt happiness, pure happiness, maybe for the first time in her life, certainly for the first time in years. Satisfying Stuart's every whim at work, she realized now, was a poor second to loving Blake.

The thought startled Jennifer into a frown, erasing the joy she'd felt just moments before. Stuart. She'd have to see him this morning. At their daily seven o'clock breakfast meeting.

Mentally, she squared her shoulders. Jennifer would tell Stuart about the conflict of interest they had in representing Denton Bio-Medical. By seven-thirty, Jennifer would be without a lover, without a client, and without a job. Slowly, she dragged herself out of bed and headed toward the shower the way Marie Antoinette must have approached the guillotine.

It wasn't until she allowed the pelting hot water to flog her skin for a full twenty minutes that she remembered today was Saturday. She could avoid the end of her life as she knew it by simply staying out of the office until Monday.

CHAPTER TWENTY

RUSSELL DENTON STOOD ON the balcony of his suite at the Don CeSar Resort, the luxurious, pink historic hotel on St. Pete Beach where, it was claimed, Scott and Zelda Fitzgerald once vacationed. Russell watched from behind his Ray Bans as the big orange sun slowly slipped into the horizon. Sunsets in August were late and lazy, and he relaxed while he sipped his vodka martini.

Russell had never been a heavy drinker, but he understood its appeal. Alcohol lifted him away from the troubled thoughts of HepZMax, Annabelle James, and Blake that occupied him constantly. If only he could get his formula back, he'd be able to get his life back on track. Blake would come around. He'd have to. He took a bigger swallow of the martini.

Russell remembered the seventies, when hallucinogenic drugs were taken to transport one to greater levels of consciousness. Now the meditation gurus said daily quiet reflection would do the same—expand your mind. Interesting concept. Sometimes Russell thought getting *out* of his mind would be the only way he could survive.

Russell sipped at his martini again, more carefully this time, and set it down on the small table next to his chair. He was beginning to relax. Patricia would be here in a minute. He looked forward to the brief interludes he was able to spend with her. Since she lived in Pinellas County, they always met at the suite he kept at the Don.

This evening he'd made reservations downstairs in the Maritana Grille at eight o'clock. At night, even in the slow summer season when it was too hot for tourists to swarm, the Don offered live music at the dinner hour. A quartet played songs that lovers could dance to. Part of the ambience. And Patricia loved to dance.

While he waited, Russell let his concerns, freed now by the unaccustomed martini, float out onto the Gulf of Mexico in front of him. He stood at the balcony parapet and watched the undulating waves sparkling in the late-day sunlight and he shuddered. The Gulf's calm water was deceiving. It would be warm and shallow near the shoreline, where the children swam. But out in the shipping channel, the water was deep and surprisingly cold. One could easily die of hypothermia out there.

Drowning would be worse, though. But at least, while you waited to die inside a car, the sharks wouldn't eat you. Russell had tried not to think about his friend Gilbert Irwin, found by the state highway patrol in the channel out there, after a report from a motorist who'd seen a car go over the bridge. When Russell was completely sober, he could keep Gilbert neatly locked away in his mental vault where Russell stored everything he didn't want to think about. Another reason not to drink. Drinking loosened his iron-fisted control.

A light hand touched Russell's back and he turned to see Patricia standing behind him. Smiling at her, he bent over only slightly to receive a kiss from his longtime lover, who was almost as tall as he.

"Where were you? I knocked, but you didn't answer," she said, returning her key to the small bag she carried.

Russell's smile broadened when he saw the bag, one of those whimsical crystal beaded things she loved. This one was a shiny silver elephant with a big red bow around its neck. She had an entire collection ranging from butterflies to a Santa's elf. He'd impulsively offered to buy her one of the bags on a long-ago shopping trip to Chicago. That bag had been a colorful hot air balloon about the size of a small Chinese takeout box. Patricia had laughed when Russell, incredulous at the price, asked if the crystals were actually diamonds. He'd felt like a fool for asking, but it was one of the reasons he enjoyed Patricia so. She didn't want or need his money; she had plenty of her own.

"I'm sorry. I was thinking about Gilbert, if you want to know the truth," Russell told her now, offering her a glass of the chilled white wine she preferred.

Patricia accepted the wine. "Yes, I noticed the funeral is tomorrow. I'm sorry, Russell."

"I wish we'd realized how troubled Gilbert really was. Maybe we could have done something," he told her.

Patricia joined him at the balcony rail and looked across the water, away from the channel where Gilbert's car had been hoisted up a few days ago.

"Maybe Gilbert didn't intend to drive off the Skyway Bridge. It could have been an accident. Didn't the police say that it looked like his car had been hit a couple of times?" Patricia was trying to make him feel better, but Russell feared Gilbert's trip over the side had been intentional.

The police hadn't been able to say whether one of the cars that hit Gilbert had pushed him over deliberately. The dents and paint scrapes could have been inflicted another time. They just weren't sure.

"Honey," she said, placing a hand over his on the rail, "We both know Gilbert had a history of depression and he usually took medication to combat it. Maybe his meds were just out of adjustment. It happens sometimes."

Russell wanted to be comforted. But he knew Gilbert. Like many geniuses seemed to be, Gilbert was fragile in a way others, less gifted, were not. Russell understood Gilbert's problems, but he hadn't been able to help solve them. Gilbert's social skills, like those of many people with impressive IQs, were underdeveloped. Gilbert had been bored in school alongside children his age who were intellectually below his skill level. Later, in the higher grades, he'd been emotionally lonely, surrounded by children who were more mature.

Gilbert had been isolated by the very intellect that he had harnessed to high achievement. That isolation could lead a genius to success or ruin, and, sometimes, telling one from the other isn't easy. Russell, himself, had gone through a similar sort of life. So had Blake. But neither had killed himself in an act of despair. Was that what Gilbert had finally done?

Russell sipped his martini again, trying to withdraw from his feeling of responsibility for Gilbert's death. Maybe if he got drunk tonight, he could forget Gilbert's betrayal, followed by his beseeching, pathetic apology the morning right before he died. Maybe Russell could forget how coldly he'd rejected Gilbert's apology and how crushed Gilbert had been.

Probably not.

"Let's not talk about Gilbert, darling. We may never know what drove him over the edge." Patricia's touch was light on

Russell's arm. "It's a beautiful evening. Let's only have pleasant thoughts tonight, shall we?" Patricia was a psychiatrist. To her, everything was drugs and thought control.

Russell's agreement with Patricia was forced. If only having pleasant thoughts were just a matter of choice. The best he could do was to indulge her by engaging solely in light conversation. He silently agreed to keep his darker thoughts to himself.

Much later, after dinner and two hours of dancing, as they sat brushed in the rosy glow of the last remnants of sunset, he told her about the three teenagers who had thrown eggs at him today as he left his home on the way to meet her. The kids had hit him twice before racing off on their bicycles.

Patricia was horrified. "Russell, that's awful. Did you call the police?"

He shook his head. "It's not the worst thing that's happened to me lately." He considered telling her how tired he'd been, a fatigue he'd put down to being heartsick over Gilbert's betrayal and then death. Instead, he asked her quietly, "Why do people hate me so much?" A small fire in the grate warmed the room. He felt amorous in the glow of the alcohol he'd consumed, but he ignored it. This conversation was more important right now than sex.

"What do you mean?" Her face reflected surprise.

"I come from a middle-class family. Barely middle-class. I've worked hard and made something of myself. I give away more money every year than the total gross national product of some third world countries," he said, no trace of whining in his voice, merely by way of framing the question. "Yet, people want to destroy me. Why is that? Where would the world be without people like me?"

Patricia leaned over, brushed his hair off his forehead and

began to nibble on his ear. "I think Ayn Rand already explored that idea."

"What?" He was startled by her response.

"*Atlas Shrugged.* The premise was, what if all the movers and shakers of the country, like you, went on strike." Leaning close, she continued, "Her point being how essential you are to the American way of life. Essential to my life." Patricia got up and moved over to his chair. She sat in his lap and wiggled suggestively.

Russell enjoyed the sensation she evoked, but he was intent on his question and willed himself to stillness. "I know. I'm a member of the Atlas Society. I understand Rand's idea. But I'm asking you, what do you think? As a psychiatrist. What's the motivation? Is it personal to me or just generalized envy? What?"

Russell felt he'd kept his promise to limit their conversation to pleasant topics through dinner and afterward. Now, he wanted a companion who would help him make sense of his world. He felt bewildered by Gilbert's complicity in the theft of the HepZMax formula. He felt betrayed.

When Gilbert had confessed to giving the formula to Annabelle James, Russell had been crushed. He and Gilbert had known each other all their lives. They'd gone through very difficult years together growing up in a rough section of Chicago.

Russell couldn't make sense of what Gilbert had told him. He had been a good friend to Gilbert, standing by him when no one else would. Why would Gilbert want to hurt Russell? What had made him do it?

Patricia sat up in his lap and put one hand on each side of his face. She looked directly into his eyes. "You ask excellent questions, Russell. Really. And I wish I knew the answers. I know you're a good man. You've done countless good deeds in your life. In fact, I wonder why you've done all those good deeds sometimes." She wiggled her bottom again so that he felt her warmth through his silk slacks.

He enjoyed the sensation and rubbed her back with his free hand while holding his drink in the other, showing his interest.

"Why do people hate you? I think *hate* is probably too strong a word. It's more like fear, really." She bent down and kissed him, long and slow.

He sighed when at last she lifted her lips. "What? Why would anyone be afraid of me? I don't even swat mosquitoes." He was bewildered by the concept that others, especially friends who should know better, might fear him.

"People are afraid there isn't enough to go around in the world. They worry that they will never get their 'fair share.'" Patricia kissed his eyes, his nose.

He waited until she stopped. "What does that have to do with me?"

"So they see you and people like you as getting way more than you should have, or could ever use or need. And then they're afraid that because you have so much, it means they themselves are destined to be shortchanged." She took her hands off him, got up from his lap and turned to the now deep-red sky.

"But that's ridiculous! This is the United States. The American dream and all that. I just did what our culture tells us anyone who applies himself can do."

"Philosophy is for people like you and me, Russell. People who don't feel need, hunger, poverty. We can afford the luxury of philosophy." Patricia turned to leave. It was late. As usual, she had a full schedule of patient appointments the next day and couldn't stay all night. Russell understood. Work demands filled his life, too. He'd been amorous before, but how he wasn't in the mood. Besides, he was tired. He needed to sleep.

Russell walked her to the door of their suite. "So, you're saying that no matter how hard I try, I'll never get to the point where I am universally loved?" His tone was ironic. He didn't want to part from her with any unpleasantness between them. He'd learned that lesson the hard way, with Gilbert.

Patricia kissed him goodnight, then threw a light wrap, against the cool night breeze, over her bare shoulders. "*I* love you, dear. That should be enough." She closed the door softly behind her and left for home.

That Patricia loved him *should* be enough, but it wasn't. Too many fearful people existed in the world. Too many who thought hurting him would, in some unknown, unfathomable way, improve their own miserable lives. He shuddered. Chilled now by his thoughts and the evening breeze, Russell moved closer to the fire.

CHAPTER TWENTY-ONE

TIM TYLER STOOD ON the porch of what used to be his home and rang the doorbell. Through the heavy wooden door, he could hear the twins running to let him in. "Daddy's here! Daddy's here!" they squealed.

When he heard them fumbling with the deadbolt, his face split with a big grin that erased the worry lines that the Annabelle James situation had etched there. Lori kept the door locked, just as he'd asked her to do. She was petrified of home invasions. To calm her, Tyler had installed an elaborate alarm system throughout the house, double locks on every door, and hidden video cameras activated by motion sensors in every room. When one of the homes down the street had been invaded last year, Lori had gotten a gun permit and learned to shoot.

That was how Tyler had first noticed Jennifer Lane. He'd picked up Lori one day at the shooting range, and Jennifer Lane—this woman who looked so much like Annabelle James—just happened to be walking out at the same time. Tyler had thought she *was* Annabelle. He loved coincidences like that. He'd long ago stopped trying to figure out where they came from. And Tampa was such a small world. Everyone met everyone else here, eventually.

Lori's target practice had paid off; she was a better marksman than Tyler was. Still, she was afraid. Tyler told her to let him move back home and she'd feel safer. So far, she'd refused. But he figured another break-in in the neighborhood and he'd at least be welcome to sleep on the couch.

He heard Lori coming now, heard her unlocking the deadbolt that was too high for the girls to reach. Together, his daughters swung open the door and jumped at him where he stood, two feet from the threshold.

He laughed, tickled them, and picked them both up, one under each arm. His girls were growing so fast he wouldn't be able to pick them up simultaneously much longer. The thought made him sad.

Walking through the entryway with the laughing, wiggly bundles, he kissed Lori's cheek. "Morning, Lin. Want to get married?" Tyler asked her.

Tyler thought his ex-wife was quite beautiful. She'd always been beautiful. When she'd divorced him, that had made her even more desirable in his eyes. They'd been divorced now for six years and he'd proposed to her every time he'd seen her since she left him.

"Hello, Tim," she answered. He thought he heard a little less frost in her voice today than he'd heard three days ago.

"What's up?"

She ignored the question, turned, and walked through the house, back toward the kitchen. Tyler followed her, still carrying the girls, nuzzling their necks and listening to their duet of tales and adventures they'd accumulated since he'd seen them last. He sat the twins down at the breakfast table.

He talked to his kids on the phone every day and he saw them as often as he could. They were typical all-American kids: overbooked, constantly going somewhere and doing something. Just to follow their girls from swimming to soccer to piano to dance classes, and on and on and on took all of his and Lori's energy. Some days, he felt like a cross between a camp counselor and a bus driver.

Tyler never complained though. He loved it all, every minute of fatherhood that he could squeeze into his life around the demands of securing Russell Denton's personal empire. Tyler missed the evenings when all four of them used to read or watch television or just have some quiet time together.

That was the worst part of the divorce. No evening bedtimes. No stories. No hugs and kisses.

He acknowledged to himself that he missed hugs and kisses from Lori as much as from the kids.

But he was working on that. He thought she was softening. She'd give up eventually. Of course, when Lori had divorced him, Tyler thought he'd win her back long before now. But Tyler was a determined ex-Marine. He'd win this war; his tactics were better than hers.

"Look, Daddy," Penny said, pulling him over to the refrigerator to see the latest paper she'd brought home with a big "A++" marked on the top.

"Me, too, Daddy," said Cindi, showing him an equally well-judged picture that she'd drawn. Every inch of the refrigerator was covered in their elementary school artwork. When did kids stop bringing that stuff home? Tyler wondered. He hoped such a time was years away. The girls were ten years old now. All too soon, they'd have better things to do than create pictures for Mom and Dad.

Lori sent the kids upstairs to put on their soccer uniforms.

"So, what's up?" he asked her again.

She fidgeted, pouring coffee, loading the dishwasher. She made a big show of disinterest in conversation. But he knew her well. She had something on her mind.

Tyler came over to pick up the full cup of coffee she'd poured and sweetened for him. Four packets of the blue stuff, just the way he liked it. "The girls will be back in a minute. The soccer game is out in Carrollwood and we'll have to get going." He was saying she should hurry up, spill her concerns. In the last six years, Tyler had learned how to draw her out. How to listen. To be patient.

Lori focused on wiping up a spot on the countertop and said nothing. Tyler sipped the coffee. In less time than he would have thought possible, the girls ran downstairs, dressed in their uniforms, literally jumping to go.

"Kids, run out to the car. Daddy will be right there," Lori told them. On their way out the door, she called, "Put your seat belts on!" Car accidents were another of Lori's fears.

Tyler stood to rinse his coffee cup and put it in the dishwasher. Lori looked up at him. "Come for dinner tonight?" she asked. Finally.

"Sure. What time?" He tried to control his accelerating heartbeat. She hadn't invited him to dinner for a long time. This could be it. He mentally made a list of things he'd bring. Flowers. Wine. He'd dress up, maybe. Would candy for the kids be too much? Too little?

"About seven," she said. One of the twins beeped the horn. Penny probably. She was the impatient one. He nodded and started out to the car. "And, Tim," she said, placing her hand on his arm as he walked past her. "Plan to stay a little after dinner, okay?"

A big grin lit his face. "Sure. See you at seven."

He kissed her cheek again before he walked out of the house, restraining his desire to jump all the way to the car. This was it. He'd bring the four-carat diamond ring he'd already bought.

CHAPTER TWENTY-TWO

JENNIFER'S CELL PHONE RANG right on time at ten o'clock in the morning. She knew before she answered that the caller was her mother, Debbie Lane. Hearing Debbie's voice was almost like being with her. Jennifer pictured Debbie in her bright yellow kitchen with the curtains Debbie had made herself. Debbie would be fixing breakfast or pressing clothes while they talked. The aroma of freshly baked biscuits or cookies would fill the air. The imagined domestic scene pierced Jennifer's heart.

Jennifer had always been close with her mother and the separation of fifteen hundred miles had the curious effect of bringing them even closer. They'd started using their business cell phones lately since weekend calling time was practically free. Sometimes, they'd talk at night during the week, too. Debbie was Jennifer's closest friend, and Jennifer missed her under the best of circumstances. Now, Jennifer's desire for her mother's comfort was palpable.

"Hi, Mom," Jennifer said, trying to keep the quaver out of her voice. She held the tiny cell phone to her ear with her shoulder, while she toweled off after her swim. She'd had a good workout.

Twenty-five laps in the pool, managing to keep ahead of her demons. The cool water felt good on her skin.

"Good morning," Debbie responded. "How are you? How was your week?"

"Good. How's Dad?" Jennifer carried the towel and the phone across the patio and found a lounge chair shaded by a bushy palm tree. She unscrewed the cap of a water bottle and swallowed half its contents.

"Oh, he's fine. He had a seven-thirty tee-off over at Mistwood this morning." This was the usual Saturday opening. It never varied. Jennifer settled in to talk with Debbie for an hour or more, holding Debbie's voice close to her.

Those conversations made her feel connected. Loved. Jennifer realized she'd left home seeking independence, but, paradoxically, she'd planned all along to return to where she'd come from someday. Jennifer thought of herself as being on a journey. What she would experience would change her forever. Change her from what, she didn't know. This was one of many things Jennifer was still attempting to discover.

Right now, Jennifer put her feet up and finished her water as Debbie rambled on with quiet conversation. Debbie talked about Aunt Peggy's recent bout of the flu and the women in Debbie's bridge club whom Jennifer didn't know. The normalcy of Debbie's life surrounded Jennifer like a cozy blanket, warming her and making her feel secure in the world. Maybe, Jennifer thought, she should just go home to be with her family. Running away had great appeal right now.

Jennifer considered telling Debbie about her troubles. Her mother was always willing to listen. Jennifer could count on support from both her parents, actually, no matter what she did. As their only child, Jennifer had been treasured. They coddled her and made everything perfect, always. Jennifer counted on her mother's kindness and her father's protection. She needed them both still, even when she was almost thirty years old. Jennifer wondered when, exactly, one began to feel like an adult, capable of taking care of herself.

Yet she couldn't, or maybe wouldn't, admit defeat and run back to her parents. She hadn't been fired yet. She hadn't been disbarred. She hadn't let them down yet. Maybe she could figure out a way to get the HepZMax formula back. If she could do that, neither the Waldens, Russell Denton, nor Stuart would be angry with her. Things could still work out. She had no idea how that could possibly happen. But she had hope.

"Mom, I've met the most incredible guy," she offered a little tentatively. This was a change in their usual routine. Jennifer never had a man to talk about and Debbie never asked. The subject was one they tactfully avoided. Her parents just wanted Jennifer to be happy, but in her parents' world, that meant married with children.

"Oh? What's his name?"

"Blake Denton. His uncle is Russell Denton." Jennifer thought it best to get this piece of information out of the way first. She knew her mother wouldn't be thrilled. Debbie believed money in extremes corrupted everyone it touched. Debbie had lived a comfortable life, but both she and Jennifer's father had worked for everything they had. They'd taught Jennifer to do the same. Debbie and Clay Lane thought making one's own way in the world built character.

"Mom, he's really the most down-to-earth man I've ever met. Having money has relaxed him. He's not so bent on making his mark." Jennifer tried to defuse the issue of Blake's wealth before it became a concern to her parents.

"Working for what you have is a good thing," Debbie said in

response. She wouldn't judge Jennifer's choice, but Debbie had her own views, too.

"I know. He does work. In his uncle's company." Jennifer was a little sorry she'd brought this up. Since nothing would probably come of the relationship, she shouldn't have said anything. But her pattern was to tell Debbie about whatever was going on in her life. The idea of drawing boundaries around such an important piece of news as her feelings for Blake just didn't occur to her. But mentioning him was a commitment.

"Tell me about him."

"He's wonderful, Mom, really. So polite and sweet. He's the nicest man I've met in a long, long time." Jennifer remembered Blake's kiss, his caress. She could imagine the smile on her mother's face as Debbie listened to Jennifer describe Blake's virtues.

Jennifer understood her parents' concern for her. Debbie and Clay had been high school sweethearts. Their love had endured for more than thirty years. Jennifer wanted for herself the deep emotional connection her parents shared, and had been looking all her life for a man who could measure up to her girlhood view of Clay Lane. She let herself believe that maybe, with a little luck and lots of prayers, she'd found that man in Blake Denton.

Eventually, Debbie said during a lull near the end of the call, "Did I tell you that we're going to take a little vacation?"

"Really? Where are you going?" Jennifer was surprised. She was glad she hadn't suggested she might want to come home. She would never want to disrupt her parents' lives.

"Your Dad's finally going to take me to Alaska this summer. We've been considering a cruise for quite a long time. Our anniversary is coming up and we never really had a honeymoon. So we thought this would be a good opportunity to do both."

Debbie seemed shyly pleased that Clay had surprised her with the trip.

"Mom, that sounds great." Jennifer's workout had made her hungry. She gathered up her towel and the empty water bottle and walked back toward her apartment. "How did Dad ever think of that?"

"Oh, you know. One of those telemarketing things. He can't ever turn anybody down," Debbie said with affection.

They talked about the vacation for a while, and then Debbie returned to the subject they most often discussed. "What's up with Stuart and the office?" Debbie didn't really understand everything about the work Jennifer did, but she was always willing to lend an ear.

When Jennifer didn't respond right away, Debbie asked her, "Honey? Something wrong?"

Jennifer stopped walking and leaned one shoulder against a wall on the way to the elevator. She closed her eyes to keep her composure. "No, not really. It's hard to say much about what I'm working on." Why didn't she just tell her mother about Annabelle James, the HepZMax theft? Why evade the subject? But she held back. She lowered her voice.

"Stuart is Stuart. We got a big new case we're working on which should be pretty exciting. I'm getting a fairly big role." That was an understatement. In fact, Jennifer still didn't feel comfortable with the size of the task she'd undertaken.

Debbie interrupted her. "Jennifer, I'm sorry. I didn't realize the time. I've got to get ready for a funeral. One of our friends from church died this week and the funeral is today. We're at that age when we attend more funerals than weddings." Debbie's tone was rueful. "I think that's one of the things that prompted your father to buy this cruise when that woman called. Life is too short. We won't be around forever, you know."

Jennifer ignored this piece of reality. She couldn't consider losing her parents. Not right now. "Okay. I'll talk to you next week then. Love you, Mom," Jennifer signed off.

"Love you, too, dear. Bye." After Debbie hung up, Jennifer stared at the phone in her hand, bereft of the one link that tethered her to a world where she belonged, where she felt comfortable. She imagined Debbie and Clay at home, having dinner together, watching television in the evening. The scene made her homesick in a way she hadn't felt in a long time. She missed her parents. She'd left home seeking adventure and to create her own life. Right now, she thought leaving had been a terrible mistake.

CHAPTER TWENTY-THREE

ON THE WAY TO breakfast, Jennifer watched Stuart do his "chivalry" thing. He walked on the outside, near the curb. Every time they crossed the street, he adjusted his position.

Once, early on in their relationship, practically running just to keep pace with his long strides, she'd failed to see him cross behind her to take the outside position and had bumped right into him.

"A gentleman always walks on the side near the curb," he'd said, as he gently moved her toward the building. Jennifer's face had burned with embarrassment. *Who did stuff like that these days?* she asked herself. The answer was, *Stuart does.*

Stuart read all the transcripts of old British trials, famous ones, and he collected the first editions of the transcripts in book form. He was an Anglophile, a sophisticated reader of everything British. Stuart might have been a king of England in a former life, Jennifer thought. He was not in the least affected, though. No faux British accent or anything like that. But his manners came straight from King Arthur's court.

The paradox that was Stuart had proved an interesting study.

Stuart was honorable, a brilliant lawyer, and a loyal friend. All in his own way.

Stuart had his own rules, his own morality. The rules were complicated. They seemed to be part old school and part navy. Stuart had joined the U.S. Navy after he'd been expelled from Harvard and was about to be drafted into the army. At the time, that had meant he'd go to Vietnam, a fate his mother thought was worse than death.

At seventeen, Stuart had apparently been quite a handful.

The prank that had gotten him expelled from college was drinking in his dorm with certain half-clothed girls present. Those were the days when three strikes meant you were out, no matter who your father was. Stuart was out and into the navy faster than he could say, "Goodbye Mr. Chips."

Now, seated across the breakfast table, Stuart stared at Jennifer as if she'd just grown an actual third eye, right between the other two.

"No," he said, returning his attention to the melon he'd been eating.

"We have no choice, Stuart," Jennifer repeated. She enunciated each sentence again clearly, as if she thought he hadn't understood her the first time. "The Waldens were our clients first. Worthington is representing them. I have personally met these people and talked to them. They are Annabelle James's parents and they will be her legal guardians when Melanie gets them appointed by the court. We simply cannot represent Denton Bio-Medical in a lawsuit against one of our own clients. And we can't represent both sides. We'll both lose our licenses to practice law."

Stuart looked over Jennifer's shoulder, staring into the sky, which was the only thing one could see straight ahead out of the windows in the Grill Room on the forty-second floor of the Bank of America Building in downtown Tampa. They were seated twenty-two stories directly above where a young boy died when he deliberately crashed a small plane into the corner of the building. The knowledge made Jennifer uneasy every time she met Stuart here for breakfast, at his favorite table, each weekday morning.

Jennifer watched Stuart, waiting for him to realize they had to stop working for Russell Denton. But, Stuart expected big things from this case, and he'd told her so, in no uncertain terms. The case was a critical one, for a hugely important client. Fees to the firm would be enormous. The stakes were perhaps the highest of his career.

Over the weekend, Jennifer had prepared herself to face the consequences. It was her own fault that she hadn't looked at the conflicts sheet; she hadn't read the Waldens' file materials; she hadn't even run a conflicts check on the Denton Bio-Medical case. Jennifer deserved to be fired, and she knew it. She just waited for the ax to fall.

When Jennifer tried to be easier on herself, she remembered that Stuart was the one who'd brought the Denton Bio-Medical case to the firm. But Stuart couldn't be bothered with mundane matters related to firm administration like conflicts checks. That was her responsibility. Jennifer's analysis always came back to the fact she should have performed the check but did not. Her lapse was unforgivable.

But what if she *had* checked? The only thing that would have been accomplished was that she'd have been in this situation a whole lot sooner. No. The Waldens came first. You couldn't just dump a client because a better client came along. Stuart had to see that.

But he didn't. "No," Stuart said again. "We'll withdraw from representing the Waldens, instead. We'll continue on as Denton's counsel." He finished his melon and focused on the hot cereal.

Jennifer blanched. "We can't do that—" she started.

Stuart looked at Jennifer, directly, straight into her dark brown eyes. "We can. And we will. I will instruct Melanie to withdraw as the Waldens' counsel." Stuart's tone brooked no argument. "I, alone, will tell Russell Denton about the problem."

He was saying he'd pull rank on Melanie, just as Melanie had pulled rank on Jennifer when she'd accidentally stumbled into Melanie's initial conference with the Waldens last week. But that wouldn't solve the problem.

"Stuart, that's not fair. The Waldens have no money. Who else will represent them in a fight against Denton? Their daughter is missing, probably dead. How can we just abandon them and then represent their biggest enemy in a case against them?"

Stuart was unmoved. "None of that is my problem, Jennifer. My problem is that I've been handed the biggest client of my career and the case that will raise me to CEO. On top of that, Denton just happens to be on the right side of this—"

"You don't know that." Jennifer interrupted here because she had to. Her convictions had overtaken her fear and her desire for Stuart's approval—at least momentarily. "It's Annabelle's work. Annabelle's formula."

"Enough!" Stuart slammed his hand down on the table, hard, making a noise like hammering stone, causing heads to turn their way. Jennifer tried to shrink back into the chair. "You have romanticized this woman and made her into some sort of deserving underdog, Jennifer. She is not. Annabelle James is a thief, a disloyal employee who has taken something that does not belong to her. I'm sorry for her parents if she's dead. But that doesn't make this formula hers."

Stuart stopped here and fixed his steady stare directly on

Jennifer again. "Hear me. You're wrong. We will not resign from this case. We don't have to. Denton is right about this and that is the end of this conversation."

Jennifer had no power to thwart Stuart in this. He was going to do whatever he wanted. The question was what would Jennifer do? She often felt as if she'd come from another planet, an outsider who didn't fit into Stuart's world no matter how much she tried to become what he wanted.

"Do you understand me?" Stuart demanded. "I may be able to salvage your career, *if* you listen to me. You will do nothing further on either the Denton matter or the Walden matter until I give you permission. Don't discuss this with anyone. Not anyone. Is that clear?"

Jennifer nodded miserably. Crystal clear. What could she do, anyway? Melanie was no longer her friend. Stuart had never been so angry with her. And the Waldens, who had already lost their daughter, would be flailing around, no match for Stuart, Denton, or the firm. And Blake? When Jennifer lost her job, Blake would go, too.

Everyone Jennifer had come to depend on would evaporate like the scent of lavender in yesterday's bubble bath.

CHAPTER TWENTY-FOUR

RUSSELL ARRIVED EARLY AND waited for Stuart Barnett to show. He'd selected the small restaurant in Tarpon Springs both because he liked the Greek food and because it was a tourist town that reminded him of the small villages near Athens he and Patricia had visited last year. Russell wore the tourist uniform of shorts, golf shirt, and Top-siders without socks, a fishing hat, and dark prescription sunglasses. His clothes were baggy on him since he'd lost so much weight. But, sartorial matters aside, this outfit drew so little attention he might as well have been invisible in it. *Perfect.*

He glanced occasionally at the entrance. He would spot Barnett a nanosecond after the attorney arrived. In the meantime, Russell studied the room. It was the lunch hour. The restaurant began to fill up with visitors to the quaint Greek fishing village. The walls were painted a bright aqua, similar to the blue-green Mediterranean Sea they were intended to represent, a color one had to see to believe could actually be found in nature. Sponges decorated the walls amid murals of tropical fish and other aquatic life. The overall effect was a caricature of the sea more suitable for a children's theme park ride than an adult eatery.

The interesting thing to Russell was why the Greek family who owned the restaurant wanted to portray the family business in this cartoon-like fashion. The food was some of the best around, but the décor was so far from authentic that Russell found it almost offensive. He came here in spite of the ambience, not because of it.

The tourists seemed enchanted with the stylized views into the sea. When had the entire state of Florida turned itself into a theme park?

Fifteen minutes later, a slight stir among the diners drew Russell's attention to the front of the restaurant. Stuart Barnett stood in line at the threshold, no doubt allowing his eyes to adjust to the interior after the brilliant sunlight outside. Russell didn't wave or gesture to him. Barnett would find him soon enough. Instead, Russell continued to observe the man. What was it about him that so appealed to everyone?

Russell watched the diners' heads turn to look at Barnett as if he were a movie star. People seemed to be attracted to him in a mystical way. Sure, he was good looking. But a lot of men were. And Barnett was getting older, aging badly, if the pictures of him in his youth could be believed. His hair held several streaks of unattractive gray and his sun-damaged skin aged him.

He carried himself like the ex-military man that he was. Ramrod-straight spine. Graceful walk. And while his clothes resembled those worn by every other man in the place, on Barnett the casual uniform seemed almost luminous. Barnett's manners were impeccable, his voice cultured, his vocabulary extensive, precise, and creative. But you needed to talk to him to experience all of that charm.

Russell realized Barnett was an intriguing package whose reputation claimed he had a gift for persuading juries with something like hypnotic manipulation. What Russell didn't understand was where that all came from. Was it a divine gift? Cultivated? What? More importantly, why didn't Russell have the same magic, whatever it was?

When Barnett's turn to speak to the hostess finally arrived, her face lit up like a child on Christmas morning. Barnett flirted with her a little, then she nodded and led him through the crowded restaurant to Russell's table in the back.

Animal magnetism. He chalked the magic up to only that. If he could bottle that magnetism, he could sell it to customers faster than Super Bowl tickets.

When Barnett arrived at the table and greetings were exchanged, he sat to Russell's left, not across, where his back would have been to the door.

"Why do you do that?" Russell asked him, nodding toward the hostess. She was facing back, smiling at Barnett as if she'd go to bed with him right now, if only he'd ask.

Barnett didn't pretend to misunderstand Russell's meaning.

"To prove I still can," he said as he brought water to his lips, holding the back of his hand under the glass to catch the sweaty drips.

Russell shook his head slowly from side to side. "I never learned the technique."

"You probably never had to," Barnett replied.

"What do you mean?"

"You've had me investigated, Russell. You know all about me. From my silver-spoon gene pool to my wealthy wife, right? That's what you think?" Barnett looked directly into Russell's eyes without flinching or dissembling. Russell had to give that to the man. He was direct.

"Well, that's the paper story," Barnett continued matter-of-factly. He could have been reciting the phone book for the little emotion he displayed. "It doesn't tell you that my parents were as coldhearted as ice sculptures. They sent me away to boarding school because they couldn't be bothered. I struggled for years to fit into life. You have no idea how lonely a young boy can be. Charming people is something I learned to do because I needed human contact. It's a learned skill. One that has served me well in life." He sat back in his chair and delivered a frosty warning to his client. "Don't make the mistake of thinking you know me."

Russell found himself less offended than intrigued. Stuart Barnett could keep some psychiatrist occupied for an entire lifetime. Russell made a mental note to himself to discuss Barnett with Patricia. As a psychiatrist, she might have some insight that would help him in his dealings with this enigma of a man.

"I'd love to hear about it sometime."

"You'd find my life story boring, I'm sure. Let's talk about Annabelle James and your nephew instead," Barnett said.

Russell's surprise was swift. "Why?"

"You know Annabelle James couldn't have stolen that formula by herself. She must have had help. I'm betting it was Blake." The waiter arrived and they placed their orders.

Barnett nonchalantly handed his menu back and, when the waiter left, he made no effort to lean closer to Russell or soften his voice.

"You said it yourself, Russell. I understand sex, women—what men will do for both. I've known a thousand Blakes. He's the kind of man who thinks he can diddle the help. In fact, I'd say he thinks he's entitled, since he'll own Denton Bio-Medical someday." Barnett reached for the bread and butter. He spoke conversationally, as if he were talking about a story on television and not offensively defaming Russell's heir.

"So, the way I figure it is that Blake had a thing with Annabelle. He helped her steal the formula. What I don't understand is why he did it. That and why you're fooling around with me and Jennifer Lane." Barnett continued to eat his bread. He seemed completely unconcerned. He took a sip of the water, holding the glass over the back of his hand again while Russell floundered for a response.

"Look, don't bother to lie to me about it. The answer really doesn't even matter. I don't mind being used to serve your purposes, as long as I get what I want out of the deal. I'm like a cab in the line. I'll take the first customer who comes along. You pay me; as long as it's not illegal or unethical, I'll represent you." Stuart's tone was light, but entirely serious. "Just remember that you're not putting anything over on me. I've met a thousand guys like you, too. I don't need you. You don't intimidate me. You never will."

Russell had no illusions on that score. If he'd underestimated Barnett or thought him a fool, Russell wouldn't make that mistake again. He struggled to regain control of the meeting he'd scheduled for his own purposes. "As long as we're laying our cards on the table, I hear you've *got* a little ethical problem going on over at your shop." Russell watched Barnett closely. Briefly, very briefly, he thought he saw a small flicker of surprise in Barnett's eyes.

"Not at all, Russell. I hope you haven't been worried about anything you've heard. There seemed to be a misunderstanding by one of our young partners. She had a couple of pro bono clients she wanted to represent. But we've cleared that up."

"How?" One of the reasons Russell had hired Barnett was to be sure he couldn't represent the enemy, if it should come to that. It was a common strategy he'd employed before in other markets.

Once a lawyer or his firm had been hired to represent his company, they could never represent someone who wanted to sue him without his consent.

Barnett raised his eyebrow, feigning shock, which both men recognized as absurd. “Why, we’ve declined to represent them and suggested alternative counsel, of course.”

“How did they take that suggestion?” Russell realized he was holding his breath. He willed himself to relax. If the Waldens were looking for free lawyers, then maybe Annabelle hadn’t sold HepZMax to the highest bidder yet. He still had time.

Barnett smiled ruefully. “Not well, I’m told. The father seems somewhat unstable, actually. I hear he’s a former soldier who likes to play with guns. I’d be careful if I were you.”

Russell said nothing, so Barnett added, “And you might pass that advice along to your nephew.”

CHAPTER TWENTY-FIVE

THE PHONE RANG WHEN she was already in bed, facing away from the nightstand, sleep almost upon her. She ignored it until the fourth ring, when she turned and picked it up. "Hi, Mom." Her parents' name had come up on the caller ID her dad had insisted she get. He still thought of Tampa as a high-crime area and he wasn't happy about Jennifer living there alone. He'd carefully inspected the tight security at Paradise Apartments for himself before she'd moved in. Trying to reassure him, she'd told him more than once that most crimes are committed by people you know, which didn't remove his concern at all.

Clay Lane worried about his daughter wherever she was. He'd insisted that she get a gun and learn to use it. He made sure her car provided keyless entry so she just had to push a button on her key fob and the doors locked or unlocked quickly. He was always sending Jennifer articles and e-mail about safety precautions for women. Jennifer tried to make light of her dad's overprotective nature, because his concern frightened her if she dwelled on it. She wondered whether Clay had passed his worry gene on to her.

"How are you?" This was always Debbie's first question.

"Fine," Jennifer said into the phone in the dark. Then, more honestly, she added, "A little tired, I guess. I've been working a lot." She didn't mention the stress or the guilt she felt over abandoning the Waldens and becoming even more entrenched in what Melanie, borrowing a phrase from Ronald Reagan, called the Evil Empire. She didn't tell Debbie how Stuart had ditched the Waldens, either. Jennifer's hero worship of Stuart had taken a hit this week, even though she had held on to her job. For now. She didn't want to talk about it.

"Well, that's to be expected for an associate, isn't it?" Debbie never thought that hard work was a bad thing. Jennifer bristled, although she knew Debbie was just trying to be supportive.

Jennifer swallowed her irritation. "Yes, it is. I just feel as if I could use a long nap." Jennifer struggled to keep her composure. She felt depressed, but she wanted to act strong with her mom.

"Well, I won't keep you. I called to let you know that we've gotten an amazing deal on the Alaska cruise I was telling you about."

"Really?" Jennifer tried to summon some enthusiasm.

"Yes, and the most exciting thing is we've decided to go right away."

"I thought you were talking about doing this in the summer, for your anniversary?" Had she simply failed to listen? Again?

"We were. But, the telemarketer called back. She made us a deal for next week that is so fabulous, we've decided just to go now." Debbie's good cheer was genuine.

Jennifer believed that any deal that sounded too good to be true usually *was* too good to be true, but she tried to be positive. "Well, that's certainly a lucky break." Jennifer suspected her parents would return from this trip with a slim wallet and a big credit card bill.

"We've both got some vacation time coming and we're going to take it." Debbie said this last a little tentatively. When Jennifer didn't answer right away, Debbie continued. "I know we were planning to use that time to visit you this fall, but I hope you won't mind. Maybe you can come to see us instead."

Jennifer didn't see how she could possibly get away until after the Denton Bio-Medical case ended, which would be at least six months from now. She tried not to be too sad about this, and didn't want to dampen her parents' enthusiasm for their plans, so she crossed her fingers and lied. "Sure, Mom. That can probably work out. This is really great. Is Dad excited about it?"

"You can't imagine. I haven't seen him so thrilled about anything in a long time. He's out shopping for digital cameras right now. He'll probably be sending you e-mail from the ship." Debbie laughed and Jennifer smiled in the dark. Clay's interest in anything technical was a standing joke in the family.

Debbie talked a little longer about the vacation and then Jennifer begged off. She really was tired and feeling somewhat sorry for herself, too. First the thing with Stuart—and now her parents were going so far away.

Jennifer depended on Debbie and Clay, even if they lived on the other side of the country in northern Michigan. She wanted to go home and have them take care of her—just give her parents all of her troubles, eat Debbie's comfort food, go fishing with Clay.

All of that sounded exactly like what she should do. She'd get on the Internet and make some reservations for right after they returned from Alaska. That decided, even though it might not fit into her schedule, Jennifer felt better. She fell back onto her pillow and into an exhausted sleep in less than five minutes.

CHAPTER TWENTY-SIX

SITTING AT A BAR with a clear view of the Channelside movie complex, Roger Riley watched Melanie Stein ride the escalator to the second floor and approach the ticket window. The outdoor shopping and dining destination on Tampa's waterfront was one of Roger's favorite spots, but Melanie was the one who had selected the unusual locale for their meeting today. She held a cell phone to her ear. Roger could hear her voice, but not the content of her conversation.

The bartender whistled. "Man, what a looker!" Roger had to agree. She was black and beautiful—but "Stein"? She looked every inch the royal African American, descended from queens and kings. Where did the Jew come in? Not that he cared. He was just curious.

Even in the bright sunlight, Melanie was stunningly beautiful. Roger had known she would be. Only a beautiful woman would have the "stones" to do what she was doing. He felt the familiar stirring in his groin as he observed her.

Melanie's request to meet here was an indication of her conscious betrayal of her employers. Normal clients met him in his office. Roger didn't trust her. But he didn't have to. They would be using each other, which suited him fine.

Once she entered the theater, Roger left Melanie alone inside for twenty minutes. Someone had told him, somewhere along the road to fame and fortune, that making the little people wait was a good way to keep them off balance so that you could maintain the upper hand. He'd been making the little people wait for over twenty years now and it was one of the tactics that kept him on top of his game.

Melanie Stein had something serious to offer, something Roger wanted. But he wouldn't let her know that any too soon.

He didn't like to lose control and, except for the pleasant physical stirrings, Melanie's beauty was irrelevant to him. He liked the scenery now, but that wasn't why Roger wanted to meet with Melanie. This was business. He wouldn't stoop to playing cloak-and-dagger with some deceitful broad, except for one thing. In her voice mail message inviting him here Melanie had said the magic words: *Stuart Barnett.*

It was no secret that Roger despised Stuart Barnett. They'd battled each other repeatedly in court over the years. And as with everything he did, Roger had kept score. Barnett was ahead. Barnett had won their very last case, causing Roger to take a bath to the tune of about six million smackers, while Barnett got paid for every nickel's worth of his time. Not to mention Roger's clients, who got nothing. Zip. Nada. They were none too pleased. Thinking about it now, Roger ordered a straight shot of tequila and tossed it back to calm his rage.

He wasn't known as Rabid Roger for nothing. Every scrap of his publicity calling him a scorched-earth litigator was deserved. He'd fought hard to earn his take-no-prisoners reputation and he was proud of it.

"I think we can be useful to each other, Roger," Melanie had said to his voice mail, after telling him she was a lawyer at Worthington, Smith & Marquette. "I have a project I think you'll be interested in."

Recalling the words sent a shiver up his spine. A shiver of anger. Roger hated people who thought they could predict what he would think or do. He made a real effort to keep everyone off guard, on the squash court and in life. Part of his cultivated mystique was that he was unknowable, unpredictable—in a highly scary way. That was how he liked to be viewed. Let them all worry.

Yet, here he was, waiting in a bar for a secret meeting with a damn whistle-blower. These days, he still helped the underdog. He represented high-profile white-collar criminals, victims of fraud and personal injury. But he never represented snitches and tattletales. Roger despised snitches. He didn't think of them as deserving reward.

When Stuart Barnett had handed Roger his balls on a platter the last time they'd crossed swords, Roger was publicly humiliated. Barnett walked out of that courtroom the victor, while Roger left with nothing but empty hands.

The hell with his clients. So they'd lost their one and only day in court. He'd taken the case on a contingent fee. They hadn't lost any money. It was a piece-of-shit case, anyway. They deserved to lose. Which didn't mean Roger planned to let Barnett get away with making an ass out of him. Not by a long shot. Roger had gone straight back to his office and screamed at his associates to look at every file in the office to find him another battle with Stuart Barnett. One he could win.

But Roger found out he had no other cases in his office against Barnett. That was when Roger really blew his cool. He screamed for six days straight every time someone tried to talk to him. Was this about a case involving Stuart Barnett? *No? Then get the hell out of my office!* Roger had been completely insufferable to everyone for months afterward. He knew it. So what. He ordered another tequila shot and tossed this one back, too.

Chemical warmth spread through his veins. Fortune now smiled on Roger Riley. Melanie Stein had called. He didn't care what her case was about. If she was willing to stab Stuart Barnett in the back, she could be a member of his team.

All Roger wanted was to sign Melanie up so that he could make Stuart Barnett's life miserable and wipe the courtroom floor with the blue-blooded asshole. He'd make Barnett gag over that silver spoon he'd been born sucking on, when Roger slammed it down his throat. Roger gloated as he visualized his victory.

But it wouldn't pay to let Melanie think she had the upper hand. Let her stew. She knew she needed him or she wouldn't have arranged this odd encounter.

Roger's life was one battle after another, more victories than losses. He loved the excitement of competition thrumming through his veins like the thrill felt by a wide receiver carrying the touchdown pass, running eighty yards down the field accompanied by a stadium full of ninety thousand screaming fans. Roger knew exactly what that felt like because he'd been the most successful wide receiver the Tampa Bay Buccaneers had ever fielded. Roger brought that same competitive drive to everything he did, from practicing law to bedding women. The adrenaline alone kept him high. When he added a little recreational cocaine to the adrenaline, Roger was unstoppable.

Ten more minutes passed before Roger stood up, buttoned his expensively casual jacket, left a twenty on the bar, and walked to the ticket window. "One, please, for *Crabapple Kids*," he told the attendant.

He made his way into the darkened theater. Only one seat was occupied. Choosing a children's cartoon movie in the middle of the school day had been a smart move on her part. They would not be seen together or overheard. It was a perfect meeting place for a woman who wanted to play dangerous games.

Melanie glanced up with big brown eyes set in a face with coffee-colored skin, surrounded by processed hair that fell straight to her shoulders.

"Mr. Riley," Melanie said, as she offered her cool long fingers to shake his hand.

"So nice to meet you in person, Ms. Stein," Roger answered, with every ounce of the private-school breeding he, as the consummate actor, had learned from watching Stuart Barnett perform. Roger took Melanie's right hand, held it, for a moment, in a warm, firm clasp, and then covered her right hand with his left, holding on from his standing position.

After a few minutes, Roger knew that Melanie's arm had begun to ache and that she felt he was making a spectacle of them both. Roger understood these were her thoughts because he used this same ploy to tilt all beautiful women he encountered off balance. It worked every time. The last of his three wives had called Roger an asshole for doing this to her best friend, right before he took the friend to bed. Roger had simply shrugged. Hard to argue with the truth, although he *would* have argued the point if someone had paid him to do it in court.

Melanie tried to pull her hand away. When he wouldn't release her, she simply stood up. Her bold countermove put *him* off balance. He released her. "You're even more outrageous than I had hoped," she said as if he'd just handed her a delicious present.

He didn't want to give her the impression that she had any control over him or their relationship. Because she didn't. Roger did whatever he wanted to do, whenever he wanted to do it, for his own reasons.

"I'm so glad you called," he told her. This statement was not a lie in the slightest. If Melanie hadn't called precisely when she did, Roger might have found himself in a fistfight with Stuart Barnett soon.

While physical violence was often effective with pretty boys like Barnett, by means of Melanie's case—whatever it was—Roger could revert to the civilized form of combat Barnett preferred. Roger wanted to beat Barnett at his best game and to have the satisfaction of proving he was better in the sport of Barnett's choice. In front of the whole damned legal world.

Roger gestured and they sat. As if the matter were insignificant, he asked her the question he'd wanted answered since she'd first called his office yesterday. "How can we help each other, Ms. Stein?"

Melanie handed him a dirty, thin Manila folder. "This file contains all the material I have on a matter that has been rejected by my firm. I'd like you to take on the case. Stuart Barnett will be representing the opposition."

Roger wanted to leap on the file, to drool over it, to shout that he'd love nothing more. He wanted to run out the door directly to the courthouse to file a complaint the way he'd once run to the goal line with a touchdown.

Instead, he played the moment nice and cool. Winning in court was all a game. If he wanted to learn everything this woman knew, especially why she was betraying one of her firm's most influential partners, Roger knew he had to show some restraint.

He'd get the file and the client no matter what. Because he

wanted it. But this was his chance to acquire inside information that would give Roger another competitive edge in his battle with Barnett. He'd charm more information out of her than she even knew she possessed. And, it might be his only chance to convince Melanie he should get laid this afternoon to celebrate their new partnership. The thought caused him to smile to himself. *Let's not forget that.*

"Why did you choose me? Surely you know that Barnett and I are old adversaries. He won't be pleased." Roger was many things, but "subtle" was not one of them.

Melanie's nostrils flared and her eyes narrowed. Then, her lips drew back, exposing bright white teeth that could have belonged to a vampire or a wolf. "Stuart Barnett is a snake. He would screw his own mother to be Worthington's CEO." It was a point upon which they could easily agree.

She patted the file folder with a well-manicured hand. "These are good people here. They have a good claim. Because he wanted to represent the other side, he rejected them after I'd already agreed to take them on. They deserve better."

Ah, Roger thought. *A woman scorned.* Roger had never known Barnett to be a philanderer, and Roger heard everything sooner or later. Maybe Barnett had applied his charm, then rejected Melanie and that was the source of her venom. Or maybe she was just a woman with a scorned client, thwarted in her career by Barnett. Roger certainly understood what that felt like.

Roger narrowed his own eyes now. He didn't worry about Melanie's hidden agenda. Roger could handle anything thrown his way by a "mere" woman. But he did want to know what motivated her. Maybe he could use it against Barnett.

Roger laid his hand over Melanie's hand perched tentatively on the armrest between their seats. "These 'good people.' What are they to you?"

Melanie's anger abated for a moment and she softened, and Roger caught a glimpse of what kind of lover she would be, if she wanted to. He felt the familiar stirring in his groin.

"I know it's ridiculous, but I get emotionally involved with my clients. I've never been able to separate their causes from mine. These parents are very close to the edge. Their daughter is missing, probably dead. And they're about to get screwed by the legal system. They need help—desperately—and I promised to give it to them. I can't break my word."

This was more than enough for Rabid Roger. He really did view himself as some sort of modern-day knight in shining armor, or Robin Hood or something equally admirable. Never mind that he was a millionaire many times over himself and his behavior was seriously less than chivalrous. Those sorts of facts never got in the way of Roger's self-image or his logic.

But still, Roger felt she had more at stake, and he wanted to see all the cards on the table. He trusted his own instincts. They had literally kept him alive more than once.

"What else?"

Melanie wouldn't look at him now. She pulled her hand away and placed it in her lap. She was having a little trouble spitting it out. Patiently, he waited. Clients had been avoiding the hard truths in their conversations with Roger for years. He could make Melanie tell him what he needed to know. She was no match for him.

Melanie lifted her head and took a deep breath. He could almost see the point at which she decided to make a clean sweep of the facts. "I knew their daughter, Annabelle James quite well. If she's dead…" Melanie stopped here for control. "If she is dead, I want her parents taken care of."

Roger considered her explanation. His instincts told him there was more. He wasn't satisfied yet. "What else?"

Melanie paused a couple of beats and lowered her voice to a growl roughened by emotion. "I was with her the night she disappeared. I should have gone home with her, but I met another friend at the bar and I let her go home alone. I'll never forgive myself." Melanie picked up her Diet Coke and took a huge swig, spilling some on her chin and throat.

Guilt, Roger thought. *What a waste of time.*

Roger pulled the pressed handkerchief out of his breast pocket, reached over, and gently wiped the spilled cola from her skin. He let his fingers graze her neck, ever so gently, as if it were an accident. She didn't flinch.

Yes, Roger thought. This is perfect. I can screw Stuart Barnett in more ways than one.

"One more thing," Melanie said, steel evident in her tone and her gaze. She returned his handkerchief.

"What's that?"

"You'll find a copy of an ethics complaint I filed against Stuart Barnett and Jennifer Lane in that file, too."

"An ethics complaint? Why?" Roger had been the subject of a few ethics complaints himself. He found them a pain in the ass and the people who filed them were usually the worst kind of snitches, the lowest life form Roger could imagine. Roger despised snitches. If a man had some business to take care of, he should do it face-to-face. Man-to-man. Like Roger did. That was Roger's view.

"Because I want them both disbarred. I want them thrown out of the firm on their asses. If they have to leave town, that would be a total victory." The hardness chiseled Melanie's features into razor-sharp edges, and Roger decided he'd be better off going home to the mistress he knew he could control.

CHAPTER TWENTY-SEVEN

RETURNING TO HIS OFFICE, Roger drove west on Brorien, ignoring the forty-miles-per-hour speed limit. He completed the trip in less than six minutes. What was the point of driving a Porsche if you couldn't free the engine every once in a while? But his dictation speed surpassed that of his driving, and he'd finished recording the formal complaint by the time he approached the parking garage of One Harbour Place, based on the information Melanie had told him.

Roger hadn't met the client yet, hadn't considered whether Annabelle James or her parents would want to sue. He hadn't even read the file. He'd figure all that out later. What mattered now was beating Stuart Barnett to the courthouse so Roger could get the home field advantage.

He'd parked the car in its reserved spot before he scooped up the Waldens' dirty file folder and dropped his digital voice recorder into his pocket. He ignored the elevator and skipped easily up the stairs two at a time to the top floor where his office provided a panoramic view of Davis Islands, the Bayshore, and South Tampa. The building was only nine stories high, so he could actually see the nubile joggers running toward him along Bayshore Boulevard.

Know it and weep, Barnett, Roger bragged to himself. Barnett's office was up about forty stories from the ground. The joggers would be mere specs in the distance from Barnett's window.

In under five minutes, Roger was striding down the corridor, through the double glass doors into his opulently appointed lobby and past his receptionist. He gave her a quick wave on the way to his secretary's desk, where he threw the grimy folder and tossed the recorder toward the secretary.

"Type up that complaint for me in the next ten minutes and prepare a summons." He looked at his watch. "It's three o'clock. I want to sign this personally. Call the process server. I want it served before the end of the business day."

The grin on Roger's face was one of the ear-to-ear varieties that he hadn't worn in front of his secretary since the days before Barnett's last win on that orange juice case had turned the grin into a grimace. She snapped the digital recorder's memory stick out of the recorder and pushed it into her computer. She watched the screen as the software converted and then transcribed Roger's verbal dictation into words on the page, undoubtedly eager to see what had so radically altered her boss's mood.

Roger walked into his lavish, large office—"ridiculously large" to quote some client gossip he'd overheard. Not wasting a minute, he reached to buzz his associate on the intercom. He took a quick glance out the window and noticed the joggers again. The fear of heatstroke kept most joggers off the payment in the mid-afternoon during summer. But the ones who had made it out today were worthy enough for Roger to dig his binoculars out of his bottom desk drawer for a closer look.

"Yes, Roger?" the young female associate he'd been sleeping with for the past six weeks asked him as she walked into the room. "You called?"

Without putting down the binoculars, Roger said, "Yes, Tommy." The young woman's name was Thomasina, but Roger couldn't take that much time to address her. She was the most recent in a long line of tall, thin, blonde beauties who took orders from Roger in the office *and* the bedroom until they couldn't stand it anymore and moved on.

"In about ten minutes, I'll have a complaint I'd like you to personally file this afternoon. Then, make sure it gets served before five o'clock." Roger was still grinning like an Olympic gold medal winner. "After that, go home and get dressed up. We're going out."

Thomasina stood quietly.

"Aren't you going to ask me what it is?" Roger knew he had been an absolute bear recently. He turned the full power of his brilliant smile toward Tommy, to thaw her out.

"What is the case, Roger?" she asked, dutifully, because Thomasina understood her role in Roger's life. She was to do whatever Roger wanted—and do it yesterday.

"That asshole Barnett is on the wrong side of this one, Tommy. He's representing Denton Bio-Medical in a whopper of a case against a young woman. Barnett wants to steal the only thing she owns outright—her own work. Like Denton needs more money." Roger's glee spilled out of him, incapable of being contained. "It's perfect. *Perfect.* Couldn't be better if I'd made it up myself. God loves me, Tommy. Oh, yes he does!"

"That's great, Roger," Thomasina said without enthusiasm. "I'll get right on it," she added as she headed for the door.

"I want to sign the complaint myself," Roger told her.

"Okay," she said, nearly out of his inner sanctum now.

"And, Tommy?" His voice called her back. She turned around.

"Yes?"

"Schedule a press conference for four forty-five. I want to make the five o'clock news."

The game was about to begin again.

CHAPTER TWENTY-EIGHT

TYLER STAYED IN THE Cellar, looking, listening, and trying to put together the evidence to fill the gaps. He'd isolated the time of the theft. From the outset, he'd believed the HepZMax theft was an inside job. Because of Gilbert Irwin's open affair with Annabelle James, Tyler believed the guilty party was Gilbert. Russell had been incredulous. He wouldn't believe that Gilbert had betrayed him.

But Tyler understood human nature. First with the FBI and now as a private security consultant, he'd been busting crime for too many years to believe that loyalty to a friend—even a childhood companion who had given Gilbert breaks in life he could never have gotten otherwise—would triumph over love. Even misguided love, like Gilbert's feelings for Annabelle James.

Tyler had focused on Gilbert around the clock for three weeks, and had put together every minute of Gilbert's time line from the moment Annabelle James disappeared until Gilbert killed himself. Tyler's dedication was personal. When he'd been hired ten years ago, he had given Russell Denton his word that nothing could be stolen from Denton Bio-Medical without Tyler's knowledge. He wouldn't be proven wrong by a slip of a woman and a misguided scientist.

Tyler had taken several days to find out exactly when Gilbert had given Annabelle the formula. Annabelle was clever, he'd give her that much. She'd had the formula for over a month before she'd finally disappeared. Tyler would have thought she'd move more quickly.

Tyler eventually found the crucial recording, taped at a restaurant in South Tampa where Gilbert and Annabelle had dined.

Gilbert's briefcase and Annabelle's purse had been wired for sound. Even before Gilbert had ripped off the formula for Annabelle, Tyler hadn't trusted his fidelity. He had listening devices in strategic places for all key employees. Fortunately, as Denton's chief researcher on HepZMax, Gilbert had fit that category. It was only after Gilbert began spending so much time together with Annabelle that Tyler had put his devices in her car and in her house.

Tyler had no method for covert video when the suspects were in public places. But from both audiotapes, he'd filtered out much of the restaurant noise and was able to get most of their dialogue.

Tyler now believed Annabelle's plan had been to make Gilbert himself look like the thief. Hoping he'd missed something important, something that would help him, Tyler listened to the dialogue again, applying his own imagination to reconstruct the scene.

Tyler knew both Annabelle and Gilbert. But to help him visualize, he put a picture of each of them, side by side, on the computer screen while he listened to them speak. Looking at the pictures juxtaposed right in front of him, their affair seemed more improbable than ever.

Gilbert had been a happy man that night. Tyler had the

audiotape of Gilbert singing in the shower, humming as he dressed, laughing on the way to Annabelle's apartment. It was probably the last happy night the poor slob ever spent.

Fortunately for Tyler, Gilbert talked to himself. Gilbert told himself everything as he prepared for his big dinner date with Annabelle James, the one where he intended to propose.

"Will you marry me? Will you marry me?" Gilbert practiced the phrase about fifty times, using different voice inflections, until Tyler began to hate the words as much as his own ex-wife claimed to do.

Tyler settled back with his headphones and started Gilbert's tape at the point where Gilbert was driving to Annabelle's apartment. "I brought you a big surprise, Annabelle," he said. "I'll tell you about it after dinner. You won't believe it."

How could Gilbert have been so gullible, Tyler wondered. Gilbert was a scientist. He knew about Pavlov's dogs, how they salivated every time Pavlov fed them and rang a bell, and, pretty soon, salivated just at the sound of the bell.

Gilbert was like those dogs himself, thought Tyler. Gilbert had salivated just thinking about Annabelle and how she would reward him.

At the restaurant, Tyler heard the pout in Annabelle's voice. He'd seen her hold onto Gilbert's arm many times and pet him like a beloved dog. It made Tyler want to vomit. "You know what this means to me, don't you, honey?" she said. Her voice was almost a purr, like a kitten's. Gilbert actually said, "Yes, kitten." It was disgusting how he fawned over her, how she led him on.

Tyler shuddered to think how conniving Annabelle was. She had to know that few women had ever touched Gilbert. Certainly none as beautiful as Annabelle. The woman was a coldhearted bitch, that was for sure.

But what about Gilbert? Every time he'd looked at her, Gilbert must have known she was too good to be true. Gilbert must have expected to wake up from his very pleasant dream any minute and find himself working alone in the lab, spending hours developing a new formula, just as he had done in the years before Annabelle. The reality was finally so much worse for him.

"Just wait, baby. I have a special surprise. After dinner," Gilbert said as if he were placating a child. Tyler shook his head in amazement. How could men be so stupid, so self-deluded? Gilbert couldn't have imagined that a woman who looked and smelled and tasted like Annabelle James was seriously interested in him. A woman like Annabelle actually loving Gilbert was too good to be true, and he should have known it.

On the other hand, maybe he did know, Tyler reminded himself. Maybe Gilbert just didn't care. He was a realistic guy. At Gilbert's age, Annabelle would have been his last chance to feel like a desirable man. Why would Gilbert have given up that feeling, voluntarily, anyway? Not many guys would have. Look at the fool Tyler himself was making of himself over his ex-wife. Men could be such idiots.

"We've got to finish the work, honey. You promised," Annabelle whined. She'd probably pouted some more. On Annabelle, the pout was absolutely perfect. Everything about Annabelle was perfectly in place. That was the whole problem—Tyler knew. If Annabelle James hadn't been so damn perfect, Tyler wouldn't be sitting here, trying to figure out why Gilbert had driven off the damn Sunshine Skyway Bridge for her.

Tyler looked down at his notes. Gilbert had brought the formula documents to dinner. He'd recited what he put in his briefcase as he'd gotten dressed. "HepZMax formula, engagement ring, cell phone," he'd said as he packed.

Maybe he'd only meant to show Annabelle that he had finished the work. But Gilbert gave her the only hard copy, and put her name on it. Tyler could imagine Gilbert wanting Annabelle to see her own success. The HepZMax formula, with its moneymaking potential, would be a powerful aphrodisiac to a woman like Annabelle. Tyler thought of Annabelle as a gold digger. She lived luxuriously. Money seemed to motivate her more than anything else. But she also wanted worldly acknowledgment and legitimacy. That much had been obvious.

Tyler pulled up Annabelle's résumé on another computer screen while the audiotape was projecting clashing cutlery and conversation about trivial matters made by several voices Tyler couldn't identify. Annabelle and Gilbert were waiting for a table alongside other patrons. Gilbert was complaining about the heat and Annabelle was ignoring him. Someone nearby was talking to his companion in the loud tones supported by too much alcohol.

Annabelle's résumé revealed that she wasn't actually much of a scientist. She was minimally credentialed, and the so-called lab rats had told Tyler that she simply couldn't do the work as well as others could. Gilbert probably thought she'd get a raise and a promotion and that would be enough to keep her in his bed. Tyler figured Gilbert had badly misjudged Annabelle, trusting in her too much.

Gilbert had probably just wanted Annabelle to get all the credit for developing the formula. It belonged to Denton Bio-Medical, anyway. Employees usually signed an agreement assigning all rights in any newly developed products to Denton. Which was only fair. Tyler knew Gilbert believed the deal was fair.

Gilbert had worked with Russell Denton for over twenty years. Denton paid him well, supported his research, and did everything possible to bring the new products Gilbert developed to market. Gilbert and Denton were friends as well as colleagues. Tyler had talked with Gilbert many times after Annabelle disappeared and before Gilbert died. Gilbert wasn't concerned that Denton was rich and Gilbert wasn't. Until Annabelle, Gilbert hadn't had anyone to spend his money on, anyway.

Besides, the formula was only one part of developing a new treatment as important as HepZMax. Gilbert knew that. This wasn't the first successful formula he'd worked on for Russell Denton, but it was the first one he'd given to Annabelle.

Tyler went back to listening when he heard the hostess tell them their table was ready. Heads must have turned as they walked through the crowded restaurant. Other diners surely watched the petite, dark beauty with the oafish older man.

Tyler figured Gilbert was Annabelle's sugar daddy; the other diners must have thought so, too. The truth was Gilbert couldn't give Annabelle much money, but he gave her the professional recognition she craved.

When they were seated and their orders taken, Gilbert's impatience finally got the better of him. "Annabelle, kitten, I have something for you." Gilbert's voice fairly crackled with emotion. "Something really special. Close your eyes."

"Ooooohh!" Annabelle squealed and clapped her hands. Tyler rolled his eyes just hearing the audio. Video would have made him nauseous. "What is it? Tell me! I love surprises, baby."

Tyler heard the clasps on the briefcase snap open. By enhancing the audio's volume, he could hear something fairly light being removed from the briefcase and the lid falling closed.

"Here. Open it," Gilbert told her.

"But what's this? An envelope?" Annabelle's disappointment was evident. *Just wait,* Tyler thought. *The jewelry's coming.*

He heard background noise for a few seconds and then Annabelle's gasp. "Oh, Gilbert!" she whispered her exclamation. "When did you finish the work? I can't believe you didn't tell me."

"This morning. Look. Look on the bottom where it says 'developer.'" Gilbert was fairly bursting with pride. "It says Roxanne Mae Walden James. Your full name. Just yours." It hurt Tyler to hear Gilbert's pathetic approval seeking.

A few seconds passed. "Don't cry, kitten. It's supposed to make you happy. Here," Gilbert said. What did he hand her? A tissue? The fool probably pictured the two of them working together forever, side by side, Annabelle helping him in the lab and Gilbert giving Annabelle all the credit. Gilbert had no need for fame and fortune. He only needed Annabelle. How stupid could such an intelligent man be?

"Oh, baby. It's perfect. I can't believe you'd do this for me," she sniveled.

"I can't, either," Tyler said to himself.

"Are you all right, miss?" The waitress's voice again. "Can I get you something?"

Annabelle's sniveling continued. "Oh, I'm just so happy."

"Give me a break," Tyler commented.

When the waitress took their orders and left, Annabelle leaned over to Gilbert and gave him a kiss loud enough to drown out the background noise on the audio. There were more "kittens" and "babys" and Tyler had to turn off the tape and refill his coffee just to keep his ire under control.

No matter how many times he heard this exchange, he couldn't just listen and let it go. Annabelle James had killed Gilbert, as far as Tyler was concerned. She'd killed him just the same as if she'd rammed into his car and run him over the side of the bridge.

What did she think was going to happen? Women like that play with a man. Treat them like pawns in a heartless game of chess. Once she got the formula, Annabelle didn't need Gilbert anymore. Of course Annabelle had never loved the poor guy. He must have figured that out at some point.

Gilbert was more than willing to be a fool for Annabelle. That much was obvious. But she still was guilty for using him to steal from his friend and employer.

When had Gilbert realized that Annabelle had played him for a complete idiot? Was it before she disappeared? Or not until later when she didn't come back, when he found out she'd stolen HepZMax?

Tyler hung his head as he thought about how Gilbert had tried to go on, tried to work on something else, tried to make it up to Denton. He'd returned to the dull, lonely, colorless life he had lived "before Annabelle." Russell told Tyler that Gilbert had apologized over and over again, in tears over what he'd done, asking Russell to forgive him in the weeks after Annabelle left and before Gilbert died.

What was Gilbert thinking at the moment he drove his car through the sheeting rain off the Sunshine Skyway Bridge? Had he convinced himself that his time with Annabelle had been too short?

Tyler tried to put himself in Gilbert's shoes, tried to realize how Gilbert must have felt. Gilbert had believed Annabelle loved him. Losing that must have been unbearable. Without Annabelle, Gilbert obviously thought life was no longer worth living. Tyler had gone through that himself, right after his divorce. It had taken him years to get over it.

Tyler returned to the audio again. "Annabelle, will you marry me?" Tyler heard Gilbert's choice of inflection from the many he had rehearsed: quiet, sincere, pleading.

"Oh, baby! I thought you'd never ask!" Annabelle accepted Gilbert's ring. Was she so heartless that she wouldn't realize how her treachery would hurt the big oaf? How could she have been such a stone cold bitch to the poor bastard?

Gilbert's death was a tragedy. Tyler hadn't meant to drive him to suicide. He'd miscalculated Gilbert's level of anxiety. Which was why he was being so careful with Blake and Russell now. Both of them were near the breaking point. Jennifer Lane seemed to be the catalyst that would resolve that conflict, one way or another.

Tyler could sense Russell's struggle with himself: Should he tell Jennifer? Not? Let it go for now. Tyler saw no immediate urgency to telling Jennifer what was going on. But they'd have to do so soon. Before Blake beguiled her, too.

Exhausted now, Tyler moved to another tape. He listened to the conversation the previous night between Jennifer and Blake. Tyler was disgusted with the man. How could he be so universally evil?

Of course, Tyler didn't believe in evil in the religious sense. Never had. He'd seen more than enough evil in his life, though. He knew that all men had the capacity for evil, however one defined it. Evil behavior was just a result of something that pushed people's buttons, and how they justified their acts to themselves.

Tyler rubbed the back of his neck and rose to refill his coffee cup. He'd been at this for thirty-six hours straight. He needed a break. He set all of his listening devices to mute, went over to the cot in the corner and lay down just to rest for an hour. In less than ten seconds, he fell into a deep, dreamless sleep.

CHAPTER TWENTY-NINE

THE CRUSH OF REPORTERS filled the lavish conference room overlooking the Bayshore at the offices of Roger Riley and Associates. Tampa wasn't the home of all that many print and television reporters, but the ones who regularly worked the court beats knew that Roger was good for a newsworthy story. He was theatrical and a media hound. He made sellable press. Every time.

Today was no exception to the rule. Roger watched the clock so that the reporters would have to make the decision as to whether to broadcast his press conference live at five o'clock. Then once on the air at five, he was pretty well assured of a taped repeat at six and eleven. Roger manipulated the news cycle with skill. He was a master at it. The reporters didn't mind his maneuvering, either. Roger Riley's agenda was good for all of them.

At precisely one minute past five, Roger walked into the conference room with a big smile on his face. He wore a camera-friendly, fresh shirt in light blue; a sincere navy blue suit; and a red, conservatively patterned tie. This was Roger's "man of the people" outfit. He kept it in his office closet for just such emergencies.

"Ladies and gentlemen, thank you for coming on such short notice," Roger said.

"Always the charmer, Roger Riley," one reporter snickered to his sidekick.

"Yeah, especially when he wants something," the sidekick whispered back.

Roger ignored them. "I wanted you to be the first to know that we have filed this complaint"—for the photo op, he held up the paper with the Hillsborough County Circuit Court time stamp on the corner—"against Denton Bio-Medical, Incorporated, today."

The reporters looked at their copies of the complaints handed to them at the door when they'd come in.

"We're seeking twenty million dollars in compensatory damages and two hundred million in punitive damages on behalf of our client, Annabelle James." A collective gasp went up from the crowd of jaded reporters. Such numbers were unusual in Tampa, but they made a juicy story practically soggy.

Tampa courts drew jurors from a conservative county where the median income of most jurors was in the hard-earned twenty-five thousand dollar-a-year range. Sometimes, they'd help a deserving plaintiff win the litigation lotto, but not all that often. Defendants won more times than they lost. Still, a big money claim brought by Roger Riley held a lot of sex appeal.

"The punitive damage award could go higher. Denton Bio-Medical has conspired, out of pure greed, to remove a new product from the market. A potential cure for a silent time bomb that might be killing everyone in this room. Russell Denton wants to keep the cure from us all. Our children—mine and yours—are at risk. Denton is a killer and a thief. We will not rest until Annabelle James is vindicated." Roger smiled into the glaring lights for the seven-second sound bite. Then he left the conference room, refusing to take the usual questions.

Roger would keep the story alive by allowing the reporters to digest the complaint, do some investigating, and come back to him later with requests for further interviews. All he wanted to do today was to get on the newscast, so that Stuart Barnett would find out in the most public way possible that he'd been screwed.

CHAPTER THIRTY

SHORTLY AFTER FIVE O'CLOCK, Jennifer was sitting in Stuart's office awaiting final suggestions on the Denton Bio-Medical complaint, when Stuart's direct phone line rang. He pushed the speaker button. "Hello." His voice was quiet, intimate, as if only his nearest and dearest could be calling.

Instead Russell Denton's voice shouted over the speaker, loud enough to wake the dead, "You must be out of your mind!"

"Russell," Stuart acknowledged, while he continued to review the draft complaint Jennifer had prepared, making a few changes with his red pen.

"How could you have let Roger Riley beat you into court? I thought we were going to be the plaintiff here? We're the victim. I thought we were going to federal court. We'd have a preliminary injunction by now if you'd gotten this case moving when I hired you. What the hell is going on?" All this from Russell Denton who was legendary for keeping his cool in hot situations.

Jennifer's stomach began to churn as she realized what Denton was so angry about. Jennifer cowered in the face of any angry man, even when that anger was not directed at her. She much preferred the protective shield Stuart Barnett provided to taking the heat herself.

Stuart didn't answer Denton's questions right away. "Russell, I don't know what you're talking about." Stuart was flush with the victory he'd won this morning in his latest case. He'd been giving Jennifer the blow-by-blow when she'd first come in. Because he'd been so busy, Jennifer hadn't been able to keep him in the loop on Denton's case until today.

"Turn on your television," Russell commanded.

"Okay." Stuart pointed his remote at his television and clicked the power button.

When the picture flashed on, Stuart swore and threw the remote at the wall so hard it broke apart. He gestured to Jennifer to walk over to the television to flip manually through the channels. With each flick, Roger Riley's devilish features filled the screen. Jennifer watched him in fascination. The man had some gall. His insincere indignation at Denton's expense might have been comical, it was so overplayed. But Roger was deadly serious. No wonder Russell was pissed. He had every right to be.

Jennifer thought for a moment that Stuart would tell Denton why he was being targeted by Rabid Roger. But Stuart kept silent and allowed Russell to continue his unabated angry tirade. Jennifer tuned Russell out and listened to Roger's statement followed by the anchor's comments. With each word, she felt herself becoming more nauseated. Rabid Roger was not a man she wanted to fight. The mere thought of it tied her stomach in knots.

Stuart whistled when he heard that Roger had asked for two hundred twenty million in damages. He pushed the mute button on the phone so that Russell couldn't hear their conversation. "What's Riley so hot about? Is it that juice case?" Stuart asked her.

"How should I know?" Fear made her snap. Jennifer had

handled that file, and handled it brilliantly. Stuart had had nothing to do with it, although his name was on the pleadings. Not that Stuart hadn't been pleased when Jennifer had beaten Roger's ass. But Rabid Roger was dangerous. "You can beat the tar out of him, can't you?" Jennifer was afraid of Riley. She wished she had her gun. It would make her feel safer.

"Litigation requires a worthy opponent, Jennifer," was his response. "Riley's a challenge to litigate against. I love a good fight, in the right context."

Jennifer envied Stuart's maleness. Stuart didn't feel threatened by Roger in any way. They'd been jousting for years now. Sometimes Roger was ahead, sometimes Stuart trounced him. Their sparring was a game to Stuart and he enjoyed it.

"Maybe so. But Roger Riley doesn't play well with others, and you know that. He takes everything personally." Jennifer was not happy at all about this ongoing argument with Riley. She understood that Roger was still trying to prove he was good enough, while Stuart had already settled that for himself in everyone's mind. Jennifer, in fact, recognized a kindred spirit in Roger. He would never be good enough in the ways that mattered.

Stuart had released the mute button, and Jennifer tuned in to what Russell was saying It was almost as if he'd heard Stuart's remarks. "My case is not going to be a brawl, Barnett. We've all got too much at stake."

"I know, Russell," Stuart said, trying to placate him.

"Don't patronize me. You told me that the preliminary injunction was a slam dunk. 'No contest,' you said." Russell's rage continued like a wildfire out of control.

Jennifer listened with a sinking feeling. Russell was right. Stuart had said Jennifer would file a complaint, write a brief, and get an injunction, just like she'd done in the orange juice case.

She'd felt all along that Stuart was overconfident, but she knew better than to say so right this minute.

No one had planned on adding Rabid Roger to this glowing picture, but, somehow, he had made his way into the scene. *Of all the lousy luck,* Jennifer thought.

Stuart pressed the mute button on the phone again. "How the hell did Roger get this client and this file so quickly?"

"I don't know. Do I look like the answer woman to you?" Jennifer was walking on thin ice here, but fear galvanized her.

Stuart raised one eyebrow at her tone, then released the mute button and responded to Russell. "A draft complaint is sitting on my desk right now, Russell. I intend to file it in federal court tomorrow morning."

"You're a few hours too late, aren't you? If you'd done it yesterday, Riley would be at a serious disadvantage. The same disadvantage you now have to dig yourself out from under." Russell refused to give one centimeter. He was right and he obviously knew it. Not that it mattered who was right. The damage was done.

Jennifer heard Stuart curse under his breath, as Russell continued to rant.

"I take your point, Russell. I won't pretend it's not a bad break," Stuart said, when he could finally get a word in.

"Bad break? You've got to be kidding me! Rabid Roger Riley on the other side of a case like this is more than a 'bad break.'" Russell emphasized the words as if they were the most outrageous understatement he had ever heard. "And you know it. It's a catastrophe. We can forget about winning quickly and we may be able to forget about winning at all."

Stuart almost laughed. He covered his mouth with his hand to hide his amusement. He waved Jennifer to turn the television off.

"I take it you've dealt with Roger before." Stuart said it as a statement, not a question.

"I think we both know the answer to that," Russell responded, with the kind of finality that acknowledged Roger's reputation and his prior acts of combat with both Russell and Stuart.

"Fax me the complaint—" Stuart started. But Russell cut him off.

"You should have it already. Don't you get your mail over there, either?"

"Let me take a look at it and I'll call you back." Stuart rang off. He stepped around his desk and covered the distance to the door in three long strides. Then he reached for the knob and opened the door, only to find his secretary standing there, holding Roger's complaint in one hand, the other poised to knock. Hilda looked like a child whose beloved dog had just been hit by a car. Jennifer put her head in her hands and vowed to apply for a concealed-weapon permit.

CHAPTER THIRTY-ONE

TYLER SAT IN HIS white Xterra in the parking lot at the outdoor shooting range, waiting. The Xterra's windows were tinted dark. He'd followed Jennifer from the office, just to keep up his skills and for something to do. He'd spent so many hours in the Cellar since Gilbert had died that he felt like a mushroom. He needed to get out, get back in the field. An instinct told him today would be a good day for this task.

Jennifer spent an hour at the range. Tyler had watched her target practice from the inside viewing room for her first round. She had scored deadly hits on the center of the target more often than not. He couldn't count the number of holes in the dead center of the circular bull's-eye from his vantage point, but he could see clear through the paper. She was good.

Tyler wondered why she was so focused, so intent on shooting to kill. What drove her? He hoped to find out. When she reloaded and began to shoot another round, Tyler went outside and let himself into her purple PT Cruiser parked in the parking lot near his Xterra. It took him only a few minutes to insert a listening device into her car and to be sure it worked with the voice-activated recorder. He reached over and turned the radio on, twisting the volume control up. He'd be able to test it when she exited the range. When he'd finished the setup, he settled into the Xterra to wait.

Now, Tyler watched her walk to her car, carrying a small briefcase. She'd come to the range to pick up her gun. Lori had a locker inside, and Jennifer probably did, too. He'd checked the records and she didn't have a concealed weapon permit, which meant she should have left the gun in the locker. Where was she taking the gun? Why did she feel she needed it?

Tyler had a clear view of Jennifer as she unlocked the car with the keyless entry, opened the door, and put the gun case in the backseat. She entered the car, closed and locked the door. He looked down at his surveillance equipment. When Jennifer started the car, her radio caused the voice-activated recorder to come on. So far, so good.

He turned up the volume on the recorder's speaker and followed Jennifer into the afternoon traffic on Dale Mabry—Tampa's all-purpose highway. Traffic was so slow, he dropped back a few car lengths to avoid being spotted. Fortunately, her purple car stood out like a big eggplant and was easy to watch.

CHAPTER THIRTY-TWO

JENNIFER REACHED OVER AND turned down the radio. Had she left the volume that loud earlier? When she did, she noticed the blinking red light on her cell phone telling her she had messages. As she made the decision to ignore them, the phone began the computerized rendition of "The Entertainer," signaling an incoming call.

The caller ID read "Ronald Walden." Jennifer swallowed and wavered over the phone's answer button. Probably it was Lila Walden, calling from home. She'd called four times today already, before Jennifer left the office. The voice mail messages were most likely from her, too.

"Oh, hell," Jennifer wailed into the empty car. "What do you want from me?" But she didn't answer the phone, which eventually stopped ringing, allowing Jennifer to breathe a sigh of relief. "Give it up," she prayed aloud.

Just as the words left her mouth, the phone rang again. She ignored it through three more sets of the tinny tune, while she was stalled in afternoon traffic. On the fifth set, Jennifer had to acknowledge that the woman was not going to stop calling her. Lila Walden was one determined female.

Jennifer shrugged, took a deep breath and pushed the talk button. "Mrs. Walden, I'm not allowed to talk to you. I am so sorry, but I just can't have this conversation." Jennifer hurried through her rehearsed lines while the traffic moved forward an inch at a time. Stuart had told her not to have any further contact with the Waldens. Jennifer already felt so guilty for abandoning them that she just wanted the whole experience to go away.

"Why can't you talk to me?" Lila asked, offended. "Is there something wrong with me?"

"Not at all. It's just that you are the plaintiff in a case that I'm defending and you have a lawyer. I'm required to deal directly with Mr. Riley—I can't talk with you. I'll get in big trouble. Please." Jennifer managed to keep the tremor out of her voice at the mere thought of how livid Riley would be if he knew Jennifer was talking to his client. "I'm so sorry," Jennifer added again, meaning it.

"Oh, for heaven's sake. Roger Riley isn't my lawyer and never will be." Lila dismissed the idea out of hand.

"What do you mean?"

"I didn't hire Roger Riley. He doesn't represent me," Lila said as if she were explaining the fundamentals of life to a dim student.

The *Annabelle James v. Denton Bio-Medical, Inc.* complaint had slithered onto Jennifer's desk this afternoon like the serpent appearing in the Garden of Eden, full of malicious intent and the capacity to destroy life as she knew it. Lila Walden was represented by Roger Riley. Riley said so right there in black and white.

"Mr. Riley filed a complaint on behalf of your daughter, Mrs. Walden—" Jennifer started.

"Yes, but it doesn't have my name on it, does it?" Lila asked her, reasonably. "As I said, I didn't hire Roger Riley. He doesn't represent me. Can you talk to me now?"

Jennifer was bewildered. How could Riley not be the Waldens' lawyer? Unless Annabelle had reappeared? Maybe Annabelle had hired Riley herself. If Annabelle was Riley's client, then Jennifer had no real ethical problem with talking to Lila. Except that Stuart had told her in no uncertain terms not to do so.

"I don't understand. Has Annabelle come home?" Traffic speed picked up a little and Jennifer gunned the Cruiser's engine to make it through the light. On the other side, she began to move about thirty miles an hour. The gods were smiling.

"Not that I know of. That's why I'm calling you," Lila said, enunciating each word very slowly.

"But then, who is Roger Riley representing?" Jennifer asked, completely flummoxed now.

"Good question," Lila said. "I can only tell you that we were never appointed as Roxanne Mae's guardians and I did not hire the man. He doesn't represent me."

"Or your husband?" Jennifer asked.

"That, you'd have to ask Ronald." Lila sounded as if she couldn't care less what her husband might be doing, or with whom. When had that happened?

"Well, don't you know?" Jennifer pressed her, annoyed, herself, at Lila's insistence and deliberate stalling.

"Look, it doesn't matter. If Riley was representing my husband, that still wouldn't make me Riley's client, would it? Because if it does, I'm going to fire him right now and hire you back," Lila told her.

An involuntary "No!" escaped Jennifer's throat. She dropped the phone into her lap and slammed on her brakes. The Cruiser swerved over to her right. Her seatbelt jerked her back into her seat. She stopped inches before she hit the old, beat-up silver Buick in front of her.

When she regained her composure, Jennifer's shaking hand found the phone in her lap. Lila was still there. Jennifer could hear her breathing. "I can't represent you, Mrs. Walden. I represent Denton Bio-Medical in this case. You see?" She righted the Cruiser on the road and started forth again, moving more cautiously this time. Her chest was sore where the seatbelt had grabbed her. She'd have a bruise there tomorrow.

"No, I don't see." Lila sounded completely annoyed. "I'm not calling about that case."

Cautiously, Jennifer said, "Then why are you calling me?"

"I know what Roger Riley is and what he's not," Lila added.

Jennifer had assumed that Riley was well-regarded among Tampa's economically disadvantaged folks, such as Lila Walden. Apparently not this one.

Lila said, "He's not interested in finding Roxanne Mae. You are. I don't care what your reasons are. I want you to locate my daughter."

Watching the taillights of the car in front of her more closely now, Jennifer cautiously considered the implications. When the car ahead stopped abruptly the next time, she realized he didn't have any brake lights. That explained why she'd almost slammed into him before. Lila had distracted her attention to the point of near disaster. She rubbed her sore chest again.

If Lila Walden was telling her the truth, Roger Riley didn't really have a client at all. Annabelle was missing. Annabelle hadn't hired Riley, hadn't authorized the complaint. Jennifer began to think about how she could use this information to Denton Bio-Medical's advantage, information she wouldn't have known without Lila Walden.

Which was exactly why she shouldn't be talking to Lila at all. Roger Riley would move to disqualify Jennifer. She'd be out of a client and probably get fired. She reached into her pocket for her antacids. Every time she turned around, she faced disaster of one kind or another. Was this what it meant to be a successful lawyer? Did she want the job?

"So? Will you help me find my daughter or not?"

Jennifer cleared her throat. She saw her digital clock click over one second, two, three. She kept her eyes on the old beater still in front of her. If she'd hit that tank, her face would bear the impression of the grille of her car. Involuntarily, she visualized her body being forced through the windshield and tried to shake off the image.

"Well?" Lila prompted her again.

"I don't know, Mrs. Walden." She heard her own weariness in her tone. "I'd have to get permission from Denton and Stuart Barnett. I don't think they'd let me do that."

"Why not? You want to find her, don't you?" Lila insisted.

Jennifer did want to find Annabelle. She just didn't know whether she could, or even should, help to find the Waldens' daughter. Jennifer hoped that Annabelle and Denton might work out their differences in mediation. They didn't need to be at war with one another. They had a great product in the making, one that could save a large number of people from terrible suffering and death. The two parties working together, not against each other, made the most sense.

And, it had the added benefit of getting Jennifer out of some serious hot water with the Florida Bar. If there was no active controversy, and no one got hurt, then the bar might be a little lenient with her. Maybe the firm's executive committee wouldn't demand her head on a platter.

As the traffic slowed to a halt again, her eyes focused on the old Buick ahead, and with the phone still held to her ear, Jennifer's mind churned with her choices.

Rabid Roger didn't care about Annabelle, her formula, or even mankind for that matter. All he wanted was to beat the snot out of Stuart Barnett, at whatever cost. Riley would carry this thing into forever, until he was finally able to ruin Stuart. Riley didn't want to just resolve the dispute favorably for his client. He wanted to humiliate and annihilate Stuart. If Jennifer took this opportunity from Riley, she would join Stuart as Riley's biggest enemy. The mere thought of being Roger Riley's enemy caused Jennifer to reach into her pocket and pop another antacid into her mouth.

Still, if Jennifer found Annabelle James, she could get Annabelle and Denton together. Maybe she could avoid the fight between Riley and Stuart. Maybe, just maybe, finding Annabelle James could salvage both her job and her affair with Blake. Lila's call could be a blessing in disguise.

But she'd have to do everything quietly, with the utmost secrecy. Stuart would fire her in a New York minute if he found out what she was up to. Russell Denton would do worse. He'd see to it that she never practiced law in Tampa again. Rabid Roger might actually kill her—really. *Okay. Now that's a little paranoid,* she thought. Her gun resting in the backseat was small comfort. She'd never have the nerve to shoot *anyone.*

Still, it was time Jennifer found some courage for herself. If not now, when? She could have died just now. Surely she'd been spared for some reason.

Jennifer squared her shoulders, sat up straight, and dug into her deepest center, looking for some fortitude. She swallowed the rest of the antacid with a big gulp of lukewarm water from the bottle that had been sitting in the Cruiser's cup holder for days. A small grimace creased her features as the water and antacid went down, along with her better judgment.

"All right, Lila, I'll consider it," Jennifer said before she really intended to do so, before she could crawl back into herself and cower behind fears even she realized were irrational. *You hope,* she thought.

CHAPTER THIRTY-THREE

LILA'S MOUTH TURNED UP into a satisfied curve as she heard Jennifer's coerced agreement. The psychic had told her that Jennifer would agree to find Roxanne Mae. Lila Walden understood the girl. Jennifer was an idealist, a real do-gooder. Just the person Lila needed.

"Come to see me this evening. About six o'clock will be fine. Ronald will be fishing until long past dark. Do you know where we live?" Lila gave the lawyer an address over on North C near Westshore.

"And Jennifer," Lila said just before she signed off, "don't drive that purple car of yours. It's too visible."

Lila replaced the phone in its cradle and began her preparations for Jennifer's visit. Lila was not only a cunning woman, she was also a planner. She wanted everything to go smoothly. Her goals depended on Jennifer, and Lila did not intend to leave anything to chance.

CHAPTER THIRTY-FOUR

JENNIFER LEFT HER APARTMENT, driving her neighbor's unfamiliar Honda in fits and starts. She hadn't driven a car with a five-speed transmission since high school, so she had to relearn its operation. After a few blocks, though, she was able to drive cautiously forward, hoping she didn't have to try reverse. She traveled west on Swann to Dale Mabry. Negotiating the stop-and-go traffic, she made her way slowly north of Kennedy Boulevard, where she turned left onto North C, traveling west again, and began to look at the house numbers.

Trying to remember to press the clutch on the floor before she shifted, and grinding the gears every time no matter how careful she was, Jennifer drove slowly through the intersection at Himes and then Lois. In the next block, Jennifer found the Waldens' small Florida ranch-style house on the south side of the street.

The house was one of the smaller ones still standing in the neighborhood. Though it had a lot of what real estate agents called "curb appeal," the house was destined to be a teardown. Like many of Tampa's older, less affluent areas, North C was cluttered with new homes that were much too large for the lots they consumed. A home like the Waldens' would be snapped up by developers, and soon replaced by a three story, zero-lot-line house.

You could pick out the first oversized homes that had arrived in these neighborhoods; they seemed more like Dorothy's house plopped down from the sky in the middle of the Munchkin patch than urban progress. Soon after, the Munchkin-patch houses disappeared entirely, replaced by faux haciendas and historic-looking tall and narrow Charleston styles built so close together that their owners could shake hands through open kitchen windows.

At the rate things were going on North C, the Waldens could probably sell their house for ten times what they'd paid for it back in the sixties when they'd bought it. Why hadn't they sold already? Obviously, they needed the money. They couldn't even afford to pay their daughter's monthly rent and they qualified for pro bono status at Worthington.

Jennifer parked in Lila Walden's driveway, which was lined on either side with well-tended red and white begonias in full bloom. A live oak tree filled the front yard with wandering branches bigger than Jennifer's waist. Red geraniums, variegated lariope, and orange birds-of-paradise bloomed around the perimeter of the small house. It was apparent that the yard had received Lila's loving attention.

Jennifer locked the borrowed Honda after picking up her gun case from the backseat. Now that she'd brought it home from the shooting range, she was afraid to leave the gun unattended anywhere. Her grip on the small, heavy case made it feel like a deadly extension of her arm. "That's what you get for catastrophizing," she scolded herself.

A heart-shaped wreath of red velvet roses surrounded a small window in the front door. Jennifer pushed the doorbell and heard it chime pleasantly inside the house. In just a few moments Lila Walden's face appeared, framed in the window, before she opened the door.

"Jennifer," she said, "come in, dear."

When the door opened, the smell of freshly baked cookies wafted out to Jennifer's nose, reminding her of her own mother's passion for baking such treats.

Lila was wearing a cotton shirtwaist dress with pink and white stripes, fitted bodice, and a covered belt. She wore flat, white shoes with open toes and panty hose. The woman looked like a fifties sitcom mom. Jennifer had seen outfits like this on late-night syndicated television programs. She wondered where Lila could actually buy such dresses now. Maybe she sewed her own clothes. Did anybody do that anymore?

"Come this way," Lila said, preceding Jennifer down the hallway through the small house into the kitchen. Jennifer felt as if she were in a time warp. She could be walking through an episode of *The Donna Reed Show* or *Leave It to Beaver*. The fifties' decor was disorienting, but somehow more comforting than twenty-first century furnishings would have been.

Lila offered her freshly brewed iced tea with mint sprigs—already laced with plenty of sugar. This was what Jennifer's Aunt Peggy would have called "sweet tea," and it was a staple of Southern households of a certain era. Again, Jennifer felt strange—as if she were walking and talking in a fantasy world.

Jennifer had never done any acting in school, but now she felt she was supposed to be someone else, not herself. Jennifer Lane's life didn't look like this. She began to feel a weird connection to Annabelle James, as though she could feel how Annabelle felt growing up.

The odd connection Jennifer had begun to feel with Annabelle

James—a woman she'd never met and was opposing in litigation, the equivalent of a modern battlefield—was strong here. Very strong.

Once they were settled at the small, red Formica-and-chrome dinette set with their hot sugar cookies and sweet tea, Jennifer brought the conversation around to the reason for her visit.

"I've decided that I do want to help you find Annabelle, if I can," Jennifer started to explain. Lila nodded as if she was not surprised. "But, I don't want you to get your hopes up, Lila. The police have tried to find her already. You've tried. Denton has probably tried, too, given how he feels about her." Jennifer didn't know whether the Waldens were aware that Denton had hired a private investigator to find Annabelle. She had to be careful not to disclose Denton's secrets or she'd be in worse trouble than she was already.

Lila covered Jennifer's hand on the kitchen table. "It's okay, dear. I know you'll find Roxanne Mae. The others weren't meant to find her, or she didn't want to be found by them." Lila's demeanor was calm, relaxed. "Everything happens for a reason. You're the one who will find my daughter. I know it."

Jennifer pulled out her yellow legal pad and one of the blue Flair pens she favored. She would write down, verbatim and in shorthand, what Lila told her. "Okay. Where do we start?"

Jennifer lifted her Dictaphone out of her briefcase and set it on the table between them. "Do you mind if I keep this on? It will help me later." The tape would record nuances of voice and word inflections, Jennifer explained in response to Lila's unasked question. Sometimes it wasn't so much what was said but how one said it that conveyed meaning.

What Jennifer didn't say was that she wanted a clear and accurate record if Roger Riley should ever try to suggest that she'd done something illegal or unethical, or both. Litigating against Rabid Roger was a very personal experience. He would attack Jennifer at every turn. She was handing him a loaded gun by simply being here.

Lila nodded her head. “Use whatever you like, dear. If it will help you to tape us, then go ahead. Another cookie?”

“Where should we begin?” Jennifer asked, pen poised to take notes between bites of fresh cookie that melted in her mouth.

“I think I should tell you why I know you’ll be able to find Roxanne Mae, don’t you?”

CHAPTER THIRTY-FIVE

JENNIFER LANE WAS AN odd little woman, Lila thought as she studied the girl sitting at her kitchen table. Jennifer was so much like Roxanne Mae in some ways, and so different in others. Lila turned her head to the side, trying to observe Jennifer's aura. The psychic said that auras were visible, but, so far, Lila couldn't see them.

Jennifer and Roxanne Mae were about the same size, but Roxanne Mae was a little older, Lila guessed. A year, perhaps. Or maybe Jennifer just looked younger because she dressed so immaturely.

One thing about Roxanne Mae, she'd always looked and acted much older than her age. Or at least, what Lila believed was her age. Lila didn't know for sure how old Roxanne Mae was. She'd been a toddler when Lila and Ronald had adopted her. But she had always been small for whatever age she was. Maybe she wasn't two years old when she first came to live with them.

The resemblance between Jennifer and Roxanne Mae was uncanny, Lila had thought the first time she'd met Jennifer, although she hadn't mentioned it at the time, of course. Could they be sisters? Lila had gotten the vibe that night in the conference room at Jennifer's office, when Jennifer first walked through the door. Lila knew it was possible, although she hadn't revealed the idea to anyone. Ronald had been so unaware of everything around him since their daughter left, he wouldn't believe Lila, anyway. And only the three of them knew Roxanne Mae was adopted.

Maybe believing the two girls were alike was just wishful thinking on Lila's part. Lila had always wanted more children. That could be it. Things had turned out so badly with Roxanne Mae. Maybe Jennifer Lane didn't look like her daughter at all. Maybe Lila had just gotten the idea because they were the same size, the same coloring. Jennifer was so much nicer, so much more like the daughter she had imagined.

But no, there was something else, too; Lila could feel it. Not simply that they both had brown eyes and those lusciously long eyelashes. Each had a dimple in her chin, in exactly the same place. A certain turn of the lips when they smiled and a few hand gestures they both made when they talked were almost identical. Even their fingernails looked the same, although Jennifer wore hers short and unpolished while Roxanne Mae's were almost claw-like and brightly painted.

This was the thing that made Lila doubt her own senses. Jennifer might physically resemble Roxanne Mae, but that was where the resemblance ended. Compared to Jennifer, her daughter was the bad twin. Lila believed genes did not control a person's destiny. Still, if they were sisters, wouldn't their personalities be at least a little alike?

Lila nibbled on a cookie while she watched Jennifer for any flicker of recognition as she paged through the photo album containing pictures of Roxanne Mae from the age of two. Birthday parties, dance recitals, beauty contests.

Like her mother, Roxanne Mae had competed in beauty contests from the time she was four until after she'd graduated from Plant High School. She was, naturally, on the homecoming court, just as Lila had been. Roxanne Mae always won the beauty contests, and that had won her a scholarship to college. She'd been smart, too. Jennifer was smart. *Another thing they have in common.*

The main thing Lila had wanted for her daughter was a better life than the one Lila had achieved for herself. Lila realized Roxanne Mae would have accomplished that much if she had married a man completely unlike Ronald.

Lila watched Jennifer study the pictures of Ronald and Roxanne Mae. How he loved that child. Even now, Ronald was beside himself with grief over their daughter's disappearance.

He had already decided that Roxanne Mae was dead. The knowledge was killing him slowly, every day a little death. Her disappearance had driven Ronald mad with grief. Lila hardly recognized him anymore. He certainly didn't look like the happy-go-lucky man in these photos. He didn't even look like the man who had sat in Jennifer's conference room just a few short days ago. Roxanne Mae was killing her father whether she meant to or not.

Jennifer kept flipping through the pages, reciting what she was looking at into the little tape recorder. "Junior Miss competition winner…junior high school graduation…Homecoming Queen…prom," and so on. Lila watched in silence, expecting Jennifer to get it, to look up and ask.

When Jennifer came to the more recent pictures, she slowed down in her flipping and reciting. "College graduation… twenty-first birthday…Ronald's fiftieth birthday…"

Lila remembered these events well. Happy times in the days

before Lila had become totally bewildered by her daughter's out-of-control behavior. Lila felt a little stab of remorse now at how glad she'd been when Roxanne Mae went away to college. In truth, Roxanne Mae's wild streak had started long before college graduation.

While she was away at college, Lila and Ronald had remained blissfully unaware of their daughter's antics. She had always been the brightest student in her class and she never had to study to get good grades. All the time that the other students spent working hard was free time Roxanne Mae could use to get into trouble. In high school, she'd been almost uncontrollable, even for Ronald.

In retrospect, Lila had to admit that Roxanne Mae must have been wild in college, too. Why else would she have run off with that James boy they'd never even met and then divorce him six months later? Lila suspected Annabelle had an abortion then, but Annabelle had never told her what happened to the marriage.

Jennifer said, "Was Roxanne happy in college?"

"'Roxanne Mae was simply too gifted for her own good,' is what Ronald used to say. I suppose that's true," she said, tentatively.

"You don't sound like you agree."

Lila stalled a little, pointing out Roxanne Mae's graduation pictures. "The most gifted ones often get into the most trouble. But she graduated *magna cum laude*, near the top of her class." It was impossible to keep the pride out of her voice.

"When did she go to work for Denton Bio-Medical?" Jennifer asked her.

"Right away. Then Denton sent her to graduate school and she got her Ph.D. in biology and chemistry before she turned twenty-nine." At the time, Lila had dared to believe her beloved daughter had come to her senses. Lila hoped that anyone holding down a full-time job and going to graduate school at the same time couldn't be getting into too much trouble.

Jennifer looked at a few more pictures, then stopped her recitation momentarily, leaving the dictating machine running. "Lila"—Lila had insisted that Jennifer call her Lila like Roxanne Mae always did—"when did Annabelle get this tattoo?"

Lila looked over at the picture Jennifer pointed to with her index finger. The photo had been taken at a picnic on Clearwater Beach. The picture showed Roxanne Mae in a very small bikini that Lila had disapproved of. Her back had turned to the camera while she played beach volleyball.

Lila looked only briefly. She didn't need to examine the picture. She remembered the tattoo low on her daughter's back only too well. It was the first one, and Lila had been furious. Not that her mother's disapproval mattered to Roxanne Mae. *To be honest, her mother's disapproval was probably the point.*

"I'm not sure exactly when she got it," Lila answered honestly. "I do remember why."

"What do you mean?"

"She got that tattoo three years ago when a man she was dating talked her into it. I didn't want her to deface herself that way, but, by then, she rarely listened to me. I wish she had." Lila realized she was decidedly conveying her bitterness. And why not? If Roxanne Mae hadn't gotten that first tattoo, she might not have started on the self-destructive path that eventually gave her hepatitis Z. But Jennifer probably didn't know about Roxanne Mae having the disease. Yet. "She had other tattoos."

"How many did she have?" Jennifer asked.

"I don't really know. I never counted them. After that first one, when she saw how much it upset me, she was gleeful about adding to her collection." Lila was bitter about the tattoos, all right. Her little daughter had been so beautiful. Why ruin the perfect body God gave her with that common trash? "I can remember about six or seven others. If you keep looking you'll see them."

Jennifer continued to flip through the photo album, naming other pictures of Roxanne Mae and her tattoos into her recorder. The tattoo on the small of Roxanne Mae's back was displayed in several of the photographs. It was a ring of Chinese or Japanese characters, about three inches in diameter. One picture of her in a bathing suit, standing near a swimming pool reflected the tattoo clearly.

"When was this taken?" Jennifer asked.

Lila looked at the picture carefully. A grimace marred her usually well-composed features. "That was a few weeks before she disappeared, a family party at her aunt's house in north Tampa."

Lila noticed that Jennifer studied this particular picture for several minutes. "Why don't you take that one? I have quite a few others. Perhaps someone can tell you what the tattoo says, since you're so interested in it."

Lila tried not to sound too disappointed. Was Jennifer really not seeing what was right in front of her face? How could she not realize that she was looking into a mirror with every photograph? The resemblance was so obvious, a blind man could see it. Lila got up to take another batch of cookies out of the oven. These were peanut butter, Roxanne Mae's favorite.

Jennifer thanked her and removed the picture from the album.

Lila came back to the table with a plate of the peanut butter cookies. There was no reason not to eat a few while they were warm. When Roxanne Mae came back, Lila would bake more, if she had the chance.

Lila then pointed out several other pictures in which Roxanne

Mae's tattoos could be seen. She had a red rose on her right shoulder, and a butterfly graced the top of her left breast. A circle of blue scrollwork encircled both wrists, like bracelets. On the outside of each ankle, something that resembled a dragon had been etched.

"Who did Annabelle's tattoo work?" Jennifer asked.

Lila frowned again. "I don't know, really. I disapproved of the tattoos, so she didn't talk to me about them. Ronald might be able to tell you that."

Jennifer closed the album and turned to ask Lila a few more questions. Lila humored her by answering, although she knew Jennifer hadn't focused on what was important. After a few minutes, Lila handed Jennifer a large stationery box.

"I gathered some things together for you in here," Lila told her. "You'll find a copy of the police reports, a few e-mail messages from Roxanne Mae written in the weeks before she disappeared, and the keys to her car and her apartment. You should go over there and look around."

Jennifer accepted the box, but didn't open it. "What about friends? Might Annabelle have kept in touch with any?"

Lila shook her head back and forth. "Not that I know of. You might find out more about that if you check the address book on her computer. She communicated with almost everyone by e-mail. She was always on the computer."

Jennifer opened the box and looked through the materials Lila had gathered. She added the pictures Lila allowed her to take from the album. Then Jennifer set everything aside and turned to Lila with her pen in hand, ready to take her shorthand notes.

"Tell me everything, in your own words. I won't stop you unless something is unclear to me," Jennifer instructed her.

Lila smiled. She'd been preparing for this moment since she'd first met Jennifer. "Where should I begin?"

"Wherever you like," Jennifer said.

Lila began at the point where she was most curious about Jennifer's own past. "Roxanne Mae was a Jacks baby. Do you know about the Jacks Clinic?" Lila asked her.

Lila suspected that Jennifer was a Jacks baby, too, although she had no way to know that for sure. But the psychic had told Lila that Jennifer had a special affinity for her daughter. Lila believed the connection was the Jacks Clinic. Lila searched Jennifer's face for the smallest sign of recognition, but it wasn't there. Jennifer simply looked puzzled at the question.

"Dr. Jacks was an angel to some of us—and, to some others, the devil himself, I suppose. But Ronald and I wanted a baby and if it wasn't for the Jacks Clinic we'd never have been parents. Roxanne Mae was a miracle to us. We never thought we'd have a child." Lila wanted Jennifer to understand how much she had loved her daughter, how wanted Roxanne Mae was. Treasured. At least, in the beginning. Lila was a good mother. It wasn't her fault Roxanne Mae had become a thief.

Jennifer's pen raced over the paper, taking down Lila's words as she recited her story, she supposed. After over an hour, Lila still hadn't gotten to Roxanne Mae's disappearance. The late summer sun was finally setting and night was approaching fast. Jennifer had filled an entire steno pad with notes and changed her Dictaphone tapes four times. Yet Jennifer never once asked the question Lila had hoped to hear.

Finally, Lila could see that Jennifer's hand was cramping and that she was tired. "Ronald will be home soon. We need to stop for now. You can come again, and we'll talk some more." Lila stood up and rubbed her sore shoulders while Jennifer packed her briefcase. Lila was disappointed in Jennifer's lack of curiosity about her connection to Roxanne Mae. She intended to give

Jennifer one more push. "But, before you leave, I'd like to show you Roxanne Mae's room."

"I thought Annabelle lived in an apartment out near USF?" Jennifer asked.

"She did. After she left home to go to college, she never came back. But you can get a sense of what she was like before she left us." Lila felt Roxanne Mae had left them years before, when she went away to college and changed her name. When she insisted on being called Annabelle James. She was a different girl after she became Annabelle. Roxanne Mae never really came home.

Lila wanted to see Jennifer's reaction to her daughter's room. She was still hoping Jennifer would realize who Jennifer herself was. Maybe then, Lila herself could have a second chance at a daughter.

Anyone can see how badly you need mothering, Lila thought. The girl was a mess. Her hair was all over the place, her clothes never looked pressed. Even her panty hose were on upside down, the reinforced heel resting on top of her foot. If Lila took Jennifer in hand, some changes would be made, and all for the better.

Lila walked Jennifer down the narrow hallway to a small bedroom in the back of the house. She turned on the lights in the dark room, bathing everything in a soft glow.

Roxanne Mae's childhood room was furnished in pink and white with eyelet lace and frills. The walls were covered with shelves where trophies for dancing, beauty pageants, and gymnastics sat, polished and gleaming.

Lila displayed her daughter's room with the pride of a mother whose child had excelled in every arena. Before her daughter had turned away from Lila and become a complete mystery to her, they had been so close. Lila had fantasized a lifelong closeness with her child. A daughter who would grow up to be more like

Jennifer. *If Jennifer was a Jacks baby, why weren't we offered her?*

It might not be too late. Maybe Lila could correct this mistake now. Maybe Jennifer didn't see her physical resemblance to Roxanne Mae because their personalities were so opposite. If Jennifer had been Lila's child, Lila's whole life would have been so different. Lila wanted to take Jennifer in her arms and hold her like she'd held Roxanne Mae as a child. Her arms were aching to be a real mother again.

But Jennifer's vibes clearly showed Lila that any move right now would be too soon. Jennifer wasn't ready yet.

When Lila walked Jennifer to the front door and out to her car, she said, "After you look at everything I gave you and go over to Roxanne Mae's apartment, give me a call. I'm sure you'll have more questions for me." Lila tried to keep the hope out of her voice and infuse it with promise instead.

She thought Jennifer seemed puzzled still, as if she didn't quite understand why she was being given this inner glimpse of Lila and her daughter that had not been shared with the police.

Lila congratulated herself on her prescience when Jennifer asked, "Why did you choose me for this, Lila? I have the sense that you've got a reason you haven't told me."

Lila looked at Jennifer carefully in the rapidly fading evening light. This could still work out. Jennifer felt the vibes, too. She had to. Lila patted Jennifer's shoulder, reassuringly. "Do your investigating first. Then, if you haven't figured it out, ask me again," she said, confident that Jennifer would understand soon, and life would be good once more.

CHAPTER THIRTY-SIX

JENNIFER DROVE DIRECTLY HOME. If she took a few extra minutes for a quick shower, she could also change into a slinky outfit and trade the dull borrowed Honda for her purple PT Cruiser. With any luck at all, she'd be less than fifteen minutes late. Surely Blake would wait that long. She'd left him a quick message on his cell phone; that was the best she could do. She dropped off the keys to the Honda at her neighbor's and jogged quickly to her own apartment across the courtyard, lugging the gun case and her briefcase, one in each hand.

As she put her key in the lock, she heard the phone inside her apartment. Jennifer rushed in and picked it up, without checking the caller ID, hoping Blake was returning her call. Instead, Debbie was on the line again.

"Oh, hi, Mom," Jennifer said, distracted, in a hurry to get to her date. She set the gun case down on the kitchen counter.

"I can tell you're busy," Debbie responded, "so I won't keep you."

Jennifer noticed the absence of her mother's usual greeting and guilt started before Jennifer could squelch it, even though she knew it was not her mother's intention to make her feel guilty. Jennifer forced herself to pay attention.

"No, really. I was just finishing up," Jennifer lied as she walked into the bedroom and began to yank off her clothes. "What's going on?"

"We're leaving for the cruise tomorrow morning, early, so I called to say good-bye," Debbie told her.

Of course. Their vacation. Normally, Jennifer would have been focused on missing them for the two weeks they planned to be gone. Usually Jennifer relied on her parents the way a diabetic relies on insulin—a regular dose of talking to them made her feel healthy and secure.

"Will I be able to call you?" Jennifer asked, sitting down hard on the bed, her slacks half off.

Debbie laughed. "Well, judging from the number of times you've called since you started this new case, I doubt you'll even notice we're gone." Jennifer *would* notice, she realized with a jolt. She'd feel their absence like the amputation of a limb.

She could hear Debbie shuffling through some papers. "Here it is. The cruise line gave us a number you can call. And we'll be picking up e-mail. The cell phones probably won't work, but you can try. Alaska is America's last frontier, you know."

The idea of how inaccessible Alaska must be was not reassuring. Jennifer rummaged through the nightstand to find an old charge receipt and a broken pencil. She jotted down the instructions Debbie gave her for contacting them on the ship.

Jennifer had lost all interest in rushing to meet Blake. "Let me talk to Dad a minute." She felt a longing for the reassurance of his voice. She worried about him almost as much as he worried about her. It had been years since he'd taken a drink. Still, the potential was always there.

"I'm sorry, honey. He ran out for more memory cards for the digital camera. He tried to call you earlier, but you weren't home. Want me to have him try again later?"

Jennifer cringed. She remembered that the phone had rung earlier as she was leaving for Lila's and she hadn't picked up. She kicked her slacks the rest of the way to the floor and walked with the cordless over to the answering machine. Three messages—no doubt one or more from her father.

"No, Mom, that's okay. You two will be back before I know it. It's just strange to have you gone. Usually, I'm the one who's traveling." Jennifer never felt bereft when she was the one leaving. Staying home while someone else met the dangers and excitement of the road was much more difficult. She forced back images of her parents in a plane crash and others of a sinking ship.

After talking for a few more minutes, they rang off. Jennifer took a big black marker and circled on her calendar exactly when her parents were leaving, then wrote down the phone number to reach them and when they would return. She missed them already. Thank God for Blake, she thought, as she rushed to get dressed.

On her way out, not wanting to leave it in the apartment unattended, she picked up the gun case. It had become like another appendage.

CHAPTER THIRTY-SEVEN

LILA WAS PLANNING HER fall garden, while Ronald dozed through the eleven o'clock news, waiting for the sports. They weren't talking to each other. They rarely talked at all these days, it seemed to Lila, but she didn't mind. Not talking to Ronald was a kind of blessing.

He'd had so much to drink today, Lila hoped he'd pass out soon. But he was still semi-awake at eleven fifteen, if a man as pickled by alcohol as Ronald was could be called awake. She thought she'd heard him snoring a few minutes before, but she wasn't really paying attention.

Lila was so involved in her garden plan that she didn't hear the anchorman read the report. When Ronald jumped up out of his chair and shouted, "Lila! Look! It's her!" Lila had to blink her eyes and bring her attention back to the room.

Footage of Kennedy Park surrounded by police cars and yellow crime-scene tape was on the screen.

"Who?" she asked, returning to her garden plan.

She was trying to place the red and white geraniums where they would get the best sun, but most of the front yard was shaded by the oak tree. If she moved the geraniums around back, she wouldn't be able to see them from the living room. This was a difficult decision and she'd been working on it for several hours. Each possibility seemed to have its problems and Ronald's interruption, just at this crucial moment, was annoying.

Ronald crossed the distance to Lila's chair in seconds, grabbed her head, placing one hand on each temple, and forced her to look directly at the television. "Listen!" he hissed.

Lila listened to the story in progress.

The remains were discovered in Kennedy Park late today by two young men playing with their dog. Authorities believe recent heavy rains washed away the top layer of a shallow grave near the river where the partially decomposed body had been buried. Tampa police chief Ben Hathaway said the woman had probably been killed about four to five weeks ago. No identification has been made. We'll bring you further details about this grisly discovery as we receive them.

"Ronald, let me go," Lila told him with forced calm. He still held her head in both hands and now he pressed his hands together, hard. "I'm watching. Let me go." Her voice was stern now.

Slowly, Ronald released her. He returned to his chair and picked up the remote control. When the anchor switched to another story, Ronald ran through the channels, seeking more information on the body found in Kennedy Park, Lila supposed. He found the same film on each of the four networks and the all-news channel, but no additional facts. Lila kept her head up, as if she were watching as intently as he was, but she wasn't.

CHAPTER THIRTY-EIGHT

JENNIFER ARRIVED AT THE Green Iguana, a hangout for singles on Seventh Avenue in Tampa's old cigar district, Ybor City, at nine thirty. She usually felt out of place here among the fun-loving twenty- and thirty-somethings looking for partners. Now, though, she had a partner and she wanted to do everything couples did.

Just a few dates and already Jennifer was thinking of Blake Denton in permanent terms. This morning, she had caught herself at her old high school pastime, absently writing her name in cursive letters along the unprinted edges of the newspaper. Jennifer was embarrassed to see that the name she'd written over and over was "Jennifer Deborah Denton." She'd then hidden the defaced paper deep into the trash bag and stuffed the entire bag down the trash chute before she'd left for her appointment with Lila Walden.

Such a fantasy was foolish, maybe even emotionally dangerous. She would never be Jennifer Denton. Blake didn't think of her that way and never would. She was setting herself up for heartbreak if she imagined otherwise. Men like Blake Denton didn't marry women like Jennifer Lane. She was a temporary distraction for him, nothing more. And she'd be much less likely to get hurt if she kept that fact firmly in mind. Have a good time, even love him if she couldn't help it. *But don't get carried away with your Cinderella dreams, Jennifer,* she scolded herself.

From the club's open doorway, Jennifer scanned the dim interior and eventually spotted Blake sitting at the crowded bar. She walked up to him as bold as brass, wrapped her arms around his waist from behind, and squeezed. Then, she kissed his neck before she could stop herself.

Blake stood and turned to face her. He gave her a long, satisfying kiss, which she was only too eager to return. Mindful of the reaction they'd attracted that first night when they were kissing by the Olde Hyde Park Village fountain, Jennifer reluctantly pulled away, though no one here seemed to notice them or to care what they did.

"Hmmm…" Blake sniffed her frizzy hair and continued to hold her, then bent his head so his mouth brushed close to her ear and said, "Hey, beautiful. You smell good enough to eat. Interested?"

Jennifer laughed, as she knew he'd meant her to do. Blake's admiration made her feel warm and desirable from her toes to the roots of her hair. "Maybe," she smiled up at him. "But you can ply me with liquor first. I've had a very long day."

After they were seated at a small table near the bar, Blake kept his arm draped around her shoulders. He stayed as close to Jennifer as he could get. He urged her to sit in his lap, but she was too embarrassed to do that. They talked for a while about nothing much and shared a plate of nachos with their margaritas, Jennifer's frozen and Blake's on the rocks, with salt, and ordered by the pitcher.

Jennifer worried about everything. Could Blake be interested in her at all? Was he just using her until the lawsuit was over? Was she one of many women he dated on a regular basis? Jennifer recognized her usual litany of *Jennifer isn't good enough* thoughts that she applied to all situations in which, even objectively, good fortune seemed to smile upon her. She'd always done that to herself. She didn't know why, but knew she had to get over doing it. She shook herself and told her psyche to stop, and it worked—for a couple of seconds.

After a few drinks and a few more kisses, Jennifer began to relax and forget her cares, to go with the flow, as Melanie often advised. Melanie, who used to be her friend.

"What did you do today?" Blake asked.

"Several things that might interest you, actually," she answered, thinking to eliminate all traces of the gun she had locked in her car, her creepy encounter with Lila Walden, and her anxiety over her parents by making light conversation with Blake.

He nuzzled her ear. "Anything you do interests me," he told her. "Actually." He reproduced her tone and inflection nuance for nuance. Blake was a talented mimic.

"You should do impressions over at the Improv. Take your act on the road," Jennifer told him, grinning.

"Ah, my *cherie,* I perform only privately, for your amusement alone," he responded in a mock French accent that had her laughing.

Jennifer took a deep breath, the trembling in her stomach making it almost impossible to concentrate. She blamed that on the margaritas, but lust was probably the real cause. "Well, I worked, of course," she told Blake now.

"Hmmmm," Blake said into her ear. "How's that coming?" He seemed politely interested, but not overly so. Every time Jennifer became convinced Blake was simply trying to persuade her to work hard, using his bedroom skills, he surprised her by seeming to be completely uninterested in the Denton Bio-Medical case.

"Okay," she said. But what she'd wanted to say was "Not too well." Rabid Roger had drafted a pretty good complaint, based on Florida's trade-secrets statute. Unfortunately, he had the better end of the facts. There had been a couple of big verdicts in Hillsborough County for individuals who'd had their secrets stolen by big companies in the past few years. Jennifer was truly worried about how they stood. Stuart didn't want to be in state court against Roger Riley, based on these precedents, for one thing, and Jennifer didn't think they would be able to win a motion to transfer the case to federal court.

The truth was that Stuart never wanted to be in state court at all under any circumstances. But in a case against Roger Riley, state court would be a disaster.

The situation could be likened to the Tampa Bay Buccaneers trying to win a football game in Green Bay, Wisconsin. For years, the cold defeated the Bucs time and time again. Stuart didn't like the climate in state court because he seldom won there. Jennifer didn't tell Blake that, although staying mum wasn't easy. She couldn't tell Blake about her concerns because Russell had specifically instructed her not to discuss the case with Blake. The tequila had relaxed her body and loosened her control. Anything Blake asked her now, she'd willingly answer.

Blake didn't seem to care at all. "Anything else interesting?" Jennifer almost told him about her visit to Lila Walden, but somehow she stopped herself in time. She believed Blake was reporting everything she said to his uncle and to Stuart, but she hoped her suspicion was more paranoia.

Yet, by helping Lila, Jennifer was walking a very fine line.

The less anyone knew about her extracurricular activity, the better.

"Your lawsuit keeps me up to my ears in alligators most of the time," she said, repeating one of her favorite local sayings.

"These lovely ears, you mean?" Blake said. Jennifer bent her head to her shoulder to avoid Blake's wicked tongue and teeth, which were attempting to nibble and caress her ears. But he trapped her arms at her sides as he quietly moved from one ear to the other, making it impossible for her to thwart him—even if she'd really wanted to.

"I have an idea," he said, close to her ear, still nibbling softly. "Why don't I meet you back at your place?"

Jennifer wanted to have the willpower to say no. But she didn't. She had already acknowledged her love for Blake, even if the relationship was a hopeless one. She had decided to live in the sunshine of his affection for as long as possible. Not only would she not kick Blake out of bed for eating crackers, she'd be willing to serve him an entire nine-course meal lasting for days there.

She fantasized for a while about doing just that, when the band started to play and the pulsing music became too loud for conversation. Blake pulled her out to the dance floor for a slow dance, caressing her everywhere and kissing her neck as he held her close.

Jennifer floated on alcohol, denial, and joy. She worried her relationship with Blake was too good to be true, but she didn't know what to do about it. The only friend she had with whom she could discuss such things was Melanie Stein. But Melanie wasn't talking to Jennifer these days. Melanie was still furious with her.

Jennifer had left Melanie several messages, but Melanie refused to return her calls. Jennifer could only hope her friend would get over her anger, eventually. Until then, without the benefit of female advice, Jennifer would throw aside all caution with her new lover, Blake. Why not? Being reckless was not Jennifer's typical method of operating, but her usual strategy hadn't been all that successful for her in the past.

A man bumped into Blake's back on the dance floor, making them both fall into Jennifer, nearly knocking her down. Blake began to curse in a tone of voice Jennifer had never heard him use before. "You asshole! Get off of me!" he shouted to the drunk, who seemed to have the loose-limbed manner of the scarecrow in Wizard of Oz.

A pulse visibly pounded in Blake's temple and anger tinted his face a bright red. "Sorry, pal," the drunk said with a silly, vacant half-smile.

The man's girlfriend tried to pull him up and away. "Come on, Larry. Let's go."

Blake took a swing at the guy, but his girlfriend had moved him out of Blake's reach and the punch didn't really connect. Blake followed the two of them, threatening to beat the man. Jennifer couldn't see everything from her position, but once she managed to push through the crowd, she approached Blake.

"It's okay, Blake. I'm fine. He didn't hurt me. He's just drunk," she said.

"It's not okay. The guy's a menace. He deserves to pay for it." Blake's tone made Jennifer even more nervous. The last thing she wanted tonight was a bar fight. That was not the end to the evening she'd hoped for.

"You're right. But let's just get out of here," she suggested, putting her hand on his arm. Something about her touch seemed to bring Blake's attention back to her. He glared at the onlookers, challenging them to go about their business. Then he glanced down at Jennifer and the tenderness she had come to expect from him returned.

"I'm sorry. Are you really all right?" He ran his hands over her body, maybe checking for broken bones, but the sensations he left in the wake of his contact were anything but comforting. Jennifer felt like a live electric wire everywhere he touched.

"Let's just go, okay?" she said in as steady a voice as she could muster. She gave him a kiss and headed toward the door.

Blake paid the bill and they walked out to their separate cars. Jennifer was far from sober and she suspected that Blake was in worse shape than she. She was usually unwilling to drink and drive, but the night and the newness of their affair inspired her to recklessness.

Jennifer snugged up her seatbelt, opened the car window so the air would rush across her face, and drove as carefully as she could manage, ten miles under the speed limit. If she got pulled over she probably wouldn't have to explain the gun in her trunk. It's legal to have a gun in the trunk of your car in Hillsborough County, even without a concealed weapons permit. Of course, the Cruiser didn't technically have a trunk at all, but the hatchback would probably satisfy the letter of the law. Still, she'd probably spend the rest of the night in the Orient Road Jail—not in bed with Blake.

CHAPTER THIRTY-NINE

"COME ON, YOU BITCH!" Ronald shouted at the television when the anchorwoman on the all-news channel began to report the weather. "Tell me about my baby!"

Ronald was wide awake now and fixated on the story. It consumed him. He became increasingly agitated when no further details about the body were reported by any of the news channels. Lila kept her face forward, as if she were watching the news, but she didn't say anything.

After a while, Ronald noticed her silence. "Ain't you worried?" he asked her. She didn't acknowledge him. "I said," his voice was louder now, "ain't you worried? About our baby? Didn't you see her body?"

What should she say? The truth was she wasn't worried, which she knew would only infuriate him further. But if she said nothing at all, that would make him mad, too. "I've told you, Ronald. Roxanne Mae is not dead."

"That's a lie!" Ronald turned on her, remote control in one hand, an open can of beer in the other, eyes bulging in his angry face. "If my baby was alive, she'd a called. She ain't called because she's dead. That woman they found has got to be her."

Something snapped in Lila at that moment. She wouldn't sit here and be forced to endure this anymore. She'd had enough. She stood up. "You're wrong, Ronald. You're wrong about her. It's just like Roxanne Mae to upset you, just for fun or whatever her own reasons are. She doesn't care about how you feel. That much is pretty obvious, isn't it?"

Lila didn't tell him that the psychic had confirmed Lila's suspicions. Roxanne Mae was just trying to torment him. The girl was mad at him for some reason—who knew why. Those two had the same temperament; no one would believe they weren't really blood-related. Roxanne Mae could be just as vicious as Ronald sometimes was.

"What kind of mother are you, anyway?" he shouted at her, throwing the remote and hitting her in the face with it. Now, his left hand was free. In two steps, he was across the room, and that was when he hit her.

Ronald hadn't been violent with her for a long time. She'd promised herself she'd kill him the next time he laid a hand on her, and a deep, boiling anger began to bubble up in her now.

Ronald stormed out of the house while Lila still lay on the floor. "Somebody is going to tell me that's my baby dead in that lousy grave!" he shouted on his way out the door.

Lila wondered whether the truth would drive Ronald the rest of the short distance he'd need to travel to insanity. Maybe she wouldn't have to kill him at all. Maybe Annabelle would do it for her.

CHAPTER FORTY

JENNIFER'S DRIVE BACK TO her apartment wasn't far and not many cars were on the road. Still, she breathed a sigh of relief after she made it home safely.

The security gate rose when she pushed the opener inside her car, and she pulled into tenant parking in the underground garage. She saw Blake take a spot in guest parking, where he locked up his midnight blue Jaguar, then walked toward her. The car was a flashy one, what she could see of it parked several rows away in the dark garage.

Money had its advantages. But she wasn't interested in money right now. Jennifer pushed the magnetic gate release to admit him when he approached on foot. After the gate again closed out the world, Blake took her hand and pulled her into the shadows.

She leaned into his mouth, as if she'd never felt so at home anywhere in her life. Which was the truth. If Jennifer had ever been in love before, those feelings were a pale second to what she now felt for Blake. If she died tomorrow, Jennifer thought, she'd die a happy woman.

Blake moved slightly away from her in order to slide his hand up under her crop top. He cupped her left breast, covered by her lacy bra, then rubbed the flat of his thumb over her nipple until it stood up taut. With his other hand, Blake reached behind her to unclasp her bra, and Jennifer pulled slightly away from him. "Let's go upstairs," she whispered against his mouth.

She could feel his smile. Blake said, "I thought you'd never ask."

Jennifer tried not to be embarrassed as he followed her to her apartment. Blake had already learned more about her body than most men ever cared to know. Under normal circumstances, Jennifer wouldn't have the courage to invite a man to her bed. She would have waited until he swept her off her feet. But this was Blake, the man she loved and would love forever. It didn't matter whether he loved her or not, she told herself. If she only had what Blake was offering her now, that would be enough.

Once in the foyer upstairs, Blake began to undress Jennifer before she could turn on the lights. He kicked the door closed with one foot while he pulled her shirt up over her head. Next, he unclasped her bra, letting it fall to the tile floor. Jennifer not only acquiesced, she lifted her arms to help him, stretched her back like a cat, and arched herself toward Blake's magic fingers.

When he picked her up and carried her to the bedroom, Jennifer remembered thinking that she hadn't made the bed today. But then she realized it didn't matter.

CHAPTER FORTY-ONE

RONALD WAS OUTRAGED WHEN he returned from the excavation site after being gone for an hour. “They won’t let me bring my baby home,” he cried. His visit to the police had done no good. The young woman’s body hadn’t been autopsied or identified. “We’re sorry, Mr. Walden,” Ronald mocked them, mimicking what they’d told him. Then his chin quivered with rage and tears streamed down his face. “I don’t want their damn excuses! They better give me my baby to bury!”

Lila didn’t know what to do or how to deal with him. When he headed for the refrigerator again, she went to bed just to get away.

Within minutes, she could hear Ronald on the phone to the police again from his bedroom, and he stayed up most of the night arguing with the person at the other end of the line.

Ronald and Lila had slept in separate bedrooms for years, but even from across the hallway, Lila could hear him. She thought they could hear him all the way to the state capitol in Tallahassee. He shouted, cursed, and opened beer after beer.

When she heard the pop-top on another can around four o’clock in the morning, Lila got up and threw the deadbolt she’d installed on her bedroom door. She pushed the heavy dresser in front of the flimsy hollow wood as well, for good measure. Locked doors didn't keep Ronald out when he wanted to come in. Lila knew that from experience.

How did our lives degenerate to this? she asked herself, lying in the dark, listening to Ronald rage. Her face hurt, her shoulder was sore, and she was exhausted. Tears leaked out of her eyes and ran down the sides of her face into her hair and onto the pillow.

She tried to think where they'd gone wrong.

He didn't drink when Lila had first met him, although in hindsight it was pretty obvious that Ronald was headed in that direction. He'd never been good enough for her; her parents had been right about that. But in high school, Ronald had carried the allure of the forbidden, an outlaw's dangerousness that attracted Lila, the good girl, the homecoming queen. She'd thought then that his blonde good looks would make cute babies.

During the early hours of the morning, she could hear him slamming around, knocking over the furniture. Lila cried harder when she heard him shatter what must have been her grandmother's vase, which Lila kept on a special table in the living room. She loved the vase and it was all she had left of her grandmother to remember her by. Ronald knew it, too, but when he was mad at Lila, he'd often break the things she cared for the most.

They'd married during her senior year. He'd already quit school and been hired on at the MECO water power plant then. They both thought they'd have all the money they'd ever need. Ten thousand dollars a year had seemed like a fortune in those days. What a joke. They'd been lucky to get this house, and they'd never put together enough money to move.

Lila quit school, too, once her future had been finalized. After all, why would a housewife need a high school diploma when her husband didn't even have one? Lila planned to be a wife and a mother forevermore. She had as much education as she would ever need for her ideal career.

Now Lila could see clearly when her life took a turn for the worse. She hadn't realized it at the time, but it was when Roxanne Mae came into their home.

After three years of marriage, Lila had still been unable to conceive, so they adopted this pretty little baby. Ronald was already drinking every day by that time and Lila should have gotten out. He loved that baby, though, with all the emotion he was capable of. And everyone knew a child needed a father. Especially a child as difficult as Roxanne Mae turned out to be.

So Lila had stayed with Ronald. She'd lived with his decay into alcoholism. She'd survived his verbal and emotional abuse and his daily temper tantrums. She'd even managed to stay out of the way of his flying fists—most of the time. Only in the past year had Lila seriously considered a radical change. Leaving her life. Starting over.

Lila knew exactly when she'd made her biggest mistake—the day she'd told Roxanne Mae she was planning to leave Ronald.

Oh, Lila knew that Roxanne Mae's disappearance was her way of beating Lila to the punch. Roxanne Mae had been competing with Lila her whole life. When she learned that Lila planned to leave Ronald, she just left first. Lila knew that was all Roxanne Mae's disappearance meant. Another chance to be better than her mother. She'd probably gone on some lavish trip or something.

Briefly, Lila considered that Roxanne Mae might have decided to try to find her birth parents. But Roxanne Mae had known she was adopted for years and she'd never shown the slightest interest in looking for those people, even if Lila had known who they were. Lila couldn't imagine that Roxanne Mae would have developed an interest in her birth family out of the blue.

Wherever Roxanne Mae was, she would be having a good laugh over Ronald's paranoia. She wouldn't care about some poor girl found dead in the park. Roxanne Mae would be happy about the extra pain the discovery of the girl's body would cause Ronald. She'd think Lila could never top that.

Ronald had idealized Roxanne Mae. He thought the girl was more loving and kind and considerate than she actually was. Lila had been grateful at first that Ronald had treated Roxanne Mae as their own child and always believed the best of her. But, later, when the facts proved that Roxanne Mae was really no angel, Ronald couldn't see the truth. To him, she was still his little girl. No matter what she did.

Lila soon realized that Roxanne Mae wasn't thinking about Ronald at all. Wherever she was, their daughter was engrossed in her own little world, whatever that might be. But she wasn't dead. Her body hadn't been buried in Kennedy Park, or anywhere else. Roxanne Mae was alive and well and playing out some game only she understood. Lila was sure of it.

And she resented Roxanne Mae for making her life a living hell.

Although she tried, Lila slept little. Her tormented thoughts kept her awake, but once she did manage to sleep, she was awakened by Ronald's rage erupting again. She could hear him in the garage throughout the night, ranting and raving with anger and frustration. Some of the words he said Lila had never heard before she'd became a full-grown woman; Ronald Walden was as common as they came. She was grateful when the sun came up and she heard him stumble out. Then she could get out of bed.

CHAPTER FORTY-TWO

THE SUN PEEKED IN through the half-open mini-blinds, casting a small straight line across Jennifer's eyes, awakening her gently. She saw that Blake still slept beside her.

Jennifer watched his chest rise and fall in rhythmic motion for a while, almost hypnotizing herself back to sleep. But then her eyes opened with a start when she thought about what she must look like. Jennifer slept soundly and in the morning her hair always looked as if she'd styled it with an egg beater. Tasting the stale nachos and margaritas in her mouth made her wrinkle her nose. She'd stink Blake out of the place if she actually breathed on him when he woke up. So she got out of bed and walked softly into the bathroom to brush her teeth.

When she looked in the mirror, her appearance was even worse than she'd thought. She noticed a small puncture wound on her shoulder where Blake, a little too excited, had bitten her skin last night. She took out some alcohol and wiped off the blood he'd drawn. It was just a small scratch. But she remembered what he'd said as he kissed the spot.

"Here, let me touch it with this cut on my finger I got fighting with that jerk. We'll be blood lovers." She'd never heard of such a thing before, and thought it was slightly weird at first. But then she liked the idea. Blood lovers. Sounded like vampires in love or something. She smiled to herself.

After taking a shower and blow-drying her hair, applying a little makeup and putting on a slinky bathrobe, Jennifer returned to find Blake still sleeping. She looked at him from the doorway, allowing her love to show in her eyes. He couldn't see her, she reasoned. Feasting on his good looks while he slept was certainly harmless.

Jennifer noticed Blake had rolled over and the sheet had fallen lower on his body, only about halfway up his thighs. She allowed her eyes to roam slowly over Blake's entire form, from the top of his beloved curly blonde head, past golden eyelashes resting on his freckled cheeks. Her gaze caressed his full lips, a little puffy now from all the activity last night.

Jennifer flushed at the memory of what they'd done together. She allowed her gaze to drift farther down, past the golden red stubble on his jaw and chin to broad, muscled shoulders defined by his regular weight-lifting workouts.

Now, Jennifer was frankly appraising every small nuance of Blake's body. She hoped he'd move again and the sheet would fall away completely. Such bold thoughts would make her blush if Blake were awake, but he wasn't.

Her gaze reached the little dimple above the cheeks of his very well-toned backside, the one she'd held in both of her hands at some very pleasant moments last night. Then her relaxed mind needed a few seconds to take in what she was looking at. When it registered, Jennifer gasped at what she finally noticed.

Without opening his eyes, Blake said in a lazy voice, "See anything you like?"

"No!" Jennifer blurted out, before she could stifle the truth.

Just below his waist and above his backside was a tattoo, a circle of Chinese characters, about three inches in diameter. A tattoo identical to the one she'd seen in pictures the day before in the same spot on Annabelle James.

CHAPTER FORTY-THREE

THIS MORNING, LILA HAD several bruises to remember the evening by. She ignored the newspaper that Ronald had left sitting on the kitchen table. It was open to the story about the body found in Kennedy Park. She moved to the refrigerator for a cold bag of frozen peas to put on her swollen eye.

She could feel the soreness in her shoulder where he'd hit her with a half-full can of beer. Lila winced as she moved the peas to a cut on her cheek and read the first paragraph of the short article in the *Tribune* with her second cup of coffee.

The newspaper said a positive identification of the body would take several days or maybe weeks. People were always reported missing in Tampa, just as in any other big city. Tourists who never made it home, drug dealers and homeless people no one would miss. Runaways. Prostitutes.

Yes, the dead woman could literally be anyone. The one thing Lila was sure of was it wasn't her daughter.

Her toast popped up from the ancient toaster she and Ronald had received as a wedding gift. Funny that it still worked all these years later, when the marriage was long dead, she thought each morning. If Ronald had been half as reliable, their lives would have been so much different now.

Lila placed the softening bag of peas on the table, lifted the toast from the toaster and put it on a china plate. She lightly buttered the bread and added, as a special treat, a dollop of peanut butter.

CHAPTER FORTY-FOUR

"ANNABELLE IS DEAD," BLAKE told his uncle with barely controlled anger. He threw the folded newspaper down on the desk in front of Russell. Then he paced back and forth in the office like a caged animal. "She's not coming back. We need to move on to the next step. If HepZMax gets tied up in Annabelle's estate, it will be years before you get it back. You have to file a lawsuit. Now. What's the holdup?"

Russell felt as if he'd aged ten years in the past week. His eyes were bloodshot; the bags underneath them lay in dark folds visible even through his glasses. Deep lines had settled in furrows on his forehead and crevices had burrowed themselves between his nose and mouth. He couldn't seem to change his expression from a perpetual scowl. He had hardly recognized the man in the mirror when he'd shaved this morning.

"You're being a little premature, aren't you? No one has identified this woman's body as Annabelle James yet." Russell was reluctant to argue with Blake. They argued constantly now. They hadn't had a pleasant conversation in days.

Blake dismissed the suggestion with a swift slice of his hand.

"Come on, Uncle Russell. She's been gone for weeks, a body is found, about the right age. It has to be her. Who else could it be? We need to act before someone else acts first." Blake's tone rose with every sentence. His impatience and hostility were hard for Russell to take.

Patricia had warned Russell about Blake's escalating anger. "He needs an evaluation and medication," she'd said. But Blake was an adult. Russell couldn't convince him to see a doctor voluntarily. Nor could he force Blake to go. Unless Blake became a danger to himself or others, Russell's hands were tied.

"When are you going to wake up and smell the coffee?" Blake fairly shouted the question.

Russell studied his nephew with the practiced eye of a shrewd businessman. He put aside the fatherly affection with which he'd always tempered his judgment of Blake. Cold analysis had revealed that Blake was flawed, just as Blake's father had been. Russell didn't know why he'd never before admitted this to himself. Denial was no longer possible.

Russell wiped his face with his hands as he stood up from his desk and walked toward the door. "I have an appointment, Blake. We'll talk about this when I come home. In the meantime, see what information you can get from the police. Start by calling Stuart Barnett. He's got connections. Ask him to find out what they really know about this body."

Blake began to say something more, but Russell ignored him. He had to get away. He needed to think. He needed to talk to Tyler.

"And Blake," he turned to look directly into Blake's wild eyes, "don't do anything else until I specifically authorize it. This is still my company. Don't you forget that." Russell turned away from the hatred in Blake's face, hatred that had been directed his way years before by Blake's father.

CHAPTER FORTY-FIVE

HE MET TYLER IN the Denton Bio-Medical facility in the security Cellar, which only Russell and Tyler knew existed. Russell stood before the retina scanner and waited for the loud click that signaled the heavy reinforced door had unlocked.

After the retina scan, Tyler had to open the door using his own palm scan, retina scan, and password. Only two people ever came here, and only Tyler was ever here alone.

Tyler released the door and a video camera photographed Russell's entry into the Cellar. The room was airtight, watertight, and impermeable to fire, hurricanes, explosions, or espionage. Russell had long ago accepted the necessity of this level of security for his business, and for himself.

Security cameras were trained on every aspect of the Denton Bio-Medical facility and on Russell's home. A man as rich and powerful as Russell Denton was always a target for some scheming thief. Or some organization, such as the IRS, the FBI—or his competitors. Not to mention every nutcase who thought his child's cure was being kept from the public because Russell had a hidden agenda, a desire for people to remain sick so that he could make more money selling existing drugs.

Where this level of crazy thinking came from was a mystery to Russell. All he'd ever tried to do was to live the American dream. He'd succeeded and now the entire world, including his own nephew, seemed to hold it against him.

The Cellar, as he and Tyler called the security room, held all of the company's deepest secrets. Some were secrets Russell Denton would have preferred not to know.

"Where did he go?" Russell asked Tyler.

"To the phone, the minute you left. He called Barnett. Probably because he knew you'd check," Tyler responded.

"What did Barnett say?"

"He wasn't in his office."

"Now what?" Russell's fatigue was born of the spirit and exacerbated by illness. This business with Blake and Annabelle James had deflated him in a way a mere business setback would not have. His already weakened health had set him up for disaster. He'd be lucky to live through this cat and mouse episode and the trial that followed.

"I put a tracking device on his car and listening devices all over his rooms, office, and both vehicles. I've already got hours of tape, but I haven't had time to listen to all of it." Tyler looked uncomfortable as he stalled over some piece of information.

"What are you trying to tell me, Tim?" Russell was beyond hurt, beyond pain. He wanted to know everything.

Tyler backed off. "Okay. Let's look at what I called you about." Tyler cued up the tape and played it.

Blake didn't know cameras were hidden in his office. Why hadn't he suspected? Maybe Blake trusted Russell and thought Russell trusted him. The relationship between the two men was complicated and Russell didn't understand it, himself. Maybe Blake wasn't so paranoid. Maybe he suspected Russell for good reason.

Although he was the one who had been betrayed, Russell was saddened again by what Tyler had found. He watched the tape filmed the day that Annabelle James had disappeared. Russell motioned Tyler to rewind and replay the video again and they watched it three more times.

"There's no chance this is a mistake, is there?" Tyler asked him.

Not because he believes he made a mistake, Russell thought. He bristled at Tyler's sympathy but let it go.

"Look at this one," Tyler said, cueing up another slice of tape. The time and date were recorded in the lower right-hand corner, showing this piece had been made early in the morning of the following day.

Russell watched Blake and Annabelle carefully examine her apartment. They discussed mimicking the recent disappearance of a Washington intern, which had been covered broadly by the national news media. Annabelle walked out of her apartment wearing jogging clothes and carrying nothing. Blake left right behind her.

"This only proves Blake saw her the day she disappeared. It doesn't prove he killed her." Russell heard the sound of hope in his voice.

He didn't know how he could let that hope go. Blake couldn't be a killer. The thought was one that he just couldn't accept. The ten-year-old Blake he'd held in his arms at his brother Donald's funeral had been so easy to love. Blake even looked like Russell's brother. Taking care of Blake all these years had been Russell's way of making everything up to Donald himself. Now Russell had to face his own guilt again. Where had he failed? How could Blake be a killer?

"It doesn't prove he killed her. It doesn't even prove she's dead," Tyler agreed reluctantly.

Russell sighed. "I hear a 'but' in there."

Tyler shrugged. "Either she's dead and he killed her—"

"Or," Russell prompted.

"Or she's not dead and he knows where she is." Tyler's voice sounded kind, gentle. "There's no other choice, is there?"

Russell was completely defeated now. He felt tears welling in his eyes. Unwilling to let Tyler see him break down, he turned and left.

CHAPTER FORTY-SIX

AS QUICKLY AS POSSIBLE, Jennifer headed over to the Worthington offices and pulled out the Tampa and St. Pete telephone books and looked in the yellow pages for *Tattooing.* She was surprised at the number of listings in both. She'd thought only a handful would be in there, but she found more than twenty-five in the St. Petersburg book and a full page in the Tampa directory. A small grin lightened her face when she saw that *Tattooing* was followed by another list labeled *Tattoos—removed.*

Some of the names were clever, such as "Balls of Steel," *Tat-em Up* and *Once Upon a Tattoo.* Others were straightforward, like *Lou's Tattoo's.* Several of the listings boasted "award-winning artists," and "hospital-type sterilization."

Knowing something about Annabelle's personality, Jennifer guessed she'd go for a little glamour—assuming Annabelle was the one who'd selected the artist. Jennifer had wanted to ask Ronald for the name of Annabelle's tattoo artist, since Lila had told her that Ronald might know. But she hadn't been able to reach Ronald or to find any information about the tattoos in Annabelle's computer address book. Jennifer thought the artwork on Annabelle's tattoos seemed especially beautiful, so she focused on the listings that bragged about their "artists." She found ten in the Tampa phone book and two in St. Pete.

Jennifer lugged the heavy phone books over to the photocopy machine and made copies of the relevant pages. When she returned to her desk, she circled the likely choices in red ink, stuffed the pages into her pocket, and headed out.

Starting with the listing closest to Annabelle's apartment, Jennifer made her way toward the University of South Florida campus. Tattoos were becoming more popular and more mainstream, but a few years ago they were a young person's rebellion. Jennifer figured the artists in the vicinity of the campus were Annabelle's likely choices, given that she'd been wearing tattoos for several years.

The first place Jennifer visited was on North Florida, north of Fowler, relatively close to both Annabelle's home and the Denton Bio-Medical facility. The store was one of those with a serious name: *Body Art and Design.* As with many of Florida's business establishments, from medical clinics to restaurants to video stores, this one was located in the ubiquitous strip mall. Jennifer parked in the small lot and made her way to the entrance. This shop, despite its name, didn't seem to be what Jennifer was looking for. The tattoo artists could have been among the cast of a Hell's Angels movie. The artwork posted around the small room consisted of skulls and flames, and the waiting customers looked like Goths. Not Annabelle's style at all.

Still, Jennifer made her way over to one of the artists and introduced herself. She showed him the picture of Annabelle that Lila had given her. The man said he'd never seen Annabelle before.

"Are you sure?"

"I'm sure. She ain't my type. Too bony." He turned back to the heavy red flame he was working on, running the design up the customer's arm from his wrist to his neck.

Jennifer tried two more shops near the campus, but didn't find anyone who knew Annabelle or would claim the work. Sitting in her PT Cruiser with the air conditioning blasting and the radio blaring louder to cover the noise of the fan, Jennifer looked again at her list. Maybe she was going about this the wrong way. Maybe she should look for someone reputable, but with a specialty in Asian tattoos. In the photographs of Annabelle, most of her tattoos had Asian design elements.

Tampa's Asian population was not large. Neither Tampa nor St. Pete had an area resembling San Francisco's Chinatown, or any neighborhood where primarily Asians lived. Yet, not many tattoo artists would know the meaning of the Chinese characters Annabelle had placed on her back.

None of the listings in either phone book had any obvious Asian connection. It was getting late and Jennifer was hot. She wanted a cool swim and an even colder beer. Though she was tempted to stop for the day, she decided to give it one more chance. She pulled out her cell phone and dialed the first number on the list.

On the twelfth try, thirty minutes later, she thought she'd found it. Over in St. Pete Beach, more than an hour's drive from both Annabelle's apartment and the Denton Bio-Medical plant, Jennifer had located an artist who said he often did Chinese character tattoos for clients who thought the designs were exotic. Jennifer pulled out onto Fowler again and headed south on I-275.

Traffic was still fairly light going through downtown Tampa and over the Howard Franklin Bridge. Jennifer made it to the Beeline Expressway exit—one of the last before the Sunshine

Skyway Bridge—in just under forty-five minutes. She was still at least fifteen minutes from St. Pete Beach, assuming the drawbridge was down and she wouldn't have to wait for it. She checked her watch. The artist said the store closed at six o'clock. It was five thirty now.

Jennifer pulled up in front of *Bobby's Artistry* just five minutes before closing. From the curb, she could see the Closed sign was already turned over in the front window. Jennifer hopped out of the car and sprinted up to the door. It was locked, but she'd told the man she was coming, so she pounded on the glass. He had to be inside.

After a few minutes, a small Asian man, Jennifer thought maybe Chinese, came to the door. He pointed to the Closed sign and shook his head, miming the word. Jennifer shouted through the glass. "I called. I've driven an hour. I just want to ask you something!" The man kept shaking his head and pointing at the sign.

Desperate now, Jennifer held up Annabelle's photograph, the one of her in the bikini with the tattoo clearly shown, to the glass. "Is this your work?" she shouted. At first, she thought the man was going to turn around and leave her there, but something about her must have conveyed her desperation. He nodded.

"What does it say?" she shouted again. He reached up and turned the lock on the door, opening just a small wedge so that he wouldn't have to shout back, but enough for her to see inside.

Jennifer was appalled at sight of the filthy shop. The other tattoo shops she'd been to had been clean, their instruments displayed in sterile wrappings. Hepatitis Z and other blood-borne diseases were well-known in the business. Many of the advertisers she'd seen had placed statements in their ads about the cleanliness of their practices. This place looked like a walking incubator for bacteria and viruses. Surely, Annabelle didn't get her tattoo here?

"It say, 'Forever, my love,'" the man told her in answer to her question.

"Do you remember this woman?" Jennifer asked him.

He shook his head. "That one very popular. I do it all the time." He opened the door a little wider and waved his hand to his display of Chinese characters behind the tattoo table. Jennifer looked up and noticed the art posted on the walls. She couldn't pick Annabelle's tattoo from the bunch, but she'd take his word for it. All the characters looked similar to her.

While she was looking, he said, "Come back tomorrow. I'll do for you."

He closed the door and relocked it, heading toward the rear of the shop.

"Not on your life, buddy," she said under her breath.

CHAPTER FORTY-SEVEN

LILA BATHED AND DRESSED in another of her crisp cotton shirtwaist dresses she'd made for wearing around the house. This one had small bunches of yellow daisies sprinkled over the sky blue fabric and was one of Lila's favorites. She brushed her hair into its French twist and applied her makeup. She then made her bed and opened the drapes to let the sunlight stream pleasantly into the room. The vase of roses she'd cut yesterday needed water, so she took them into the kitchen to freshen their stems. Afterward, she'd have tea and cookies.

Ronald's truck roared into the garage, hitting the front wall so hard Lila felt the whole house shake. He was already swearing before he stepped down from the cab and slammed the door.

In the ensuing silence, Lila heard him open the small refrigerator he kept in the garage and pop the top on a can of "Bud." Lila hadn't bothered to count how many cans of beer Ronald had opened since the six o'clock news last night. He was running on pure alcohol, fatigue, and fear but didn't seem to realize it. Lila felt powerless to stop him.

"I'm not an alcoholic," Ronald had said to her the first few times she'd suggested he be careful with his drinking. "I only drink beer." But his father had died of "drinking beer," as had his uncle and his only brother. Ronald had probably been an alcoholic back when they were both in high school. Now, thirty years later, Ronald was living pickled, preserved in a solution that kept him looking alive when he was already dead.

This was one of the reasons Lila had changed her mind about leaving him. She figured he'd die soon, anyway. Then, with Roxanne Mae gone and Ronald dead, Lila could stay in her own home and start a new life. A life that could include Jennifer Lane. Jennifer could be her daughter this time around.

"Lila!" Ronald yelled, his noise preceding him into the house. "Lila!"

Ronald walked through the small house and out to the screen porch where Lila now sat with her sweet tea and Lorna Doones, once again mapping out next year's flower garden.

"Would you believe those cocksuckers won't tell me a damn thing about my own little girl?" Ronald demanded, almost crying as he fell into the chair across from Lila. "I been sitting in the police station all day and they won't tell me nothin'."

Lila had given up trying to reason with Ronald. From experience, and the fresh blue bruises, she knew she should stay out of the way. He was already repeating himself. He would continue to rant until he wore himself out and went to sleep. He hadn't slept in more than thirty-six hours. Lila expected him to collapse any minute.

Ronald began to cry. Just quiet tears at first, the kind he'd been crying every day since Roxanne Mae left. His tears turned to sobs and finally to keening. Ronald, still holding the beer can, fell down on his knees on the hard tile floor of the porch. He rocked back and forth, back and forth, his hiccupped curses and shouting interrupting his tears.

Finally, Ronald must have realized that Lila was ignoring him. She continued reading and working out her garden plan, paying no attention to him at all. The knowledge ignited his fury into flames.

Ronald stood up and threw the beer can, still half full, onto the floor. Beer flew all over the tile and splashed everywhere. Beer drenched the bodice of Lila's favorite, sky blue dress.

She blinked the beer out of her eyes. She sat as still as a piece of the furniture. Her calm demeanor was the shield she'd raised years ago to deflect Ronald's tantrums.

"Goddamn it, Lila! Maybe you can sit there while our little baby is lying dead in some morgue, but I'm going to do something about it!"

Lila didn't move, even to wipe the beer off of her face, even after Ronald stormed into his bedroom. Lila heard him open his bedside table and pull out his gun, the one he'd used for shooting practice every week since he'd returned from Vietnam. He'd been drafted into the infantry, an experience that had turned him into a man who thought all problems could be solved with a gun.

The gun was cleaned and loaded. Lila knew. Maybe he'd come back and shoot her dead. She should move, hide somewhere, leave. But she didn't. She sat. If he wanted to kill her, Ronald would find her and do it, wherever she went. She waited.

Ronald stomped through the house and she heard him return to the garage, where he stopped to grab another beer from the small refrigerator. Lila heard the fizz when the top popped.

Ronald started up his truck, twice, the second time grinding the starter for a full five seconds before he realized the truck was already running. He swore loudly enough to be heard over the powerful engine. Then he backed the truck out of the driveway and peeled off down the street, tires shrieking like a bad start to the Daytona 500.

Only then, careful of her makeup, she dabbed the beer from her face with the slightly damp lace handkerchief pinned to her bodice. Then she sipped her tea, took a bite of her cookie, and returned to her garden plans.

She considered calling the police, but they already knew about her husband. He'd been there all day. The police had let Ronald leave the station this afternoon, as drunk as he was. If anything happened to Ronald while he was driving, the police could just deal with it. She touched her sore eye through her makeup. Lila had long ago been depleted of sympathy for her husband.

CHAPTER FORTY-EIGHT

JENNIFER PULLED INTO THE Ybor City Walk-in Clinic parking lot and found an open space near the entrance. She reached down and turned off the ignition. The cold air inside the PT Cruiser quickly dispelled as the car's roof absorbed the sun's heat. Jennifer began to feel a trickle of sweat roll between her breasts.

She stopped a moment and tried to calm herself. She'd already made up her mind that she wanted to know, whatever the result was. She couldn't live in ignorance.

Once her heartbeat had slowed to the point where she no longer felt a jackhammer was pounding her to death, she forced herself to open the car door and step out into the sauna of the day. Looking up at the sky, she observed clouds gathering in preparation for the usual afternoon storm. Jennifer tried to breathe around the heavy air, but managed only to inhale enough to keep from suffocating.

Slow forward steps led her to the clinic's front door and, then, when she stepped over the threshold, into the relief of coolness. But her breathing became shallower, her inhalations more difficult, resulting in less to exhale. Then she knew the close summer air was not the source of her shortness of breath.

"May I help you?" A pleasant heavy black woman with a lilting accent and beautiful smile asked from behind the glass window. No one else was in the waiting room.

Jennifer swallowed. Her first attempts at speech were mere squeaks so that the receptionist opened the windows and patted her hand. "It's okay, honey. Take your time."

Jennifer nodded. She swallowed her saliva, gathered her breath, and put some force behind her words. "I need to have a blood test."

"Okay. We can handle that. What do you need to be tested for?"

"For, um, hepatitis Z." She struggled with the concept that she, Jennifer Lane, would be saying those words.

The woman shook her head, almost involuntarily. "Okay. Here you go." She handed Jennifer a clipboard with a new patient information form on it. "Fill this out and we'll get you in right away."

Fifteen minutes later, Jennifer was sitting in an examination room, waiting for the doctor. A nurse had taken her blood pressure, and was obviously trying not to show her concern at the results. She told Jennifer she was probably just nervous. They'd check her blood pressure again before she left. Jennifer knew she was in the throes of an anxiety attack, but she couldn't turn back. She had to know. Just face the fear and move through it.

A quick knock at the door preceded a youngish looking man's entrance to the examination room. "Hello! Jennifer Lane, right? I'm Dr. Fernandez," he said, not offering to shake her hand. Maybe he thought she was contagious. Jennifer nodded, not able to summon her voice.

"Okay, you think you may have been exposed to hepatitis Z? You know we need to report this sort of thing, right? It's a public-health issue." He didn't wait for an answer. "So, tell me where you think you may have contracted the virus." He stood poised with his pen over the clipboard, waiting for her answer.

"I think my boyfriend may have it."

"Why do you think that?"

"I just do."

"You know hepatitis Z isn't sexually transmitted, right? You need to have blood-to-blood contact. Have you had that?"

Blood Lovers, she thought. "Look, just test me," She snapped. "If I have it, then I'll tell you where I got it. If I don't have it, then we don't have to involve him."

"I'm not supposed to do it that way," young Dr. Fernandez said.

Jennifer spoke more firmly this time. "If you don't do it my way, I'll just go to another clinic and another and another until I find one that will."

Dr. Fernandez was probably not used to patients with a will of their own. He seemed ill-equipped to deal with any kind of outright refusal of cooperation. He tried to talk Jennifer into the usual procedure, but, after three more attempts, he left the room.

Jennifer was about to jump down from the exam table when the door opened again and another nurse, carrying a small blue plastic basket filled with syringes, entered. She told Jennifer her name, then stood near the sink and began to prepare a needle to draw blood.

Jennifer's anxiety began to dissolve. She wouldn't have to give Blake Denton's name. At least one of her problems had disappeared, for the moment.

Jennifer paid cash for the lab test. With new courage, she

refused to give even her phone number. She told the kindly receptionist that she'd call back in one week for the results. She left the clinic and was on her way to meet with Russell Denton and Stuart. It was time to face her future.

CHAPTER FORTY-NINE

STUART BARNETT AND RUSSELL Denton sat across from each other in the main conference room of the Worthington offices on the forty-second floor in the 100 North Tampa building. Jennifer Lane sat at the head of the table.

Jennifer was explaining why the motion she'd drafted seeking a temporary restraining order preventing further action in the matter of *Annabelle James v. Denton Bio-Medical, Inc.,* which Roger Riley had filed in state court, was a loser. Argument on Jennifer's motion was set for tomorrow in federal court. If they lost the motion, as a practical matter the case would be over. Annabelle James would be able to sell HepZMax to the highest bidder. Denton might win the war eventually, but the success would be all too late. Everything depended on their winning now. And, right this minute, they had strategic decisions to make, Jennifer said.

Russell Denton, unimpressed by the luxurious surroundings or the spectacular view, tuned her out. He couldn't concentrate on Jennifer's words, because what she said didn't matter to him in the light of his more disturbing problems. His concern over Blake's mental deterioration and his possible role in Annabelle James's theft and disappearance—he still refused to believe Blake had killed her—had not left his thoughts for a single moment in these last few days.

He could add nothing to this conversation, anyway. The ineptitude Jennifer had shown so far in handling the case and Stuart Barnett's lack of effective strategic planning were both beyond belief. Russell questioned his own judgment at hiring them. Only knowing how much stress he was under kept him from making the snap decision to replace the two right now. If he could, he would simply drop this case.

When he'd started on this course of action, using Jennifer to find Annabelle and his HepZMax formula had seemed quite clever. Now, with Blake involved somehow and Annabelle missing, if not dead, Russell wanted to let it all go hang. And he couldn't. Because now he had Riley's lawsuit to defend. Why hadn't he hired some New York lawyers experienced in patent litigation for this job?

Dark black coffee sat in a china cup and saucer in front of Barnett on a mahogany table so highly polished that it reflected everything in the room as if in a mirror. Russell had declined the coffee and everything else he'd been offered since. He was not in a social mood. Barnett, on the other hand, appeared completely relaxed, as if they were all discussing an intellectual problem, not the very life of Russell's business.

Russell stuffed his irritation down even farther, into his already acidic stomach. He waited, almost without hope, for Barnett to demonstrate some of that finely honed legal acumen for which he was renowned. Barnett had won a big corporate case recently. So Russell knew that Barnett could win. The question was whether he would win for Russell.

Jennifer was wrapping up, rushing her conclusion, no doubt, because she knew how unacceptable her vote of no-confidence in their position was. "So, we had no enforceable contract to begin with and no real federal court jurisdiction. Our local federal courts are already overburdened and they look for good reasons to dismiss a case. There's no reason for the judge to take on this case now. Riley will stay in state court, where he's got an excellent chance of getting to the jury. I have the motion and we can file it, but I don't think it's a winner."

She stopped and looked at each of the two men in turn. "If we lose, we'll be down another battle with Riley. It's not a good idea to let Riley win," she said, as if this were something Russell or Barnett might have otherwise found acceptable.

Russell tuned in long enough to hear Barnett begin to question the facts in support of the motion, testing Jennifer's logic. Russell knew Jennifer's reasoning was flawless, and he made his decision right that moment: Unless Stuart Barnett could pull this rabbit out of his hat, he was about to be fired. He would no longer represent Denton Bio-Medical.

Russell had more at stake now than he'd had at the start. If the body they'd found in Kennedy Park was Annabelle James, as Blake had said, Russell needed to move quickly. Indeed, it might already be too late. Russell felt he was under the pressure of a ticking clock. He needed better lawyers. Lawyers who would get the job done.

He listened to Barnett's continuing monologue with skepticism. Russell had been a very successful businessman for a good long time. He'd clawed his way to the top of his industry and he'd learned to trust and follow his gut. He could smell a shit sandwich when he was being force-fed one. He buried his impatience a little longer while he waited to hear Barnett's recommendation.

Half an hour later, Russell's patience was exhausted. He was about to tell Barnett to cut to the chase, when the telephone near the antique mahogany server in the back of the room buzzed. Barnett ignored it, continuing to discuss the options with Jennifer like a law professor giving an oral exam to a student.

The telephone buzzed a second time. Again, Barnett ignored the sound. When it buzzed the third time, Jennifer walked over to the phone and jabbed the speaker button.

"Yes!" she snapped, revealing the same impatience Russell had kept in check.

A female voice responded. "Mr. Barnett, Mr. Ronald Walden is here, demanding to see you." Jennifer turned a sickly shade of pale.

Russell recalled meeting Hilda, Barnett's secretary, earlier today. About sixty, she'd seemed to Russell the type who would be unperturbed by a hurricane blowing directly into the room. Her voice now was not calm. Russell briefly wondered what could have possibly upset her.

"We can't see Mr. Walden right now," Barnett said, gesturing to Jennifer to disconnect the call. She pushed the speaker button with a shaky hand, this time to hang up.

A few seconds later, the door to the conference room burst open. The polished red-oak door slammed against the wall hard enough to rattle the priceless oil paintings and the small gold-tone lights above the chairs that sat with their backs against the papered walls. A man Russell assumed to be Ronald Walden, whoever that might be, stood in the open entryway. At first, Russell didn't see the gun in his left hand.

"But you *can* see Mr. Walden. Right now," the man said to Barnett, mimicking the words Barnett had used just seconds ago. Walden waved the gun toward them as if it were an extension of his left arm.

"Mr. Walden?" Barnett said. Russell realized Barnett had never met the man. Who was he, then?

"Don't act like you don't know me, Barnett," Walden said. "You and your firm were my lawyers 'till you kicked me out to represent Mr. Fat Cat here." Walden pointed the gun directly at Russell, but then waved it around and pointed it back toward Stuart Barnett again. Russell wondered what he was talking about. Was this man Annabelle James's father? *How could that be?*

"And she," Walden said, pointing the gun toward Jennifer now, "was supposed to help me find my baby. Well, none of you are helping me, and my little girl is gone forever." His face began to collapse into sobs, but he got hold of himself before the tears began to fall. He took one deep, ragged breath. "The police won't let me see her, either. They won't give me my baby back."

Barnett remained outwardly still and seemed unconcerned. Russell remembered that Barnett had seen combat in Vietnam. No doubt he had had guns pointed at him by lunatics before. He seemed to know what to do.

"Mr. Walden," Barnett began, standing up to face the man and the gun, giving Walden a bigger target.

"Ronald," the man interrupted, still pointing the gun straight at Barnett.

"Ronald," Barnett amended. "It sounds like maybe you think that body they found yesterday in Kennedy Park was your daughter."

"Damn straight," Ronald Walden said, pointing with the gun for emphasis.

Barnett never flinched. "Well, it might be her, I'm sorry to say."

Russell thought admitting that possibility at this point was a mistake. Barnett must believe step one in dealing with a lunatic was to agree with his own warped version of reality.

"I know," Walden said, tears beginning to fall now from red eyes that had obviously been crying earlier.

Walden wasn't close enough for Russell to smell him, but Russell had seen his share of drunks. This jerk was plastered, as well as armed and dangerous.

Russell felt for the cell phone in his pocket and silently pressed *9-1-1*. The sensitive microphone on his high-tech phone would pick up the man's loud voice. The operator would only be able to locate the cell phone, not his physical location. *At least there will be a recording of my last moments on earth,* Russell thought.

"Ronald, I'll call the police chief for you, if you'd like. He's a friend of mine. Let me use the phone. I'm sure we can get to the bottom of this." As he made the offer, Barnett moved toward the phone near the server. But Walden became more agitated at Barnett's offer and waved the gun again.

"Sure. Of course, your friend would be the police chief. You people make me sick. You think you're so goddamned special. Special rules for people like you. For me? They ignore me." Ronald Walden was still crying, but his anger had returned. His voice was harsher, louder. He took a step toward Barnett and suddenly, without warning, shot the gun.

Russell felt the deafening explosion as the bullet punctured the plate glass that, just seconds before, had stretched from floor to ceiling behind him. Or at least, that's what he assumed; he didn't have time to look. A rush of air swept in through what was now a fifteen-foot hole in the wall. The structural integrity of the wall of glass must have been weakened already from some prior damage, or it would never have shattered like that from a single gunshot. But whatever the reason, a stiff breeze was blowing into the room from the hot afternoon outside.

Russell involuntary jumped away from the window and crouched behind the shiny mahogany conference table. He couldn't hear anything except a loud ringing in his ears. He glared over at Barnett, who remained standing and motionless like a mannequin.

Through the now open hole in the wall, the sound of approaching sirens became loud enough to penetrate the loud ringing in Russell's ears.

Walden, too, must have heard the sirens' noise. His face flushed bright red and his eyes bulged with anger. "That bitch! She's your secretary, right?" he said to Barnett, waving the gun around. "She called the cops, didn't she?"

"She probably did, Ronald. When they get here, we'll ask them about your daughter."

Barnett was holding up well. He stood directly in front of Walden. Russell was still hunched down behind the table, but he could see clearly. He glanced around for Jennifer and found her cowering in the corner, her hands over her ears and her eyes filled with terror.

Ronald Walden's eyes were mad, his mouth slack. He held the gun in his left hand and gestured with it as if it were a pointer.

"Yeah? Well, how would your family like it if you were dead like my baby, huh? How would they like it?" Walden asked Barnett.

Russell and Jennifer's eyes met as they realized at the same moment that Walden intended to shoot Stuart Barnett. Barnett, apparently deciding that, too, lunged forward toward Walden. The gun went off a second time. The noise, even with the now open hole in the wall, was deafening. Russell ducked.

When next he looked, he saw Stuart Barnett lying on the floor in a widening pool of blood, a hole in his chest big enough to pour his heart out.

Walden stared at Barnett's bloody body on the floor, then scanned the room with wild eyes, waving the gun in a wide arc from Russell to Jennifer. Russell couldn't just stay there and let Barnett die.

He stood up slowly and faced Walden directly. The two men stared at each other for a few seconds, and then, his decision made, Russell ignored Walden and rushed over to help Barnett.

Barnett's body felt cold already. So quickly. Or maybe it was Russell's misperception. Pulling off his own jacket to cover Barnett's chest, Russell checked Barnett's pulse. It was still there.

When Russell looked up to assess the level of remaining danger, Ronald Walden was gone.

CHAPTER FIFTY

THE EMERGENCY MEDICAL TECHNICIANS rushed Stuart into the elevator and down to where the ambulance waited outside.

The ambulance doors were closed before Jennifer could reach Stuart. She raced back upstairs to grab her car keys from her office, located two floors below the beehive of activity in the main conference room. If she returned to where all the hubbub was, police would detain her and try to get details of the incident from her. But she needed to get to Stuart—now.

Jennifer rushed back out to the fortieth floor lobby, keys in hand, and literally ran into Russell Denton where he stood near the glass door, deliberately blocking her exit. She bounced back off him like a banked pool shot.

"Let me go! I have to get to Tampa General," Jennifer said, attempting to move around Blake's uncle. Tampa General Hospital was a level one trauma center and less than a mile away. The ambulance would have taken Stuart there. In her head, she could still hear the ambulance siren start up as its doors closed on Jennifer, who was left outside on the street. The ambulance had taken Stuart away, alone. But Stuart needed her. He depended on

Jennifer. Stuart told everyone, "Jennifer is my strong right arm." She absolutely had to be with him. Now.

Russell reached out to Jennifer with both hands. He held onto her arms, gently but with the firmness of knowledge, until his silence attracted her attention away from the door. Jennifer finally looked straight into Russell's eyes and read in them the insight she'd rejected.

"Let me go," she said again, but this time, without urgency. Russell's eyes told Jennifer that Stuart no longer needed Jennifer, no longer relied on her. If she went to the hospital, Russell's steady gaze said, Jennifer would find only Stuart's grieving family and the body she didn't want to see.

Jennifer pictured Stuart's lovely wife, his four teenage children. They had often chided Stuart for his devotion to the law. They told him he would die at the office with only his colleagues left to mourn him. Jennifer imagined their grief when they learned that Stuart had indeed died at work as they had innocently foreshadowed.

No one could have known that Ronald Walden would kill Stuart Barnett. The moment this thought surfaced, Jennifer tested its truth. Should she have known? Would a better lawyer have figured it out? When Jennifer sat directly across from Ronald's wife in his home, asking questions about his daughter, should she have asked about Ronald Walden's mental state? Or, when he had walked into the conference room today, could she have done more? Taken him outside and tried to reason with him? Called for help? Used the gun she had in its case in her office? Should she have killed Ronald Walden first?

"No." Russell seemed to answer her very thoughts, shaking her gently to focus her attention again. "Don't blame yourself," he told her. "There was nothing you could do." She thought he was trying to believe that he, too, was innocent of Stuart's murder. Was either of them innocent?

Jennifer shivered. She remembered the look on Ronald Walden's face when he burst into the conference room. The anger. His fierce eyes. How drunk he was. She began to shake her head, almost reflexively. Never had she believed Ronald Walden would shoot Stuart. Never.

She hadn't believed Walden would shoot his gun at all. The first shot, loud, deafening, unanticipated, was such a shock, Jennifer couldn't process it at first—she was too amazed. Once she'd figured out how angry and distraught Walden was, Jennifer thought he'd come to kill *her*. *She* was the one who had breached his confidence by refusing to represent him and then by meeting secretly with his wife.

All the time Jennifer had had to save Stuart, she'd spent thinking about herself. Jennifer was sure Ronald had found out about the meeting with Lila. Maybe Ronald was furious with Jennifer. Maybe he believed Jennifer was conspiring with Lila or Russell—or both.

Jennifer hadn't seen Ronald shoot Stuart because she had cowered down behind that stupid old piece of furniture and closed her eyes. Jennifer had crouched there, like a child, praying that Ronald wouldn't shoot her in the back. And he hadn't. After the second shot, she'd realized that she had never been Ronald Walden's target, even if she should have been.

"Why didn't he kill *me*?" Jennifer asked Russell now, her voice breaking as he led her back into her private office and sat across from her in the cramped space.

Russell dropped his head into his hands. "I don't know. Why didn't he kill *me*? In his mind, he must feel I'm the one who's caused all his problems." He looked at her, with a quizzical expression on his face. “The man wasn’t thinking clearly, Jennifer. You must realize that.” To Jennifer, Russell seemed to be seeking a sign that she was grounded in his reality, seeing events the way he’d interpreted them.

At the time, she had, of course, realized Ronald Walden was not in a rational state of mind. That’s why she was hiding in the corner when Stuart was killed.

When she thought the words *Stuart is dead* for the first time tears welled up in her eyes and she knew she was going to lose her composure. She didn’t want to break down in front of this man.

“Russell, I won’t go over to the hospital. I promise. You can leave me alone now. I really want to be alone.” When she saw he was going to protest, she said, “Really.”

Jennifer didn’t think she could hold up much longer. Soon, she would be sobbing for Stuart, and for herself. How could she go on without Stuart? Stuart was always there for her, always her teacher, always protecting her from her enemies as well as his. Stuart was Jennifer’s whole life at the firm. She had no idea how to be a lawyer without Stuart.

Everything Jennifer knew about practicing law, he’d taught her himself. Most of the things she knew about how a good man behaved, she’d learned from Stuart, too. There hadn’t been many good men in Jennifer’s life, except her father. Stuart was the gold standard by which she measured all the males she met, usually finding them lacking.

Jennifer would miss Stuart more than anyone else did. She would mourn more than Stuart’s own family and certainly more than his law partners or his clients. Stuart was irreplaceable. He couldn’t be dead; Jennifer knew she’d never survive it. Ronald Walden might as well have killed her, too.

Russell, raising his head, looked up at her. He kept both

forearms on his knees and clasped his hands as if in prayer. Jennifer hadn't thought Russell was a religious man, but what did she know about him, really?

Maybe his precious company wasn't worth saving. The cost was too high. Maybe Russell Denton was just another corporate pirate. Maybe Stuart and Annabelle James had died because of this man. Whatever Denton thought his HepZMax formula was worth, Jennifer would have been willing to pay any ransom to have Stuart back.

Russell seemed to reach some sort of decision. "I hate to mention this now, but we do have that big hearing tomorrow on the motion…" Russell said, letting his voice drop. Jennifer looked at her client in horror. "Look, I know Stuart was going to argue the motion. But he can't do that now. You wrote the brief; you know the case. You'll have to do it."

Had he lost his mind? Jennifer couldn't argue this motion. She'd given up litigation after the mere scheduling of her very first court appearance had sent her to the psychiatrist for Valium weeks in advance, and to the ladies room to vomit right before a single word had escaped her lips in the courtroom. Stuart understood her deep fear of public appearances, and it was one of the reasons their partnership worked.

Stuart loved the courtroom. His ability to compose and deliver persuasive arguments extemporaneously was legendary. Overcoming insurmountable obstacles was Stuart's forte. They had planned that he would argue this motion. Jennifer couldn't possibly do it on her own. She threw her head back and forth, almost violently, rejecting Russell's plea.

"No one else can get up to speed quickly enough, Jennifer." He said only what Jennifer already knew to be true. "Time is of the essence here. We can't wait." Then he looked at his watch. "It's after seven o'clock. You can't cancel now."

"Yes, I can. I can call Roger Riley and he'll agree. He doesn't want to fight with me. It was Stuart he wanted to beat. Now that Stuart is…" Her eyes filled with tears again. This time, those tears spilled over onto her cheeks and ran down her face. She cleared her throat but made no attempt to wipe away the wetness, even when Russell handed her a tissue.

"Now that Stuart is…unavailable…Riley will agree to reschedule," she finished. "And even if he doesn't agree, the judge will give us another date. This is Tampa. Litigation is still civilized here." Jennifer had allowed her emotions to escalate to near panic. "The judge will give us more time. Stuart was shot, for God's sake."

"I thought you said the judge was in Riley's pocket?" Russell's question reminded her that the judge assigned to their case was one of Riley's former law partners. A man Riley played golf with three days a week. The judge they'd been unlucky enough to draw was one of the reasons Jennifer had concluded the motion was a loser.

"And you told me that in federal court the procedural rules are more strictly applied," he added, repeating her own words back to her.

Jennifer felt the door closing on her opportunity to run away. The shock of the shooting, Stuart's death, and the fear she experienced at going into the courtroom, any courtroom, began to close in on her. She felt dizzy; the room was getting inexplicably blacker.

"I can't do this, Russell," Jennifer said, with quiet desperation. "Please don't ask me to."

"You said we would need to argue this motion quickly if we were to have any hope of winning it. You said we needed to do it now, because of the schedule. You said that we'd only have a narrow window to win before Riley could thwart us again in state court."

Jennifer's head began to pound and the nausea she experienced with her migraines returned, stronger than anything she'd felt in a long time. Her stomach started to heave. She took several deep breaths, trying to get herself under control. She didn't want to vomit on Russell's shoes and she was close to that point.

Russell reached over and took her hand. He played his final, winning card. "Putting the motion off is not the best thing to do for either of us. We need you, Jennifer. Stuart would want you to do it," he told her. "You know he would. He would say you know the case well, and no one else has a chance." Jennifer felt herself slipping from the chair. "Do it for Stuart," Russell said, as Jennifer fell, unconscious, onto the floor.

CHAPTER FIFTY-ONE

"FIND HIM, TYLER. FIND him now," Russell Denton said into the cell phone.

"The cops are better equipped for that," Tyler told him. Tyler was on his way to pick up his kids. He'd already disappointed them three days this week because of his work schedule. Lori was freezing up again on the marriage proposal, although she'd accepted the ring he'd bought her. He didn't want to blow it.

Russell's rebuttal interrupted his thoughts. "They might be, if they already had the equipment in place the way you do. Anyway, the cops are still in the building, interviewing witnesses and trying to get a handle on the thing."

"Where are you?"

Tyler heard Russell's patience slipping away. "I'm at Jennifer's apartment. Blake's on his way over. Then, I'll head home. Keep me posted there."

"Do you think that's wise?"

"What else can I do?" Russell snapped at him.

"Look," Tyler said, "I'm sorry you witnessed a murder today." Tyler had witnessed murders and human death too many times. He knew the horror of it. But Blake could be dangerous to Jennifer. You don't want that on your conscience, do you? I don't want it on mine."

"Just find Ronald Walden. Do it now." Russell hung up.

Tyler looked at the cell phone and pushed the end button. He thought about sending the police over to Jennifer's apartment, but if he did, Russell would be livid.

Tyler crossed his fingers and hoped for the best, as he turned his car toward Denton Bio-Medical and the Cellar where he could sort out the tracking device he'd put on Ronald Walden's truck right after Annabelle disappeared. Maybe he could find Walden more quickly than the cops, but he thought not. They had arrived at the scene almost instantaneously. They'd been looking for him for an hour already.

He pushed a button on the cell phone. Lori answered on the fourth ring. "Honey, I'm sorry. There's an emergency. I can't pick up the kids."

Frosty silence.

"It's not like I have a choice," he started to explain.

"You never do, Tim. It's always business before family," she said, and hung up.

Tyler pounded his hand on the steering wheel. "Shit!" He threw the cell phone on the seat and paid attention to his driving.

The radio's all-news station rattled on as he sped north on I-275 toward the Denton Bio-Medical plant. He listened to stories about the oppressive heat wave that had been suffocating the city for the past two weeks, the upcoming football season, and the latest shenanigans in Tallahassee.

Nothing was reported about a former client shooting a lawyer in a downtown high-rise. Either they didn't have the story yet, or they'd decided for some reason not to run it.

Either way, Tyler took that as good news. It wasn't like this was the first time a disgruntled client had decided to take the law into his own hands and shoot his lawyer. Still, a prominent man had died today. You'd think it would at least make the cheap AM news ahead of a story about the weather, for God's sake. Whatever happened to the newsman's motto: if it bleeds, it leads?

Tyler exited the expressway to Fowler and headed east. The local news stories continued and began to repeat themselves. By the time he reached Denton Bio-Medical, still nothing had been reported about Stuart Barnett's murder. He took that as a bad sign, an indication that the police didn't have much to report or wouldn't report the news that Barnett had died before the family was notified.

He made it down to the Cellar in a little more than an hour after Barnett was killed. Walden could be on his way to Cuba by now, if he'd left the city by boat. Tyler didn't have a lot of hope for his technology. After all, Walden had had experience as a soldier. He knew how to escape enemies intent on killing him. He was a formidable opponent for the Tampa Police Department.

It took Tyler several minutes to locate and isolate Walden's truck signal on one of the computer screens. The signal showed the truck heading north, near where Tyler was sitting. Why would the man stay around town? Why not try to get the hell away?

While Tyler was watching the moving signal, he reached over and flipped through the contact database on another computer screen until he found what he was looking for. He dialed the number through the computer, slipping on his headset.

"Chief Hathaway," he requested of the operator. "Tim Tyler calling. Tell him it's urgent."

In a few minutes, Hathaway came on the line. He sounded

distant, as if he'd been patched in from the station to his cell phone. "Tim. What do you have?"

Their relationship was a professional one. They had no need to make small talk. Hathaway, by this time, must have figured out who killed Stuart Barnett. "I have reason to believe that Ronald Walden is driving his red 1998 Ford pickup truck north on I-275, headed toward the University of South Florida," Tyler told him.

"Headed toward Denton Bio-Medical, you mean," Hathaway said, matter-of-factly. "We're on it already. I won't ask you how you know that. But you tell your boss I'm going to need a statement from him. I'll come out to the plant or we can do it at his house. I figure we'll have Walden in about twenty minutes. Then I'll have time to talk to you."

Tyler swore under his breath. He'd wasted his time on the call and tipped his hand to boot.

"Right now, I've got to go deliver some very bad news to a widow." Hathaway clicked off.

Tyler continued to follow the beeping red signal on the computer with his eyes, watching Ronald Walden come closer and closer to where he was sitting. When Walden turned into Bruce B. Downs and headed toward the Denton Bio-Medical parking lot, Tyler flipped the switch to allow his quick exit, pulled out his gun and took off at a trot, not wanting to alarm everyone in the plant, but in a hurry to get outside.

Tyler could hear the sirens as he exited the building and headed toward the parking lot nearest the Bruce B. Downs entrance. Tyler was running full out now. He could see the old red truck, stopped at a traffic light north of the plant entrance. Tyler pulled out his cell phone and dialed Hathaway again.

"The cellular customer you have called is not available. Please try your call again later," the computerized voice said into Tyler's ear.

"Damn!" he said, flipping the phone closed and slipping it into his pocket. He stooped down behind an SUV bigger than his first house, gun drawn, both eyes watching Ronald Walden's truck move through the traffic light and turn into the Denton Bio-Medical parking lot.

The sirens came closer, getting louder. There were three or four of them now, coming from different directions. Tyler could hear them, but he couldn't see the police cars from behind the SUV.

Tyler stuck his head out, quickly looking in the direction of the driveway. Walden's truck sped around the turn on squealing tires. Tyler heard the growling eight-cylinder engine from two hundred feet away as the truck barreled down the driveway, heading directly toward the employee parking area.

What the hell is this moron trying to do? Tyler moved away from the SUV and held his gun in front of him, ready to shoot Walden through the windshield of his truck, if he had to.

Walden must have seen Tyler because he swerved down one of the aisles of the parking lot toward the other side of the building, toward the executive parking lot.

"Where are the damn cops, already?" Tyler shouted aloud into the air, as he ran around the parked cars to get to the executive parking zone. He could see Walden's truck circle the lot, speeding, looking for what?

The truck didn't stop, but drove toward the south entrance. Tyler hesitated a few seconds too long, and in that few seconds, the truck growled out of range. He dropped his gun and watched the truck fly out of the south driveway and head south onto Bruce B. Downs. Three police cars that never made it to the plant must have seen Walden's truck exit. Sirens still blaring, all three followed him.

Tyler stood impotent, the unfired gun at his side now, as Walden blew the red light and kept on going. As Tyler watched, three police cars were forced to stop by a young mother who, oblivious to the world around her, had stepped into the crosswalk pushing a double baby stroller. Tires screeched, the mother screamed, the babies cried, and cars slammed on their breaks and blew their horns: pure chaos.

From his vantage point at the top of the drive, Tyler saw Walden's red truck speed away and turn down a side street. The police cars resumed the chase, but they seemed unfocused now. Tyler thought they didn't see where he'd gone.

Tyler hotfooted it back into the building, running full out this time to reach the Cellar. Dodging people and desks and hurriedly pushing all obstacles out of his way, he no longer cared whether the employees became alarmed. Tyler needed to get back to his equipment and find Walden again before the man got away.

Once he made it back to the Cellar, the damned security system slowed him down at the door. After what seemed like a lifetime, Tyler was seated, looking at the computer screen where Walden's tracking device had been sending a steady stream of red flashes only moments before.

The screen was dark. "What the hell?" Tyler said, frustrated. He looked down and saw that he must have pulled the plug from the wall when he'd tripped over the cord in his haste to leave the room.

He reached down and plugged the machine back in, turned it on to reboot, and waited the interminable two minutes for the computer to set up the program again. When he did, Walden's red signal revealed the truck to be heading out of range. Tyler flipped on his police scanner. He could hear the cops talking to each other over the static.

CHAPTER FIFTY-TWO

BLAKE SAT BESIDE JENNIFER on the bed in her apartment, changing the cold compress on her forehead. Jennifer looked at him briefly through lowered eyelids, pretending to be asleep. She felt his comforting weight on the bed. He took care with the compress, then placed a warm hand over hers. Jennifer hadn't been so vigilantly tended since childhood. She wallowed in it. She felt relaxed, safe. She wanted to stay here, just like this, forever.

After a few minutes, Blake left the room and the troubling thoughts that had roared in her head since Ronald Walden shot Stuart to death returned.

For starters, exactly how had she gotten home? The last thing she remembered was the enveloping panic she'd felt sitting in her closet-sized office with Russell Denton. He'd been pressuring her, pushing her too hard. Making the ridiculous suggestion that she appear in court the next day. Maybe he had some idiotic notion about getting back up on the horse after you've been thrown, or something. But the man was crazy if he thought she'd go argue his motion tomorrow. No way.

Jennifer had had panic attacks before. They were caused by

her own anxious imaginings and not by some real, external situation. Intellectually, she understood. Emotionally, her anxiety became simply unbearable.

"Anxiety attacks, like other forms of mental illness, are caused by chemical imbalances in the brain," she told herself and everyone else who asked. Why she'd rather consider herself mentally ill was easy—it meant she wasn't in control, that her feelings were not her fault.

Jennifer had prescription medication, but she hated its side effects. So, most of the time, she suppressed her anxiety by controlling her environment. Today, everything had literally been out of control, and the anxiety had returned with a vengeance.

Sometimes, she'd get killer migraines that lasted for days. Tonight's headache was just a dull thudding in her head. She tried to get up. Dizziness caused the bed to move and toss her back. She'd try again later. Unfortunately, the headache wouldn't protect her from the world.

To deal with her anxiety, Jennifer had taken a workshop a few years ago. She'd learned techniques to embrace reality. Her psychologist had suggested that Jennifer's anxiety attacks were caused by the real world's failure to reflect what she believed the world should be. He showed Jennifer how to control the attacks by accepting reality and embracing it before changing her behavior, and thus achieving the desired result. In calm times, Jennifer could use the techniques she'd learned at the workshop to survive in her world. She tried to apply them now, but every attempt ended in failure.

Lying back on the pillow to keep her headache at bay, Jennifer's uncontrollable mind continued to run the events of the past few days through her head like a movie, altering the behavior of the characters, changing the outcome.

Whatever she did, she couldn't resurrect Stuart. Returning Stuart to her life was the only thing she really wanted to do.

The more she thought about it, the more her anxiety escalated. How could Stuart be dead? How could Jennifer have witnessed his murder and failed to stop it?

She applied her coping techniques. Strictly speaking, Jennifer hadn't actually witnessed Stuart's murder, she reminded herself. She'd been hiding in the corner like a frightened six-year-old.

She shook her head violently from side to side. There was no way she could have done anything while Ronald Walden was in that conference room.

She tried a different subject. Okay, Stuart was dead. Jennifer wasn't. She had to go on. How long would she mourn for Stuart? Always. Jennifer's entire life since law school had revolved around Stuart. She had done whatever he wanted, whenever he asked.

The bad angel on her pillow, near her left ear, said, "But it's your fault that Stuart's dead. You failed. Again." Jennifer nodded her head miserably. It was true. She had failed to trust her instincts. She had known better than to take on the Denton Bio-Medical case. She'd tried to tell Stuart that taking the case was a mistake. She tried to get him to let it go. Ambition killed Stuart.

The bad angel kept up its incessant, negative chatter. "You could have prevented this, you know. You could have insisted, stuck to what you knew was right. Then, you'd both be back at the firm, working side by side. Your life would be unfolding as you planned. You'd still be Stuart's perpetual personal aide. Life would be normal. You should have insisted." She wanted to scream.

"What is reality, Jennifer?" she heard her doctor asking inside her head. Jennifer tried to focus. To consider. The reality was that

Stuart had made all of the professional decisions for their team of two. Jennifer's role was to execute the parts of the cases assigned to her, to be the assistant.

To be fair to Stuart, whenever he did consult her on major decisions, she was always afraid of taking a risk and advised against it. Risk taking was Stuart's role and why would he have understood that this situation was different? How would he have known that he should have listened to her this time?

Jennifer's thoughts continued to circle around her headache, resolving nothing. She deliberately switched herself to another channel. She tried to think positive thoughts and her mind lit on Blake.

Jennifer easily conjured up love and desire for Blake Denton. She was glad that she wasn't alone, regardless of how she'd come to be lying here. Her body re-experienced his hands, comforting her, giving her caring attention.

When had Blake started to be such a big figure in her life? If she truly loved him, why wasn't he enough to make her forget Stuart now?

Incessant questions with no answers exhausted her again. She fell back into sleep.

CHAPTER FIFTY-THREE

WHEN JENNIFER RESURFACED, SHE heard the stereo playing quiet music in the living room and the unmistakable clink of ice in a glass. The sun was low. Dim light illuminated the closed mini-blinds. Jennifer saw that she was dressed only in her bra and panties. Color rose into her cheeks as she realized Blake must have undressed her while she was—what?—unconscious? Sleeping?

Jennifer got up and belted on her blue silk robe. She walked out into the living room. Blake was watching an old movie on television. Bette Davis, or maybe Deborah Kerr, lounged on a sofa, a drink in her hand. A man stood at the doorway to her apartment, talking angrily to her. The volume on the television was muted, though, while the stereo played quietly. Jennifer walked up behind Blake and caressed the back of his neck.

"Hey. It is alive!" he joked, turning to look at her.

Jennifer gave him a sheepish smile. "What're you drinking?"

"Scotch. Want some?" He poured her a glass of Dewar's, neat, and brought it back to her where she curled up on one end of the couch.

Jennifer took a sip of the strong liquor. She relished the

burning as it traveled to her empty stomach and rested there. Liquid warmth spread to her chilled limbs. It was the first pleasant sensation Jennifer had felt since the last time she and Blake made love. Before she'd discovered the tattoo.

Jennifer took another sip of the Scotch and pushed aside the unhappy thought. Discovering the tattoo wasn't a memory she wanted to experience at the moment. She wanted to think about Stuart instead.

"Want to talk about it?" Blake asked her.

"How did I get here?"

"Uncle Russell brought you home. Your keys were in your hand when you passed out. He called me and I came over." Blake looked down at his watch. "I've been here about four hours."

Jennifer sipped her Scotch. She tried to orient herself. "How did he know where I live? Did you tell him?"

He shrugged. "He always knows everything. I gave up asking him for his sources years ago," Blake said with a trace of bitterness, confirming what Jennifer already believed.

Russell Denton was not a good man. He was full of secrets. He had his own reasons for hiring her to handle the Annabelle James case. He was a careful man. He'd checked her out before he'd hired her. He knew she was not experienced enough, not strong enough. The Dewar's made her see this all clearly.

But what did Russell Denton ultimately want? And was Blake another part of that hidden agenda? Jennifer didn't believe in coincidences. She believed Blake had been assigned to her, just as she had been assigned to the Annabelle James case. What irony that she had fallen in love. Maybe Russell Denton did know everything, but he couldn't control everything. That was for sure.

She had the guts to acknowledge to herself that she wasn't sorry. Jennifer loved Blake. She'd had her best times, ever, while with him. Though she distrusted his motives and didn't believe he loved her in return, she wasn't sorry for any of it.

Unless Russell Denton's hidden agenda had gotten Stuart killed. Jennifer had sipped quite a bit more of the Scotch by this time, and she recognized the effects of the alcohol. She felt bolder, wiser. These were dangerous feelings.

"How long had you known Stuart?" Blake asked. The sound jarred her. Jennifer wasn't used to having another person in her apartment. Usually, all of her conversation was with herself.

Jennifer sipped. "Forever. Not long enough." Blake looked interested. The Scotch made Jennifer want to talk about Stuart with someone who wanted to know, whatever his reasons.

"I'm an only child. Did you know that?" she asked him. Blake shook his head to say no. Jennifer didn't believe him, but she was too drunk now to care.

"Well, my parents loved me, but they were young and they worked hard, all the time. So I felt abandoned, even though once I was old enough to understand their situation, I realized I was wrong to feel that way." Jennifer held out her glass out for more of the Scotch. Blake filled the tumbler and added a couple of ice cubes. He also added a little water. "I was raised mostly by my grandmother, who adored me, until I was six years old. Then she died."

Jennifer thwarted his effort to slow down her drinking by taking a bigger gulp of the amber solace. "I was about five when I figured out that my dad was a functioning alcoholic. I never saw him without a glass in his hand. I thought it was ice water. But it wasn't. Vodka was his anesthetic of choice." Jennifer kept drinking. Soon, she held her glass out for another refill.

Blake poured more Scotch in the tumbler. "Was he abusive?" Blake asked in a knowing tone.

Jennifer shook her head. "Just the opposite. He was quiet, loving. Cried a lot. Pretty sad about something, but he'd never say what. He never caused any trouble at all. Until he got fired for being drunk on the job. Then, Mom had to work more."

"None of that was your fault, Jennifer," Blake said, sounding like her therapist. "We're not our parents. And we're not to blame for the mistakes they make. Usually, someone else has pushed them to the breaking point. Trust me on this. I've seen it, firsthand."

"I thought everything was all my fault. I wasn't pretty, not athletic, not artistic. I had nothing to offer, except constant compliance and hard work. I thought if I was a good girl, my dad would get better. Our family would be okay. I never made trouble. I just tried to stay out of the way. So no one noticed me. I faded into the atmosphere." Jennifer saw that Blake was about to contradict her, but she was quite drunk and intent on telling him her story.

"There was a good side. Dad was home with me a lot and he treated me like an angel. Eventually, when I was about eight, he joined AA and stopped drinking. He went back to work. Mom was working, too. After that, I never felt special again." She took another big swig of the Scotch, emptying the glass.

"Until Stuart. Stuart saw something in me that no one else ever had. He let me be myself. He never tried to push me or to make me do more than I could. But he nurtured my talents and what little ability I had. He was like a father to me," Jennifer said. Then she shrugged in defeat. "Or at least he was like what I imagined a father should be."

"Sounds to me like he used you. He kept you on a leash, like a pet," Blake said. "You could be a lot more than Stuart let you be, Jennifer. I wouldn't be so quick to canonize the guy."

"That's crap. I know what I'm capable of. Stuart appreciated me for what I was." This time, Jennifer got up and poured more Scotch herself, leaving out both the ice and the water. She hiccupped. "Of course, Stuart wasn't much of a father himself, if his wife and children are to be believed." She staggered back to her seat, laughing a little.

"Are you sure you should be drinking this much?" Blake asked. "You know, alcoholism runs in families. And you've taken some drugs today, too."

Jennifer all but sneered at him. "Why? Worried that I won't show up for your Uncle's all-important motion tomorrow?"

Blake arched back, as if she'd thrown cold water on his concern. "I'm just worried. You've had about half that bottle already. I've never seen you drink so much before."

"Well, Mr. Perfect, I never saw Stuart lying on the ground with a hole in his chest before, either," she snapped.

Jennifer continued to drink, but all conversation between them ceased. He returned his gaze to Deborah Kerr. Jennifer sat alone on the couch now. She filled her glass twice more with liquid courage before she managed to get past her internal censor and ask him what was on her mind.

"Where did you get that tattoo on your back?" She finally slurred her questions out of lips that were numb with the effects of alcohol and Valium: "I'd like to get one just like it. What does it say, anyway?"

"Don't do that, Jennifer," he warned her, in a tone meant to discourage her from asking about the tattoo along with any further questions. "Why don't you go back to bed." Under normal circumstances, Jennifer would have been cowed and abandoned the topic. But these circumstances were anything but normal and Jennifer didn't let it go.

"Why not? I've never had a tattoo. I like that one. Does it mean long life or what?" Jennifer pushed him. Something in her befogged brain warned her against mentioning Annabelle James, but she burned to destroy Blake's pretenses. She knew he had an agenda with her and she feared he'd had one with Annabelle, too. She wanted to know what that agenda was. This was a test. He was failing.

Blake set his own glass down on the side table and rose to leave. "I'm going now. I'll call you tomorrow, when you're feeling better," he told her.

Just like a man, Jennifer thought. *If it looks like an uncomfortable moment, bug out. Good to find out Mr. Apollo has clay feet like all the rest.*

"I want to know why you won't tell me about that tattoo," she demanded. Jennifer hardly recognized her own voice. Then she realized that she sounded like her mother in the days when her father had been drinking. It was a time she'd buried in the deep recesses of her consciousness, along with much of her early childhood. She hadn't thought about those times in years.

Blake walked to the door. He reached for the doorknob. Jennifer knew she'd never work up the nerve to ask again unless she did so right now. "Blake. What is the big deal about that tattoo? I'd really like to know."

He looked at her, shrugged, and came back into the living room. Blake stood looking over the back of the couch where Jennifer was splayed out as Deborah Kerr had been in the movie. The Scotch glass dangled, half full, from her left hand. Jennifer felt surreal. Was she herself? Or was this the movie? She didn't know anymore.

"I don't want you to get this tattoo, or any other tattoo. They're dangerous," he said, as if explaining to a child.

"But why?" Jennifer insisted once too often.

Blake's demeanor changed instantly, as if she'd thrown a switch. His face suffused with blood, giving him a crazed look. His eyes were enraged and his nostrils flared. He sneered at her.

"It's none of your business, Jennifer. I said 'no,' and I meant 'no.' Now get off my back." He turned and strode to the exit. Blake pulled the heavy door open in one swift jerk, walked through, and slammed it behind him.

Jennifer stared at the closed door in disbelief. She put her hand up to her face. She felt as if he'd actually slapped her.

CHAPTER FIFTY-FOUR

AFTER BLAKE LEFT, JENNIFER tried the toll-free number Debbie and Clay had given her for calling the cruise ship. When she dialed it, she got a recording and an automated menu, but she was too drunk to follow the directions. It took her three tries to work her way through the menu. She ended up at a voice mailbox and left a message.

Her parents had been gone too long. She'd tried to call twice before, with the same results. Nor had she gotten any e-mail from them. Jennifer told herself they were simply having too much fun to keep in touch with their only child. The entire trip would last just two weeks. They'd be back soon. She'd survive until then. She had to hang on.

CHAPTER FIFTY-FIVE

ROGER RILEY DRESSED FOR court. As he put the gold pin through the collar of his sharply starched and pressed pinpoint oxford shirt, he whistled a happy tune. "Roger. You're a winner," he said to his reflection in the mirror. He knew it. Everybody knew it.

"Today is the day, my man. Today, you'll beat Stuart Barnett's ass in federal court. Barnett will be finished. Dead in the water."

A big wide grin split Roger's face as if he'd won the biggest prize in the world. Roger would conquer Barnett, once and for all. When Roger finished with Barnett today, Barnett would never practice law effectively in this town again. "Ladies and gentlemen, may I present the one, the only 'king of courts,' Roger Riley," he exclaimed, mimicking a boxing promoter, as he examined his appearance for tiny flaws. He found none. He could almost see a crown on his head. He laughed.

Roger had worked all day the day before, sequestered in his study at home until the wee hours of the morning. He had studied like he hadn't done since he'd passed the bar exam. He ignored his office, his telephone calls, and all forms of distraction. No television, radio, or even newspapers. No sex. He trained like an athlete, with the single-mindedness of the big stars. Nothing was more important than his preparation. Roger was ready. Barnett didn't have a chance.

Alive with anticipation, Roger felt every nerve cell in his body tingle. He smoothed down the bright orange Hermes tie he'd bought on his last trip to Palm Beach, slipped on the fine Italian custom-made suit jacket, and stepped back to admire the total effect.

Roger liked what he saw. The outfit would be perfect on video for the news cameras. He'd ordered his staff to get the cameras to the courthouse this morning, pronto. They would film him on his way into and out of the building, both. He'd prepared appropriate sound bites for his confident entrance and his victorious exit, and right here and now he practiced them once more.

One thought temporarily soured Roger's good mood. Damn federal court, anyway. In state court, the cameras could be right in the courtroom. They could record, for posterity, the excellent performance he'd deliver. In state court, Roger could get a copy of the game tape. He could splice it in a continuous loop and play the tape in his office, day and night. But for federal court, he'd have to be satisfied with the video of his before and after sound bites. All the drama would be sucked out of his victory, like one of those space-saving bags that flattened a down body-pillow into the size of a cereal box.

Well, Roger reminded himself, it couldn't be helped. His good mood returned. Barnett had chosen the forum for their standoff. And Roger knew why Barnett had chosen federal court. Barnett was a wuss, that was why.

So what if Barnett had once been a navy fighter pilot? He'd

gone soft. Too much cerebral work across the bridge in that tall office building with the rarefied air. Too many fawning people bowing to his every whim.

Barnett only wanted to play on the field where he thought he had the advantage. Where he believed he could win. Never mind. Roger's victory would be all the sweeter for the extra effort that would be required. Roger would beat Barnett on his favorite turf.

The doorbell rang. Roger had scheduled his driver to pick him up at home in the Rolls Royce Silver Cloud, his favorite of the three luxury cars he owned. He'd managed to wrestle it from the third Mrs. Roger Riley in their divorce. Roger had bought the Rolls from a CEO he'd stomped into submission during the tobacco cases, so the car had special significance. Roger smiled at the memory, which filled him with pride.

The Rolls was a part of today's carefully choreographed public performance. Roger would be seen in the Rolls, but not driving it. *How gauche. No.*

The entrance he wanted to make was meticulously framed: important, successful, champion of the people, Roger Riley arrives at the coliseum to eviscerate the king lion, for once and for all. Roger grinned to himself at the image and resisted the urge to break into song.

CHAPTER FIFTY-SIX

JENNIFER'S ALARM CLOCK WOKE her with shrill, incessant screeching from across the room. When she tried to raise her head from the pillow, pounding nausea kept her plastered to the bed like steel to a magnet.

A few minutes later, the timer turned on the television in the living room at full volume, blasting her senses with sickeningly cheerful introductory music for the morning news. Jennifer had deliberately turned up the volume to maximum last night so she wouldn't oversleep. For a few moments, she couldn't remember why she had to get up.

Then yesterday's events dragged her back to life like the undertow sucks a surfer to his death. Even the momentary recollection of the day before threatened to plunge Jennifer into an abyss of despair. But she had only two hours to get ready and get to court.

Jennifer forced her legs over the side of her bed and her feet to the floor. When she reached a sitting position, nausea propelled her to the bathroom where she vomited her dinner: a disgusting amount of Dewar's and a bag of microwave popcorn.

In fiction, people always feel better after expelling noxious substances. Jennifer didn't. She felt as if she were on the brink of death. Jennifer wished for death. She believed in heaven and she knew that no one in heaven would feel as bad as she felt today, so she wanted to get there. Jennifer looked in the mirror and groaned out loud. How much had she drunk last night, anyway?

She'd seen terminally ill patients who looked better. Her hair stood out all over her head as if she were a cartoon character who had stuck her finger in a light socket with shocking results. Her face was a sickly shade of pale and the dark circles under her eyes looked like bruises. Her mouth tasted like something had died in there—some weeks ago.

Jennifer looked back at the bed longingly. Why not return to bed, cover her head, and never come out? Only for Stuart could she consider going to court or anywhere else today. Whatever else he was, Russell Denton had hit the nail on the head when he'd told her that Stuart would want her to do this thing. "The client comes first, Jennifer," Stuart had told her over and over.

She marched herself into the shower stall and stuck her head under the merciless spray.

After a thirty-minute shower, Jennifer did her best to ready herself to go to court. She put on her makeup and more or less tamed her hair. Dressed in a blue suit and white blouse, she slipped on her pumps, picked up her briefcase, and walked down to her car without bothering to look in the mirror again. What was the point? This was the best she could do.

As she pulled out through the security gate, Jennifer considered going to the airport and flying to South America or Africa, or anyplace where Russell and Blake Denton and Ronald Walden could never find her. Somewhere that would let her grieve for Stuart. She'd go home to her mother if her mother were there.

Jennifer didn't want to go to court, or to face Rabid Roger Riley. She had never wanted to face Riley, in court or anywhere else. And certainly not today, of all days.

Jennifer turned her car away from the airport road and headed downtown.

CHAPTER FIFTY-SEVEN

A GAGGLE OF REPORTERS MILLED around the outside of the Sam M. Gibbons Federal Courthouse on Florida Avenue. News vans with satellite feeds to networks and the all-news station were parked near the building's entrance. Reporters holding microphones faced photographers carrying cameras on their shoulders, filming their leads.

Roger had instructed his own video people to record all of the major news broadcasts on all channels. He wanted a montage of coverage to savor later in bed with Thomasina—along with the magnum of French champagne he'd been saving for Stuart Barnett's demise in the courtroom at Roger's hands.

Roger asked his driver to circle the block so he could get a feel for the reporters. On the second pass, the driver stopped in the traffic lane, put on his flashers, and pressed the horn a couple of times, giving the photographers time to get their lights ready and to focus. Then, the chauffeur walked around to the right passenger door. Roger stepped out of the car regally, the king of courts.

When he emerged from the Rolls, Roger wore a serious face, an expression that said, "I'm here for justice." Gone was his glee.

He delivered his prepared remarks like an actor, making sure he looked straight at every camera at least once. He'd trained himself not to blink.

Roger never once mentioned Stuart Barnett's name, which would have been bad form. Like every game, this one had rules. For the public view, Roger's job was to represent his client zealously, within the bounds of the law.

Roger's remarks were carefully limited to the clients and the merits of Annabelle James's case. When he was asked whether he'd say more after the hearing, Roger simply answered, "I'm sure we'll be able to report a complete victory for Annabelle James when we return."

After the cameras were stilled, Roger talked off the record with the reporters for a while. When he left them to enter the courthouse, they settled in to await his return. Later, Roger wondered why no one mentioned that Stuart Barnett was already dead—literally. Maybe they had thought he'd surely known.

CHAPTER FIFTY-EIGHT

JUDGE WILHELMINA CARSON LOOKED down on Jennifer and Rabid Roger from her perch on the bench the way an eagle regards a couple of small ducks left alone by their mother, Jennifer thought. She felt, indeed, like easy prey.

Jennifer knew she should have been pleased that her case was reassigned to Judge Carson, through some miracle of God. The original judge had inexplicably recused himself late yesterday. Judge Carson was, thankfully, impartial. She would give Jennifer a level playing field.

Reporters filled the gallery, their writing pads in hand. Jennifer was unnerved by their presence. Why were they here? Stuart was already dead. They would have nothing to see. No reporter would be interested in her.

Clients were not present. She and Stuart had discussed this bit of strategy. This type of motion was usually a routine legal matter that did not require client participation. They'd felt Russell Denton would be better served by his absence, especially since they knew Rabid Roger would have no client to bring. Jennifer could challenge Riley to produce his client, but unless she could prove that Annabelle hadn't hired him, Jennifer would look like a fool. Riley was too wily for that. He'd have a successful countermove planned.

Consistent with their desire not to appear to be overpowering Annabelle James, the "little gal in this farce," as Stuart had described her, they'd decided that only the lawyers should appear.

That was then. Right now, Jennifer was living out her worst nightmare. She was in court, alone, against Rabid Roger Riley, with an audience of reporters who would record her every mistake. She wasn't with Stuart. Even Russell Denton was absent. How could her life get any worse?

Judge Carson's reputation as strong but fair was small comfort to Jennifer. This judge brooked no nonsense of any kind, regardless of its source. Rabid Roger would not be allowed to engage in any of his shenanigans. But neither would Jennifer get much of a break. Justice was evenly applied in Judge Carson's courtroom.

Jennifer gathered her notes and approached the podium when the case was called. It was her motion and she was first. The podium was too tall, and Jennifer was dwarfed by it. She could only see the judge if she stood to one side and looked up because the judge was elevated on her bench. Rather than feeling at a disadvantage this way, Jennifer felt a little better being able to hide behind the tall, wooden box.

The microphones used to record the proceedings amplified Jennifer's reticent, quiet words. She read her entire argument from the prepared text in a quaver that sometimes lapsed into complete, utter silence. Judge Carson paid close attention to every word.

When Jennifer had finished, Rabid Roger took the stage. In stark contrast to Jennifer, his delivery was masterful, his arguments cogent, his reasoning sound.

When Riley returned to his seat, Jennifer was granted time to rebut. She could think of nothing to say in response to his eloquence, even if she could have forced herself to get up there again. She declined.

Judge Carson turned toward her microphone. "Normally, on a matter so recently assigned to me, I might take a motion such as this under advisement."

Jennifer gave silent thanks for these opening remarks. That was one of the outcomes they had hoped for. Sometimes, it took months or years to get a ruling from a federal judge. As long as the motion wasn't denied, it was still alive and could be used in litigation and settlement strategies. If Judge Carson took the motion under advisement it wasn't the out-and-out win Russell Denton wanted, but the result was usable. Jennifer crossed her fingers under the table and offered up a desperate prayer.

Judge Carson looked at Jennifer with something like pity. Jennifer cringed. Was it so obvious to everyone that Jennifer was no match for Roger Riley? She was ill, suffering from Stuart's loss, and had totally disappointed everyone with her horrible performance. Jennifer tried to think positive thoughts, to influence the judge. Fortunately, most federal judges didn't believe in oral arguments anyway. Usually, they relied on the papers and Jennifer had filed a pretty good brief. She told herself she hadn't failed yet.

"I'm sorry for your recent loss, Ms. Lane," Judge Carson said. "Stuart Barnett was a fine man and an excellent lawyer. We all mourn his passing."

Jennifer looked over at Riley and was gratified to see that he looked as if a bayonet had just been ripped into his gut. Jennifer had thought Stuart's loss meant little to Riley. Or Riley felt relieved that his only true opponent was permanently removed from the game. Now, he looked like a fish left to die on the beach when the tide receded. Jennifer felt something like satisfaction.

"Do you have anything more to add?" Judge Carson asked Jennifer. Although she was grateful for the judge's consideration, Jennifer didn't believe she would ever do any better on this motion than she'd done today. If she had two or three weeks to think about it, she might die of anxiety. She was better off just relying on the papers she'd filed and hoping for the best.

Jennifer stood and leaned into the microphone at the counsel table. She was amazed that her voice emerged at all from her constricted throat. "No, Your Honor. We filed an extensive brief that I know the court will consider. We'll rest on our papers."

Judge Carson looked at Jennifer again. "Are you sure? I'm prepared to rule, but I will wait if you have anything more to offer."

Jennifer's heart fell to her feet. She knew what was coming. She'd known it before she ever entered the courtroom. "I'm sure, Judge. But thank you."

"All right, then. After carefully considering the papers filed by the parties and listening to oral arguments in open court, Denton Bio-Medical's motion for a temporary restraining order is denied. We'll prepare and send an order. We're adjourned." With that, Judge Carson left the bench, and the courtroom broke into absolute bedlam.

Before he turned to perform for the print reporters seated in the gallery, Roger Riley approached Jennifer. She prepared herself to accept the equivalent of the tennis "good game" handshake offered to the loser by the champ.

Instead, he reached over, patted her cheek, and said to her, "Don't feel bad, sweetie. Your case was always a loser. Even Stuart Barnett wouldn't have pulled it out. He was good, but not that good."

Maybe Riley was trying to make her feel better, but Jennifer took the comment as a slam against Stuart, not a sop to her ego. Her head pounding, her heart broken, her tail between her legs, Jennifer had nothing more to lose.

"Roger," she said as she passed him, loud enough for the reporters to hear. "You are a horse's ass."

CHAPTER FIFTY-NINE

RUSSELL DENTON SAT IN a high-backed green leather chair behind his formal, black lacquered desk, looking every inch the multimillionaire. He wore his habitual casual clothes. A melon-hued silk golf shirt, Egyptian-cotton khaki trousers, and bench-made loafers all looked like JCPenney to the untrained eye, but they were custom-tailored originals and very expensive. The deliberately staged picture was one of money and power. He gazed across the desk at Jennifer Lane seated on his left side and Blake on the right in matching leather club chairs.

Russell listened as Jennifer reported on the hearing. Losing the TRO motion had angered Russell, but his anger was directed at himself. He should never have hired this woman in the first place. She had been outmatched from the start. Instead of following his better instincts, he'd allowed Tyler to convince him that Annabelle James might return the HepZMax formula if they hired Jennifer. It had seemed like an acceptable tactical decision while Stuart Barnett was alive. Now, Russell very much regretted his choice.

In his left hand at this moment, Russell Denton held the premarket approval application for HepZMax that had been filed yesterday with the FDA by his biggest competitor. While he had sat in a conference room discussing tactics for the hearing, Roger Riley had been girding himself for the real battle. But Riley had also laid down his trump card. The man was a master strategist. Once he filed the FDA application, Denton Bio-Medical's chances of quietly retrieving HepZMax died. Riley won twice.

Russell's life was falling down around him. Two days ago, when he'd seen Blake on tape betraying him, the last of his illusions about his nephew had been shattered. Yesterday, he'd been in the presence of a madman and watched another man gunned down in cold blood. Today, he held in his hand the death of his company and everything he'd worked to build. He looked again at the FDA application. It might as well have been the signature on his own death warrant.

Russell looked up from the application toward Jennifer, then to Blake and back again. Jennifer's love for Blake was almost a separate presence in the room. Russell felt like a voyeur. And he felt guilty. Jennifer deserved better than his nephew. She wasn't Blake's type. At the outset, Russell had tried to thwart Blake's womanizing. He'd hired Jennifer, in part, because he'd believed Blake wouldn't be interested in her. Something else he'd been wrong about.

As Jennifer described her morning in court, she was a different woman from the one who'd fainted yesterday in her office. What had happened? The fire in her eyes, the flair of her nostrils, her harsh tones, all suggested a strength he'd never seen her display before.

"What I'm telling you, Russell, is that I've decided to win this case," Jennifer said. "Roger Riley is a jerk. Stuart was the only lawyer in town who could keep him in line. Now that falls to me. I will beat Roger Riley for you in court. We will win this case."

Jennifer's resolve was wonderful to behold. If she'd simply had that level of confidence at the beginning, Russell might have been able to stick with her. But not now. Every competitive advantage had been lost. Russell had no choice but to get rid of her.

He shook his head. "I'm sorry, Jennifer," he told her. Better to come right out with bad news, like ripping off a scab. The faster you do the job, the briefer the pain. "I'm going to have to replace you."

Both Jennifer and Blake looked shocked at his words. Blake was the first to protest out loud. "But Jennifer is the best lawyer for us here. We already decided that. She needs to stay on the case."

"I can do this, Russell. Let me prove it to you." Jennifer said, with more conviction than he'd ever heard from her before.

"I'd like to do that. But I can't. Not now."

"What do you mean?" Blake asked, the now familiar hidden anger bubbling up to the surface.

"Why?" Jennifer asked, simultaneously.

Russell threw the HepZMax application across the desk to his nephew. "Because Alabaster Medical has our HepZMax formula. They've filed a PMA. I'm sure they're paying Riley's legal fees. When we lost the motion for a temporary restraining order today, that gave them the green light. They'll go ahead with their clinical trials. We'll never recover."

Blake glanced at the application and then handed it over to Jennifer. He pinched the base of his nose and creased his forehead. He was the picture of concern. Russell would have laughed if the matter were less serious.

"We need seasoned, hard-assed New York lawyers to get this job done and get it done quickly. We need some regulatory affairs folks in D.C. on our side. We need political clout." Russell looked at Jennifer directly now, in a kindly way, but with firmness. "You can't do any of that, Jennifer, and we both know it."

Russell watched Jennifer start to object to his statements. She tried to do so, but could not. Stuart Barnett might have pulled off a miracle at this point, but he wasn't here anymore. And Jennifer didn't have the experience or the strength. She didn't have the full support of her own firm, either. As much as she'd hate to admit it, Jennifer had to know Russell was right. She was the wrong woman for the job.

Blake continued to argue against Russell's decision, and, although Russell remained respectfully silent, he tuned Blake out. He'd made up his mind before he'd called them into his office. As soon as he heard about the decision on the TRO and opened Alabaster Medical's hand-delivered document minutes afterward, Russell knew that he had lost. Damage control was required now, and he had to do it quickly. He'd already placed the necessary calls.

When Blake finally stopped his futile arguing, Russell said, "Jennifer, I'll let you know where to send our files." He stood, his hand outstretched, and came around the desk to walk her to the door. "I'm sorry. This is a purely business decision. It's not a personal one. I've truly come to respect you. We may be able to do business together again, sometime. I hope you and Blake will join me for dinner one day next week."

Jennifer looked at him directly, anger still fresh, obvious. "Is that why you hired me? To get a date for Blake?"

In response, Russell laughed heartily. "I assure you, Blake has no problem getting dates." Then a troubled expression clouded his face. "Or we might not be in the mess we're in now."

"What do you mean?" Jennifer asked.

Russell made another decision. It was time to do the right thing regarding Jennifer. He should have told her long ago. Russell's list of regrets was growing longer. "Because if he hadn't slept with Annabelle James," Russell told her, still holding her hand, "she wouldn't have come to hate him when he dumped her. And we'd still have our formula, as well as a chance to save my life."

Jennifer pulled her hand away and stuffed it in her pocket. "Blake? Is that true?" she asked him, in the voice of a young girl who has been betrayed by her best friend.

Blake looked away, then back toward Jennifer. "Annabelle wasn't what I thought she was. When I found out, I broke it off with her. That's when she took the formula."

Russell marveled at Blake's ability to lie that smoothly. He was so convincing, Russell might have believed him, if he hadn't known better. Russell continued, "But she blamed me. She thought Blake dumped her because I told him to do it. That's why she took HepZMax. She wanted to hand me a death sentence."

His own lies sounded as plausible as Blake's. Maybe because Russell's lies were almost true.

"Why?" Jennifer leaned against the door now, seeming to be unable to stand.

Blake said, "Don't worry, Jennifer. I don't have Hep Z and it's not contracted like that anyway. It's not like AIDS. You're not in any personal danger."

Russell looked at his nephew with real sadness, and with love. "But I do. That's why I can't waste any more time, Jennifer. I have to get HepZMax back and I have to do it my way. I'm sorry. I never meant for you and Stuart to get hurt."

Jennifer looked at them both, all the loss and anguish she felt in full view. She opened the door and exited through it, her back ramrod straight. Blake followed. Russell stood watching them walk down the hall for a few seconds, until they turned the corner out of sight, then he returned to his desk and picked up the phone.

CHAPTER SIXTY

"WHEN WERE YOU GOING to tell me, Blake? How long were you going wait?" Jennifer asked. She made no effort to hide her consuming anger. They stood outside the Denton Bio-Medical plant, in the visitor's parking lot.

She wanted to be shocked and outraged, but she wasn't. The tattoo on Blake's back confessed long before. Everyone knew Blake had been involved with Annabelle. Jennifer felt mortified, betrayed. But she couldn't deny she had only herself to blame. She'd known Blake's affection for her was too good to be true from the beginning.

Blake hung his head but the gesture looked rehearsed. He must have anticipated Jennifer would find out about his affair with Annabelle James at some point. He didn't seem to care about the outcome.

"Well?" she repeated. "Can't you have the decency to tell me about it, even now?"

"I didn't know how to bring it up. I wanted to tell you." Sincerity fairly oozed from his pores.

Jennifer cocked her head and looked at him critically. She

wanted to believe him. She'd already admitted to herself that she loved Blake. Right now, after losing Stuart just yesterday and the Denton Bio-Medical case a few minutes ago, a breakup with Blake was simply too much for her to cope with.

Jennifer's anxiety returned all at once, full force, landing with the speed of an asteroid striking the earth. Her head began to pound and she felt the all-too-familiar nausea. Pain shot bright lights between her eyes and narrowed her vision. For the second time in as many days, Jennifer felt she might faint.

She opened the door to her car, turned on the ignition and flipped the air conditioner to full blast. She rummaged around in her purse for her prescription Xanax. Sometimes Xanax relieved her symptoms, if she took it early enough.

"I have to go, Blake," she told him, trying to close the door. His body was between the door and the car, preventing her from getting away, and he wouldn't move.

"Not yet. Let me tell you." His pleading was excruciating to hear. "I thought I loved Annabelle, but I didn't know her. She was evil. Truly evil."

Jennifer felt no compassion. She felt as if she might die herself, if she didn't get home and go to bed. She said nothing, because she couldn't muster the ability to speak. She stared straight ahead, both hands on the wheel to support herself, her face absorbing the cold air from the vent.

"Annabelle is out of my life, Jennifer. I swear. Don't leave me. Please. I love you." Blake sounded so sincere. He wouldn't get away from the car. Jennifer couldn't close the door. She had to say something, if she could summon her voice.

She whispered. "Ronald Walden thinks Annabelle is dead, Blake. He could be right. Not everything is just about you. Maybe Annabelle was only trying to teach you a lesson. Someday, maybe you'll learn not to stomp the heart of a woman who loves you," Jennifer told him. She was too ill and too heartsick to sugarcoat her words for him now.

And she was through being a victim.

Blake jumped back from the inside of the car door, angry now. Just like yesterday, his mood changed as if she'd flipped a switch. The effect scared her, but there was not a thing she could do to change him.

"How can you say that? I've been nothing but wonderful to you since we met. Even before we met. I'm the one who talked Uncle Russell into hiring you in the first place." Blake pounded his left hand on the top of the door. "You'd never have gotten this case at all if it wasn't for me!"

For the first time since they'd met, Jennifer said exactly what she was thinking. "Well, don't do me any more favors, okay? Because of you, two people are dead and I just got fired. So stay out of my life."

Blake slammed the door shut, shaking the entire car.

Jennifer backed out of the parking space and squealed her tires in the turn onto Bruce B. Downs Boulevard. When she glanced back in the rearview mirror, Blake was still standing there, hands on his hips, color high. Jennifer focused on her driving. For the first time in her life, Jennifer Lane had gotten the last word in an argument and walked away from a man. She felt good about that. Really good.

She made it all the way home on the strength of her anger. Then she walked into her empty apartment and collapsed onto the bed in painful tears.

CHAPTER SIXTY-ONE

AT ST. PAUL'S EPISCOPAL CHURCH, Stuart's casket commanded attention. Jennifer had arrived late and sat in the back pew without speaking to anyone. She didn't want a front-row seat at Stuart's funeral. She didn't want Stuart to be dead at all. As the organ began to play, Jennifer's lips turned up in a sad smile. Stuart hated that hymn. If he were here, he'd have insisted on something different. How she wished Stuart were here. But she couldn't think about that now or she'd never make it through the next two hours.

When she'd settled into her seat, the wild thoughts she'd been battling resumed chasing each other around in her head. She became barely conscious of her surroundings.

Jennifer spoke to no one. She fell into the silence habit she'd developed too easily during the week she'd spent closeted at home, refusing visitors and phone calls. Her emotions fluctuated wildly from anger to sorrow to self-pity and back again. Each piece of news sent her careening like a sharply struck billiard ball. She'd stayed mired in turmoil with no way out for days.

First she'd been fired by Russell Denton, single-handedly losing the firm's biggest client. The next piece of news came by fax from the Florida Bar. That bitch, Melanie Stein, had filed an ethics complaint against her. Jennifer had lost her protector when Stuart died and Melanie's complaint was the straw that made the remaining Worthington partners wash their hands of Jennifer Lane faster than a surgeon scrubs dirt from his nails.

The partners, cowards all, hadn't had the balls to tell her in person. No. The office manager had called.

"You're suspended, Ms. Lane," the pompous bastard said.

She'd listened in silence as tears streamed down her face, desperately trying to muffle her pathetic mewing.

"Perhaps you'd be better suited elsewhere," he said before he hung up.

After that, she'd accepted no further calls.

She was aware that the organ played on, filling the church with hymns meant to comfort. The sonorous music failed to crowd frantic thinking from Jennifer's mind. Without her job, who was she? Where would she go? What would she do? Solutions continued to evade her.

She'd spent hours imagining scenarios in which Stuart had survived Ronald Walden's gunshots. He was under FBI protection at the hospital. Maybe he'd left the country. Perhaps he was recovering at home with his family. All of the plots she devised had happy endings. She could barely stand to leave them. She might have stayed secluded forever had not respect for Stuart and one other thing pulled her here.

When the service began, perhaps she could concentrate on her purpose instead.

Mourners continued filing in. A few nodded toward Jennifer, but she ignored them. Her bench filled with people who pressed closer until her body was shoved uncomfortably against the pew's outside end. She said nothing.

Still they came, flooding the open spaces of the church and finally standing outside. The organ played on, a sonorous soundtrack for her guilty conscience.

Again, she pushed her focus to her purpose. She'd devoured the television news and read every word of the newspapers left at her door. "Ronald Walden still at large," they claimed. A situation she intended to rectify today.

Posted at the church exits, Jennifer saw several men who could only be cops. They'd come hoping Walden would attend Stuart's funeral. She'd read that killers often do. She hoped he would.

Jennifer knew Walden. She'd recognize him, if he showed his face here. She'd make sure he was caught. Her plan was tenuous, but the very least she could do for Stuart. Maybe, once Walden was arrested, Jennifer could find at least a beginning of peace.

The organ never waited a moment to catch a spoonful of silence. Nor did Jennifer's relentless brain. Replayed in her mind's eye, she saw the televised interviews with Lila Walden. Dressed like the fifties housewife, Donna Reed, Lila had appeared poised, seemingly unconcerned by recent events. Lila's daughter and husband were both missing, and she repeatedly said, "No, I haven't seen them." She didn't seem worried in the slightest, which was doubly odd. Was she in shock?

Jennifer worried enough for them both, though. She worried about where Ronald Walden was and what he would do next. Jennifer worried about her own personal safety. Would he try to kill her, too? She stayed inside secure, locked doors and gates wherever possible. She kept her gun by her side constantly. She felt naked without it right now, but guns were not allowed in church. Police officers posted at the doors made her feel only slightly safer. After all, they hadn't protected Stuart, had they?

A large woman wearing spike heels muscled her way toward Jennifer from the middle of the pew. "Excuse me," she said, a bit too loudly.

Jennifer heard, drew her knees closer to her body, and let the woman struggle past leaving a whiff of Chanel No. 5 in her wake.

The scent renewed a migraine that had started the day Stuart died and raged for five days, exacerbated by Melanie's complaint and Worthington's phone call. For three of those days she couldn't leave her bed, let alone her home. She hadn't spoken to Blake, although he'd left several messages on her answering machine. She lacked the stamina to deal with him.

Maybe the poets were right. Maybe there was only a thin line between love and hate. If so, she was on the negative side with Blake at the moment. Would she be able to get over her hurt and her anger? She didn't think so. The moment she'd heard him admit his affair with Annabelle James, the love she'd thought she felt for him shriveled up and blew away. She could never love a man without trust, and she would never be able to trust Blake again.

"Excuse me," the overwhelming perfumed woman said before she stepped on Jennifer's foot on her way back to her seat.

The noxious odor and sharp pain pushed Jennifer's thoughts toward Melanie.

Melanie had dropped Jennifer like a hot skillet right after she'd stabbed Jennifer in the back with that ethics complaint. She was told to report to the grievance committee of the Florida Bar in two weeks. Everyone knew Jennifer had no defense to the charges of conflict of interest. The best result she could hope for would be a reprimand—a result the firm would never accept. One thing was certain: her career at Worthington was over.

Melanie would answer for that. Somehow.

Jennifer's parents had called once while she was sleeping, but she had been unable to get a return call through to them. Where were they? Their absence made her feel even more bereft. She was alone in the world, and she wasn't learning to cope with it.

She felt the mood in the church shift like a change in atmospheric pressure. The organ completed one hymn and began another. She recognized Stuart's favorite "Peace in the Valley." Jennifer began to cry. A man behind her placed a calming hand on her shoulder, but failed to comfort her.

The tears, once released, refused to stop. She cried through Stuart's entire funeral, sadness and loss threatening to overwhelm her. Everyone noticed. Stuart's wife and children were less upset than Jennifer was. Stares, ranging from curious to mean, were cast her way. But Jennifer didn't care.

Stuart Barnett had been more like a father to her than a mentor. Her own dad was too far away, too fragile; not as wise; not physically or emotionally available for a long, long time.

The funeral forced her to accept that Stuart was truly gone. Jennifer cried for Stuart and for her own loss.

Embarrassed but unable to control either her tears or her deep despair, her sobs echoed in the high-ceilinged house of worship at every silence in the service, winning every battle she waged to stop them.

Jennifer looked around the church for distraction and it didn't take long to find the perfect one. Blake and Russell Denton. She saw the backs of their heads in one of the middle pews. Melanie was there, too. Even Rabid Roger had made an appearance. The gall of the man was unsurpassed in Jennifer's experience. How could he even think about coming to Stuart's funeral?

Without conscious effort, Jennifer's crying abruptly stopped. She felt welcome anger, hatred almost, radiating from every heartbeat through the remainder of the service.

She did not see Ronald Walden. If he'd attended, he'd concealed himself from her view. There were so many people crowding the grounds, hiding wouldn't have been difficult. Another failure.

Afterward, Jennifer slipped quickly out the door before the casket returned the length of the aisle, in the same direction that couples traveled after marriage. Jennifer's beloved Stuart was no more, and she was forced to embark on a new life in sad parody of those hopeful brides.

Once outside she didn't linger. She couldn't bear to watch Stuart's last "repose" inside the hearse or at the graveside. Nor was she capable of speaking to Stuart's friends or enemies. She could not make conversation, and she wanted no condolences, so she hurried away to walk the few blocks home.

Jennifer hadn't spoken a single word.

She was bewildered. Lost. Numb. Ignoring the pain of losing Stuart would mean she'd feel nothing at all. Jennifer had spent five long years trying to fit into Stuart's foreign and inhospitable world. He was the only reason she'd stayed at Worthington. With Stuart gone, she simply didn't know what to do.

Consciously putting one foot in front of the other, Jennifer considered what to do next. She knew she should snap out of it, find some purpose for her life, and get herself together, all those pop psychology phrases Melanie used to feed her. But she just couldn't do it. She couldn't bring herself to shed her sorrow. It had become a comfort to her; an enveloping sensation that she could rely on. And it made her feel something.

Jennifer walked along Morrison Avenue, head low, still thinking about losing Stuart. She vaguely registered an old blue Nissan pulling over to the curb in front of her and the passenger door opening.

When she reached the car, Lila Walden called out, "Get in. We'll go have a cup of coffee."

Exhausted by the service, the heat, and her fragile emotions, having failed to find Ronald Walden, weary in body and spirit, Jennifer simply followed her habit and did what she was told.

CHAPTER SIXTY-TWO

TYLER WATCHED FROM HIS Xterra as Jennifer left the church and walked half a block toward home. He saw Lila Walden's blue Nissan pull over to the curb and Jennifer get in the car. Tyler had installed a listening device in Lila's car, but he couldn't access it from the Xterra. This working as a one-man operation was a real handicap. At the FBI, he'd have had backup. Someone would have been monitoring all this shit for him. He slapped his hand on the steering wheel. "Crap!"

The exclamation made him grin. Lori had been hounding him not to swear in front of the kids, so he'd been trying to break the habit. Perhaps better curses had abandoned his vocabulary. Lori would be glad to know it.

Tyler followed Lila Walden to a rundown house on Davis Islands. The street lacked a satisfactory surveillance point, so he watched from the corner as Lila parked the car and the two women entered the unkempt house. Then he drove around the block seeking to park and wait.

Ronald Walden's truck was not in the immediate area. When the truck had fallen off the radar, Tyler had had a tough choice to make. He'd picked Lila as the one most likely to lead him to Ronald. So Tyler had been following Lila for days, but Ronald's old red truck never returned home. Tyler hadn't caught sight of it, even once. Maybe he'd get lucky here on Como Street.

When Jennifer and Lila left the house about an hour later, the truck still had not appeared, dashing Tyler's hopes. "Crap!" he said again. He started the car and followed Lila back to Jennifer's apartment. After that, he followed Lila home.

Once back in her neighborhood, he settled into his favorite spot on North C, down a couple of blocks from the Waldens' but with a clear view of the front of the house and the driveway. He was almost invisible there, he knew. And he was a patient man. He could wait.

An old drunk like Ronald Walden wouldn't find it easy to start a new life. He'd come home eventually. Tyler was a patient man.

CHAPTER SIXTY-THREE

"I DON'T REALLY WANT to talk now, Lila," Jennifer said, after she had settled into the passenger seat. Her voice sounded rusty. "Can you just drop me off at home?"

Lila said, "I'll take you home, but there's someone I want you to meet first." She turned away from Jennifer's apartment and drove south to Bayshore Boulevard.

Jennifer noticed the direction the car was taking, but didn't protest. She'd muster the energy soon. Very soon. But not yet.

Lila continued driving east until she reached the long bridge to Davis Islands. She eventually parked on Como Street in front of a small ranch-style house that resembled Lila's own home. Hundreds of these small ranches must have been built around South Tampa in the sixties. This one was not as well kept as the Waldens'. No flowers lined the driveway and the paint was peeling in many places. The doors and windows were shut tight against the summer heat. The air conditioning inside was presumably on high.

"Where are we?" Jennifer asked, surprised to feel a small spark of curiosity.

"You'll see. Come on." Lila parked the car and got out. Jennifer followed. Lila rang the doorbell and waited a few moments before she opened the glass storm door and then the solid aluminum door and entered the frigid house. Jennifer followed.

Lila sat down in the living room on a couch that the Salvation Army wouldn't have accepted. The arms and the cushions were frayed at the edges, and the entire sofa sagged in the middle. The fabric upholstery was a synthetic plaid that looked like a man's flannel hunting shirt.

The house was cluttered with well-used, or simply worn-out, mismatched furnishings. Dirt thick enough to plant tomatoes had settled on every available surface. The vague odor of incense hung in the brittle air.

Jennifer stood, hands folded in front of her, unwilling to touch anything, and simply waited. She had no idea why they were there, but she knew Lila well enough by now to realize she wouldn't be pushed. Resisting Lila was futile.

Minutes passed. Lila read a magazine while Jennifer resisted sad thoughts of Stuart's funeral. She was tired of crying, tired of being sad. Back when they were friends, Melanie had tried to convince Jennifer that her thoughts were what controlled her world. Melanie was a New Age convert from Judaism. She was always giving Jennifer advice on how to improve her life.

Melanie told Jennifer many times that she could change her life simply by changing her approach to situations as they appeared. Jennifer wanted to believe her, but her efforts to resurrect Stuart through positive thinking had failed. The silly idea made her smile.

For a few minutes in Russell Denton's office, Jennifer had thought maybe things could change. She actually felt powerful then, as if she could take on Roger Riley and win. But Russell wasn't willing to give her another chance.

And why should he have? It's not as if you've done anything to gain his confidence. You hid in a corner with your eyes squeezed shut while Ronald Walden shot and killed Stuart. You lost every battle on Denton's case you were asked to fight. He'd have been crazy to keep you.

Yet something in Jennifer clung to the hopeful words the otherwise treacherous Melanie had gifted to her. Jennifer hoped her feelings were simply a matter of lack of support and love in her life. Stuart had supported her in his own way. He'd played Nero Wolfe to her Archie with genuine affection. She knew he had. Knew it. Without Stuart to rely on, she'd need a big change. She welcomed that idea. Craved it, really. She felt now was the time. But what change? And how?

As quickly as the seeds of her optimism began to germinate, Jennifer was overcome again with grief. How would she function without Stuart? Emotions washed through her like ocean waves hitting the sand. The pounding guilt receded for a minute and calm intervened, and then harsh reality returned with stronger force than the previous onrush.

She looked at Lila calmly reading a magazine. What was Jennifer doing here? Allowing Lila to lead her was easier than fighting to rise above the emotional tide. Easy sounded great at the moment. She'd be ready for the fight soon. But not yet.

A door opened down the small hallway and Jennifer heard voices coming toward her. She looked up to see two women, one a visitor, walk past the living room entry and out the front door. The two women stood to talk briefly on the front porch.

The smaller woman came back into the house and joined

Jennifer and Lila in the living room. She nodded at Lila, then, extending her hand to Jennifer, she said, "I'm Abby Barnett, Ms. Lane. Welcome. Come this way."

Lila said, "Go on. She won't bite you."

Jennifer felt silly thinking maybe Lila was right. Could Abby Barnett have something, anything, helpful to give her? She had very little to lose and she was willing to try at this point. She couldn't simply walk home now. She shrugged. Why not?

She straightened her spine and followed Abby down the short, narrow hallway and into a small room on the right furnished with examples of eclectic spiritualism. Two large posters of book covers decorated the wall. *Abigail Barnett* was prominently printed on the bottom of each. The books were typical of several Melanie had given Jennifer to read. *Be Your Own Guide* was one of the titles. The other was *How to Manifest Your Dreams.*

So Abby Barnett was what? A therapist? A psychic?

Jennifer felt silly now, letting Lila lead her anywhere. She should have known better. She'd wait this out, get through it, and get the hell out of here.

Abby looked the part of a spiritual adviser. She resembled the descriptions of gypsies in stories for children with her wild, curly dark hair, small stature, dark eyes. Abby exuded a positive, soothing calm that enveloped Jennifer like a cocoon. Almost against her will, she felt relaxed, as if she'd known Abby all her life.

Abby handed Jennifer a deck of Tarot cards and told her to hold them in her right hand and shuffle with her left. "I want to get you out of your head for a while," Abby instructed. Jennifer did as she was told not simply through habit; getting out of her head seemed like a fine plan. She'd love to get out of her head.

"You're a Gemini, right?" Abby asked her.

Surprise widened Jennifer's eyes and prompted a quick response. "Lila told you?"

Abby smiled gently. "You seem to be two people to me. You have a tough side, and a weak side. But your weak side predominates."

Jennifer felt she must be wearing a sign on her forehead that said, "Ambivalence is my name."

"I'm very intuitive. I sense much about you and your life," Abby said.

"Like what?" Jennifer was intrigued, even though she figured Lila as Abby's information source.

"It's easy to see how unhappy you are right now. A friend died, and you feel abandoned," Abby told her. "But this will be a good thing for you."

Jennifer stopped shuffling the cards immediately and stared.

Abby said calmly, as if stating the most obvious logic, "Every soul must follow its own path. Stuart chose his fate. You must accept his choice."

Jennifer thought the woman must be insane. She said, "Why would Stuart choose to die? He had everything to live for. *Everything*."

"I can't answer that for you, Jennifer. Only Stuart's soul knows the actual answer. But, what I can tell you is that no amount of mourning on your part will bring Stuart back into your life. What matters now is how you deal with the situation that has been gifted to you."

Jennifer's anger overflowed like pent up lava. "*Gifted* to me? Are you kidding? My best friend is *dead* and I let it happen. How in the *hell* is that a gift?" But she didn't storm out of the room. Against all reason, she wanted to know Abby's answer.

Blunt words were softened and made more powerful by

Abby's quiet delivery. "The reality is that Stuart is no longer a part of your daily life. How are you going to deal with that?"

Jennifer had no idea how to answer. She would miss him forever—his laugh, his keen intelligence, his wit, his sense of honor. Stuart had, indeed, been one of a kind. He was irreplaceable.

Abby said, "Stuart will always be special to you. Nothing will change the feelings you have for him. You will always have those memories and that foundation to fall back on. Yet, he is gone and your destiny is to continue on your own journey."

Jennifer's heart knew Abby was right. Jennifer wanted to live in the past. At some point she'd have to let Stuart go. But not yet.

"You can continue to love Stuart, Jennifer. His spirit will be with you as long as you need it," Abby told her, still gentle. "But Stuart left you to set you free. What will you do with his gift, with that freedom?"

This time, Jennifer considered Abby's words. With Stuart gone, Jennifer's loyalty to him was released. She no longer needed to try to fit into his world, a world that didn't value her, didn't want her, where she couldn't excel. Worthington had never been the right place for Jennifer, as much as she'd wanted it to be. With Stuart gone, she could leave the firm forever. She actually began to feel a bit free. For a moment.

And do what? Go where?

Abby waited, allowing Jennifer to think things through. After a minute or so, she asked, "What will you do now?"

Jennifer had no idea what she would do next. She had been wallowing in pain for days. She felt comfortable there. Too comfortable.

Are you just going to die, too? Follow Stuart wherever he went? Is that who you are?

Abby gazed at the opposite wall, then spoke again, more forcefully. "I know it seems too soon, that you need to grieve Stuart longer. But I urge you not to do that, Jennifer. You'll never get over Stuart's death, not really. Don't waste any more time indulging your misery. Let it go. You must dust yourself off and move forward. Stuart's given you a growth opportunity for you, but *you* have to use it. What doesn't kill you makes you smarter, Archie."

Jennifer felt her mouth flop open. She stared into Abby's brown eyes as if she might see a twinkle of someone else there.

Stuart used to say that just to piss her off.

Immediately, Jennifer felt her spine straighten and her chin jut in the old response to Stuart's challenge. The rush of adrenaline was just what she needed.

CHAPTER SIXTY-FOUR

JENNIFER HAD NEVER BEEN inside the Denton home before and she wasn't quite sure what she was doing here now. Russell had asked her to come. She didn't owe him anything; she could have refused. But somehow, she felt maybe this was the first test of what Abby Barnett had called her life after Stuart. Or something.

She'd admired the house from Bayshore Boulevard whenever she drove past. You couldn't miss it. It was large enough to be a hotel. Gardeners worked daily on the park-like grounds. Flowering annuals appeared and disappeared with seasonal regularity Mother Nature would envy. Several buildings, each visible from the road, stood proudly for passersby to enjoy or despise, depending on their point of view.

Jennifer drove her PT Cruiser through the open gate and around the brick-paved circular drive. She parked in the center of the circle, at the foot of the steps leading to the front door, then flipped the visor down on the driver's side to check her appearance in the mirror.

Her hair curled wildly in the summer humidity; what little

makeup she'd applied had melted and slid off her face. She considered dabbing a little lipstick on her mouth again, but discarded the idea immediately. She wasn't a big city lawyer anymore and she could dress as she pleased. Russell Denton had summoned her; she was curious about his reasons. She hadn't promised to come bedazzled. She might never go anywhere uncomfortably bedazzled again. *Who knows?*

At the top of the outside steps, Jennifer rang the doorbell. She heard the chimes inside. While she waited, she turned and looked out across Hillsborough Bay. She could definitely get used to that view.

A small Latin woman opened the door. "Hello," she said in heavily accented English. "Mr. Russell is waiting." She gestured Jennifer into the foyer. "I'm Rosa," she told Jennifer after she'd closed the door. "Come."

Jennifer followed her deeper into the house, down a long corridor lined with Florida art. Several original works by Thomas McKnight, bold and colorful with strong Caribbean flavor. They seemed comfortable in the Mediterranean-style house.

They reached double doors more than eleven feet tall, dwarfed by the high ceilings.

"Mr. Russell, a woman to see you," Rosa called and knocked briefly before opening the door and waving her into the darkened room.

Jennifer's breath caught when she saw him. If Rosa hadn't used his name, she wouldn't have recognized him as the same man who had so terrified her such a short time ago.

Russell Denton sat in a Spanish-style wing chair close to a fireplace that, despite the heat outside, had a small fire burning. The room was uncomfortably warm, but he was dressed in a long-sleeved flannel shirt, trousers, socks, and shoes. Jennifer's flimsy

T-shirt and shorts felt damp in this heat, but Russell also had a sweater thrown over his shoulders.

"Come in, Jennifer," he told her.

Even his voice sounded weak. Gone were the commanding tones he'd used to dismiss her a few days before.

"Sit there." He gestured to the other Spanish armchair opposite his, closer so he didn't have to project his speech farther than he could manage.

She sat. His appearance had robbed her words.

"Thank you for coming. I wouldn't have, in your shoes." A faint wheeze escaped his lips. He pulled an oxygen cannula up from its resting place around his neck and placed it under his nose.

"Russell, are you all right?"

"Emerson said, 'The first wealth is health.' He knew what he was talking about." He wheezed again, longer this time.

Jennifer felt bewildered, as if she had fallen through Alice's looking glass again. It seemed her entire world was coming unglued. "But what's wrong with you? You looked great a few days ago. More than great, actually."

He struggled to breathe between short sentences. "Vietnam. Years ago. Like yesterday to me. I'm almost seventy now. In my heart. As young as Blake."

His choppy narrative stopped with his failing voice and he seemed unable to focus on the present. In a few seconds, though, he brought his attention back to Jennifer and tried again. "I was wounded. Blood transfusion."

Instantly, Jennifer understood so much that had baffled her before. His desperation to retrieve HepZMax and to get the formula from theory to treatment as soon as possible finally made sense.

She said, "You have Hep Z."

Russell coughed, a racking sound that Jennifer could feel inside her own chest and seemed to continue much too long. When he'd sipped water and could speak again, he said, "I was functioning well on treatment. Until I developed a hepatoma."

Liver cancer. She could think of nothing to say. The painful breaths and coughing made more sense to her, but were no easier to watch him struggle through.

"On a transplant list. New liver soon. Extend my life. Until HepZMax comes out."

If you live until then, Jennifer thought to herself, and felt sad for him, which she'd never have thought possible. "I'm really sorry, Russell. I should have guessed that you were sick, but I didn't."

Russell's laugh became another hacking cough that hurt to watch. How much worse it must be to experience.

He sucked more oxygen, filling his lungs, expanding his chest, sitting straighter in the chair. "I'm not that close to death yet. Although my liver is bad enough, what's bothering me now is a disease of my heart."

His voice was stronger, more determined. Maybe he was not as sick as he'd seemed. She hoped. He coughed again, but controlled it quicker.

Jennifer reached over to the table and picked up a tea cookie from the tray sitting there, more for something to do than because she wanted to eat anything. She poured herself a small glass of lemonade and refilled his. Again she noticed the room's stifling heat and the smell of burning wood, each oppressive in its own way.

What did he want from her?

While she busied herself with these small duties, Russell was able to regain control. She glanced at him. He'd fallen back against the chair, seemingly exhausted by the effort of mastering the last frightening cough.

She handed him the lemonade. He took a small sip, holding it in his mouth for a few seconds to subdue the involuntary coughing spasms.

"I wanted to talk with you about Blake."

Jennifer's back stiffened. She hadn't seen Blake since the day she'd left him standing alone in that parking lot—the day after Stuart died. She hadn't completely sorted out her ambivalent feelings for Blake yet, and she certainly didn't want to dissect them here with his uncle.

Now that the coughing was vanquished for now, his words came more easily. "There are things about Blake that you don't know. Things it pains me to recall, much less to share with you."

She knew Russell felt she wasn't good enough for his heir. Jennifer wasn't sure she was good enough, either. Nor that she wanted Blake at all. Stuart's death and her visit to Abby Barnett had given her a great deal of perspective on a lot of things. Had she been so desperate as to fall into a relationship with the first attractive man who pursued her? Obviously, she'd leaped into the situation before she knew everything about Blake that she should have.

Russell spoke again, firmly, as determined as she'd ever heard him. "I had one brother who died years ago. Blake is Donald's only child. We enjoyed an excellent relationship for years, but Blake now believes I'm somehow responsible for his father's failures in life. He intends to destroy me and everything that's important to me."

Jennifer didn't believe him and she didn't want to listen. His words were inconsistent with what she knew of Blake. He'd been tender and caring toward her, fun-loving and sweet, really. If

Blake was angry with Russell, he must have a reason—a good one. She half-rose from her chair.

Russell's next words felt like ice pellets hitting her sweat-soaked skin. "Donald was schizophrenic. Self-destructive. It's hereditary and manifests in young men around Blake's age. Do you understand?"

Russell's accusation plopped Jennifer hard into the chair. A moment passed. Two. She gathered her wits enough to argue.

"There's nothing wrong with Blake." But even as she defended him, was she sure? She'd witnessed his sudden, unexplainable mood swings. She'd seen him angry at a level far above what situations required. And he'd deliberately lied to her about his affair with Annabelle. A lie of omission, but a lie just the same.

Still, that didn't mean he had a debilitating mental illness and it was horrifying to hear his uncle say so. She was used to dealing with her own anxiety, but schizophrenia was something entirely more serious.

Russell shook his head sadly. "Blake is a fine man. Sometimes. Other times, he's convinced that he's being pursued by demons of his own mind. I resisted the diagnosis for a long time, but I was wrong."

Another coughing spell, this one lasting several minutes, caused Russell to double over in pain. Jennifer picked up the bell to ring Rosa when Russell finally regained control. Still, he looked frighteningly frail. More frail than when she'd arrived. This conversation was draining his energy in potentially dangerous ways.

He said, "I wasn't able to save my brother Donald from his illness. I want to save Blake."

"I should go, Russell. You need some rest." Jennifer began to rise from her chair; he waved her down with his hand. She complied because she worried another coughing jag might kill him. He seemed able to control it only with great effort; any agitation caused his control to slip.

"Listen to me. Blake is dangerous. He needs medication. Without it, he's very, very violent. If he contacts you, please let me know. Please."

Rosa entered just then with a tray of medicines, allowing Jennifer an excuse to leave. "If I hear from Blake again, I'll ask him to contact you," she murmured too quietly for Rosa to overhear.

She wasn't sure if she meant what she said. The situation seemed bizarre to her—unreal. She didn't know who—or what—to believe.

At the doorway, she turned and met his eyes. "And if you hear from him, will you let me know?"

Russell stared back into her steady gaze, but he didn't return her promise.

CHAPTER SIXTY-FIVE

TYLER HAD TOLD HER where to meet him. Jennifer flashed her Florida driver's license at the ticket counter and received the resident's discount for her entry to Busch Gardens. She examined the illustrated map handed to her by the gate attendant.

She located the winding path through the park leading past the Cheetah Run and the Crown Colony Restaurant, ending near the Montu roller coaster in Egypt, and set off.

It was her first trip and she wasn't prepared for the size of the place. She'd always intended to visit the famous park, but for some reason had never made time for it. Like she'd failed to make time for a lot of other things while she was living out what she thought she *should* be doing.

The day was hot and steamy. Jennifer had made the mistake of wearing her casual business clothes. The wrong choice of clothes reminded her again that she'd never felt comfortable in suits of any kind. What did she feel comfortable wearing? She'd have time to explore that and a lot of other things now that she was unemployed.

Jennifer peeled off the tropical-wool blazer and carried it over one arm, blessing her silk shell and cursing the hot slacks and uncomfortable heels. In her new life, whatever that would be, Jennifer promised herself she'd never wear panty hose again. At least, not outside in 95 degree heat with 98 percent humidity.

The grounds were well stocked with blooming annuals in bright colors and one cluster of rocks seemed filled with every known variety of orchid. The delicate blossoms flourishing in hard rock crevices was one of nature's many paradoxes. Jennifer studied the incongruity, wondering whether some metaphor for her own life was being revealed, as Abby Barnett would undoubtedly suggest.

Since her visit to the psychic, Jennifer had been examining every nuance of her existence. After she'd spoken to Russell Denton, Blake's regular phone calls halted abruptly. Maybe he'd given up, or maybe he knew she'd spent time with his uncle and suspected what she'd been told. She wasn't sorry his calls had stopped. Not hearing his voice on her answering machine made it easier to put the embarrassing romance behind her. This was one decision she felt good about. No doubts.

Otherwise, Jennifer felt different, disoriented, as if she'd been jerked into another world. Her work schedule had always provided order to her days and purpose for her life. She needed to figure herself out. She hoped Tim Tyler would provide some of the answers.

Eventually, Jennifer made her way around the open area set aside for the line of thrill seekers who would ride the monstrous Montu and found a bench in the shade, though it wasn't actually much cooler under the banyan tree. The sticky, heavy air enveloped her like a wet towel, and she fanned the hot air around her face with the folded map. She'd paid an exorbitant price for a bottle of water from a vendor close by and she pressed the cool plastic against her face.

Tim Tyler, according to his history from the Annabelle James file Russell Denton had given her, had been a sergeant with the U.S. Army's 101st Airborne Division in Vietnam. He'd returned in 1972, long before Jennifer was born.

Like many vets, Tyler brought the war home with him. He'd joined the FBI and stayed there until an unlucky bullet provided a disability pension, retirement in Florida, and a PI license. Blake had told her that Tyler's investigation had failed to find Annabelle James. He was still looking.

"Thanks for meeting me here," Tyler said from behind her. "I don't get much time with my daughters and they love this place. We had the day planned before you called."

Tim Tyler was a normal looking, middle-aged white guy, about six feet tall—a couple inches more or less. He had a full head of salt-and-pepper hair and wore small black-rimmed glasses. He was dressed in dark green shorts and a muted green and white checked shirt. The man was not at all what Jennifer had been expecting.

"You have children?" She asked. Another surprise. The file said Tyler was single.

"Twins. They're ten next week. They'll be with their mother on their birthday. This was our only chance to celebrate." Everything about Tyler contradicted Jennifer's assumptions. The tone of his reports was very dry, very "just the facts." Yet, here was a pleasant man, celebrating his daughters' birthday.

Jennifer shook her head, as if clearing the cobwebs. She had begun to question all of her beliefs in the last few days. She'd thought Stuart was her life, Worthington her career, and that she was destined to be alone. Now, Stuart was dead, she'd been fired by Russell Denton, suspended by her firm, and for a while there, she'd had a lover. Nothing was as it had been or as it seemed. She strived to remember that.

Here she was, sitting in a theme park with an ex-FBI man, discussing a murderer and a missing person, floundering in her new circumstances.

"Now," Tyler said, turning to face her after checking on his kids who apparently were involved in one of the thrill rides, "what can I do for you?"

Jennifer had practiced her questions in the car, but was unable to begin. She tried to articulate exactly what she wanted. It seemed silly to believe what Lila had said, that she had some innate ability to find Annabelle James, when so many others had failed to do so. Including Tyler. He was experienced. Capable. How could she expect to do better than he?

"You look like her, you know." Tyler said into the void, startling Jennifer.

"Like who?"

"Annabelle James." Tyler studied her closely. "That's why Blake picked you to have an affair with, because he was so taken with Annabelle. When she left and he saw you, looking so much like her, he grabbed the chance to repeat his fantasy life with Annabelle."

Her heart stopped. She couldn't breathe. The air, already close, began to suffocate her. She felt like a fool.

Jennifer had seen pictures of Annabelle James. Quite a few of them, in fact. She rejected Tyler's terrible suggestion. "We don't look anything alike. Annabelle was glamorous. I'm so plain."

"Fishing?" Tyler smiled at her. Jennifer blushed. "Annabelle *was* glamorous. A scientist in short skirts, high heels, and red lipstick was a big turn-on to Blake."

Jennifer remembered Blake's lust the night she'd dressed up

for their date. Had she unwittingly reminded him of Annabelle? Was that why he'd taken her to bed? Why he was still interested?

"We knew you'd be smart. But we also think you're related to her. We hoped she might contact you." Tyler watched Jennifer closely. "She hasn't contacted you, has she?"

Jennifer shook her head. "As far as I know, I've never met the woman. And she's not related to me."

"Are you sure?" Tyler asked.

Taken aback, Jennifer said, "I don't have a sister."

Tyler looked at her critically. He seemed to be making a mental decision. He leaned his forearm over the back of the bench, put one leg up on the seat and faced Jennifer directly.

"Yes, Jennifer, you do have a sister. Maybe a fraternal twin. At least she's very near your age."

"That can't be true." Jennifer's hand flew to her mouth, stopping her words before she blurted things she'd regret.

Her mind raced. If she had a sister, she'd have known. Her parents would have told her. A sister would have been raised with her. A sister would have made all the difference in Jennifer's lonely life. Sisters have a supernatural connection. They *know* each other. Jennifer would *know* if she had a sister. She was sure of it. Right?

"Let's walk," Tyler said, after he'd given her room to think a minute. He stood and waited for Jennifer to follow him, then he led her toward the roller coaster. "My girls are over here. They would spend all day on this ride if they could. Cindi is fearless, and Penny is afraid, but she won't be left out. There they are," he told her, proud of his kids, pointing to two heads with blonde ponytails barely seen above the backs of seats near the very top of the big apparatus.

Jennifer saw them waving to their father. "They look identical from this distance," she said.

"They're not, though. I mean, they look like sisters. Penny has her mother's green eyes, but Cindi has my blue ones. Penny looks like me, but Cindi looks so much like her mother that I sometimes feel Lori is staring at me when Cindi talks." Tyler described his family affectionately.

How lucky his wife was to have him, Jennifer thought. Would she ever find a man who loved her that much?

Tyler seemed to be sensitive to Jennifer's feelings. "Fraternal twins are just siblings. They have none of that creepy look-alike stuff. Their personalities are different, they like different things, excel at different subjects. Penny counts absolutely everything, plans everything out, sticks with her plan. But Cindi is a free spirit. She lives totally for the moment." He put his arm around Jennifer's shoulders. "You can be sisters, even twins, and be different from Annabelle."

Jennifer's ambivalence resurfaced. She didn't want Annabelle James to be her sister, but, at the same time, she would love to have a sister. She didn't know exactly what to think. Or how to feel about his outrageous suggestion. She felt sweat trickling down her sides and her neck and dotting her forehead.

"How much do you know about Annabelle James's background?" Tyler asked her.

"I've read your report. I've talked with her parents. I've heard Blake and Russell Denton's points of view," Jennifer told him matter-of-factly.

"But you didn't interview Gilbert Irwin," Tyler said.

"Who's Gilbert Irwin?"

Tyler took a minute to give his daughters a thumbs up when they looked over from the roller coaster's exit and gestured a request to get back on again. After they returned to the line, Tyler continued. "He was the man who really discovered HepZMax."

"I thought that was Annabelle's work? Her name is on the documents." Jennifer became more confused as the conversation continued.

Tyler shook his head. "Annabelle was very bright, but no way could she have developed HepZMax by herself. The formula is too sophisticated, too complicated. And she would have required access to data that wasn't given to her. No. She didn't do it."

Jennifer heard Tyler's use of the past tense: *"Annabelle was."* Did he know Annabelle was dead?

"Did she steal the formula from Gilbert Irwin?" Jennifer would not believe that one slight woman could have stolen anything from a male coworker determined to keep it.

Tyler shook his head again. "Gilbert gave it to her."

"Why?"

Tyler shrugged. "He loved her. She played him for a fool."

"I don't get this, Tim. What do you mean?"

"It was a classic situation. An older man, almost pathetically introverted. A beautiful woman shows some interest. Hell, I knew Annabelle James. Even I would have given her the formula to make her love me. Gilbert didn't stand a chance."

Again, she noticed the past tense. Tyler looked at Jennifer, raised his eyebrows in question. She didn't understand. She shook her head.

"Look, Jennifer. All a middle-aged guy like Gilbert wants is an attractive woman on his arm who will have sex with him all the time and make him look good. That's it. We're not that complicated. It takes very little to make us happy. Trust me. This is something I know about." A lopsided grin warmed his face and softened his judgment.

"From personal experience?" Jennifer asked him with sarcasm.

Tyler seemed not at all offended. He grinned. "How do you think I ended up divorced and standing in a steam bath at Busch Gardens celebrating my daughters' birthday? Lori threw me out." He shrugged.

"Good for her," Jennifer said. And they both laughed. The laughter broke the tension and she relaxed a little. But she couldn't get her head or her heart around the idea that Annabelle James might be her *sister*. No. Impossible.

"Jennifer, look. You're smart. Think it through. Why would Annabelle want to manipulate Gilbert into putting her name on the documents, claiming she'd discovered HepZMax?" He let her work it out a moment. "She planned this, don't you see? She wanted it to look like it was her formula, her work, so she'd have a legal claim to HepZMax when she stole it."

Tyler's words made sense, but still Jennifer resisted. If Annabelle was her sister, as he claimed, then she couldn't be a thief and a manipulator. Jennifer wouldn't believe that a child of Clay and Debbie Lane could be that depraved. No. Either Annabelle wasn't related to her or Annabelle didn't steal the formula. One or the other, but not both. No way.

"But why would she do that?" Jennifer's question seemed stupid to her the second she'd uttered it.

Tyler didn't call her stupid, though. "Who knows? Money. Fame. A desire to hurt Russell or Blake. There are probably a few more."

Jennifer clicked into her lawyer mode. "Let's say you're right. Not about the motive. I don't know what that is yet. There's not enough evidence to prove any of that. But, for the sake of argument, let's say you're right about Annabelle having manipulated Gilbert into putting her name on the documents and about her stealing the formula."

Tyler nodded. "I am right."

The man's certainty was maddening. "Then, how did she steal all the data and what, in God's name, happened to her?"

Tyler waved to a nearby bench. They sat. He studied Jennifer's face and seemed to come to some conclusion. Finally, he said, "Blake helped her."

"What?" Jennifer's exclamation of shocked incredulity caused several heads to turn their way. She waited a few minutes for the curious onlookers to go back to their business. "That makes no sense."

"Yes, it does. And I'm not guessing."

"But how do you know?"

Tyler's tone became urgent, forceful. "Just take my word for it for now. The point is, we have to find Annabelle and get that formula back. You saw Russell. He needs a liver transplant to survive. But the transplant won't cure the virus. He'll still have Hep Z. He needs that formula, Jennifer. And I have to help him get it."

Jennifer asked, "What is it that you want me to do?"

While Tyler's girls rode the roller coaster again, he turned to face her. "Find Annabelle James if she's still alive. Or, if she's dead, find a way to get the rights to that formula back from Alabaster Medical and let Russell's lab rats produce HepZMax."

She didn't consent. "What are you doing in the meantime?"

"I'm on it, trust me. But you are Annabelle James's sister. She's got a connection to you. And I think she knows it." Tyler pulled a large, thick envelope from his pocked and handed to her. "You'll need this information. My contact numbers are in there. Keep in touch."

Maybe she wouldn't help find Annabelle. But she needed to know what made Tyler so sure. She accepted the envelope; he looked at her as if he could transfer his conviction to her through sheer willpower alone.

"One more thing, Jennifer." Tyler warned, "Except for your appearance, you're nothing like her. Don't let Lila Walden make you over into Annabelle James. And don't let Blake Denton do it, either."

"Blake loves me. He would never do that." Jennifer's words sounded weak, even to her own ears. She realized she was really finished with her misguided infatuation; the knowledge was not as comforting as she'd hoped it would be.

Tyler gave her a hard look to match his hard warning. "Blake is using you. Annabelle trusted him. Look where it got her."

CHAPTER SIXTY-SIX

JENNIFER'S RIGHT ARM LIFTED over her head and made a smooth cut into the water as her left arm passed silently by her side. She kicked both feet, forcing her body through the water. When she reached the edge of the lap pool, she ducked under the surface and disappeared, only to resurface ten yards out to continue swimming. Despite having performed the same strokes for twenty laps, she was not aware of her fatigue. It was after midnight and she was alone, but Jennifer wouldn't have noticed a full class of splashing children. She focused all her attention on her strokes, her form, her speed. She refused to think about her life.

Her concentration held for thirty second intervals. Then her thoughts carried her into the land of "what if."

What if Annabelle James was her sister? What if her parents had lied to her? Could she ever believe her parents again? Had her whole life been nothing but a lie? What if she'd known about her sister? How would that have changed her life?

Jennifer pushed her body to physical exhaustion. After forty more laps, she couldn't, simply couldn't, swim one more stroke.

Only then did she stop. It was one o'clock in the morning and no one was around to save her from drowning.

When she stopped swimming, she floated over to the shallow end of the pool and pulled her aching limbs up the steps. On the pool deck, she collapsed into a poolside lounge chair, where the warm summer breeze cooled her body. Hopefully, she was finally tired enough to sleep.

The early morning sun began to lighten the sky about five thirty. Jennifer slept in the chaise through the first hints of daylight, but the combination of full sunlight and noise from the other apartments, as people opened their windows to capture the early morning cool temperatures, awakened her.

By nine o'clock, the thermometer would register in the mid-eighties and the humidity eighty percent. The bearable early morning would be captured much too soon by the sweltering day, turning the pool deck into a wet sauna as water evaporated and added weight to the already heavy air.

Jennifer awakened disoriented. When she opened her eyes fully, the soreness in her limbs reminded her of how she'd spent the night. She rose from the lounger and walked slowly down the stairs into the shallow end of the pool. She floated, then swam a few slow laps to limber up her stiff arms and legs and to wash the sleep from her face.

Jennifer was too exhausted to be angry at her life anymore. She walked back to her apartment, removed her wet swimsuit, and dried off with the towel she'd slept on. She lay face down on her bed and dissolved into exhausted sleep.

The next time she awakened, it was late afternoon. Jennifer got up and splashed water on her face, then made her way into the kitchen where she dumped coffee into the basket, added water and turned on the coffeemaker. While she waited for the caffeine transfusion to jump-start her energy, Jennifer picked up the newspaper from outside her door.

The smell of freshly brewed coffee brought her alive again. She carried a big cup of liquid energy over to her favorite chair, where she planned to sit and read the paper. But, she was so tired the letters swam around the page.

Jennifer noticed, but ignored, the papers on the table that had tumbled out of the Pandora's Box disguised as the thick envelope Tyler had given her, damning evidence of the lie her life had been.

No matter how she tried to explain it to herself, she could not understand her parents' betrayal. Why had they never told her the truth about her sister? And the wasted time—that was the worst thing. She could have known Annabelle all those years. Both sisters could have been part of a full family, instead of lonely girls and solitary women.

And maybe, just maybe, she could have made a difference in Annabelle's life. Maybe Annabelle wouldn't have become the thief and heartless bitch Tyler and the Dentons described if Jennifer had had a chance to be a real sister to her.

Jennifer could have taken care of Annabelle. She could have given Annabelle a real family, guidance, and love. Annabelle would have been different. Jennifer would have been different, too. She knew it.

Tears neared the surface again and threatened to spill down Jennifer's face one more time. She wiped her eyes and forced her thoughts back to the present.

"Jennifer," she said aloud, attempting to shake herself into reality. "You know you're engaging in pure fantasy. Who do you think you are, anyway—Hercules? You're so strong that, single-handedly, you could change the course of Annabelle's history? Come on!" She wiped her eyes with the back of her hand.

"What is the reality of the situation?" she wondered, again aloud. Then she answered. "The reality is that both you and Annabelle were raised as only children. Your parents loved you both and did the best they could, under the circumstances. Everything that happened to you happened exactly the way it was supposed to." She tried to believe the answer she'd given. But doubts plucked at the edges of her resolve.

"Even if your lives could have been better, that's in the past. You can't change any of it. Deal with what is."

What doesn't kill you makes you smarter.

"Yeah, yeah, Stuart. Shut up."

Knowing that she couldn't change the past, that she was wasting her time by trying to go back, didn't make her feel any better. But Jennifer continued her self-talk. "The reality is that today, right now, Annabelle is missing. What are you going to do to find her?"

Jennifer began to think about what to do right this minute to help herself, Annabelle, even Russell—and maybe, just maybe, her parents. First, she had to get dressed. Then, she'd make a serious attempt at finding Annabelle James. She would figure out whether Annabelle was her sister. After that, she'd make the next decision—whatever it was. One step at a time.

But first she had some unfinished business. She picked up the phone and dialed Blake's numbers, first the home, then the cell. She got the voice mail both times and left the same message: "Blake, I'm going out of town for a couple of days. When I get back, we need to talk. In the meantime, please call your uncle, if you haven't already. He's very worried about you."

She didn't know how she felt about Blake now, but she realized that what she'd thought was love must have been something else. *'Lust,'* the old Melanie Stein reprise sounded in her head. She couldn't possibly have loved the man Tyler and Russell Denton described. If they were right—and they'd known Blake much longer than she had—then Blake was not the love of her life. Some part of her was glad. *Let Annabelle have him*, she thought.

But, as she hung up the phone and headed toward her closet, Jennifer puzzled over Blake for a few more minutes. He hadn't called for several days. Russell Denton hadn't been able to find him. Where was he? What was he doing?

After dressing, she dialed the number Tyler had given her. He wasn't around, either—didn't anyone answer the phone anymore? "Tim. Jennifer Lane. I can't find Blake. Sorry. I'm going to look for Annabelle. I'll leave Blake to you."

CHAPTER SIXTY-SEVEN

JENNIFER REFILLED HER COFFEE, grabbed a handful of jelly beans and reexamined the map of North America tacked up on the wall in Annabelle James's apartment, located about ten miles from where Jennifer had been living for the past five years. Could the woman who lived here really be her sister?

She'd been staring at the map for several hours, as if it would reveal Annabelle's secrets. Annabelle had the map here for some reason. But why? Jennifer could see the map on her eyelids, but she didn't know what it meant. She swiped a hand over her eyes to erase the image burned into her brain.

"Where are you, Annabelle? Where did you go?" Jennifer asked aloud. She walked around the apartment, examining the shelves and the closets. She considered the possibilities one at a time, testing Tyler's hypothesis that Annabelle must have had help running away.

On Jennifer's first visit to Denton Bio-Medical, Blake had told her that Annabelle's access to data was limited. Tyler said Gilbert had given Annabelle the HepZMax formula and then Blake helped her steal the data.

But if Gilbert gave Annabelle the formula, then why did she need to disappear? Why not just sell it and then hire Roger Riley, or someone like him, to help her keep it?

Was Annabelle dead? The body the police had found in Kennedy Park remained unidentified. But Annabelle's dental work or DNA should have been readily available. If the woman was or wasn't Annabelle, why not just say so? Were they keeping the information quiet because Ronald Walden was still at large? Would Walden become any more dangerous if the body was Annabelle's? He was already a killer. He'd killed Stuart. How could he get worse than homicidal?

Jennifer gulped the last of the coffee and sat down again in front of the map. Okay. Whether Annabelle was dead or not, she hadn't stolen HepZMax by herself. That much was obvious, once you thought about it. She didn't have the security clearance that would have given her access to the data, and the place was closed up tighter than Fort Knox. No way could Annabelle have done this alone.

But Tyler's opinion that Blake had been the one who helped her wasn't unassailable. There were other choices. There had to be.

Did Gilbert really just simply give the formula to Annabelle, as Tyler said?

Jennifer doodled on her pad. She wrote *Gilbert* with an arrow to *Annabelle* and then an arrow to *Alabaster Medical*, and left Blake out of the picture. This was her working theory. But Jennifer didn't believe the links she'd just written on the page. Somehow that theory just didn't fit together right, either.

For starters, Gilbert was dead now. If he'd helped Annabelle disappear, why had he killed himself? Why not simply join her, wherever she went?

And if Gilbert had killed Annabelle first, where was her body?

And why would he do that after the two of them went to all the trouble to steal HepZMax, and got away with it?

No. Jennifer had to agree that Gilbert was only part of the answer. Some pieces of the puzzle were still missing.

But what were they? Was a third person who was not Blake involved in the scheme? Someone who had stayed behind, negotiated with Alabaster Medical? Hired Roger Riley? It made sense.

Jennifer drew an *X* on her legal pad. Who was X? She wanted it to be someone other than Blake, although now that she'd drawn out the options for herself, she understood Tyler's logic all too well.

The same facts led Jennifer repeatedly to the same conclusions. She needed to know whether the body found in the park was or was not that of Annabelle James. Whether Annabelle was dead or alive would change the picture, she felt sure, without knowing how or why.

She looked up at the map again. "Where did you go, Annabelle? Where are you now?"

Jennifer picked up her cell phone and dialed Tim Tyler's number. He answered on the fourth ring. "What can I do for you, Jennifer?" She looked around involuntarily. Was Annabelle's apartment under surveillance? Was Tyler watching her? The feeling creeped her out.

"How did you know it was me?"

"Cell caller ID, Jennifer. You should get it," he responded.

Jennifer said, "Have you heard anything about the identity of the body they found in the park? The woman Ronald Walden thinks is Annabelle?"

She heard Tyler's breathing, and noises that sounded like

television in the background. She thought she recognized Blake's voice. Were they together?

"Tim? Do you know whether the body is Annabelle?"

Tyler sighed. "If I tell you the answer to that, can you keep it to yourself? The police are playing beat the clock with this thing, trying to keep Walden from wigging out even more before they find him."

Jennifer felt the cold bands of fear constrict her lungs, making breathing difficult. She didn't promise. "Is it Annabelle or not?"

"It's not her," Tyler said.

Jennifer's cold fingers pushed the disconnect button. After a while, she felt her heart beating normally again.

Two hours later, Jennifer's pad was full of lines and doodles, but she was no closer to answers than she'd been all day. She needed to find a fresh approach. A completely different tack. She drummed her pen on the table and stared into space. Then she made up her mind.

In less than twenty minutes, she was home, stuffing her files into her oversized briefcase on wheels. She went into her bedroom and packed a small duffel bag. She picked up the gun case, turned on the alarm, and started out.

Within an hour of making her decision, Jennifer was headed north on I-275 in her PT Cruiser, her gas tank almost full. The little car could go a long way on a full tank of gas. She shouldn't have to stop until she got to Valdosta, Georgia. With any luck, she'd be in Birmingham by morning.

Jennifer plugged her cell phone into the car's cigarette lighter, and then placed the call. She'd tell Tyler. She didn't want him to think history had repeated itself. She wouldn't disappear without a trace.

And she'd feel more comfortable if someone, at least, knew where she was.

Tyler didn't answer. Maybe he had been with Blake and was still with him. She hoped so. At least Blake would be accounted for. She trusted Tyler to know what to do about Blake. She had all she could think about with finding Annabelle.

After she'd left the message, Jennifer turned on her radar detector and set her cruise control at eighty miles per hour. She turned up the volume on the radio and sang along with Patsy Cline. "Your cheatin' heart..."

CHAPTER SIXTY-EIGHT

RUSSELL WAS SITTING IN his study, a brandy in his hand and an unread book on his lap, when his private cell phone rang at two o'clock in the morning. Russell hated cell phones, and for that reason only one person had his number.

"Yes," he said into the small device.

"She's gone," Tyler told him.

"Where?"

"The Jacks Clinic, if I had to guess."

"Excellent," Russell answered.

He almost asked Tyler if he'd found Blake, but he didn't want to cause unnecessary alarm.

Blake had disappeared before, sometimes for days.

When he was off his meds Blake was irrational and volatile. But he always came home.

Russell flipped the phone closed and put it back in his pocket.

CHAPTER SIXTY-NINE

BONE WEARY, JENNIFER PULLED into the parking lot at the Embassy Suites shortly after ten o'clock in the morning. When she straightened up from behind the wheel, she actually heard her bones crack as they released some of the stiffness. She stood beside the car and stretched her tired muscles, then grabbed her cell phone, the duffel bag, and the rolling briefcase and made her way to the front door.

Jennifer had stayed here on business several times during a case she and Stuart had defended. The Embassy Suites was the most convenient business hotel in Birmingham, and it had the added benefit of a decent restaurant in the lobby.

She'd called ahead for a reservation in a nonsmoking room with a king-size bed. She registered under her own name at the front desk and plunked down her credit card. After she received her key card, she trudged to the elevator and got off at the sixth floor, where she found room 631 on the far left hallway. Once inside, she dropped her luggage and walked straight through to the bedroom. She fell onto the fully made bed and instantly passed into a deep state of sleep. If her exhausted dreams answered any of her questions, she was blissfully oblivious.

Waking spontaneously around three o'clock in the afternoon, Jennifer called for room service and spread out her files on the suite's small kitchen table. Then, she went into the bathroom, peeled off her clothes, and stepped into the pounding, hot water of the shower.

An hour later, she was seated in an armchair, reviewing the notes she'd made for herself about the Jacks Clinic. She had long since finished the complimentary coffee, along with the continental breakfast. Her files covered the table. The gun rested near enough to grab.

Jennifer's meticulous legal training had many advantages. When Lila first told her that Annabelle had been adopted through the infamous Jacks Clinic, Jennifer had started a file on the place, including legal database research. One of the things she'd found was a list of litigation the clinic had spawned. She now carefully examined the printouts she'd made.

Dr. Jacks had died years ago; his clinic was closed. But once the full story of the small rural facility became known, people affected by the activities there had united in rage. Jennifer skimmed the articles. Eventually, she found what she was looking for—the name of the woman who headed the grassroots group formed to locate the Jacks babies and reunite them with their birth families.

Jennifer picked up the hotel's phone, dialed "*9*" for an outside line, and then called information. "The Jacks Baby Project, in Birmingham, Alabama, please."

When she had the telephone number. She dialed again. On the third ring, a woman answered. "The Jacks Baby Project. How can I help you?"

"I'd like to have a package hand delivered. What is your street address please?"

Jennifer marveled at the trust people put in a telephone call. She hadn't said or been asked what she wanted to send. Given the irrational anger evidenced by some of the lawsuits filed against Dr. Jacks, she could be someone with a vendetta. Still, the woman volunteered the address without a pause.

"Do you need directions, honey?" After answering yes, Jennifer took down the woman's words verbatim in shorthand.

Thirty minutes later, Jennifer had packed up her bags and files, and checked out of the hotel, and was back on the road.

CHAPTER SEVENTY

JENNIFER TURNED LEFT INTO the parking lot of what she noted was a suburban-style strip mall. A Piggly Wiggly grocery store sat on one end of the shopping center, while a series of typical small businesses filled the other retail spaces: a mailbox store; a 99 Cent discount place; a card shop. Two doors from the end was a unit with no sign out front.

She checked her notes. Nothing identified this one as the Jacks Baby Project, but the woman had said this was the place.

Jennifer parked near the grocery store and spent a moment in indecision. Should she take the gun? Or leave it in the car where it might be stolen? Neither choice was perfect, but the neighborhood didn't seem especially risky.

She left the gun in the locked car and walked to the small door, where she reconfirmed the address. White vertical blinds covered the storefront window and the glass double door. But a small sign turned to the side that said, "Come in, we're open" hung from a plastic suction-cup holder.

Jennifer pulled the door open; a small chime announced her arrival. The interior was decorated like a waiting room in an unsuccessful doctor's office. Four tattered and mismatched armchairs were arranged in two groupings on either end of the room and a dusty silk flower basket overwhelmed the particleboard coffee table between. A few framed pictures of babies and parents hung on the walls. The worn carpet had been stained and cheap to start with; the walls were painted an all-purpose gray.

A small glass partition between the waiting room and the back office slid open. Jennifer approached a small, plump woman with a tightly bound and lacquered hairstyle sitting at her desk behind an ancient computer.

"May I help you, honey?"

Jennifer recognized the voice from her earlier phone call.

"Yes, ma'am. Is this the Jacks Baby Project office?"

The woman nodded. Her smile oozed concern. "Yes, honey, it is. Are you the one who called a little while ago?"

"Yes, ma'am."

Now that she was here, all of her rehearsed lines seemed stilted and wrong. Jennifer didn't know exactly what to say. She'd taken matters into her own hands, acted decisively, to get here. Now what?

The woman patted Jennifer's hand resting on the track of the glass. "That's okay, honey. I see this a lot. When someone first finds a link to their past, it takes guts to come looking. You think you might be a Jacks baby, is that it?"

She was so kind, Jennifer's new courage dissolved on the spot. How had she ever, ever gotten involved in all this?

Jennifer shook her head. "I'm not sure. But I think maybe a friend was. Can you help me?"

The woman smiled again. "I'm Betty Lou Norton, honey. Why don't you come on in here and we can talk about it. I might be able to help you."

Jennifer walked through the interior door and sat on a folding chair opposite the single desk inside. Betty Lou asked Jennifer if she wanted coffee. "Make yourself comfortable while I get it for you."

The office was decorated similarly to the waiting room. But on every wall were framed newspaper photographs of positive stories about the Jacks Baby Project and the clinic. Many of them Jennifer had found during her research—but a few she didn't recognize.

Betty Lou had chosen not to frame the overwhelming number of negative stories Jennifer's search had also turned up. She took out her notepad and quickly recorded the names and dates of the newspapers and magazines the stories appeared in, so she could find them later on.

Jennifer's hostess returned with a tray containing two thick, chipped mugs of coffee, a green cream pitcher, and a yellow sugar bowl. She set the tray on the corner of her desk and rolled her secretarial chair closer before she plopped into it.

Jennifer guessed Betty Lou had talked to men and women in this situation many times before. According to the reports Jennifer had read, Dr. Hiram Jacks had facilitated over a thousand illegal adoptions from his clinic. With the idea that they would find their roots, many of those adoptees had undoubtedly come here seeking information.

Betty Lou patted Jennifer's hand again and said, "Why don't you tell me your story, honey, and I'll see if we can help you."

Jennifer's rehearsed story was close to the truth. Maybe she, too, was looking for her roots. Unlike many of the Jacks babies, though, she could ask her mother about Annabelle—if she could find Debbie floating around on a cruise ship somewhere in Alaska. But she wasn't ready for that. Not yet.

"I don't know a lot, really. I met this woman who was a Jacks baby. Her parents think she looks so much like me that we must be cousins or something."

Betty Lou looked at Jennifer carefully now. "What does the woman say about it?"

Jennifer hadn't expected Betty Lou's compassion. She'd anticipated resistance and created a plausible tale, but maybe the truth would be better. Her errand was almost legitimate. Lila Walden *had* asked her to find Annabelle once. If Annabelle had gone searching for her roots, this would have been a logical first stop.

"Her name is Annabelle James and she's missing. Her adoptive mother asked me to help locate Annabelle because she thinks Annabelle and I are related." Jennifer's voice broke when she seemed finally to absorb the full meaning of her words. "But I just don't know how that can be true."

"What do your people say?" Betty Lou wanted to know.

Jennifer shook her head

"You haven't asked them about this. Why not?"

Even when they returned, how would she approach her family? How could they have lied to her all these years? How could they have given Annabelle away? And if Tyler was wrong, if Annabelle was dead, and Jennifer never got to meet her in this life, how could Jennifer live with herself? The tears Jennifer had been holding back now rushed out of her eyes and down her cheeks.

The tears come from exhaustion, Jennifer consoled herself. *Or hormones. Or Stuart's still very recent death.* She couldn't be crying in front of a perfect stranger. She never did that. Never. No matter what.

Betty Lou calmly reached over, grabbed a tissue box, and offered it. She picked up a clipboard on which a form rested. She began to ask Jennifer questions and to fill out the form with the answers. The questions gave her some room to control herself.

"What's your name and address, honey?" was the first one, followed by "Where and when were you born? What were your parents' names?" and so on, to collect basic information that would allow some sort of database search.

When she'd filled in these preliminary responses, Betty Lou said, "Now, what do you know about the girl you're searching for? Any data at all?"

"I know her approximate age. I've seen pictures of her. She looks like me, but she's much more glamorous."

Betty Lou patted Jennifer's hand again and then moved over to her computer. She pulled up a database questionnaire and entered all the information Jennifer had given her into onto the screen. Then she began to run various searches. The computer was old and slow. Each search seemed to take forever. Jennifer used the time to pull herself together. *Enough of that.* She tossed the tissues into the trash.

Betty Lou began by searching for matches on Annabelle's parents' names. "I have Ronald and Lila Walden adopting a baby girl, age two," Betty Lou said, smiling at her success so far.

Lila had given Jennifer documents proving Annabelle's adoption. The birth certificate, though, was blank in the important particulars, such as mother's and father's names and Annabelle's place of birth.

"Okay. Now, if we match your age with Annabelle's age, we see that you're about the same. Maybe a year apart." Betty Lou looked up from her computer. She tried to reassure Jennifer. "But the ages could be just misinformation. Families often provided the wrong facts in those days."

Jennifer kept herself from saying, "Don't I know it."

"Okay," Betty Lou set up the next search, but in a few minutes she said, "Nope."

"What?"

"I don't have a record of any adoption of a baby girl by Deborah and Clay Lane." Betty Lou sounded sorry.

"I'm not adopted!" Jennifer blurted out, spilling coffee all over her hand and the papers on the desk. Betty Lou ignored her and kept working on the computer while Jennifer pulled tissues out of the box to wipe up the sticky mess.

"Well, sometimes parents would give Dr. Jacks two children and they'd be adopted by different families. That was one of the tragedies of his work. That's what happened to me."

Jennifer knew Betty Lou's history from articles she'd found during her research. Betty Lou's mother had come to the Jacks Clinic to give her children up for temporary foster care. Dr. Jacks sold both children to different families and told Betty Lou's mother they had died. Even now Betty Lou was still searching for her brother. It was her motivation, her mission, she said, to reunite the Jacks' babies because of what had happened to her.

Jennifer put the cup down because her hands were too shaky to hold it without spilling the coffee again. She had never considered that her parents might have adopted her. Now, though, she realized it was a possibility, if Annabelle was her sister. The two of them could have been left here at the same time. That could explain why she and Annabelle looked alike, but Jennifer didn't look at all like Debbie and, of course, Annabelle didn't resemble Lila at all.

"But it doesn't look like you were adopted from the Jacks Clinic. Not at the same time as Annabelle, anyway." Betty Lou seemed pleased with this answer, but Jennifer couldn't muster the same joy. "In fact, I can't find any record of Deborah or Clay Lane adopting at all."

Jennifer felt relieved that her parents weren't listed. Since she'd entered the door, she'd experienced more emotional ups and downs than a hot air balloon. This relief lasted only a moment before the next question.

"Let me try your mother's maiden name. Shaw, wasn't it?" Betty Lou read the name off the clipboard, clacked the keys, and explained while the computer did its work.

"Sometimes, Dr. Jacks would have a baby sale all arranged. And no baby to sell. So when a woman came in just for her delivery, Dr. Jacks would tell her that the baby died."

Jennifer felt a mixed twinge of nausea and hope. Maybe her parents didn't know Annabelle had survived. Maybe they thought she'd died at birth. That's why they didn't tell Jennifer about her sister. That had to be it.

Betty Lou, oblivious to the optimism she'd unwittingly generated, dropped Jennifer in a free fall again with her next words. "No. Sorry. Deborah Shaw wasn't a Jacks Clinic patient, either."

Jennifer vised her head in her hands and squeezed hard. Would this never end?

"Now, let's see if we can get any other information about Annabelle." She worked her computer for about thirty minutes, trying first one search and then another. She couldn't find any more about Annabelle.

After exhausting her search ideas, Betty Lou turned to Jennifer with a smile. "This is good news, honey."

"If you don't have any information, how can that be good news?" Jennifer felt more deflated by the minute. Every road she chased down was a dead end.

Betty Lou patted her hand again. "Because, honey, if Annabelle had been born in the Jacks Clinic, we'd never find out who her family was. Since she was born somewhere else, there'll be records."

Jennifer was bewildered. "What do you mean?"

"Well, when Dr. Jacks took in a woman who wanted to have her baby in secret and give the baby away, one of the ways he kept her anonymous was to say the baby was born at his clinic, but to falsify the baby's birth records, see?"

Jennifer began to understand, she thought. Maybe. "But when people brought him babies to find good homes for, he wouldn't have any birth records to change?"

Betty Lou smiled as if Jennifer was her brightest pupil. "Right! He issued a new birth certificate altogether. That's what happened in Annabelle's case. She was born somewhere else, and they will have real birth records. All we have to do is find the place."

Betty Lou fairly beamed with this "good" news, but Jennifer suppressed a groan of pain. Annabelle could have been born anywhere. How would she ever find her original birth records?

CHAPTER SEVENTY-ONE

ROGER RILEY LOOKED ACROSS the desk at Melanie Stein. She'd made an appointment and acted as if she were all business, but Roger could smell her. She wanted him. He knew it. He felt himself getting hard. What would she be like? Sometimes these hard-to-get bitches were hotter than hell in the sack. He salivated just thinking about it.

"Will you do it, or not?" she asked him again. He hadn't answered because he hadn't figured out whether the sex depended on it. "*Well*? I need an answer."

"Barnett's dead. I don't think even the Florida Bar can do anything more to the guy."

"Maybe not. But that leaves Jennifer Lane." Melanie wet her lips with her tongue and pouted.

"I thought she was a friend of yours. Remind me never to get too friendly with you," Roger joked. Why would Roger want to snitch on a lawyer? Cowardly. He preferred the full frontal attack. More sportsmanlike.

Melanie's eyes narrowed into golden slits and the light glinted off her irises as if she wore reflective contact lenses. The effect was deliciously devilish. "You won't think it's such a joke when you have to tangle with her the next time, Riley. Jennifer looks like a weak-willed woman, but appearances, as we both know, are deceiving." She trained her glinting eyes on Roger's crotch. He felt himself shrivel under her wilting stare.

Melanie stood, picked up her briefcase, and strode to the door. "You'll regret not helping me, Riley. Jennifer Lane deserves to be disbarred. Everyone's feeling sorry for her right now because of Stuart's murder, so the ethics committee will probably let her off with a slap on the wrist. But she'll be back. Don't you forget I told you so." Melanie walked through the open door and slammed it hard behind her.

Roger, left with his now shrunken libido, said a little prayer to the Virgin Mary. He'd been brought up Catholic. Every now and then, he returned to his childhood religion. This time, he prayed that he'd never be on the wrong side of Melanie Stein. The woman was a viper. And he said a little prayer for Jennifer Lane, too. How could one small woman have inspired such an enemy, he wondered. If he knew, maybe he could do the same thing to a few of his enemies.

CHAPTER SEVENTY-TWO

"DON'T WORRY, HONEY. IT'S not as hopeless as it sounds," Betty Lou patted her hand once again. She must be comforted by the gesture somehow.

"Why not?" Jennifer asked.

"Honey, I've been doing this a long time now. I'm a Jacks baby. That's what got me started. I know, for instance, that Dr. Jacks kept a fairly low profile. He only took babies for adoption from the immediate area. He ran a women's clinic and the adoptions were only a small part of his work. He didn't have the time or the resources to spread out too far."

Betty Lou stopped to refill Jennifer's coffee. "Annabelle was probably born in one of the four or five counties around Birmingham. Did you ever have any people living around here?"

She no doubt meant this news to be reassuring, but to Jennifer, it wasn't. Her parents did have family close to Birmingham. Too close. Her ambivalence swung her emotions again. One minute, she wanted no possibility that Annabelle was her sister. A few minutes later, she felt just the opposite.

Betty Lou was positively beaming now. The woman loved her

work, for sure. "And the better news is that all of those counties are cooperating with us. They have online databases now going back to the years when Dr. Jacks was running his clinic."

Jennifer's expression must have reflected her painful feelings. Betty Lou stopped her work to explain. "So with a little more checking, I can see whether Annabelle was born in or around Birmingham, Alabama, or not. That information may lead us to her parents."

Betty Lou was so pleased with herself that she looked as if she'd just won first prize in a contest of some sort. And in a way, she had. Finding Jacks' babies was her life's purpose. Reuniting families, giving them their histories back—Betty Lou considered her work a noble calling, according to the information Jennifer had found. Jennifer shuddered. All of the lives Dr. Jacks had ruined were being destroyed again by this well-meaning woman.

If Annabelle was her sister, her parents' child, would they want to know about her now? If they had wanted to know, wouldn't Clay and Debbie be sitting here themselves? And if her parents had knowingly given Annabelle away, was it Jennifer's place to interfere?

The dilemma was impossible to resolve. She felt the blood in her ears begin to pound in protest. She checked her watch. Two more hours before she could safely take another Xanax for the migraine about to envelop her. The dull thud began behind her eyes and quickly grew into the thundering tympani that filled her head with consuming pain. She reached for an eight hundred milligram ibuprofen and swallowed it with the cold, sweet sludge remaining in the bottom of her mug.

Her body remembered doing the same thing the night she'd first met Ronald and Lila Walden. The night she'd first learned about Annabelle. How far she'd traveled since that moment. How long ago and far away that night seemed now.

"Just give me a few minutes and I can get at those databases," Betty Lou said. "I've done this so many times, I know exactly where to look."

Jennifer agreed. She'd come this far. There was no turning back and she'd regret it if she did. She left Betty Lou working while she found a sink for a cold compress and more caffeine to boost the ibuprofen. She sat and closed her eyes to wait things out while Betty Lou and the drugs did their jobs.

An hour later, she walked unsteadily away from Betty Lou holding a copy of Roxanne Mae Thomas's birth certificate, listing Margaret and Herbert Thomas as parents, in her hand. Maybe, finally, this thing was starting to make sense.

She felt a thousand times better. Annabelle was not her sister, confirming what she'd believed all along. How could she have doubted Debbie and Clay? Jennifer thought of all the things she'd have to do to make it up to them. Questions remained, but she intended to find the answers soon.

Jennifer returned to her car and after a few minutes found herself driving north on Alabama Highway 39 toward Lake Bearden.

CHAPTER SEVENTY-THREE

RUSSELL PULLED THE RINGING cell phone out of his pocket and flipped it open. He'd stayed up until near dawn, expecting Blake to come home. Lack of sleep had left him exhausted, but Russell had made up his mind to confront his nephew. Tyler hadn't figured it all out yet, and Russell didn't want to falsely accuse Blake, but how long could he wait? And what difference would it make now? Alabaster Medical had HepZMax. Roger Riley had descended on him like a vulture. He needed to mend his rift with Blake. They should stand together.

"Yes," he said into the phone.

"Jennifer has found the Jacks Baby Project."

"How long has she been there?"

"About three hours so far."

"It's taking her longer than we thought."

"Betty Lou talks a lot. She's lonely. Don't worry. Jennifer's a smart girl. She'll figure things out."

Russell sighed. "Keep me posted. I want to know the minute she gets back to Tampa." Russell flipped the phone closed and returned it to his pocket, then pushed the intercom button to buzz the kitchen.

"Yes, Mr. Russell," answered Rosa, the housekeeper who'd worked here since he'd brought Blake to live with him.

"Rosa, is Blake home?"

"No, Mr. Russell. He didn't come back last night."

"Okay," he said.

When would he be able to talk with Blake, to work this out? Blake had been drifting farther and farther away from him. First, the distance had been caused by Blake's ill-advised affair with Annabelle James and, now, this rift over Jennifer had worsened their relationship. Russell understood that young men were bound to make mistakes in love, but Blake was thirty-five already.

Russell looked again at the documents Tyler had sent over the day before. Yes, Blake's judgment seemed to be seriously flawed where women were concerned. He couldn't be trusted.

Blake's father had been the same way, though. Russell's brother had died broke and almost literally in the gutter. All Russell had wanted was to give Blake everything, to make up for Donald's lousy parenting and Russell's own guilty conscience over what he'd believed at the time was his tough love approach with his brother. The result had been Donald's disastrous marriage and—worse—death.

Russell didn't like Tyler's plan, but what else could he do? He didn't have any better ideas.

Russell flipped open the phone and pushed the redial button. At the other end, Blake's cell phone rang until his voice mail answered. Russell hung up. He'd already left several messages that Blake had ignored. Leaving another would be useless.

That boy was as stubborn as Blake's own father once was. Russell and Donald had been as different as two brothers could possibly be. Donald was younger, so Russell was supposed to take care of him—and he had tried. But it soon became obvious that Russell couldn't handle the job. Donald was too intent on self-destruction.

Just like Blake.

Russell rescued Donald from one scrape after another, throughout their childhood. When Russell got a scholarship to college, Donald was left without anyone to watch over him and keep him from trouble. Ultimately, Russell had been to blame. He could have stayed home, gone to a local school. But at the time, he'd just wanted to get away.

Was that when Donald had first started using drugs? Russell didn't know anymore. But by the time Russell graduated, Donald was severely addicted to narcotics—most often heroin. One rehabilitation program after another failed. Donald would get clean for a while, then return to using.

During one of his rehab stints, Donald met another junkie, a woman named Marie. The two conceived Blake and, after his birth, ignored him. Donald never married her, but they kept living together, God only knew why. While together, the couple fought like cats and dogs.

Russell had no idea where Marie was now. She'd disappeared a long time ago. And he was glad. When Donald killed himself, Russell took Blake and raised him as if Blake were his own son. Blake had been such a good child then. His accident of birth was not his fault, and Russell had believed Blake understood that.

His relationship with Blake had been a good one, Russell thought, although it had been bumpy at times. Blake went through the same adolescent rebellion that all boys did. He tried drugs, too. He'd even tried to find his mother.

But all of that was in the past. He and Blake had been good

friends for years. Until Blake decided he wanted to marry Annabelle James.

Russell had to object. How could he let Blake marry that woman?

Yet the argument had driven a wedge between them even before Annabelle left. And ever since that body had been found in the park, Blake had refused to speak to him. Blake blamed Russell. That much was obvious. He stopped taking his meds. His delusions had become frequent and pervasive, his paranoia more pronounced.

For the first time in his life, Russell was afraid of what his nephew might do. But he didn't want to give up on him. Russell owed it to Donald to take care of Blake.

Dammit! Where *was* the boy?

Russell didn't want to call the police. He didn't want to tell Tyler. He closed his eyes and, for the first time in years, began to pray.

CHAPTER SEVENTY-FOUR

JENNIFER DROVE DIRECTLY TO the picturesque little resort town of Lake Bearden. As she traveled over the bridge crossing the lake, she came upon the small town nestled in the foothills. A slice of heaven, her father had always called it.

The few times Jennifer had visited here had been extremely happy ones. Her grandmother's sister, Great-Aunt Peggy, was one of the most wonderful women on the planet as far as Jennifer was concerned. Jennifer had transferred all of the affection she'd had for her grandmother onto Aunt Peggy when her grandmother died. The *halo effect* was the psychologist's term for it. What it meant was that Jennifer's love for her grandmother cloaked Aunt Peggy in the glow of transferred affection.

Aunt Peggy had actually never been a big part of her life, but Jennifer always told herself that it was because Aunt Peggy lived so far away.

Jennifer's mother had been Peggy's favorite, though. When Jennifer's grandmother died, Debbie had turned to Aunt Peggy, too. Jennifer was glad she'd get to see Aunt Peggy today, but she wished she had a happier reason for the visit.

During the too-short drive from Birmingham, Jennifer had practiced several approaches. None seemed right. Only momentum kept Jennifer driving toward the inevitable confrontation. Momentum that had already taken her past the point of no return.

Jennifer drove through the small town and found her way onto Blaine Street, where she drove up the hill. She parked in front of the small building housing the Bearden Public Library.

What right do I have to do this? This woman has never been anything but good to me. How can I just march into her life and turn it upside down this way?

Jennifer could ask herself great questions, but she didn't have any good answers.

She locked the car and walked the short distance uphill to the library entrance where she stopped and looked around.

A more beautiful spot for a child to grow up she couldn't imagine. Aunt Peggy had moved here when Uncle Herbert had been transferred to nearby Huntsville to work for NASA in the space program. When Uncle Herbert died twenty years ago, she'd stayed on. Debbie had asked her several times to move to Suttons Bay with them, but Aunt Peggy always refused, saying this was her home now. And she was still the town librarian as she'd been since before Jennifer was born.

Jennifer took a deep breath and entered through the front door of the library. She made her way to the small office in the back where her aunt could usually be found. She stopped in front of the glass windows and watched the small woman, whose white hair was piled on top of her head in an old-fashioned style they'd once called a "Gibson Girl" a million years ago. Aunt Peggy wore full makeup, including bright lavender lipstick, and a chiffon dress smothered in lavender cabbage roses. Lavender low-heeled pumps on her feet rested beneath the desk bearing her nameplate: Margaret Thomas.

Jennifer's heart fairly burst with love as her eyes threatened to leak silent tears. If she didn't say something now, she never would. She couldn't wait another minute.

She approached the door and knocked gently. "Aunt Peggy?" she said, careful not to frighten the elderly woman.

The woman looked through glasses that made her bright eyes, shining and alert, appear larger than marbles. A big smile parted her painted lips and her false teeth sparkled in the lamplight cast from her desk.

Aunt Peggy jumped up and ran over to Jennifer, hugging with all of her strength before she said a word. Jennifer squeezed back. She felt the frail bones inside the pretty summer frock. Aunt Peggy was a mere wisp of a woman, yet she had a strong spirit that Jennifer had always envied.

"Jennifer! What a wonderful surprise! It's so good to see you. Why didn't you tell me you were coming?" Aunt Peggy's exclamations ran one after the other, allowing Jennifer no time to reply—as usual. Jennifer laughed. The loving familiarity warmed her soul.

"I know, Aunt Peggy. It's so good to see you, too."

Aunt Peggy held onto Jennifer's waist and stood close beside her, as if moving even a fraction would separate them by as many miles as Jennifer had just driven. As a child, Jennifer had held onto Aunt Peggy in exactly the same way.

Aunt Peggy lived in a small brick ranch-style house around the corner from the library so she could walk to work; she'd never learned to drive. When they were settled in Aunt Peggy's kitchen—after Jennifer had told Aunt Peggy all about her life in Tampa, or at least, the edited version, and after Aunt Peggy had made hot tea and put out a plate of her favorite lemon pound cake—Jennifer pulled the folded birth certificate out of her pocket.

"Aunt Peggy, I have something I need to ask you about." Jennifer lowered her head and reminded herself that Annabelle was missing. Finding her was important. She didn't want to hurt Aunt Peggy. She was a wonderful woman and she'd always been so special to Jennifer. Would Aunt Peggy forgive her?

"I'm not quite sure how to say this," stalling.

"What is it, dear? Are you going to ask me before I die?" Aunt Peggy teased.

Alarmed, Jennifer asked, "You're not sick, are you?"

Aunt Peggy smiled the guileless smile that reached her lustrous eyes. "No, dear, but at my age, it's usually best to get right to the point. One never knows."

"Aunt Peggy, you're not old."

"Of course I am, dear. I'm ninety! How long do you think I'll live, anyway?" Aunt Peggy took Jennifer's hand and held it tight. "It's okay, dear. Just tell me what you want to know. I'm a lot stronger than you think. Most women are. Like you." Peggy sipped her tea and chewed on another piece of cake that she held with two hands, like a child.

Jennifer took a deep breath. "Okay. I need you to look at something for me and then I have to ask you about it." She pressed the creases from Annabelle's birth certificate, which Betty Lou had found in the public records here in Jackson County.

Aunt Peggy exchanged her distance glasses for her reading glasses—both of which dangled from chains around her neck. She took Annabelle's birth certificate and read it. Slowly. She read it through a couple of times. Then she dropped her hand to her lap, still holding on to the certificate. She changed her glasses again and then looked at Jennifer.

"Old secrets never go away, do they?" she sighed.

"Did you have a child, Aunt Peggy? A girl?" Jennifer asked her.

"No. I didn't."

"But that birth certificate says you and Uncle Herbert had a baby girl. About a year before I was born."

"I know. But it's not true." Aunt Peggy looked at her with concern.

Jennifer's confusion returned along with her headache. Birds sang outside in the pecan trees. She noticed a television playing somewhere in a back room of the house. It sounded like a game show. Aunt Peggy loved *Wheel of Fortune*.

CHAPTER SEVENTY-FIVE

TYLER'S HOURS IN THE Cellar were wearing him down. He spent every minute down here when he wasn't required to be somewhere else. He'd barely seen Lori and the girls since Walden had killed Stuart Barnett. Tyler's absence wasn't going to help him any in his will-you-remarry-me campaign. He looked at his watch, stood, and stretched his aching muscles.

"Ah, the hell with it," he said as he picked up his car keys and grabbed his wallet. He knew he'd find it. Would it matter so much if he found what he was looking for tomorrow instead of tonight?

He picked up the cell phone to call Lori. If she'd let him come over, he'd pack it in now. After the anticipation, though, he got her answering machine and left a message. He shrugged, dropped the cell, keys and wallet, and turned again to the video tapes.

So far, he'd looked at every minute of tape from all the obvious places. Nothing in the lab, Blake's office, Gilbert's cube, Annabelle's workbench. Nothing in the lunchroom. He'd looked at all the tapes from the executive wing, since computer access to the data Annabelle had stolen could be reached from there. Nada.

Now, he was down to watching tapes within seven days either

way of Annabelle's disappearance, in all the unlikely spots in the plant.

"Tonight's movie, folks, is the exciting world of the closed-files and old-furniture storage room," he said aloud, in the voice of an announcer for a movie trailer.

"Yep, here we have the storage room where Russell Denton, the pack rat, keeps every old thing he owns. On this side is the lava lamp collection," his voice trailed off as he watched the screen.

"What the hell?" he exclaimed, zooming in closer.

Tyler whistled low and slow.

"Gotcha, you son of a bitch."

His cell phone vibrated off the table and fell onto the floor. He didn't notice.

CHAPTER SEVENTY-SIX

WAS IT LATE ENOUGH for the evening television shows already? Jennifer listened to the wheel turning, a letter shouted, the unmistakable *"ping"* of a correct guess. The wheel turned again. Another successful letter was called and it allowed the contestant to solve the puzzle. Jennifer could hear the contestant's squeals and visualized her jumping up and down, hugging the host.

"Well, then why does the birth certificate say you had a child?"

Aunt Peggy searched Jennifer's face, seeking what? After a while, she left the couch and went into a back bedroom toward the television sounds.

What the hell? The woman was ninety, as she said. Maybe her mind was not as sharp as Jennifer believed?

She could hear Aunt Peggy shuffling around, the dragging sound of a chair being moved across a hardwood floor. A door creaked open. After a few commercials, another round of the game show started. A few spins of the wheel later, Aunt Peggy returned, carrying a thin brown leather book. She held it to her chest for a few more seconds, and then handed the book to Jennifer.

"What's this?"

"I thought you'd ask me these questions someday," she said.

Aunt Peggy gestured toward the small photo album. Jennifer took it and opened to the first page, where she saw a picture of her mother. Pregnant and radiant and young. The next picture was of her parents, seated outdoors in the back garden of this very house with Uncle Herbert. Jennifer looked up at Aunt Peggy, perplexed. The older woman waited.

In the next photo, Jennifer's mother and Aunt Peggy were looking at a flower garden. They wore dress clothes instead of casual ones. It was spring. Maybe Easter Sunday.

Jennifer examined the pictures of her newlywed parents awaiting the birth of their only child. Of course, they hadn't known then that Jennifer would be their only child. Debbie had wanted many children. So had Clay. But something had gone wrong and no more children would be born.

The next few photographs were of Jennifer's parents in a hospital room. Mothers stayed hospitalized with their babies for a while in those days. Debbie had explained that she'd been drugged for Jennifer's delivery and didn't remember any of the labor or even the actual time of Jennifer's birth.

Her parents looked happy and baby Jennifer seemed peacefully quiet in her mother's arms.

The last picture was of Aunt Peggy and Uncle Herbert, her parents and the baby. Aunt Peggy and Uncle Herbert were dressed for church. Debbie and Clay looked nicely groomed, too. Baby Jennifer wore a cute spring outfit with a little bonnet. She was wrapped in a pink blanket decorated with white flowers.

Jennifer flipped through the photos again and closed the book. "I've never seen these pictures before. When were they taken? I thought Mom told me she was bedridden for most of her pregnancy and couldn't travel. That's why I was born in Michigan, she said."

Aunt Peggy pressed her finger into the last crumbs of her pound cake and sucked them into her mouth. *Wheel of Fortune* continued in the rear of the hushed house. But whatever hints the pictures contained, Aunt Peggy seemed to want Jennifer to solve the puzzle herself.

Jennifer reopened the small album. She looked again, carefully this time, seeking information, if any was there to be found. All of the pictures had been taken in the spring. One captured Aunt Peggy cutting daffodils for a bouquet.

The final round of *Wheel of Fortune* was being played. One letter after another was called quickly, in succession. Time was running out. Aunt Peggy seemed excited to learn who would be the first to solve the puzzle and take home the prize money.

Jennifer was born in September, not spring.

In these pictures, her mother's hair was long, but in Jennifer's baby pictures, Debbie had a very short pixie cut. She'd said taking care of a baby and having long hair were mutually exclusive when Jennifer had asked once.

She studied the images closely. There were other discrepancies, now that she knew what to search for. She had never seen this baby blanket before. Clay appeared a little younger, maybe, than in pictures she'd seen at home.

Jennifer picked up the birth certificate again. Roxanne Mae Thomas was born on February 14—Valentine's Day. She flipped back to the hospital photo in the album. *I Love Annabelle* was pictured on the hospital room's television.

Wheel of Fortune ended. A new winner solved the final bonus round. The music closed the show, and still Aunt Peggy sat and said nothing, allowing the silence to linger.

Until finally, she got it. Understood and accepted the proof right there in front of her.

"Why didn't anyone ever tell me?" Jennifer tried to control herself, but her hysteria mounted as she voiced each unbidden question. "This was my parents' baby. My sister. What happened to her? Why didn't you tell me?"

Aunt Peggy grabbed her hand. Her sharp, bright eyes glistened with unshed tears. "We should have told you. We meant to. The story doesn't have a happy ending, Jenny. It just never seemed like the right time to make everyone sad again."

Jennifer drew back her hand as if Aunt Peggy's grasp had burned her skin. She shouted to hear herself over the roaring in her ears. "Never the right time? For nearly thirty years?"

Aunt Peggy's frail body seemed unequal to the strength of Jennifer's anger. But she didn't shrink from the truth. "At that time, pregnant high school girls had only one of two choices. Your mom could have dropped out of school to get married. Or give the baby away. Debbie wanted to be a teacher. Clay needed to go to college. They couldn't be parents. Not then."

Aunt Peggy tried to make Jennifer accept the unacceptable. Aunt Peggy should not have had to bear this task alone, but she did it bravely. "Debbie finished high school in December before she started to show. She came here for the rest of her pregnancy. Clay visited when he could. They were both here for Annabelle's birth and they stayed through the summer. In the fall, they had to give Annabelle up. It nearly broke all of our hearts, but we didn't know what else to do."

Jennifer could barely speak. "And what happened to Annabelle?"

"We didn't know anyone here then, Herbert and I. We'd just moved to this area a few months before. When we went to the hospital for Annabelle's delivery, Debbie and Clay used our names. There was no shame on us. We were glad to do it." Aunt Peggy's voice was strong.

"But why give Annabelle away at all? Why couldn't you have kept her?" Jennifer knew how Annabelle had grown up, who had adopted her. Jennifer knew how Annabelle had turned out. And she realized that her parents and this precious old woman sitting here were at least partly responsible.

Aunt Peggy hung her head in a gesture Jennifer herself so often used, twisting her linen handkerchief in her hands. She took a deep breath and tried to make Jennifer understand. "I know it seems so easy now. But then, Herbert and I were older. We'd never wanted children of our own. And we all thought that Annabelle would just be a constant reminder of a bad time in your parents' lives."

"A bad time? A bad time? That's all you could think about?" Jennifer felt her hysteria mounting but she didn't want to control herself, even if she could have.

Aunt Peggy tried to take Jennifer's hand again, but Jennifer jerked away. "We honestly believed Annabelle was better off with a family that would love her and want her."

"So what did you do? Give her to Dr. Jacks?" Jennifer knew her voice was filled with accusation caused by profound hurt. She didn't care.

For the first time, Aunt Peggy acted as if she felt uncomfortable. "Dr. Jacks was doing a lot of good in those days. He promised us Annabelle would go to a good home. We believed him."

These admissions were too much for Jennifer to get her thoughts around. She just couldn't accept it. When Betty Lou had given her Annabelle's birth certificate, Jennifer had been relieved that Aunt Peggy and Uncle Herbert were Annabelle's parents. That explained Annabelle's physical resemblance to Jennifer. It explained Lila Walden's hopes, Tim Tyler's confidence. And the explanation was one Jennifer accepted because she loved and trusted her parents so much.

Now, she was bewildered, betrayed, devastated. Who were Debbie and Clay Lane, really? And who was she?

Aunt Peggy spoke again into the silence. "The next year, when Debbie got pregnant again, they decided to go ahead and marry."

"They had *two* accidental pregnancies?" Jennifer's incredulity raised her voice again. "They did this not once, but *twice*?"

"Good girls get in trouble, too, Jennifer. Your parents loved each other. They've been married almost thirty years. That proves something, doesn't it?"

"But what about Annabelle?"

"A few years later, they tried to find Annabelle. But Dr. Jacks said he had to protect Annabelle's privacy. We all went to court, but the records were sealed away from us. Don't judge them too harshly," she said, reaching for Jennifer's hand again. Jennifer jerked away. "They never forgot Annabelle. I know they didn't. I never did. Why, when I saw Annabelle again, it was wonderful! It was just like seeing you! Debbie and Clay must feel the same way."

What Aunt Peggy had said didn't penetrate at first, but when the message slithered its way into her mind, Jennifer's eyes widened and her breath caught. "You've seen Annabelle?"

The older woman nodded, a big smile on her face, as if she'd just discovered she was the *Wheel of Fortune* winner. "Annabelle was here a few weeks ago. Didn't she tell you? She said she was going to call you." Once Aunt Peggy realized Jennifer's ignorance, she became alarmed. "I thought that's why you were here. Oh, honey, I hope I haven't spoiled Annabelle's surprise."

What was she talking about? Jennifer felt as if her head were filled with loud, pounding cotton balls, muffling everything around her. Her synapses didn't seem to be firing. "Surprise?"

"Annabelle said she was meeting your parents in Alaska. She said you were all going to be there together. Didn't she tell you?" Aunt Peggy was upset, now. Small red splotches covered her face and neck. Jennifer feared she might have a stroke. The worry instantly brought Jennifer back to a small measure of control.

"Oh, Aunt Peggy, I'm sorry. I haven't talked to her, but maybe she went to meet Mom and Dad there," Jennifer said, trying to calm the old woman. Jennifer remembered Debbie telling her about the offer for their trip. How it was too good to pass up. No wonder. Annabelle must have arranged it. What was Annabelle up to?

Jennifer looked outside. For the first time, she noticed how dark it was. She'd been gone from Tampa too long. Now that she'd learned what she'd come to discover, she'd need a new plan. She tried to call Tyler, but he didn't answer.

Jennifer knew she might never see Aunt Peggy again and she didn't want to leave her too soon. At Aunt Peggy's insistence, they had dinner together. Jennifer told her happy stories about Tampa. When Aunt Peggy's eyelids seemed too heavy for her to hold up, Jennifer left for home, protesting that she couldn't stay. She got back on the road, pointed the car due south and drove.

During the long, silent hours, Jennifer had time to think. Questions popped up every few miles and none were resolved by her answers.

Aunt Peggy suggested Jennifer ask Debbie and Clay about their first child. Of course, Aunt Peggy thought her parents should have told her long ago. Jennifer went back and forth on the issue.

Maybe she should respect their privacy, on the one hand. On the other, this was her sister. She had a stake in the matter, too.

What would her parents think if she struck up a relationship with Annabelle? Would they be happy? Horrified? Of course, that assumed she could find Annabelle.

She had to be alive. If Jennifer only just found out she had a sister and now that sister was dead… It didn't bear thinking about. But what had her great-aunt meant about Annabelle meeting her parents in Alaska? Had Annabelle really said something about that to Peggy, or was Peggy dreadfully confused? Jennifer hadn't wanted to worry Peggy more by pressing her on the issue.

Jennifer made up her mind. When her parents returned from Alaska, she would tell them what she knew. She would go home and discuss it with them in person. The delay would give her some time to absorb the implications for her own life.

Betty Lou had told Jennifer that adopted children often hold on to the contact information for their birth parents for months or years without making contact. The emotional strength necessary to step over that chasm takes time to develop. Maybe by the time her parents returned from Alaska, Jennifer would have found Annabelle and she'd have more to talk about.

Late in the evening, she stopped for gas near Macon. She located her cell phone and checked for messages, but she had none. She dialed Tyler again. When he answered, she said, "I know where Annabelle James is."

CHAPTER SEVENTY-SEVEN

THE LIMO DRIVER DROPPED Russell off at Peter O. Knight Airport and handed him his briefcase at the gate. New federal safety regulations didn't apply to Russell Denton. He didn't stand in lines, hold out his picture identification, or run his briefcase through metal detectors. He didn't have to.

Normally, Russell would have flown in his own jet. Not today. He didn't want to broadcast to anyone that he had taken this trip. Only Tyler knew and would be joining him shortly.

Once they were settled in the private plane Tyler rented, Russell said, "Have you found her?"

"Not yet. But we're close."

"How close?"

"Jennifer knows that Annabelle is her sister. She's found out Annabelle manipulated Debbie and Clay Lane into going to Alaska. We think Annabelle intends to meet them there. When she does, we'll grab her."

Russell shook his head at this very curious Lane family. He didn't understand these people. He had tried to discuss the Waldens, the Lanes, and the bizarre circumstances that tied them together with Patricia. But the situation was too complicated. Patricia was as baffled as he was.

Russell trusted Patricia. But not with everything. He had learned the hard way that no one was completely reliable. He shook off thoughts of Blake, of how Russell had trusted him, and how that trust had been violated. "So, what's next?"

"Annabelle pretended to be a telemarketer to make the Lanes an offer they couldn't refuse. They're cruising in Alaska. She intends to see them, maybe talk to them."

"Why, after all this time?"

"Hard to say. We'll be meeting them in Juneau. Maybe we'll find out." Tyler brought out a portable DVD player and opened it on the table in front of Russell. "Let me show you something else. This is the video of Annabelle's last day at the plant."

He played the video camera's recorded scenes—with the synchronized audiotape—of Annabelle's authorized entry to the lab and locker room, and then her exit. She'd been in the building nine hours on her last day. Not uncommon.

The snow on the screen signaled a change. "Here's Blake's movements that same day."

Again, the screen showed his authorized entry, Blake going into his office, an exit and return at lunchtime, and his exit at the end of the day. The same nine hours had elapsed, but he'd only spent six of those hours inside the plant.

"Here's the overlap." The video now showed a period of ten minutes beginning at 11:56 a.m. Blake and Annabelle were together in an empty closet in the seldom used storage area. Like every square inch of the Denton Bio-Medical facility, this room was under constant surveillance. Only Tyler and Russell Denton were aware of the extent of the video coverage. Most employees believed video surveillance was aimed only at sensitive areas of the plant. That was obviously what Blake and Annabelle had thought, too.

Tyler turned up the volume, but no words were exchanged between the young couple. One view of their backs made seeing what they were doing impossible, although Blake did bend down to kiss Annabelle at one point. The interlude might have looked like a quick game of grab ass in the closet, and that's what Tyler had thought when he'd seen it the first time.

The next view was a repeat of those same ten minutes, however.

"This time, we can see that Blake entered the closet first." Tyler narrated the next few minutes of the film. "Annabelle followed two minutes later."

Tyler froze the next frame so Russell could see the picture clearly. Once inside the closet, Blake handed Annabelle a small, flat, round object.

"What is it?"

"Probably a CD or DVD."

The object was so small that it was almost completely hidden by Blake's hand. Tyler increased the frame size. In Annabelle's smaller grasp, the thing looked like a compact computer disk, a CD. The florescent light caught the shiny surface and reflected the glint off the camera lens. The flash made the frame hard to see, but Russell thought Tyler was right.

Russell watched Annabelle put the CD into her lab coat, then lift her head to receive Blake's kiss. "See you tonight," he whispered to her. He opened the door.

Annabelle left the room, Blake remaining. The next frames showed her walking down to the locker room where she lifted the CD from her lab coat pocket and slipped it into her purse. Then she returned to the lab.

The next sequence showed Blake leaving the closet. He went directly out into the parking lot, climbed into his dark blue Jaguar, and drove away for his lunch break.

Russell looked again at the automatic date on the screen just to be sure. Confirmed. The date Annabelle had disappeared.

The final scenes were those in Annabelle's apartment he'd already seen—Blake and Annabelle preparing to make Annabelle disappear. Russell shuddered at his own choice of thoughts. Make Annabelle disappear. God, he hoped Blake hadn't killed her to make her disappear forever.

Russell pushed the stop button and then played the entire disk again. After three more viewings, he convinced himself that Tyler was right. Blake had helped Annabelle to steal everything about HepZMax from him. Blake knew Russell had Hep Z and was counting on HepZMax to bring him back to health. Blake had stolen the cure to hurt him, maybe kill him. The knowledge made Russell soul-sick.

The flight to Juneau would take ten hours. Russell retreated to a small bedroom at the back of the plane. He needed sleep. Fatigue had overwhelmed him lately, and he was afraid he knew why. His symptoms might have been caused by stress, but his skin had been more jaundiced than usual. He felt like hell. The cancer was progressing. He checked with the transplant people daily. Nothing yet.

How much longer could he wait?

CHAPTER SEVENTY-EIGHT

"WHY DO YOU THINK Annabelle will make contact with the Lanes in Juneau?" Russell asked Tyler later, when they were eating the catered meal served by the flight attendant. The nap had revived him and he felt better. The drugs helped, but they weren't a cure. He'd tried all the available drugs on the market. His Hep Z was the resistant type. It had destroyed his liver. If he could get HepZMax and produce even a few doses, he would be his own guinea pig. It was his only chance for a real recovery and he was eager to get started.

Since his competitor and enemy, the president of Alabaster Medical had filed his PMA application, Russell had been in negotiations to buy back the HepZMax formula, or at least to buy enough for his own use. The cretin was unwilling to sell him the formula, at any price. Nor would he break the law by selling Russell an unapproved drug. Russell knew his time was running out.

"It's the last place she called Ronald Walden from. We don't know why she hasn't contacted him since," Tyler reminded him.

"So you're just guessing." They'd had this conversation before, but Russell was a man who liked to understand everything as well as possible. Sometimes, in the retelling, new information emerged. He listened closely while Tyler ran through the facts again.

"Educated guessing. We've checked the private planes, the cruise lines. We can't find any evidence that Annabelle left Juneau. We know she's the one who arranged to get the Lanes on this trip. We checked with the travel agent and confirmed that Annabelle paid without their knowledge. Debbie Lane told Jennifer that a telemarketer had made them an offer too good to turn down. Annabelle must have made it seem like they were getting a believable deal." Tyler repeated his logic so that Russell could see it, too. "It doesn't make sense that she would bring the Lanes to Alaska and not try to contact them."

Russell flashed Tyler the same "don't bullshit me" stare Stuart Barnett had given Russell at their lunch in Tarpon Springs a lifetime ago.

Tyler responded as if Russell had commanded him to do so. "Juneau is a city that can only be reached by air or boat. No accessible roads go in or out. Annabelle could have taken a private plane somewhere. That's fairly easy to do in Alaska. But why would she? Having gone to all of the trouble to get there, to bring the Lanes, why try to leave?" Tyler reinforced his original arguments. "Jennifer said Annabelle had been two steps ahead of her, searching for her parents. Annabelle had some reason to go looking for the Lanes, some new motivation. We just don't know what that reason is yet."

When Russell didn't answer, Tyler said, "Look, Russell, I know it's not perfect. But it's the best we have. You don't want me to press Blake. We discussed this. It's our best shot."

"No, Tim," Russell said. "At this point, it's our *only* shot."

Russell returned to the DVD player and to build his resolve watched Blake betray him over and over again. Russell had nothing much to lose. They'd tried everything else. Almost.

CHAPTER SEVENTY-NINE

RUSSELL AND TYLER WAITED in the parking lot about three miles away from the cruise-ship harbor in Juneau, watching as the tourists walked past. They'd studied the photos Tyler had stolen from Jennifer's apartment. They knew what they were looking for.

Deborah Lane was a small woman, dark complexioned with soft wavy hair, about fifty. Both of her daughters resembled her in stature. Clay Lane was a tall, thin man with a fringe of silver hair around his head and sharp blue eyes. In the photos, Clay Lane was smiling, displaying the dimple in his chin that he'd passed on to both daughters. Maybe they'd spot the two of them alone, but perhaps the Lanes would be with other tourists—or with Annabelle herself.

"Why are we waiting here?" Russell asked.

"My contact on the cruise ship said Debbie and Clay Lane took the early wildlife tour. He said they'd be returning here to catch a bus for the trip back to the ship," Tyler said.

"Which of the catamarans did they embark on?"

"There's no way to tell. About six catamarans were filled with people from their cruise ship alone. We'll need to wait until all of the small boats return, unless we find them sooner." Tyler sat on the bench, a bag of peanuts and a soda in his hand.

Even in August, the air outside was cold, the wind brisk. Russell buttoned his coat closer to his face. How did people live here? Tampa's summer heat had thinned his blood. Sixty-five degrees and drizzling rain along the shore penetrated his clothes and chilled him to the bone. He ducked down into his jacket and stuffed his hands in his pockets. The heavy mist threatened to turn into a full rain shower that would be nothing like Tampa's hot summer thunderstorms. Russell missed home. Even his heart felt chilled.

After an hour of waiting, tourists funneled like cattle from one conveyance to the next, and Tyler elbowed Russell in the arm.

"Over there," he said, nodding in the direction of the final group disembarking from the very last boat of the morning.

Russell spied Debbie and Clay Lane talking with another couple who, from this distance, appeared to be Hawaiian. He sat up straighter when he noticed the single woman with them. He recognized the walk first. She was bundled up in a jogging suit and a coat. Her hair was pulled back in a ponytail, which looped through the back of a navy blue baseball cap, embroidered on the front with the gold stars of the Big Dipper—the same as the Alaska state flag.

The cap and the big sunglasses she wore hid most of her face, but even in disguise, Annabelle James was unmistakable. Russell would have recognized her anywhere, especially after looking at her on that damned DVD player for hours on the plane. Through sheer force of will and sixty years of training, Russell didn't move an inch.

Tyler focused his digital camera toward the group and took a quick stream of photographs. The camera didn't click and there was no flash or film to wind. Tyler would get good photographic evidence that they could examine later to be sure. Proof. But Russell didn't need it. It was her.

They watched the four tourists and Annabelle walk toward the bus. "She can't get on that bus," Russell said.

"She won't. Annabelle's been in Juneau for weeks. The bus is returning to the ship. She didn't come from the ship, so they won't take her back," Tyler told him.

Annabelle waved goodbye to the Lanes and headed toward a Jeep Cherokee parked farther down the lot. Tyler rose and moved toward their rental. Russell followed as quickly as he could. Annabelle got in the car and the two men quickly slid into their vehicle. They'd agreed they would not confront her in the parking lot while the Lanes were there, so they followed her.

Annabelle drove toward downtown Juneau and eventually pulled into the Best of Juneau Motor Lodge. Tyler parked on the street behind a tall shrub. Because of the long summer growing season, the annual vegetation was so huge here that the shrub completely hid the car from view.

Russell watched as Annabelle exited her Jeep and walked toward a room on the first floor of the motel. She reached in her pocket for her key, slipped it into the slot to unlock the door, and began to turn the doorknob.

Tyler, silently coming up behind her, shoved the door open and moved Annabelle into the room with the same momentum. He pushed her down onto the bed, lay on top of her, and held her there.

"What?" she cried, startled, squirming, ready to fight.

She was such a little scrapper, Russell thought, watching the scene from the doorway. Even now.

"Take it easy. Take it easy. No one's going to hurt you," Tyler said.

"Get off me! What do you want!"

Russell Denton came into the room slowly and spoke at last. "Hello, daughter-in-law. So nice to see you again. Sorry I missed the wedding."

CHAPTER EIGHTY

JENNIFER SAT IN HER car on the westbound side of the Garden, a local drive-through convenience store. She'd never seen one of these stores until she'd moved to Florida, but she loved the ease of stopping, shopping, and never leaving the car. Great concept.

The Garden was housed in a building only about ten feet wide and twenty feet long, and it was glass enclosed; sliding doors opened on both sides so that customers could see straight through from one side of the store to the other.

As she waited her turn, Jennifer barely noticed the beautiful summer evening, the sun still high enough to heat the air. She had the radio up loud. Bob Seger blasted out that old time rock and roll. She loved the oldies, particularly anything out of the Motor City.

"Hey, Jenny!" Sammy said from his position behind the cash register at the center of the store. Sammy was a good kid with a face full of freckles and a head of violent red curls. Flashing his best grin, he asked, "What's shakin' with the big city lawyer?"

"Not much," she lied while she smiled at his reference to her work. At one time, she had believed her work was worth everything. She loved being a big city lawyer. Now, that very life had evaporated, slipping through her fingers as if it had all been a dream.

"How's your mom?" Jennifer asked him. She shopped here almost every day and Sammy had become a friend of sorts. His mother was fighting breast cancer these days, and Sammy was having trouble dealing with it. Discussing his troubles with strangers seemed to help Sammy, and it got Jennifer out of her own head for a few minutes, too.

"Mom's good. Her hair is starting to grow back. For a while there, she had this really cool baldy thing goin', but now it's more Shade, you know?" Sammy told her as he walked to the other side of the store to take an order from the driver in a vintage yellow Beetle at the opposite window. Sammy had those silly sandals on his feet the kids seemed to be so fond of, and he wore denim shorts with a "Go Bucs" T-shirt that was a couple of years too old.

On the way here, Jennifer had picked up the envelope containing her blood test results from the walk-in clinic. So far, she hadn't found the courage to open it. She literally held her future in her hands and she wasn't brave enough to face what it could be. She envied Sammy's mother her courage.

Sammy handed the Beetle driver a bag filled with milk and soda and took her money, saying, "Thank you, ma'am"—always polite. The yellow Beetle pulled away, allowing a dirty midnight blue Jaguar to replace the Beetle at the drive-up doorway. Sammy returned to Jennifer's side of the store.

"Have to take everyone in turn, you know," Sammy told her. "What can I get you, good lookin'?"

"I'm in no hurry," Jennifer smiled up at him. "Give me a Lotto form and I'll fill it out while you help that gentleman." She nodded toward the Jaguar. It was a lot like the one Blake drove, but dirtier, she thought. But she wasn't good with cars.

Besides, the guy in the Jaguar seemed more than a little impatient. He'd tapped the horn twice already. Jennifer hoped he was in a hurry to get to the car wash. The car looked as if it had been sitting in a mud puddle for a month. She could wait.

"You got it!" Sammy gave her his saucy grin again, along with the Lotto form and a small pencil. "Good luck. When you win, don't forget your friend, the struggling college student," he said.

She laughed with him. "You'll be my first charitable donation, Sammy," she promised, as he turned away and approached the Jaguar.

Now, she looked more closely through the open doorways at the car directly opposite hers. Could it be Blake's?

The beautiful machine sported a big dent in the front fender, just behind the headlight. The deep blue paint was scraped off and the metal was crumpled around streaks of red left there by whatever had collided with the car. What a shame to damage a fine car like that. Drivers had killed for less.

She shrugged and turned her gaze to her future. Sure, lotto tickets were a tax on the uneducated—defined as anyone silly enough to think she might win. But fifty million dollars would go a long way toward solving her problems. With that much money, she wouldn't need to be a big-city lawyer anymore. Whatever her new life was going to be, fifty million dollars would make it a lot better. She checked her status in line.

Two cars were lined up now on Jennifer's side of the store, a red Miata convertible and an old Ford truck. On the opposite side, behind the Jaguar, was a black Regal. Sammy was getting behind in his work.

The kid was a little slow sometimes, maybe even mentally handicapped. He often seemed just a little off, although not in any way menacing. Sometimes he mixed up her order or her change. Jennifer was patient with him and she'd noticed most other customers were, too. Under pressure, he faltered now and then. Who didn't?

Jennifer had rolled the window up to keep the cool air inside her car. She'd propped the lotto form against the padded steering wheel and was carefully coloring inside the lines of her chosen numbers. She was superstitious. She always played the same numbers and each had sentimental value. It was hard to come up with six numbers between one and fifty-three that had sentimental value, but she'd done it. As she blackened in the small squares with the lead pencil, she spent a few moments recalling the reason for each number she chose and said a little wish for luck.

Everything happening around Jennifer was blocked out by her concentration, the song on the radio, and the air conditioning blowing in her face. When she heard the first loud *crack* she didn't recognize it for what it was.

Two more quick *cracks* followed the first, grabbing her attention and pulling her gaze through the door of the convenience mart toward the sound, toward the Jaguar.

Even though it was seven o'clock, it was bright daylight—a typical summer night. She saw the driver clearly, full in the face. For the first time, she looked directly into his fierce eyes.

He was just twenty-five feet from her, staring point-blank at her from his car. His features had grown wilder and she'd been put off by the likeness to Blake's car, but she now recognized Ronald Walden, and every nerve in her body jumped to full alert.

She saw Sammy lying on the ground, face down, in a pool of

rapidly spreading bright red blood. It seemed an echo of the last image she'd had of Stuart Barnett.

Ronald Walden concentrated a fierce challenging stare of intimate contact toward Jennifer that froze her in her seat. His lips curved up in a sneer of a smile while he pointed his gun directly at her. Jennifer could not move. She'd seen him kill before; she was about to die.

The silly things people said about seeing her life flash before her didn't happen. She didn't scream or duck or jump out of the way. She simply sat there, staring at him, waiting.

He squeezed the trigger a fourth time.

Nothing happened—no noise at all.

After a moment, she realized she hadn't died. She didn't feel searing pain anywhere on her body. She heard no gunshot. The gun had failed to fire this time. She got a second chance.

Her heart pounding and hands trembling, Jennifer reacted without thinking. She reached into the backseat, feeling for her gun case. This was it. She'd been carrying her gun around for days in anticipation of such a moment. Her intuition—or maybe just her fear—had told her the moment would be coming. Now, it had arrived.

Jennifer quickly opened the case by feel while she gazed steadily into Ronald Walden's malevolent eyes, afraid to turn away, even for a moment, and give him a clear shot at the back of her head.

She pulled out the gun and raised it quickly, refusing to give herself time to falter. Thinking of Stuart and Sammy, Jennifer pointed at Walden, and, sick at heart, fired without further hesitation.

Her bullets hit the roof of the sleek, dark car.

Walden laughed at her and lowered his own weapon. The Jaguar's electric window rose smoothly. Then, he opened the back door and pushed a man's body out onto the ground near Sammy.

Jennifer's hands were shaky. She'd never shot at a live target before, but she fired again. This time, she shattered the glass in the Jaguar's back window.

He gunned the Jaguar's powerful engine in reply and roared away. Jennifer wanted to take one more shot at the retreating car, but she was afraid she'd shoot a bystander. Filled with impotence and adrenaline, she placed her gun on the car seat and jumped out.

She watched the Jaguar make a quick left turn out of the parking lot onto Bay-to-Bay Boulevard, blowing through the red light while ignoring the blaring horns of angry drivers who had the right of way. He narrowly missed a head-on collision and took a sharp left onto MacDill. Walden sped north and was gone.

It didn't matter if he got away, Jennifer thought. She bent over Sammy, the wonderful young man lying wounded in the doorway, while other customers dealt with the second victim.

Jennifer had seen Ronald Walden's face quite clearly, a face she'd recognized, a face she knew she'd never forget. She was cursed with an excellent eye and memory for detail, and the event replayed in her head like a video. How could she have such an uncanny knack for being in the wrong place at the wrong time? Or had he followed her here? The idea started waves of revulsion she recognized as delayed shock.

Quickly, she glanced toward the customers attending the man Walden had pushed out of the Jaguar. She began to scream without control.

"Lady, lady." One of the bystanders ran over to where she knelt and put his arm around her shivering shoulder.

Jennifer's screams had turned to babbling incoherence. The bystander seemed finally to understand.

He pointed at the second victim. "You know this guy?"

CHAPTER EIGHTY-ONE

ANNABELLE JAMES SEATED HERSELF in the room's only armchair after Tyler released her. She straightened her clothes and her spine.

"This isn't much of a living arrangement, Annabelle," Tyler said.

"What do you care?"

Like a petulant child, one used to always getting her own way. Which was exactly what Tyler thought she was.

"I don't. But Mr. Denton here does. He wants you to give back what you took from him." He moved into the corner of the room to allow Russell free reign to conduct the interview as he wished. Russell had focused on this one moment for weeks. Tyler wouldn't get in the way for anything.

Annabelle glared in Russell's direction. "What are you talking about? I didn't take anything from you. And I'm not your daughter-in-law. You're not Blake's father, and don't you ever forget it."

She rubbed her wrists where Tyler had grabbed her when he held her down on the bed. She acted as if he'd hurt her, but he knew he hadn't. Her behavior was pure Annabelle. Petulant. Childish. Her eyes shot daggers at Russell Denton. Tyler marveled at how much she hated Russell; he had to admire that level of passion about anything. He rarely saw such energy in anyone except his daughters.

"Why would you care if I took something from you anyway?" She threw her remark Russell's way. "You have more than any man can use in this lifetime."

"How much I do or don't possess is irrelevant, Annabelle. But as it happens, I only have one nephew."

Tyler noticed again that Russell was exhausted. He'd been running on adrenaline for weeks, but now that they'd found Annabelle James, surely he realized how inconsequential she was. Annabelle hadn't held Russell captive all this time. He'd done it to himself. Tyler had tried to tell him so, but Russell had refused to listen. He'd wanted Blake back and he'd wanted to believe Annabelle could return the boy Blake had once been. Tyler knew it was way too late for that; when would Russell admit as much?

"Is that what you think?" Annabelle demanded. "That I somehow enticed Blake away from you?" Her tone was contemptuous, dismissive. As if Blake's privilege was Russell's fault. Which, of course, it was. "Wise up. Blake Denton hasn't done anything he didn't choose to do his whole entire life. You should know that."

The old man didn't strike back; Tyler respected his control. Or maybe he simply didn't have the strength.

Russell said, "So he chose the tattoo that gave him hepatitis Z? No. He did that for you. You talked him into it."

This was what Blake had told his uncle, and Tyler knew Russell wanted to believe it. The point was hopelessly intertwined with Russell's guilt in a way that Tyler didn't fully comprehend.

Somehow, Russell thought he should have told Blake about his own hepatitis Z and that would have made a difference in Blake's behavior. Annabelle was right, though. It wouldn't have mattered to Blake. He thought he was bulletproof because Russell had always made sure he was.

Bitterly, Annabelle said, "You're crazy. It was Blake's idea for us to get the tattoos together. He's the one who forced the issue. I didn't want to do it. Then I got Hep Z. He didn't." She sneered, "I guess he was just *lucky*. Like he's always been *lucky*."

Tyler saw the naked hatred in Annabelle's face. She hated Russell at a level well beyond the man's understanding.

Russell ran a hand over his face. Tyler worried that Russell's fatigue would become unbearable. The poor old guy had lost his edge. Despair defeated him in a way nothing else ever had.

"Just give me that CD with my formula on it and sign this affidavit." Russell nodded to Tyler, who pulled out the affidavit and held it in front of Annabelle.

"What's this?" She looked at the page as if it were a snake that might bite.

Russell's gray pallor alarmed Tyler; they needed to get this over with quickly. Before Russell collapsed. Tyler answered, "It says you're returning the HepZMax formula of your own free will and that you never sold it to Alabaster Medical. It also says you did not hire Roger Riley as your lawyer and are terminating his services."

Annabelle turned to face Tyler. "You must be as crazy as he is. What are you talking about? I never sold that formula. I took it out of the plant for Blake. I don't even have it. I don't know anything about Roger Riley. What does he have to do with anything?"

Tyler had interviewed a lot of suspects. He knew when they

were lying and he knew techniques to make them tell the truth. He was sure Annabelle James was lying now, but he didn't care.

"Just sign the affidavit and we'll let you go about your business," Tyler told her, weary now of her theatrics. The last thing he needed was Russell's collapse here, in the back of beyond. Who knew what kind of medical care they had up here in this frozen tundra?

Annabelle picked up the pen and signed her name on the affidavit. "I don't know what you think you're going to do with this. No court in the world will enforce it. You practically killed me to get me to sign."

"I can't wait to hear you explain that under oath." Tyler photographed her signing the paper. Then, he set the digital camera to video record. "Roxanne Mae James," he intoned, "are you executing this affidavit of your own free will?"

"Yes," Annabelle said, defiant as always. "I am. Because if I don't, you probably *will* kill me." She threw it at Tyler and it wafted to the floor.

Tyler turned off the video; he could edit that last part out.

"Hand it over, Annabelle." He held out his hand.

"Hand what over?"

"The CD. With the data on it." Tyler said.

"I don't know what the hell you're talking about." She fairly spat the words.

"Either give it to me, or I'll tear this place apart looking for it." Tyler wasn't kidding and he was through fooling around. Russell's color was getting worse by the second.

"Suit yourself." She folded her arms over her chest and sat quietly—but with the fuming energy of the wrongly accused pulsing off her body like radioactive waves.

Tyler searched the entire room quickly but thoroughly; as

Annabelle predicted, he didn't find a CD. Which meant Annabelle had told the truth. She didn't have the CD with her. But where was it? Had she given it to Blake after all?

"Now, leave," Annabelle said, her voice as icy as an Alaskan wind in January.

Tyler ran a hand through his hair. He looked around the small room once more, seeking missed hiding places, but found none. "I'll check your car on the way out," he said.

"You do that."

Tyler picked up the affidavit and stowed it in its envelope. He put the envelope in his breast pocket. Russell Denton had already risen and was standing by the door. Tyler watched as Annabelle and Russell took each other's measure for a moment. Had either of them gotten what they wanted? Tyler thought not.

He gestured to Russell that it was okay to leave. At the door, he turned for one last look. Annabelle still sat in the chair, staring at the table where the affidavit had been signed.

"Annabelle," Tyler said to her, gentling his voice a bit now that Russell was outside. She twisted her face up to glance at him. She looked so much like Jennifer. Surely, some of Jennifer's good nature had to be in that bundle of hostility somewhere. Seeing Annabelle like this, Tyler was glad he'd refused Jennifer's request to come along. "Go home. See your sister. Talk to your father. He's worried sick about you. There's nothing for you here. Blake's not coming."

Her defiance never wavered. "He will. He'll be here."

Tyler shrugged and followed Russell to the car.

CHAPTER EIGHTY-TWO

LILA OPENED THE DOOR to Chief Ben Hathaway. She'd been canning tomatoes and was wiping the mess off her hands on a kitchen towel. She knew who the chief of police was, even though he wasn't wearing his uniform, because she'd seen him on television.

Lila made no move to let him inside. Cops in the house were never a good thing in Lila's world. No cop had ever served and protected her. She had no reason to expect this one to do so now.

"What's he done?" she asked through the screen.

Chief Hathaway held his hat in front of his ample stomach. After he introduced himself and asked nicely, she let him inside because she didn't know how to reasonably refuse. He followed her into the kitchen where the canning supplies and tomatoes covered every flat surface and filled the air with acidic aroma.

"Ma'am we need to find your husband. Have you heard from him in the last few hours?"

Lila shook her head and turned back to stir the large pot of red pulp on the stove. "No. He lit out of here a few days ago like he was being chased by a rabid dog. I haven't seen him since."

"You don't seem unhappy about that," Hathaway said.

"I'm not. Ronald was drunk and mad. I'm not surprised he's in trouble again," she added.

Hathaway nodded as if he knew this already. "Do you mind if I look around?"

Lila did mind. She didn't like people messing up her house, tramping dirt all over the place. She kept her house clean. She wanted it to stay that way. In the short time Ronald had been gone she'd found she liked her solitude. She liked the control being alone in the house gave her. The last thing she needed was intrusion of any kind.

She looked Hathaway over. He was well-dressed, clean-shaven. His nails were chewed off below the quick, but otherwise, he seemed tidy enough. He sure was a big man, though. He could do damage just walking through the narrow rooms of her small house.

"It's important, Mrs. Walden," Hathaway said, pressing her. She figured that meant he didn't have a warrant. If he had one, he wouldn't be asking, he'd be telling.

"You didn't say what he's done," Lila reminded him. "Why are you looking for him? He was in your police station for hours just before he left here. None of the cops seemed to care, he said."

Hathaway nodded again. "He was at the station. We tried to help him, but he didn't like the way we do things there. That's true." He seemed to be considering something. Then he said, "We're investigating a shooting. We think your husband might be involved."

Lila cocked her head to one side while she stirred her tomatoes and thought about this information. "Who did he kill this time?"

"This time?"

"Well, your people have already been here about him killing

that lawyer. I figure it must be someone else now, or you wouldn't be here in person." Lila was no dummy. She watched television. She knew the police chief didn't make house calls. Not for the likes of Ronald Walden, anyway.

Hathaway cleared his throat. "We think he may be involved in the shooting of Blake Denton," he told her. "Haven't you seen the news?"

Lila was flatly amazed. She didn't know whether to laugh or argue. Had Ronald finally gone completely around the bend? Totally? Kill Blake? Ronald would never, ever do anything to make Annabelle so mad. Figures. Cops were either wrong or stupid most of the time.

She shrugged and returned to her canning. "He's not here. I haven't seen him in days, thank the Lord. But you're free to look around if you want to, Chief."

Hathaway nodded. He left her in the kitchen and walked quickly down the small hallway. Lila could hear him walking around first in her bedroom. He didn't stay long. Next, he went into Annabelle's old room. Lila heard only silence while the chief was inside Annabelle's room and wondered what he was doing there. Making notes, maybe.

She heard his heavy footsteps as he walked a few paces then opened the door to Ronald's room. The closet door opened, boxes were shuffled around.

Lila washed her canning jars and counted out the flat lids. She'd grown the tomatoes herself—organic. She figured she'd get twelve pints this time, the best her little stand of plants had ever done. It was that new natural fertilizer, for sure. She was right proud of herself.

Hathaway stopped off in the living room on his way back to the kitchen. She glanced at the clock. He'd been looking around maybe a total of twenty minutes. When he returned, he held nothing but his hat in his hands. Whatever he'd been looking for, he must not have found it.

"Would you mind letting yourself out, Chief?" Lila asked him. "I've got my hands back in the dishwater now."

Chief Hathaway studied her from behind. She could feel him standing there, staring at her. It had been a while since any man admired her from behind. She kind of liked it.

"What made you change your mind? About letting me look around, I mean," he asked.

Lila rinsed the jars one at a time, making sure she had all the soap out of them. She didn't want soapy tomatoes. "What do you know about my husband, Chief Hathaway?" Lila responded with a question of her own.

"Not as much as I need to," he said.

"Well, there's just no way Ronald would have shot Annabelle's fella. Not unless he thought Blake had killed Annabelle. Does he think that?"

Hathaway seemed to digest this information. If he'd known that Annabelle and Blake were involved, he didn't say anything one way or the other.

"Thank you, Mrs. Walden. I'll be going now, but we may need to come back. We need to find your husband." When Lila failed to reply, Hathaway headed toward the kitchen door, the same way he came in.

"Chief," Lila called to him when he'd stepped outside. He turned his head in her direction. "He won't come back here. You're wasting your time watching the house. If Ronald finds out Annabelle's dead, he's not through killing yet."

"What if Annabelle's still alive?"

Lila shrugged. "Hard to say."

CHAPTER EIGHTY-THREE

TYLER SAT WITH RUSSELL in his home office where he waited for Blake's return, a vigil that seemed foolish at best and deranged at worst. Tyler worried that Russell's fine mind had become affected by his disease, which was progressing at an alarming rate.

Russell replaced the phone when Blake's secretary once again conveyed the lie Blake had instructed her to tell. "Blake left the plant several hours ago. I don't know where he is right now."

Blake hadn't been at the plant for days. Why ask the secretary to lie? Blake wasn't required to answer to Russell and he'd made that fairly clear. The question bothered Tyler, but he hadn't had the time to run down the answer.

Russell had won his war of wills with Annabelle James over HepZMax's ownership, but the victory seemed to have given him no joy. His skin pallor had gone from gray to yellow. When he picked up his glasses or tried to walk, he was unsteady. Tyler had noticed, too, that Russell fatigued too easily and barely made it out of bed before eleven in the morning. His car used to be the first in the plant parking lot. Some days, almost unbelievably, Russell didn't show up at all.

"When is the last time you saw Blake?" Tyler asked him now.

"I don't know. A few days ago."

Tyler's radar went up. "Did you have some kind of argument?"

Russell sounded weary. "We don't seem to have any other kind of conversation these days."

Tyler swore under his breath. He stood up and went to the telephone in the corner of the room. "Tyler here," he said into the receiver. "Where is Blake Denton's Jaguar? Yes, right now." Tyler covered up his anger with difficulty. "Well, find out. And let me know when you find it."

"What is it?" Russell asked.

"The bug on Blake's car is offline. The last time it transmitted was from a parking lot in Coral Hill. What would he being doing in a neighborhood like that?"

The question was rhetorical. Russell Denton knew less about his nephew than Tyler did, a fact that both of them had finally been forced to acknowledge. Blake wasn't a child, looking up to Uncle Russell. He'd long since passed that threshold and, clearly, the two had some heavy issues between them. Tyler wasn't a shrink. He had no idea what the source of Blake's hatred was. He only knew that Blake was one angry and vindictive young man. In Tyler's experience, that was a lethal combination.

He changed the subject. "I think it's time we let Ronald and Lila Walden know that Annabelle is alive, don't you?"

Russell was preoccupied, probably with thoughts of Blake, and didn't answer.

"How would you feel if you thought Blake was dead?" Tyler couldn't even imagine how he would react if anything happened to

Cindi or Penny. He understood Ronald Walden's murderous rage at anyone he considered responsible for harming Annabelle. Tyler thought Annabelle's silence toward her parents was unnecessarily cruel, but he wasn't surprised by her behavior. At the same time, he didn't want to be a part of it, either.

"Walden is unstable, Tim. Even if you could find him, you wouldn't be able to talk to the man. He's crazy. Stuart Barnett thought he could reason with Walden, too, and look what happened to him." Russell wiped a hand over his face. He poured a glass of water and drank it as if he hadn't had water in days. "It's none of our business. Let's stay out of it. We don't need one more thing to worry about right now."

Tyler opened his mouth to argue; a knock at the door interrupted. "Yes?"

Rosa walked tentatively into the room. "Excuse me, Mr. Russell. There is a gentleman here to see you."

"I'm not receiving visitors right now, Rosa."

"I know, sir, but he said it was important."

"Who is it?"

"He said to give you this." She handed Russell a business card.

Russell read it and passed the card to Tyler, who looked at it and said, "Shit."

Chief Hathaway and Tyler were well acquainted. They'd had several opportunities to work together over the years. Tyler respected the man, but preferred not to involve Hathaway in Russell Denton's business. Sometimes, he had no choice. He'd hoped this situation was not one of those times.

"Show him in, Rosa. Thank you," Russell said.

Ben Hathaway filled the room like a small elephant fills a stall at the zoo. "Tim," he said, coming over and shaking hands.

Tyler made the introductions.

Russell struggled to rise and offered his hand. "What can I do for you?"

Hathaway had removed his hat, but remained on his feet. "Sir, I'm sorry to have to tell you this. There's been some trouble."

Russell and Tyler looked at each other. Tyler responded cautiously. "What kind of trouble?"

"The worst kind, I'm afraid."

"What's happened, Chief?" Russell asked him.

"I'm afraid it's your nephew. There's no easy way to say this. He's been shot. We transported him to Tampa General, but it doesn't look good."

Hathaway's news forced Russell down into his chair. He blinked hard then. He shook his head rapidly, as if he hadn't heard, although Tyler recognized the move as a stalling device. "What?"

"What happened?" Tyler asked, realizing that Russell's famous poker face had just slipped badly. There was no way Russell would be able to handle this interview.

"We're not sure. Someone apparently stole his car. He was shot at some point, either before or after that. We don't know much yet." Hathaway quickly filled them in on the events at the Garden. He told them Jennifer Lane had been there and identified Blake, who had no other means of identification with him.

"Jennifer Lane?" The name penetrated the fog that Russell Denton seemed to be sitting in. "Why was she there?"

Hathaway said, "Coincidence, maybe. She was buying a Lotto ticket on the other side of the store. She saw the killer, sir. We're looking for him now."

"Who was it?" Tyler didn't believe in coincidence and he'd bet his last nickel Hathaway didn't either; no good lawman did. If

Jennifer was there, it was because someone followed her there. Tyler's gut told him who that someone was before Hathaway got the name out.

"She identified a fellow named Ronald Walden. Do you know him?"

Tyler felt the news hit him hard in the gut, followed instantly by remorse. Why hadn't he followed his instincts on Walden? He could have prevented this. He knew he could have. *Dammit!*

Instead of answering, Russell began to cry. Hathaway's look was purely incredulous, as if such a man as Russell Denton would have no tears to shed for the nephew who was like his only son. Tyler's guilt deepened and he shoved it out of the way to allow Russell his privacy.

Tyler led Hathaway into the foyer. When the door was solidly closed, they heard the wealthiest, most successful man in Florida sobbing as if his own life had ended.

Tyler and Hathaway went outside into the opulent gardens surrounding the twenty million dollar house. The most expensive house in Tampa, the press had reported many times. Hathaway shared the few details he'd learned, but Tyler barely listened. He knew everything he needed to know already.

After Hathaway left, Tyler couldn't face Russell again. He called Patricia. She would take care of getting Russell to the hospital and stay there with him as long as necessary. Tyler had work to do. He could find Ronald Walden; Hathaway couldn't. At least, Tyler wanted, needed to believe as much. Finding Walden was the very least he could do and he knew it. Still, he'd get the job done.

What a waste, he thought, speeding back to the Cellar. Russell would give everything he owned to bring his beloved nephew back home, to erase the past two years and start anew. Was that even remotely possible now?

CHAPTER EIGHTY-FOUR

TYLER REVIEWED THE PRINTOUTS reflecting the movements of Blake's Jaguar for the past few days. He pulled out a detailed map of South Tampa and placed a red pin on the map at The Garden where Blake had been dumped. Next, he used a green highlighter to mark the routes the car had taken from the time it was driven from Denton Bio-Medical's parking lot. The tracking device had a digital readout that could be projected onto a computer screen, but Tyler liked the old-fashioned visual approach.

After the Jaguar had left the parking lot, it had traveled north on I-275 toward Dade City, where it had left the freeway at State Highway 52. Had Walden been driving then? The audio transmitter inside the car had picked up no conversation, only the country music Blake favored. But maybe Walden liked country music, too, so that didn't prove anything.

The car continued past the small north Tampa suburb of San Antonio, and even farther, out into rural and unoccupied land. The car pulled off Highway 52 at a location that Tyler's map suggested open land. He assumed there was a dirt road, though, from

Hathaway's recounting of Jennifer's statement about the shooting. Apparently the Jaguar had been beat-up and dirty, not the sleek vehicle Tyler remembered. He pulled up still photos from the parking lot's cameras to be sure the Jaguar was pristine when it left the parking lot. It was. Next, Tyler found a more detailed map of the vehicle's departure point from Highway 52 on the computer and printed it.

The small road must have been nothing more than an overgrown dirt trail. There were plenty of those north of the city. Florida had a population of over eighteen million people, yet a lot of land remained undeveloped. A murder could easily happen out there with no one to witness it. Bodies could be fed to the alligators that were ubiquitous in all Florida waters. Walden could have killed Blake, disposed of the body, and gotten away with it.

So why shoot Blake and bring him back to South Tampa and dump him in plain sight? Why use Blake's car? Why show the entire program to Jennifer Lane?

Walden wasn't a genius, but he wasn't an idiot, either. He had a reason. Tyler thought about the possibilities and come up with only one that made rational sense: Walden wanted Jennifer to know that he'd shot Blake.

He probably had wanted Blake to die in her arms, which might explain why Blake wasn't dead now. Was he sending some sort of message to Jennifer? Or was this the act of a grieving father out of his head? Or was it something else?

Tyler felt his personal guilt kick in again. He'd tried to argue himself out of the equation, but if Walden believed Annabelle was dead and Tyler had told Walden otherwise, Blake might be alive now. Stuart Barnett, too. He'd have to deal with his guilt, but finding Walden was more important right now.

He returned to his data. The tracking device on the Jaguar was lost or removed after Blake's body had been literally thrown at Jennifer. The data ended there. Where was the car now? Where was Walden?

Tyler returned to the computer and reviewed Blake's travel patterns for the past few weeks. Blake's movements lately were like the man, erratic and unpredictable. So what had Walden done to find him? Simply staked out the parking lot until Blake appeared? Probably.

Walden should have abandoned the car somewhere. He'd know the police were looking for it. And since Jennifer had positively identified Walden as the driver of the car, they'd be looking for him, too, and he'd know that. So, at the very least, Ronald Walden would need different transportation.

Tyler didn't have the manpower to locate the Jaguar by physically searching. He'd leave that to Hathaway and his team. What Tyler had was weeks of Blake's travel history which, at this point, was worse than useless. He threw the map across the room and ran his hands over his head. He needed a more creative solution but he hadn't slept for thirty-six hours and his brain was foggy. He paced. How to find Walden? What did Tyler know that would bring Walden to him?

The epiphany, when it came, made him feel stupid and slow.

Tyler knew the one and only thing that would draw Walden into a trap. He picked up the phone and called Ben Hathaway.

CHAPTER EIGHTY-FIVE

NOW THAT HE HAD a plan, Tyler began to execute it methodically. He called the Best of Juneau Motor Lodge where he and Russell had met with Annabelle James.

"Ms. James has checked out, sir," the desk clerk said.

He called ten more hotels in Juneau. If Annabelle was still in the city, she had not registered anywhere under her own name.

Next, he canvassed airlines, using techniques his bosses at the FBI would never allow. Few commercial flights took off from Juneau, and he found Annabelle's booking late in the day, when eyestrain had left him unable to read and fatigue hoarsened his voice beyond recognition.

Yet, he felt triumphant. Annabelle had departed from Juneau, changed airlines in Anchorage, and arrived in Miami yesterday. Good news and bad news. Miami was not that far from Tampa, but it was a big city with a major airport. Annabelle could have gone almost anywhere from there, but he thought he knew precisely where she was headed. He might not have to use Annabelle as bait to trap her father; she might do all the work for him.

He checked his phone to be sure he hadn't missed a call from

Hathaway. Nothing. No messages from Jennifer or Russell, either. God, he was tired. He stretched his body, splashed cold water on his face, and drank a gallon of coffee before he returned to work.

Tyler listened to the audio wiretaps he had in place and realized he'd taped several "hang-ups" on Blake's home answering machine and his cell phone voice mail. Tyler assumed Annabelle had tried to reach Blake, but wouldn't leave a message. Although Tyler tried, he was unable to trace any of the phone numbers from the hang-up calls. Another dead end.

Still, Tyler felt he knew Annabelle fairly well by now, after all the hours he'd spent mired in her business. When he'd seen her in Juneau, he'd told her to go home because Blake wasn't coming to get her. It was a deliberate attempt to push her buttons and he thought it had worked. Blake would never have met Annabelle in Alaska even if he'd remained unscathed. She'd been up there for weeks and she hadn't seen him. She had to be thinking Tyler was right, that Blake wasn't coming after all.

Annabelle would have worried. She was an insecure bitch, but she had good reason to be insecure where Blake was concerned. Blake had married her, sure. Still, she must have known he'd be unfaithful. After all, he'd been engaged to someone else when he'd started his affair with her. She'd keep trying to find him; she wasn't the kind of woman to give up on something she wanted.

Why she wanted Blake was a complete mystery to Tyler, though. Blake had always been uncontrollable and always would be. Any woman involved with him would come to heartache. Dozens already had. Annabelle would be no exception.

Now that Ronald had shot Blake, Tyler figured Annabelle was on her way to Tampa. It made sense. Annabelle had been tracing her real family. He'd followed her when she went to the Jacks Clinic and to see her Aunt Peggy. She'd gone to all the trouble of luring Clay and Debbie Lane to Alaska and then meeting up with them there, albeit anonymously.

Tyler was sure she'd try to contact Jennifer at some point. He'd put this whole plan in motion, convinced Russell to hire Jennifer initially, because he believed Annabelle would eventually contact her sister. Nothing had happened to make him change his mind. In fact, he felt more strongly about that now than he had before.

But he hadn't expected Walden to go berserk. He'd never planned to intercept Annabelle, merely to wait for her. Waiting was unaffordable now. He'd adjusted his goal.

Now, Tyler planned to catch Annabelle when she contacted Jennifer. But how would he do it when he had no idea where she was?

It was a good goal, if it could be accomplished before Ronald found Jennifer and tried to kill her, too.

CHAPTER EIGHTY-SIX

"YOU'RE NOT GOING to find him. Not until he wants to be found," Tyler told Hathaway.

Tyler and Ben Hathaway stood in one of the stores in Old Hyde Park Village, watching Jennifer Lane's apartment. Tyler had been posted there for almost two days now. Hathaway came by from time to time. The statewide manhunt for Ronald Walden had yielded nothing yet. The man had been in Vietnam, a regular infantry soldier who survived. He knew how to hide.

"Maybe," Hathaway said. "But sooner or later, he'll make a mistake. They all do."

Tyler didn't argue, but he had more faith in his own plan.

His illegal wiretaps and videos were in place, which he didn't disclose to Hathaway. That was how he'd heard Annabelle's phone call to Jennifer the previous afternoon. Bingo. Right again. He'd expected Annabelle to contact Jennifer, and she had; but she'd hung up when Jennifer answered and they hadn't agreed on a meeting place.

He figured that Annabelle would be on her way here, not to Lila Walden's house. But Hathaway had a stakeout there, just in case. And he knew Annabelle would lead them straight to Ronald Walden. Once they found her. If Hathaway didn't screw things up by interrupting.

Fortunately, Paradise Apartments had only one entrance for visitors. The other entrances required a security card. Annabelle would need to walk or drive by the store where Tyler and Hathaway stood to get to Jennifer.

Here, too, Tyler had the advantage. Although he'd never met Annabelle when she worked at Denton Bio-Medical, he'd seen her just a few days ago. He'd watched her for countless hours on videotape. He'd recognize her walk, her size, even if she'd changed her appearance. But why would she do that? Just like in Juneau, she wouldn't be expecting him.

About ten minutes past three, a white Chevy drove past the store window where Tyler stood and pulled into the visitor's garage. The car looked like a rental. After several tourist killings in Florida, the car rental agencies in the state were no longer using distinctive license plates. Still, the car was a nondescript sedan, driven by the right-sized woman with the right dark hair. It could be Annabelle.

Tyler lifted his binoculars and watched as she parked the car in the guest lot. She pulled down the visor and removed her sunglasses to check her reflection in the mirror. He saw her eyes for a positive identification, but he'd have guessed anyway. The gesture was pure Annabelle, vain to the exclusion of all else.

Yet, Annabelle's appearance was more subdued than Tyler had ever seen. She'd added a little weight, too. Some sort of disguise, perhaps? She was about to meet her sister for the first time; the Annabelle he knew would have wanted to make a flashy first impression. Curious. But not fatal to positive identification.

Tyler poked Hathaway in the arm and gestured out the window. "It's her."

Annabelle exited the car carrying a large leather tote bag and walked toward the security phone. Tyler and Hathaway trotted out of the store and across the street just as Annabelle was pushing the intercom button to Jennifer's apartment.

"Who is it?" Tyler, now ten feet away, heard Jennifer's voice through the tinny intercom.

"It's me," Annabelle said. He heard the buzz releasing the magnetic lock on the iron gate. She began to pull the gate open just as Tyler reached her.

"Hello, Annabelle," Tyler said. "Long time, no see."

She whipped her head around and stared as if he'd risen from the depths of hell.

"This is my friend, Chief Hathaway. Let's go up and see your sister."

CHAPTER EIGHTY-SEVEN

LILA COULDN'T BELIEVE HER ears when she heard the powerful engine as the car pulled into the garage. When the car hit the back of the garage wall, she knew who it had to be. Why had she left the door unlocked?

Ronald slammed the Jaguar's door and opened the garage refrigerator for a beer. There were none; Lila had thrown them all out when he left that last day and didn't come home. She'd had enough of drinking. She wouldn't stand for anymore. She'd made up her mind about a few things since he'd walked out and drinking was one of them.

He made no effort to sneak into the house. Why would he? He owned the place.

She heard the door open and close and his heavy footsteps on the kitchen floor. She was ironing in her room, and she quickly decided since there was no way to get out of the house without going past Ronald, she'd try to bluff her way through the encounter.

She made another decision, too. When he left this time, she'd change the door locks and get a restraining order. She should have done that long before, but she'd counted on Chief Hathaway to take care of Ronald before he came back. She should have known better. Cops were useless. They'd never helped her before. She wouldn't rely on them to help her again.

"Lila!" he shouted. "Lila! Where are you?" It didn't take him long to find her. The house just wasn't that big.

She stood with her back to the doorway of the small room, but she could smell him long before he reached her. The combined odor of unwashed-male and stale alcohol churned her stomach. "How in the world did I ever stay married to such a coarse pig for thirty years?"

"What did you say?" Ronald shouted, enraged.

Lila hadn't realized she'd spoken aloud. Living alone, she'd gotten into the habit of talking to herself, as natural as breathing. There had been no one to hear her. Until now.

Faster than she could turn around to reply, Ronald grabbed Lila by the throat. "Coarse pig?" he said. "Who are you calling a coarse pig? Is that how you talked about me to Annabelle? Is that why she left me?"

Ronald shook Lila back and forth like a rag doll, choking off her breath. Lila felt woozy. She tried to hold her head straight, but he shook too hard. She reached up to pull his viselike fingers from her throat. She could barely breathe. He released one hand and used it to raise the cold steel of a gun barrel to her head.

She felt herself losing consciousness. She tried to wiggle free. He lifted her off the floor. She wiggled wildly but he seemed to have superhuman strength.

"You've always been jealous, Lila. This is all your fault. Your fault!"

He shook harder while resting the gun on the side of her head. Did he intend to shoot her?

She'd scream, but she couldn't get enough air to make noise.

"Your fault!" He pressed harder on her throat.

The room went black.

CHAPTER EIGHTY-EIGHT

JENNIFER LANE AND ANNABELLE James were not carbon copies of one another, but no one would doubt they'd come from the same gene pool. Of course, Tyler didn't need to guess. Long before, he'd compared their DNA using Jennifer's saliva from her glass that first day at the club and a few hair roots from Annabelle's hairbrush. When he'd told Jennifer they were sisters, he'd been certain.

Watching both women, Tyler got an eerie feeling close to clairvoyance, as if he might be looking at his twin daughters twenty years from now and thinking exactly the same thing.

Somehow, Jennifer seemed larger to him than before, though. Stronger. She sat in her living room on one of the dining chairs, allowing Hathaway the couch to himself. Hathaway filled it the way liquid mercury spreads to cover all available space. Annabelle sat across from Jennifer.

Tyler stood; better for a quick reaction, should he need one. He'd placed listening devices strategically throughout the apartment, too. Just in case. He didn't expect to lose this battle, but better prepared than left holding nothing but empty air again.

"You don't look like your pictures," Jennifer said.

Devoid of her trademark red lipstick and talons, Annabelle seemed faded. Her outfit was Florida beachwear. Not her usual expensive, flashy style. But the shirt was a tight tank crop top, the better to show off her protruding stomach sporting a pierced navel and the disastrous tattoo on her back.

Tyler saw Jennifer's gaze fall to the engagement ring and wedding band on Annabelle's left hand. She'd believe now that what he'd told her was true. Annabelle and Blake were married; he'd been married to Annabelle when Jennifer had slept with him.

If Jennifer had harbored any further illusions about loving Blake, Tyler watched them die in that moment.

"Neither do you," Annabelle said. "When I found out about you, I was so excited. I thought we'd be so much alike. But we're not. How disappointing. You're nothing like me, little sister."

Thank God, Tyler thought.

Hathaway cleared his throat. "I know this is an emotional moment for you two," he said, somewhat sarcastically, given Annabelle's snide comment. "But I need to find Ronald Walden. Soon. Before he kills someone else."

Annabelle turned to him bewildered. "What do you mean?"

"You don't know?" Jennifer said, obviously incredulous.

Annabelle shook her head. "Know what?"

For the second time since they'd arrived, Tyler saw Jennifer's armor had been pierced. Her eyes glazed over. She blinked several times.

"Ronald killed Stuart Barnett, one of my firm's partners," Jennifer began to explain.

Annabelle jumped up from her chair, the spitfire returned. "That is not true!"

Jennifer simply looked at her.

"How can you say that? Ronald is the kindest, gentlest man you've ever met. He would never, ever, *ever* kill anyone."

Jennifer might have believed her, if she hadn't been in the room when Stuart was murdered.

"Annabelle, the things you don't know about men would fill a New York City phone book," Tyler told her.

She spit at him, but she couldn't spit far enough to reach. He didn't move, but his eyes narrowed and his temper flared.

Tyler was through playing around with Annabelle James. If he'd handled her in his own way at the beginning, Stuart Barnett would still be alive and Blake Denton wouldn't be on life support at Tampa General. Annabelle's feelings were no longer important to Tyler and he no longer believed he could protect Russell. Tyler had promised himself the Annabelle James debacle would end today.

"Annabelle," Jennifer must have felt the shift in Tyler's mood; her tone was stern. "We need to find Ronald. He's not at home. Where does he go when he wants to be off on his own?"

"You people are crazy." Annabelle took a cell phone out of her purse. She pushed the redial button. She said, "Daddy? Daddy where are you?" She paused to listen. "Stay there. I'm coming."

Before she could say more, Tyler grabbed the phone. He listened as Ronald Walden, crying and incoherent, babbled his relief that Annabelle was alive. When he noticed her lack of responses, Walden shouted into the phone. "Baby! Baby! Where are you? Are you there?" Tyler waited until he heard Walden drop the phone before disconnecting.

Tyler used his own phone to dial another number.

"Where is that cell phone located?" he asked. After a couple of seconds, he said, "Thanks."

Annabelle's cell phone rang. Tyler dropped the phone into his pocket and turned to Chief Hathaway.

Hathaway stood and took Annabelle's arm. "Let's go."

Jennifer stopped at the door to pick up her gun case. Tyler saw her do it, but didn't comment. She'd been taking the gun with her everywhere; no time to argue about it now.

They hustled downstairs and piled into Tyler's car. The women sat in the back, while Tyler occupied the driver's seat. While Hathaway wedged his bulk into the passenger side, Tyler heard Jennifer ask the toughest question first.

"Does Blake know you're pregnant?"

Annabelle, argumentative as always, said, "Of course, Blake knows. He's thrilled about it. We've already picked out names for the baby." She folded her hands over her protruding stomach, protectively.

Tyler saw Jennifer staring at Annabelle with an expression he could not define.

CHAPTER EIGHTY-NINE

WHEN SHE REGAINED CONSCIOUSNESS, Lila found herself on the floor in Annabelle's old bedroom. Her throat felt sore and raw. She could hear Ronald shouting into the phone. "Baby! Baby!"

So, she'd finally called. Now maybe Ronald would stop acting like such an animal.

Lila tried to get up off the floor. Her first few attempts to stand were failures. Her legs were bent at an unnatural angle and she'd lost some of the feeling in them. Her right leg was especially numb. She rolled around onto her stomach and tried to push herself up onto her knees first.

"Where are you? Are you there?" Ronald yelled in the other room. He must still be talking to Annabelle on the phone, Lila figured.

She pushed herself onto all fours and then raised herself up little by little. She was kneeling now, trying to get her balance. Ronald marched down the hallway toward her. She could see him coming, but she couldn't get out of the way.

He stopped two feet in front of her and threw the cell phone at her head. It hit Lila squarely in the forehead; she staggered back, fell off her precarious perch, and landed on the floor. When she caught herself with her right hand, she heard a sickening snap in her wrist and felt pain shoot up her arm. She screamed.

"What are you screaming about?" Ronald shouted at her.

Lila grabbed her wrist, writhing in pain. "I think I've broken my wrist, Ronald. I need to go to the hospital," she said through clenched teeth.

A crazy gleam entered his eye. "To the hospital? The *hospital*? You know what happens to horses when they break a leg, don't you?" Ronald raised his gun and pointed it at her, his hand on the trigger.

Lila began to cry. "Ronald, I'm hurt. Help me. I need to go to the hospital." She tried to rise, but without using her hand and with both legs still numb, she couldn't rise.

Ronald stood looking down at her with the same crazed expression on his dirty face. She smelled his rancid breath from four feet away. Her stomach started to roll with the stench, the pain and the fear. She couldn't control herself. She vomited, splashing his shoes.

"You bitch!" he screamed as he raised his left arm, extended the gun, and pulled the trigger.

CHAPTER NINETY

THE WALDEN HOUSE WAS lit up by flashing lights atop several squad cars and three EMS units spaced along the road on both sides. Tyler found a space behind the two units already parked in the driveway. Hathaway hadn't called for backup, which could only mean something had already happened inside. Tyler knew they had only a few moments to resolve this situation before the scene turned into all kinds of carnage.

He parked and jumped out of the car. Jennifer, Annabelle, and Hathaway followed quickly.

"Domestic," he heard one of the uniformed officers tell Chief Hathaway, as the four of them approached on foot. "Husband's in there with a gun. Wife's inside, too. Neighbors called it in. They heard one shot."

Law enforcement had established protocols to follow in such circumstances. Tyler didn't. Before Hathaway could stop him, Tyler drew his gun and crouched to sneak around to the side of the house and enter the carport. Hathaway wouldn't yell to bring him back because no one wanted Walden's attention drawn to Annabelle's presence yet.

Tyler heard movement behind him. He glanced back. Jennifer crouched low, gun in hand.

"Go back," he whispered as loudly as he dared. She shook her head no. He had no time to argue with her. He grabbed her arm and tried to push her toward the driveway.

Jennifer didn't budge. "Lila is in there. She trusts me."

"No."

"I'm not standing by while Ronald Walden shoots someone else." Jennifer held her gun up in her right hand and darted past Tyler, entering the house first before he could stop her.

Tyler had no choice but to follow her. They were stuck in the house together now and he knew she could shoot straight if she had to.

"Ronald won't shoot me," she said, edging her way into the kitchen.

"Yeah. That's what your pal Stuart thought." Tyler could hear nothing inside the house and the silence was worse than gunshots. At least shots fired would tell him where Walden was hiding. He saw Jennifer across the open doorway, peering down the small hallway to the back bedroom, grasping her gun as if she'd be able to use it when the time came. He hoped to God she would.

"Ronald Walden! Come out with your hands up!" Tyler heard Hathaway shouting from the bullhorn out front.

Still, an eerie silence covered the house.

The neighbors reported one gunshot had been fired before the police were called. Not a good omen. They'd heard one shot; could there have been more? Tyler pictured a murder-suicide. Plenty of times, that's how these calls turned out. Too much alcohol, hair-trigger tempers, a crisis. Death was only a short distance down the domestic violence road and these two had been on the trail for years.

Leaving Jennifer behind, he crept into the hallway. He listened carefully for noises he could identify. He thought he heard a muffled television in the back of the house. Then he remembered that Hathaway told him the Waldens had separate bedrooms, one in the back.

Tyler flattened himself against the wall. When he did, Annabelle's cell phone pressed against his thigh. *Good idea*, he thought. He carefully retrieved the phone from his pocket and turned it on. He pressed the redial button and waited.

The next few seconds passed like hours.

Finally, finally, he heard another cell phone ring in one of the back rooms.

He tossed Jennifer the phone. She caught it without releasing her grip on the gun, nodded, and put the phone to her ear.

Pick up, pick up, pick up, Tyler repeated in his head as he crept toward the ringing sound.

"Baby?" Walden called, "is that you?"

Tyler heard Walden's voice in stereo, one loud voice from the back of the house and the second emanating from the phone speaker.

In a steady, normal voice, she answered. "It's Jennifer, Ronald. Annabelle's with me. She's my sister, you know."

Walden started to cry. "Is she okay?"

"Yes," Jennifer replied. "Why don't you come out here and see her? She misses you."

"Let me talk to her. I don't trust you."

Tyler crept toward the bedroom. He stole a glance toward Jennifer, who hadn't moved from her spot around the corner. She held her gun down and out of sight, too.

Tyler was almost there.

"She's too upset to talk," Jennifer replied to Walden. "Come out and see her."

"Put her on the phone, I said!" Walden's rage had reached a boiling point, or maybe he was used to shouting at women to make them do his bidding. Could have been either one, but having crossed the line with Jennifer, he wasn't likely to go back.

Tyler took a deep breath, raised himself up only as far as necessary, and pushed the bedroom door, holding his gun in shooter's stance while yelling, "Walden! On the floor!"

Jennifer had thrown down the phone and, out of the corner of his eye, he saw her standing behind him, aiming her gun directly at Ronald Walden's chest.

Walden looked up, bewildered, the cell phone still held to his ear, as if he couldn't comprehend what he saw. His eyes were wild, his hair matted down and filthy. He was covered in dark blood stains. His stench slammed Tyler like a physical presence.

"On the floor! Now!" Tyler repeated. Walden's body swayed to the left, Jennifer's gun fired. Tyler may have heard a small scream whiz past his ear, but he'd never be sure because of the deafening noise. The shot hit Walden in the arm and he dropped the cell phone, but he didn't cry out or drop his gun.

"Now! On the floor!" Tyler ordered again, without looking at Jennifer.

Walden turned his vacant gaze from Tyler to Jennifer and back again. He shook his head from side to side.

Staring Tyler right in the eye, Walden said, "Not a chance," raised his gun and shot himself in the head.

Tyler glanced back at Jennifer who stood watching as Ronald Walden's blood splattered and pumped all over Lila Walden's body and Annabelle's pink gingham bedspread until his heart stopped beating.

Immediately after that, Hathaway's men flooded the house.

CHAPTER NINETY-ONE

Three weeks later

JENNIFER WAITED IN THE conference room where Stuart had been fatally wounded, feeling as if she'd landed in a different world. The window had been replaced and the bloody carpet had been changed. It seemed to her that she watched from a great distance, not a part of the scene. Could she really have cowered right over there, in that spot, while Ronald Walden killed Stuart? It didn't seem possible.

As a tribute to Stuart, this had to be the place where his last case ended, where he won his final battle with Roger Riley. That much, she owed her beloved friend and mentor. That, and so much more. *Thank you, Stuart. For everything.*

Jennifer had completed and rehearsed every inch of the preparations herself. She'd choreographed the finale as if directing a huge cast in a musical show, a fitting tribute to Stuart. She would do this for him and then move on with her life.

Russell Denton and Tim Tyler waited in the conference room where she'd first met Ronald and Lila Walden. Jennifer's memory of that night was vivid. If only she'd done things differently at first. If she'd known then what she knew now, Stuart would not have died.

A quick knock at the door interrupted.

"Yes?" She was expecting refreshments. Instead, Melanie Stein entered. Jennifer turned to face her.

"I'm not sorry," Melanie said, without any preamble. "What you did was wrong. And look how it turned out. Don't be thinking this was anyone else's fault."

Melanie glared, but her emotions seemed mixed.

Jennifer's emotions were crystal clear. "My license to practice law has been suspended for thirty days."

"Not enough. Stuart's been suspended forever."

Jennifer stared at Melanie for a few terrible seconds. At one time, she'd imagined Melanie her closest friend. She'd believed Melanie was smart and sexy and a great lawyer. She'd followed Melanie around like a puppy.

She shrugged. She was wiser now. She wanted Melanie to know that.

Jennifer said, "How long had you been in love with Stuart?"

Melanie looked at her with cold contempt. "None of your goddamned business. Stay out of my way, Jennifer. Don't screw with my life. Ever again." She slammed the door behind her.

Jennifer felt a sad little smile invade her lips. She and Melanie were more alike than Melanie knew.

"A thin line divides our best intentions from our worst natures," Stuart used to say. "We don't know what we're capable of until we're faced with the wrong circumstances."

Melanie had crossed that line and Jennifer had, too. She had actually shot a live human being. How was that possible?

Stuart's secretary, Hilda, knocked quickly and then entered the room with the refreshments. Jennifer gave herself a mental shake. She accepted the small key from Hilda and left the room.

She had one more thing she needed to do before Annabelle arrived with Roger Riley and the executives from Alabaster Medical.

Jennifer walked the short distance to Stuart's office, which had been locked since his death. Using Hilda's key, she let herself in. An almost overwhelming sense of déjà vu filled her heart as she stood in front of Stuart's empty chair.

"How can I be of service to you, Archie?" she wanted to hear him say.

She'd spent so many happy hours here, matching wits with Stuart, solving client problems, discussing art and books and movies and restaurants and politics and everything in between. He had given her advice on life, cared for her in a way no one else had ever done. Stuart Barnett was one of a kind. Her heart ached. The hole Stuart's absence left in her life was as big as his towering presence had been. No one would ever fill that space again.

The smoked museum-glass armoire that contained Stuart's revered collection of first edition bound British trial transcripts stood undisturbed. No one in Stuart's family would want or understand these. The collection would probably be sold. Jennifer considered making an offer on the books, but she couldn't bear to have them, really. She had the one that Stuart had given her in appreciation for work she'd done on a particularly tough case: *The Trial of Oscar Wilde.*

Stuart had inscribed the book in his distinctive hand. Thanks, Jennifer. *Remember: Speak No Evil,* he had written. Because, of course, Wilde had been a victim of enemies who spoke evil of him. When Stuart had discussed the trial with her during dinner one night, talk turned to the evil perpetrated by our enemies, especially the ones who believe they are morally right.

"Think no evil should have been the first commandment," Stuart had said at the time.

"Why?" Jennifer had asked.

"Because everything starts with thinking. Evil thoughts, evil deeds." What had followed was a long discussion of history and philosophy and justice. Always justice. Stuart's views were prescient, incisive. She missed that about him, too.

Jennifer rubbed her hand across the high back of Stuart's black leather chair. She thought of him sitting there, his shoes off under the desk, reading through his half-glasses, quizzing her before a hearing or a client meeting.

Stuart, she thought, *I will miss you for the rest of my life. There will never be another you.*

His intercom buzzed and she pushed the button.

"Roger Riley and his clients have arrived. I've put them in the conference room," Hilda said. Jennifer clicked off the speaker and took one last look around.

Her gaze rested on a small framed photograph of Stuart and her the day she was admitted to practice law, just a few months after she'd joined the firm and taken up residence in the office next door to his. *Goodbye, my friend.*

"This one's for you, Stuart," she whispered, as she turned off the lights, closed and locked the door behind her.

CHAPTER NINETY-TWO

JENNIFER SAT ACROSS THE table from Riley, Annabelle James Denton, and the CEO of Alabaster Medical, a man whose name she had not bothered to ask. Hilda perched at the end of the table with her notary implements. A court reporter was seated next to her, recording every word.

Jennifer felt infused with Stuart's confidence. She looked at Rabid Roger and wondered why this man had once terrified her so.

Russell Denton, a shadow of the man who'd summoned her to the University Club a few short weeks ago intent to turn her world upside down, sat to her left. Tim Tyler was seated on Russell's other side, as ready as ever to help no matter what Russell wanted done. Jennifer wondered whether she would ever see them again after today.

Stuart had taught her that going through a trial forged a strong bond between client and lawyer, like galvanizing steel, he said. Her experiences with Denton and Tyler felt different.

Jennifer said. "Now that we're all here in the room, just to recap briefly, Annabelle James did not own the HepZMax formula, and she's attested to that under oath. She couldn't have sold something to Alabaster Medical that she didn't own, as you claim, which means your case is frivolous. The original copies of the documents we sent you yesterday are in front of you. Hilda will notarize your signatures and we'll dismiss the case without filing counterclaims against you, as we agreed. There's also a mutual confidentiality order preventing any further discussion of this matter outside this room. I'm sure I don't need to repeat the consequences for violating the agreement?"

Roger said, "Right."

"And your clients?" Jennifer pressed.

Annabelle said, "I understand."

Alabaster's CEO said, "We agree."

Roger pulled out his expensive pen and signed his name everywhere it was required before he passed the documents along to the others. The stack was substantial; signing would take a while.

Tyler had coerced Annabelle to sign the affidavit, but it didn't matter because she agreed not to contest it. She'd helped Blake steal the formula because she loved him, not for any other reason. Annabelle wanted her baby's great-uncle to live and HepZMax might cure him. Annabelle still disliked Russell, but she'd learned the value of family.

Jennifer watched the signatures appear on the documents as they passed by her on the long table. As the piles moved around the table and stacked up in front of Hilda, Jennifer realized her time at Worthington was ending, once and for all.

Blake remained on life support. Annabelle prayed her child would not be an orphan. If Blake recovered, his uncontrolled schizophrenia might keep him out of prison.

"We'll meet again, Jennifer. I'll get you next time." Roger grinned his most predatory smile as he handed over the last of the signed papers.

"Perhaps." She stared unflinching at his pugilist mug.

EPILOGUE

"PLEASE REMAIN SEATED UNTIL the plane has stopped at the gate and the captain has turned off the seatbelt sign," the DC-9's flight attendant repeated the rote statement in a singsong tone.

Jennifer was landing into a new life. She'd traveled from a world where she struggled to fit into Stuart's vision to new, uncharted territory. She didn't know what would become of her life now, but today's mission was another step in the right direction.

She stuffed the lab report back into her jeans. She'd need clean blood tests for several years to come, but this one was negative for hepatitis Z. Annabelle was asymptomatic. Should they need it someday, HepZMax would be a reality.

Jennifer had fretted over how to handle this situation during the entire trip to Traverse City International Airport, the nearest small city to the smaller village in Michigan where her parents lived. Wearing headphones to avoid conversation with her seatmate, she'd planned the surprise.

After the passengers deplaned and collected their luggage, Jennifer picked up a car in the rental lot. She used every minute of the drive along Grand Traverse Bay toward her childhood home to think about the past and the present.

This time of year, swans paddled close to shore in pairs, mated for life, like Debbie and Clay Lane. Like Lila and Ronald Walden, too.

Annabelle and Jennifer had become close in the past few weeks. Jennifer had helped Annabelle bury the only parents she'd ever known. Blake was recovering slowly and he had a long road ahead, both for his recovery and his part in Gilbert Irwin's death. Jennifer was slowly wrapping her mind around having Blake as a brother-in-law, but she wasn't there yet.

As Annabelle's belly grew, so had Jennifer's understanding, which led her to forgive her parents for deceiving her. Only one reconciliation was left to be completed before Jennifer could begin to rebuild her life.

The beautiful drive over M-72 to Sutton's Bay passed too quickly. Before long, she was turning the car into her parents' driveway.

Jennifer sat in the parked rental car in front of the house where she'd spent all her early years. Homes more stylish than her parents' own abounded in this area now. The small town had grown into quite a resort. Old places like the one she'd grown up in were disappearing, sacrificed to the gods of gentrification.

Her parents might renovate one of these days, but she hoped they wouldn't. From outside, she could see her mother moving around in the living room. Her dad was probably working on the digital photos from their cruise in his home office. Jennifer tried to see them with new eyes, to experience the fresh look Annabelle would provide.

Jennifer took a deep breath and opened the car door. The path to her family wound down the driveway and up three steps to a wood deck leading to the back door of the house. She stood for a moment with her hand on the knob, fully aware that this moment was the last time their relationship would be the same as it had always been.

When she opened the door, she would no longer be an only child. But, she'd never been an only child anyway. They had known that. Only Jennifer had lived the fantasy.

Jennifer's childhood would always be hers. But from now on she had a sister. And she would soon be an aunt. She turned the doorknob and shouted as she and Annabelle entered together, "Mom! Dad! I've brought a guest!"

THE END

ABOUT THE AUTHOR

Diane Capri is a *New York Times*, *USA Today*, and worldwide bestselling author.

She's a recovering lawyer and snowbird who divides her time between Florida and Michigan. An active member of Mystery Writers of America, Author's Guild, International Thriller Writers, Alliance of Independent Authors, and Sisters in Crime, she loves to hear from readers and is hard at work on her next novel.

Please connect with her online:

Website: http://www.DianeCapri.com
Twitter: http://twitter.com/@DianeCapri
Facebook: http://www.facebook.com/Diane.Capri1
http://www.facebook.com/DianeCapriBooks

If you would like to be kept up to date with infrequent email including release dates for Diane Capri books, free offers, gifts, and general information for members only, please sign up for our Diane Capri Crowd mailing list. We don't want to leave you out! Sign up here:

http://dianecapri.com/contact